GW01425116

close attention paid to JMC's art

- MYTH   MADNESS 45
              (racism as 39)

suspect that the balance between
argument is off : frustration
underb/understated 'and those that feel insufficiently
unpacked
                        (of others)

can we really equate all these forms of madness? how is Bayner
going to bring them together, if at all?

controversial + perhaps unfounded conclusions, see 61 62
                                                          70
                   disputes/tangents.
lots of references to obscure/outdated work → eg. 74 Greenwood
                                                      (perhaps)
      ~ maybe she'd have been better off sticking
         to her own argument, based on few "heavyweights"
             eg. Freud/Fanon etc.

for a reader who is already familiar in the field of Coetzee studies.
not enough close readings for my taste (but see 81)

- how is her theoretical framework positioned?   DECON ?
                                                  PSYCH ?
- expects an encyclopedic knowledge of SA lit,   INTERTEXT.
     eg. 86

✱ reading of Foe is good (seems to get better as it goes on)
                 book
     also more confident, eg critique of Sanny 106-107
- strays too much from her own argument, but only to
    engage superficially in others - see AOI chapter esp. 124

- not sure that she fully engages in the nuances of JMC's
    "postcolonialism"

J. M. COETZEE AND THE PARADOX OF POSTCOLONIAL AUTHORSHIP

For Mehdi and my mother

J. M. Coetzee and the Paradox of Postcolonial Authorship

JANE POYNER
University of Exeter, UK

ASHGATE

Published by
Ashgate Publishing Limited
Wey Court East
Union Road
Farnham
Surrey, GU9 7PT
England

Ashgate Publishing Company
Suite 420
101 Cherry Street
Burlington
VT 05401-4405
USA

www.ashgate.com

British Library Cataloguing in Publication Data
Poyner, Jane.
J. M. Coetzee and the paradox of postcolonial authorship.
   1. Coetzee, J. M., 1940– – Criticism and interpretation. 2. Postcolonialism in literature.
   3. Politics and literature – South Africa – History – 20th century. 4. South Africa – In literature.
   I. Title
   823.9'14–dc22

Library of Congress Cataloging-in-Publication Data
Poyner, Jane.
J. M. Coetzee and the paradox of postcolonial authorship / Jane Poyner.
   p. cm.
Includes bibliographical references and index.
ISBN 978-0-7546-5462-9 (alk. paper)
1. Coetzee, J. M., 1940 – Criticism and interpretation. 2. Coetzee, J. M., 1940 – Characters – Authors. 3. Authorship in literature. 4. Postcolonialism in literature. 5. South Africa – In literature. 6. Narration (Rhetoric) – History – 20th century. I. Title.
PR9369.3.C58Z873 2009
823'.914–dc22

                                   2009011742

ISBN 9780754654629 (hbk)
ISBN 9780754696742 (ebk)

Printed and bound in Great Britain by
MPG Books Group, UK

Contents

Abbreviations

D	*Dusklands*. 1974. London: Vintage, 1998.
HC	*In the Heart of the Country*. 1977. London: Vintage, 1999.
WB	*Waiting for the Barbarians*. 1980. London: Minerva, 1997.
MK	*Life & Times of Michael K*. 1983. Middlesex: Penguin, 1985.
F	*Foe*. 1986. Middlesex: Penguin, 1987.
WW	*White Writing: On the Culture of Letters in South Africa*. London & New Haven: Yale University, 1988.
NT	"The Novel Today", *Upstream*, 6 (1988): 2–5.
AI	*Age of Iron*. 1990. London: Penguin, 1991.
MP	*The Master of Petersburg*. 1994. London: Minerva, 1995.
DP	*Doubling the Point: Essays and Interviews*. Ed. David Attwell. Cambridge, Massachusetts and London: Harvard UP, 1992.
GO	*Giving Offense: Essays on Censorship*. Chicago: Chicago UP, 1996.
B	*Boyhood: A Memoir*. 1997. London: Vintage, 1998.
DIS	*Disgrace*. London: Secker & Warburg, 1999.
LA	*The Lives of Animals*. Ed. and Intro. Amy Gutmann. Princeton: Princeton UP, 1999.
SS	*Stranger Shores: Essays 1986–1999*. London: Secker & Warburg, 2001.
Y	*Youth*. London: Secker & Warburg, 2002.
EC	*Elizabeth Costello*. London: Secker & Warburg, 2003.
SM	*Slow Man*. New York: Viking, 2005.
DBY	*Diary of a Bad Year*. London: Harvill Secker, 2007.

Acknowledgements

This book, which explores what I call the "paradox of postcolonial authorship" in the fiction of the South African writer J. M. Coetzee, would not have been possible without the support of the following. My dear friend and mentor, Benita Parry, guided me through my apprenticeship as a doctoral researcher and has remained perspicacious in her criticism and warm in her support. Likewise, Neil Lazarus has been an inspiration and kindly read some of the early versions of the chapters. Other friends and colleagues who generously leant their critical eye to parts of this book or to work that fed into it include Michael Bell, Sam Durrant, Kai Easton, Regenia Gagnier, Rashmi Varma and Laura Wright.

Thanks go to the then Arts and Humanities Research Board (now the AHRC), which generously provided a full doctoral scholarship, and to the Department of English at the University of Exeter for granting my sabbatical when the final revisions were made.

Thank you to Ann Donahue at Ashgate for her support of the project and for her true professionalism.

I would also like to thank colleagues (now friends) at Exeter who helped to make the transition to my new post all the easier, particularly: Julia Copus, Sally Flint, Jo Gill, Helen Hanson, Helen Taylor, Ana Vadillo and Helen Vassallo. Friends at my Alma Mater, the University of Warwick, with whom I shared the trials and the thrills of an early research career, are too many to mention here but include Chris Campbell, Mary Deane, Sharae Deckard, Lucy Frank, Pumla Gqola, Jim Graham, Kerstin Oloff, Jenny Terry and Rashmi Varma.

A special thanks is reserved for my family, for their laughter and their support: Liz, John, Cliff, Jill, Cathy, Chris, Ewan, Grace, Esmé, Rory, John, Rach, Anna, Isobel, Joe, Mark, Teresa, Kerry, Jack, Ollie, Sarah, Ella, and not least George. Above all, thank you to my dear mother who graciously proofread the book in all its stages and to Mehdi, who weathered the process of my writing and unstintingly gave his moral support.

Chapter 8 is a substantially revised version of the following essay, reproduced with the kind permission of *Scrutiny2* and Unisa, South Africa: Jane Poyner, "Truth and Reconciliation in J. M. Coetzee's *Disgrace*", *Scrutiny2*, 5.1 (2000), pp. 68–77.

Thanks to the United Nations for granting permission to reproduce the cover image, "A segregated beach in South Africa, 1982" (UN Photo).

Jane Poyner. 3 July, 2009.

Introduction
Positioning the Writer

That he was the 2003 Nobel Laureate in Literature and the first novelist to win the Booker Prize twice, with *Life & Times of Michael K* in 1983 and *Disgrace* in 1999, as well as having the gamut of major South African and international literary prizes conferred upon him, has guaranteed J. M. Coetzee's reputation as one of the most important writers living today.[1] He is also one of South Africa's most controversial. He was awarded the Order of Mapungubwe in Gold by the ANC-led government in 2005 for his "exceptional contribution in the field of literature and for putting South Africa on the world stage" (The Presidency n. pag.) despite the fact that only a few years earlier his eighth novel *Disgrace* was presented by the African National Congress (ANC) to the South African Human Rights Commission (SAHRC) as illustrative of racism in the media, its protagonists deemed representative of whites' attitudes to race in the "new South Africa".[2] His fiction and critical essays have generated a plethora of scholarly research both in South Africa and abroad and have challenged readers globally, not least for the contentious interventions the oeuvre makes through Coetzee's singular, modernist mode into South African politico-cultural discourse and the field of postcolonial studies. Even with only five of the eleven novels being set in South Africa, they all, to a greater or lesser extent, address themes and issues pertinent to the (post)colonial and apartheid situations: colonial discourse, the other, racial segregation, censorship, banning and exile, police brutality and torture, South African liberalism and revolutionary activism, the place of women, the relationship of South Africa's peoples to the land and, not least, the ethico-politics of writing all figure prominently in the oeuvre. Because the later works largely leave behind a specifically postcolonial paradigm, marked

---

[1] Coetzee has been awarded the following literary prizes: South Africa's prestigious CNA Literary Award for *In the Heart of the Country* (1977); the CNA, the James Tait Black Prize and the Geoffrey Faber Memorial Award for *Waiting for the Barbarians* (1980); the CNA and the Prix Étranger Femina in 1985 for *Life & Times of Michael K* (1983); the Jerusalem Prize in 1987 for *Foe* (1986); the Sunday Express Award for *Age of Iron* (1990); the Irish Times International Fiction Prize in 1995 for *The Master of Petersburg* and, in addition to the Booker, the Commonwealth Writers Prize (Overall Winner) in 2000 for *Disgrace*. *Slow Man* (2005) was shortlisted for the Commonwealth Writers Prize (African Region) and the International IMPAC Dublin Literary Award and his most recent novel, *Diary of a Bad Year* (2007) – eligible because Coetzee is now an Australian citizen – was shortlisted for the Adelaide 2008 Festival Awards for Literature.

[2] For conflicting interpretations of this report, see Attwell "Race in *Disgrace*" and McDonald "*Disgrace* Effects".

coincidentally by Coetzee's departure from South Africa to another postcolonial locale, Adelaide, Australia, in 2002, in this present study I focus on the first eight novels up to and including *Disgrace*, and conclude with a chapter that addresses the later works, *Elizabeth Costello* (2003), *Slow Man* (2005) and *Diary of a Bad Year* (2007), within a wider frame of intellectualism and authorship that nonetheless speaks to the field of postcolonial studies.

These thematic nodes dovetail into what I argue is the premise of all Coetzee's fiction and many of his essays and which is a problem with which postcolonial critics have grappled, that through the portrayal of a series of writer protagonists, Coetzee stages the paradox of postcolonial authorship: whilst striving symbolically to bring the stories of the marginal and the oppressed to light, stories that heretofore have been suppressed or silenced by oppressive regimes, writers of conscience or conscience-stricken writers risk re-imposing the very authority they seek to challenge. The task of the postcolonial writer therefore is exacting. I should qualify this argument by saying that a number of Coetzee's protagonists are only minimal, symbolic authors of their texts: the alienated Magda in *In the Heart of the Country* (1977) resists writing as a means of outwitting the patriarchy and literary history that entrap her but finally succumbs because it is only through writing that she can re-enter society and break free from the fetters of her alienation; Michael K in *Life & Times* is author of his life because he bespeaks the familiar postcolonial tropes of writing the body and writing the land. *Life & Times* also embeds the "white writer" in the sense that Coetzee would have it: "white writing is white only insofar as it is generated by the concerns of people no longer European, not yet African" (WW 11). The Medical Officer initially imperiously assumes the right to speak on the other's behalf. Coetzee's ("white") writers typically agonize over the ways in which the authority authorship engenders will always compromise their ethico-political conviction because authorship, for Coetzee, is always already imbued with power, mastery and colonization.

The trajectory of the oeuvre teases out the problem of authorship in ways that correspond with the novels' contemporary milieus so that this problem is gradually distilled in two of Coetzee's latest offerings, the quasi-novel *Elizabeth Costello* (2003) and *Diary of a Bad Year* (2007), which present radical instances of what I call Coetzee's "acts of genre": captured in the word "act", performances of genre that are at once contrived, duplicitous and yet agential. *Elizabeth Costello* is comprised of eight "lessons", in six out of eight of which the idiosyncratic and forthright novelist Elizabeth Costello delivers invited lectures which were originally presented by Coetzee as meta-generic public lectures at a series of international venues. In *Diary* the writer and academic J. C. offers a series of "strong opinions" in the genre of the opinion piece, and this public voice is offset at the bottom of each page by a number of more personal ones, including J. C.'s own. Costello uses the lecture forum to air her often eccentric (ex-centric) views on subjects ranging from animal rights to the problem of representing evil, and the curmudgeonly J. C.'s aphorisms diversify across subjects such as Al-Qaeda, "national shame" and the business-like enterprise of the modern-day university. Whilst the substance

of these novels clearly is ethico-political, it is in the acts of genre, I argue, that the
real intellectualizing is done. By filtering public interventions through the prism
of fiction, and by Coetzee fictionalizing himself within the narratives, the reader
is left uncertain about who is speaking, Coetzee or his characters, and this enables
Coetzee to get two jobs done: first, to raise questions about authority and the
capacity of intellectuals to "speak truth to power" (Said, *Representations* 85), and,
second, to nurture a critical readership which is obliged to participate in the life of
the text. As Edward Said has put it, the public intellectual's "whole being is staked
on the *critical sense*" (emphasis added; *Representations* 23).

Typically in Coetzee the public defers to the private sphere, as he discloses to the
interviewer, David Attwell, in *Doubling the Point*, "the contest of interpretations
… the political versus the ethical [is] played out again and again in my novels"
(DP 338). However, while Coetzee claims that, where the public maps on to the
political and the private to the ethical, he resists championing the ethical over
the political because this would reify ethics as lack (DP 200). Derek Attridge is
right when he contends that in Coetzee "it is evident that it is the political that
is to be corrected by the ethical, and not vice versa" ("Trusting the Other" 70):
Coetzee's writer protagonists are consistently marginal figures resistant to the ebb
and flow of the tides of political rhetoric. Michael K's quest for meaning in *Life
& Times*, for instance, is drawn to a close with a parable in which, envisaging
subsisting using a teaspoon to draw water from a well, he would live minimally off
the land. Mrs. Curren in *Age of Iron* (1990) is on a quest of another kind, this time
for "home truths": in the letter she is writing to her daughter, she carves out an
intellectual space for herself with an almost pedantic regard for language: "These
are terrible sights … But I cannot denounce them in other people's words. I must
find my own words, from myself. Otherwise it is not the truth" (AI 91). Through
a confessional mode and motifs of "demon-possession" and "heart-speech", the
novels address Coetzee's own very private response as an "anxious intellectual"[3]
to working under the pressures of an oppressive regime and those of conformity,
even conforming to the tenets of the progressive left with which he makes clear he
sympathizes (because conforming means on some level reining in the creative as
well as the ethical faculty).

For these reasons, Coetzee is often charged with being evasive: in the eyes of
his critics the obliquity and rarefication of the works are evidence of his disavowal
of politics in spite of some obvious sorties into the political fray (cf. Attwell, "Life
and Times" 26). This criticism stems from the difficulty critics have of positioning
an author who, attentive to the pitfalls that postcolonial authorship implies,
hews himself the precarious position of "nonposition" (GO 84), but one that is
ethico-political because it gesturally resists the authority that white South African
masculinity bestows (GO 84). I realize that in labelling him ethico-*political* I am
drawing Coetzee down a road he would be averse to travelling. Characteristically

---

[3]   *Anxious Intellects* is the title of a book by John Michael that David Attwell refers to
in an essay on Coetzee's "public" intellectualism ("Life and Times" 29).

referring to himself in the third person and revealing an abiding preoccupation with the paradox of postcolonial authorship I am mapping here, Coetzee observes that "all political language" leaves him cold: "As far back as he can see he has been ill at ease with language that lays down the law, that is not provisional, that does not as one of its habitual motions glance back sceptically at its premises" (DP 394). His use of the third-person to speak about himself, a device that resurfaces in the memoirs, *Boyhood* (1997) and *Youth* (2002), suggests that not only is he "ill at ease" with political rhetoric but, as he concedes in interview, also is uncomfortable being made to answer for his novels (DP 205). Such a position becomes thorny in postcolonial contexts, because, ironically as Coetzee's oeuvre time and again reveals, the integrity of the postcolonial author is staked on being available to redress lest the systems of power embedded in colonial writings are reproduced.

The charge of political evasion laid at Coetzee's feet has particular resonance within the South African contexts from which most of the novels were penned because under apartheid not only political and cultural but also personal freedom was restricted and often denied, thus necessitating an active struggle against the state. Draconian censorship laws were passed by the regime, including the Publications and Entertainments Act (1963) and the Publications Act (1975, amended in 1978). Indeed, Coetzee's own novels, *Waiting for the Barbarians* (1980), *In the Heart of the Country* (1977) and *Life & Times* (1983) were brought before the Directorate of Publications and threatened with the blue-pencil of the censor (McDonald, "The Writer" 45). Within some quarters of resistance culture was deemed in that now hackneyed phrase a "weapon of the struggle" and, in fiction, social realism was perceived as the best mode to convey this objective. Numerous progressive critics like Nadine Gordimer, who employs a sophisticated Lukácsian realist model that contrasts the consciousness of its protagonist with objective reality (in Georg Lukács' words, "the duality of inwardness and outside world" [qtd. in Gordimer, *Essential Gesture* 277]), voiced their misgivings about the silencing and degrading effects of protest literature that Gordimer nicely termed "conformity to an orthodoxy of opposition" (*Essential Gesture* 106). Lewis Nkosi claimed that such writing was debased by "journalistic fact parading outrageously as imaginative literature" ("Fiction" 222) and Njabulo Ndebele argued that the complexities of the combination of content and form in much contemporary South African fiction had been neglected for political posturing, resulting in "an art of anticipated surfaces rather than one of processes" (*Rediscovery* 32). Albie Sachs's ANC speech "Preparing Ourselves for Freedom" (1990) fuelled the debate by raising the question: "whether we have sufficient cultural imagination to grasp the rich texture of the free and united South Africa that we have done so much to bring about" (19). Sachs concluded that "solidarity criticism" risks being prescriptive and limiting (20). Indeed, on this point these writers reach consensus, though unlike Coetzee, their concern lies in part with the integrity of the resistance movement itself. Critics like David Attwell and Michael Chapman, however, have shown that such a position itself represents a "critical orthodoxy" (Attwell, *Rewriting Modernity* 177) that overlooks the complexities of committed literature, which

[handwritten: need to read Attwell's book]

[handwritten: but is this not distinct from "white writing"?]

at times reveals a distinct African modernism and is capable of combining self-reflexivity with political critique.

Coetzee bridges the gap between the "West" and the so-called Third World, yet because the novels are steeped in the dominant Western literary tradition some critics have questioned his postcolonial credentials. Benita Parry, for instance, argues that because the fictions are underpinned by Western cognitive frameworks, Coetzee is unable to craft marginal characters that are outside and beyond Eurocentric discourse ("Speech and Silence" 150). The oeuvre has even been read by a number of critics as "allegorized theory", as Graham Pechey points out ("Post-Apartheid" 66), drawing as it does upon the work of European philosophers and theorists like Blake, Rousseau, Lévi-Strauss, Levinas, Foucault, Sartre, Benveniste, Lacan, Freud, Derrida – a so-called "pied noir" – and Irigaray. From the European literary tradition, Dante, Defoe, Dostoevsky, Kafka, D. H. Lawrence and Beckett number amongst Coetzee's acknowledged influences. Not only is all his writing steeped in the European literary tradition, the novels also borrow from thinkers from the so-called Third World: Fanon, Ndebele, Césaire, Gordimer and Breytenbach amongst others make sometimes veiled appearances. Coetzee's often acutely self-reflexive mode even led one critic to suggest that "Almost all the initial difficulties of [Coetzee's] novels vanish when one happens to have read the same books that he has" (Watson, "Colonialism" 25).

[handwritten margin notes: + others, eg Attwell; ?I really?; don't think so.; ? where?; X]

Many of the works subvert the genres of the white South African canon. This is the premise of the first monograph that appeared on Coetzee, *The Novels of J. M. Coetzee: Lacanian Allegories* (1988), by Teresa Dovey (who combines this analysis with a Lacanian psychoanalytic reading of the act of narration in the early texts) and one subsequently rehearsed by other Coetzee scholars (for instance, Attwell, *J. M. Coetzee*; Head, *J. M. Coetzee*). Coetzee's fiction extends and, in its oppositional aspects, puts into practice his thesis outlined in *White Writing*. Concerned with "certain of the ideas, the great intellectual schemas, through which South Africa has been thought by Europe[,] and with the land itself, South Africa as landscape and landed property" (WW 10), Coetzee recognizes the failure in the white South African pastoral to represent Africa or its (indigenous) peoples authentically. The mythologized relation of the Afrikaner to the land, that struggles to fend off the threat of urban development by invoking the motif of the farmer toiling on the land, for instance, betrays a "Blindness to the colour black":

[handwritten margin note: see Attwell's 2007 article for this.]

> As its central issue the genre prefers to identify the preservation of a (Dutch) peasant rural order, or at least the preservation of the values of that order … Locating the historically significant conflict as between Boer and Britain, it shifts black-white conflict out of sight[.] (WW 5–6)

Coetzee argues that the only early "English" novels to explore the farm motif, Olive Schreiner's anti-pastoral *The Story of an African Farm* (1883) and Pauline Smith's *The Beadle* (1926) and short story collection *The Little Karoo* (1925, rev. 1930), write against the grain of this prevailing mode: "At the very least they provide a foil to the *plaasroman* [farm novel], throwing its preconceptions into relief" (WW 63–64). Representing a "critique of colonial culture", Coetzee suggests, Schreiner's novel distinguishes between the farm and nature (elements that in the *plaasroman* exist "in synthesis"): the farm is in a state of decay and the wilderness is "inhospitable". Smith's farm, on the other hand, nostalgically re-imagines an unattainable Eden; though securely lodged in a historical tradition, it registers a marked distillation of authority, patriarchy and capital, which situates it, Coetzee propounds, in a "pre-capitalist organization" (WW 64–65; 66–67; 70–71). However, these novels inadvertently reproduce the hegemonic tendencies of the *plaasroman* because they too erase South Africa's marginal majority (WW 71). The radical potentiality of the anti-pastoral genre sanctioned by Schreiner is reappraised in Gordimer's *The Conservationist* (1974) and Coetzee's *In the Heart of the Country*, *Life & Times*, *Foe* and *Disgrace* as well as his first memoir, *Boyhood*, works that not only demythologize white South Africans' relationship to the land but are inclusive of colonial and apartheid South Africa's other voices, albeit in the early Coetzee, voices of silence and subjugation. *what does this mean?*

At stake is whether Coetzee, in his deployment of the writing practices of the West and white South African genres, adequately – that is to say, ethically and politically – accommodates the contexts he chooses to address: do the novels, for instance, inadvertently read the "Third World" contexts through a misappropriated "Western" or Eurocentric lens that therefore necessarily would be myopic? By the end of *Disgrace* the problem of relevance begins to dawn on the protagonist Professor David Lurie, so that it isn't Byron or Teresa who will re-awaken his creativity but the sound of a toy banjo – "plink plunk" – that he bought his daughter "on the streets of KwaMashu" (DIS 184). In his 2005 monograph on Coetzee, Attridge argues that the importance of the early novels, *Dusklands* and *In the Heart of the Country*, doesn't even lie in an analysis of colonialism per se; as readers, Attridge claims, we don't need to have this spelled out to us, though for me it is in this analysis, which is staged *en abyme*, where the narratives triumph. Rather, Attridge contends, their power resides in the dramatizing of debates about responsibility to the other, "how otherness is engaged, staged, distanced, embraced, how it is manifested in the rupturing of narrative discourse, in the lasting uncertainties of reference, in the simultaneous exhibiting and doubting of the novelist's authority" (*J. M. Coetzee* 30–31).

Coetzee addresses issues such as these, albeit often circuitously, in the volume of essays and interviews collected in *Doubling the Point* (1992). Turning upon the concept of doubling (Dostoevskian "double thoughts") and autocritique, the volume provides insights into Coetzee's intellectual background that has coloured his novels and which is drawn from both the "West" and his South African heritage – both Attwell and Rita Barnard read the collection as, in Attwell's words, "intellectual autobiography" (Attwell, "Life and Times" 28; Barnard, "Imagining" 11). In the Dutch poet Gerrit Achterberg's sonnet sequence "Ballade van de Gasfitter" (DP 69), Coetzee analyzes what he calls the "poetics of reciprocity": the relationship between the "I" and the "You", the self and other, in literary texts, constituted

DOUBLING THE POINT

Positioning the Writer 7

by the relationship between character and author (DP 69). Fiction that Coetzee diminishes as "radical metafiction", if failing to take account of the ethical, is in danger of "swallowing its own tail", of becoming a "poetics of failure" (DP 86). He reads the defamiliarization of time in Franz Kafka's short story "The Burrow" (1923–24) as a means of "thinking outside language", and explores the subversive potential this might hold for the alienated writer who writes about alienation (DP 199). In "The Taint of the Pornographic" he suggests that D. H. Lawrence's *Lady Chatterley's Lover* (1928) is an exercise in exorcizing words that society has "made dirty" or taboo, particularly those words of a sexual and excremental nature. Yet he concludes that Lawrence's work depends upon taboo to maintain its substance. In the section devoted to South African writers Coetzee utilizes Gordimer's thesis in *The Essential Gesture* to define his own position of resistance to conformity in art. "Into the Dark Chamber" explores what Coetzee perceives as South African writers' morbid fascination with the torture chamber, a fascination which he admits sharing (DP 363). This preoccupation necessitates an ethic of representation, "how not to play the game by the rules of the state, how to establish one's own authority, how to imagine torture and death in one's own terms" (DP 364). "Confession and Double Thoughts", which he regards as his defining essay up to this moment, analyzes the confessional writing of Tolstoy, Rousseau and Dostoevsky to identify the problems that encumber confession: finding the truth about the self which, in turn, is imbued with problems of deception and self-deception and the problem of closure: how to end the infinite cycle of truth-telling and self-abnegation into which the confessant is likely to be drawn. Elsewhere, Coetzee links the emphatic assertion that "All autobiography is storytelling, all writing is autobiography" with the problem of "how to tell the truth in autobiography" (DP 391–92): writing is constituted by acts of self-disclosure that are plagued by the problem of where and when to draw a line.

Coetzee's highly cerebral and meticulously crafted prose revels in aestheticism yet is perspicacious in its treatment of the socio-political milieu from which it speaks: primarily, the colonies and postcolonies. It is in this complex knit of aesthetics and thematics that readers of Coetzee will find themselves most rewarded, neither aspect being compromised by the other. Although the writer-protagonists in the oeuvre engage with the apparent tensions between art and politics, the fictions' elaborate textuality suggests that Coetzee refuses fully to endorse the ethico-political by negating the literary. In "The Novel Today", a talk given to the *Weekly Mail* Book Week in Cape Town in 1987, Coetzee argues that polarizing commitment and aestheticism is, indeed, counterproductive (NT 4). What is more, aesthetics, he argues, play a constitutive part in the politics of a text: in the case of the argument forwarded in "The Novel Today", Coetzee's target is the discourse of history. What is intriguing, as David Atwell has pointed out ("Life and Times" 28), is that this short piece has never been anthologized or subsequently acknowledged by Coetzee, leading us to wonder whether he has revoked this perhaps earlier position on novelistic practice and the kind of literary commitment it apparently promotes.

Many of Coetzee's protagonists are at some level writers by profession, aware of the demands that the ethico-politics as well as the aesthetics of writing and reading might entail. The author Foe, for instance, is accused by Susan Barton in *Foe* of embellishing the facts of her island adventure: "Once you proposed to supply a middle by inventing cannibals and pirates. These I would not accept because they were not the truth," she says (F 121). It is Barton's conviction that "Till we have spoken the unspoken we have not come to the heart of the story" (F 141). Yet Foe warns that in choosing a path such as this, Barton risks being "lost in the maze of doubting" (F 135), the endless spiral of self-doubt into which the writer questing for truths is likely to become embroiled. Racked by the demons of guilt, the Coetzean writer of conscience typically is lost in just such a maze. Under the pressure generated by the conflicting demands writing imposes, an implosion of self occurs: the writer is "demon-possessed" or psychically (and sometimes textually) unstable. Tracing the genealogy of Coetzee's author-narrators, Jacobus Coetzee is exceptional because he remains entirely unself-reflexive but, as Attwell observes, once Coetzee has registered the existence of such blind authoritarianism, he leaves the Jacobus Coetzees of this world behind (*J. M. Coetzee* 57) and conjures instead more complex, contradictory characters.

Coetzee sketches a novelistic practice in "The Novel Today" that is anti-historical, which is not to say a-historical because several of the works engage explicitly with historical events. Some are therefore also "anti-realist", though *Age of Iron* and *Disgrace* are notable for Coetzee's "return" to realism. Situating his argument in "times of intense ideological pressure like the present", Coetzee advocates a novel that, through processes of "rivalry" rather than "supplementarity", would expose history as an ideologically inflected discourse (NT 3). A novel such as this would resist replicating certain kinds of historical "truths" pervaded by the oppressive state.

In the present study, though I aim to preserve the historical-material contexts of the works in my efforts to produce a *postcolonial* critique of the act of writing in Coetzee's fiction, historicizing is not my primary focus because this task has been amply met in the monographs by Attwell and Susan VanZanten Gallagher. Attwell identifies Coetzee's fiction as "situational metafiction" (*J. M. Coetzee* 3) and asserts "again and again the historicity of the act of storytelling, continually reading the novels back into their context" (*J. M. Coetzee* 7). Attwell's monograph, which ends with *Age of Iron*, is philosophically and aesthetically in tune with Coetzee's writing in what, to my mind, remains one of the best book-length studies of the author. Gallagher's analysis, firmly rooted in a cultural materialist critique, painstakingly situates the texts within their historical as well as literary contexts. Sue Kossew in *Pen and Power* (1996), like Attwell and Gallagher, assesses Coetzee's political engagement, this time focusing on the postcoloniality of the works through a comparison with another well-known white South African author, André Brink. Kossew chooses to focus on the relationship between the literary and the political, rightly insisting, as the title to her book suggests, on the politic weight of the writing.

Coetzee states that he is not endorsing writing that is apolitical: "am I saying [these things] in order to distance myself from revolutionary art and ally myself with those people who think there is nothing nicer than cuddling up in bed with a novel and having a good old read …? I hope not" (NT 4). What is important to Coetzee is the staging of debate, challenging orthodoxy and nurturing an agential, critical readership but one that nevertheless is not expected to forego the pleasure of the text. Yet Attridge, writing in his monograph about the ethics of reading in Coetzee, expresses skepticism towards the tendency within postcolonial studies to endow the literary with political currency; he argues that *Disgrace,* perhaps Coetzee's most disturbing work to date, "is disturbing in many ways, and among the things it disturbs is any simple faith in the political efficacy of literature – a faith upon which some styles of postcolonial criticism are built" ("J. M. Coetzee's *Disgrace*: Introduction" 320).

The efficacy of literature for effecting change may be a moot point but calling into question the dominant tendencies in writing, be it historical or fictional, is crucial to understanding the legacy of colonialism and apartheid given that under hegemonies such as these, historiography and fictional narrative form part of the ideological ammunition used to control and subject colonized and segregated peoples. To avoid replicating such tendencies, constant and evolving criticism of intellectual practice must be therefore fostered if the postcolonial project is to remain credible; questioning the writer's authority, even if through the medium of fiction, is one way of illuminating this endeavour.

Coetzee's writing, both his fiction and essays, acknowledges the gravity of writerly engagement, yet cautions against conformity in resistance lest, through complacency, artists allow the new order to degenerate to the oppressive standards of the old. As a committed ANC member, Sachs understands this problem of internalized "censorship", a kind of self-censorship, as a threat to the integrity of progressive politics (22). Gordimer, herself active in the anti-apartheid struggle, was censored under apartheid (DP 298) and attempts apparently have been made by some to censure her in the "new South Africa". As Coetzee notes in *Giving Offense,* Gordimer's *Burger's Daughter* (1979) was deemed in the words of the Publications Appeal Board (PAB) to "contain various anti-white sentiments" (GO 197) whilst in April 2001, four teachers sitting on an educational evaluation panel in Gauteng Province recommended that *July's People* (1981) be removed from school syllabuses because, in the words of Justin Cartwright who recorded the event, "any condemnation of racism is difficult to discover – so the story comes across as being deeply racist, superior and patronising" (Cartwright n. pag.). Education Minister Kader Asmal, however, was quick to come to Gordimer's defence on the grounds that the comments were anti-intellectualist and pedagogically suspect (South African Government, "Spotlight on Matriculants" n. pag.). The panel backed Asmal.

Coetzee makes the throwaway remark in *Doubling the Point* that he finds political debates about censorship at best tedious and at worst stupid: his interest lies in the psychological effects of censorship, which works like a disease infecting the mind of both censor and censored alike (DP 299). Coetzee's essays on censorship collected in *Giving Offense: Essays on Censorship* (1996) engage with his signature modernist, double-edged critique of *Doubling the Point*. In "Breyten Breytenbach and the Reader in the Mirror" he explores the ways in which Breytenbach's mirror-writings are structured by notions of contagion and complicity, embodied in the figure of the censor as *doppelgänger*: locked in the defining self/other dialectic, censor and censored metamorphose into dark twins or "mirror-brothers" (GO 228; Breytenbach, *Confessions* 260). Writer and text ("mirror/page") reproduce the dynamic between "cooperative prisoner" and interrogator (GO 228). In "Erasmus: Madness and Rivalry" Coetzee draws upon René Girard and Michel Foucault to reformulate notions of "madness" that in Enlightenment discourse have been read as antithetical to reason and served as a means of state control. In the hands of the apartheid regime "reason" is itself irrational and therefore "mad" and madness and rationality (unreason/reason), as forms of "mimetic violence", are reduced to "warring twins" (GO 90-92). In "Apartheid Thinking", Coetzee understands the writing of the progenitor of apartheid ideology, Geoffrey Cronjé, as a kind of insane confession that allow us to "follow the ravings, from inside" (GO 165).

Much scholarship on Coetzee has been preoccupied with the problem of how to define and systematize his fiction. In spite of the criticisms of evasion levelled against him, the consistently Janus-faced portrayal of the writer in the encounter with alterity throughout the oeuvre evidences Coetzee's profound sense of responsibility and accountability to his subject. Indeed, when Coetzee accepts Attwell's label as "late-modernist" rather than postmodernist, he ascribes a certain ethicality to his writing. Neil Lazarus in an early article on Coetzee registers the intellectual integrity of his fiction, which can only be called modernist, Lazarus argues, not postmodernist, because the novels represent reality, rationalism, the ethical and a humanist critique of the *status quo* ("Modernism and Modernity" 148). On this point Attridge would agree: as a "late modernist" Coetzee "does not merely employ but extends and revitalizes modernist practices, and in so doing develops a mode of writing that allows the attentive reader to live through the pressures and possibilities, and also the limits, of political engagement" (*J. M. Coetzee* 6). Attridge's monograph on Coetzee is notable, amongst other things, for its deconstructive turn that borrows from formalism and an emphasis on what he calls the "singularity of literature" experienced in the "reading event". Ethically responsible reading, he argues, involves sensitivity and attentiveness to the workings of a text. The text that is experimental and estranging is more demanding of its reader and hence such a text is more ethically charged (Attridge, *J. M. Coetzee* 11). Attridge's reading of the estranging text is not unlike Theodor Adorno's concept of literary commitment, crucially distinguished by Adorno's concern for politics rather than simply ethics (Adorno, "Commitment"). Dominic Head understands Coetzee somewhat differently by defining the fiction as "ethically oriented postmodernism" (*J. M. Coetzee* 19). I read Coetzee as a postcolonial late-modernist but would tend to agree, however, with Elleke Boehmer that, if stalled at the level of terminology, the debate risks being unproductive (*Colonial and Postcolonial Literature* 244) and detracts from the thrust of Coetzee's writing and from its achievements (not something, it has to be said, of which the aforementioned critics are guilty).

As a white South African writer, Coetzee is acutely aware that he speaks from a position of beneficiary of the apartheid regime, palpable in the string of anxious intellectuals that populate his novels. At the same time, he has tacitly positioned himself as marginalized, as a modernist writing against the grain of oppositional writing and, in childhood, as an English speaker of part-Afrikaner stock and a Protestant attending a Catholic high school (DP 393–94). In *Boyhood* the young John experiences alienation at primary school as well: when questioned by his teacher, he precociously announces he is a Roman Catholic, in this instance at a Protestant establishment, only to be excluded from assembly. (He hopes that the next day he can revise this choice and become a "Christian" [B 19].) However, whether today Coetzee can be talked about as marginal is doubtful given the intense global interest in his work.

In broad terms, I identify four phases in the trajectory of the oeuvre which can be mapped on to the political contexts of each. These phases guide the organization of the chapters that follow. I discuss the first phase, *Dusklands, In the Heart of the Country* and *Waiting for the Barbarians*, in terms of the "madness of civilization" (Foucault). The mythologies of colonial and imperial enterprise that energize the protagonists' narratives and that allow Coetzee to "historicize madness" (GO 165) are offset in these novels against the motif of madness. This early phase centres on the unremittingly Draconian power of white hegemonies – colonialism, apartheid and U.S. imperialism in Vietnam – and on the modern-day myths these hegemonies have circulated. In turn, myth mutates into forms of madness in its distortion of certain kinds of "truths", be they political, historical, social or economic.

Against the backdrop of the ANC beginning its defence campaign in 1952, D. F. Malan's Afrikaner National Party that was elected to power in 1948 implemented the major apartheid legislation between 1950 and 1953 through which it endeavoured to silence the political voice of South Africa's marginalized majority. Black opposition, according to the historian William Beinart, reached its height between 1958 and 1960 (with the Sharpeville massacre), but in 1961 the ANC and Pan Africanist Congress (PAC) were banned and thus forced underground. Though the 1960s saw rapid economic growth in South Africa, this only served to worsen the black majority's plight, bringing with it the implementation of homeland and forced removal policies. The government's violent response to the Soweto student protests of 1976 and the death in police custody of student leader Steve Biko in 1977 fanned the flames of dissent. Written in the 1970s and early 1980s, when the strong-arm of the apartheid regime may have seemed unassailable, these novels explore the problems both produced and encountered by the white writer who peddles or presses against imperialist, colonialist and apartheid ideologies. Under extreme pressure the colonizer's and colonized's sense of self, that in this early phase turns upon the motifs of contagion and madness, is fractured and insanity results. Frantz Fanon's "black

narrative wreckage.

skin/white masks" formulation speaks to this condition by elucidating the site of otherness: confronted by the racist, Fanon experiences "crushing objecthood" and is "completely dislocated" (*Black Skin* 109; 112). In this phase Coetzee establishes the unwarranted and unearned authority of the "white" writer to expose it as a kind of madness.

The second phase, *Life & Times* and *Foe*, centres on Coetzee's paradoxically resisting but utterly subjected others, a theme that converges in the Robinsonade parable as well as, in *Life & Times*, Kafka's parables and paradoxes. Thinking through what islands signify to the resisting other, my readings of the texts show how this was a necessary phase in Coetzee's writing, coming as it did at the height of the apartheid struggle, before the end of the regime, when attempts were being made to stifle the voices of the marginalized majority and before the reality of democracy was in sight. Nevertheless, black resistance was significant during this period and this fact has provoked criticism of these texts, as I subsequently explain.

The insurrection beginning in 1984 that led to the States of Emergency from 1985 to 1990 posed the most significant threat to apartheid rule, consolidating black opposition that had begun in the 1960s; but this also led to internal divisions within the resistance movements. Rural removals and the new configurations of urbanization that resulted peaked at this time and in 1986 the pass laws were rescinded in response to the population explosion in urban areas (Beinart, xiii–xvi; 238).

The stubbornly passive resistance of Coetzee's black protagonists during this phase is figured in their silence, but problematically this denotes a loss of political voice. Yet if, as Peter Hulme argues, the island motif in literature provides the vessel in which the self is distilled (*Colonial Encounters* 186; 189), both Michael K and Friday experience their islands of isolation in a similar way: identity is reconstituted in the silences they weave around themselves as authors of their lives. In spite of the "white writers" they encounter at first believing Friday and Michael K are nothing until they are fashioned in discourse, they are, in fact, resisting others who hold the colonizer out.

The penning of the first two novels of the third phase, *Age of Iron* and *The Master of Petersburg* (1994), roughly coincided with the release of the figurehead of the anti-apartheid struggle Nelson Mandela and the unbanning of the ANC in 1990 by F.W. de Klerk's regime. *Disgrace* came quick on the heels of democracy. With the end of apartheid a very real possibility when Coetzee wrote *Age of Iron*, a certainty with *The Master of Petersburg* and reality with *Disgrace*, it is not surprising that this phase is increasingly preoccupied with confession leading to truth and reconciliation, questions that clearly were working themselves out on the national plane. As South Africa moved irrepressibly towards democracy and apartheid laws were gradually repealed, the residual effects of apartheid left a nation struggling to come to terms with the past and the problem of how blacks and whites could now live peaceably as neighbours.

Questions of truth and reconciliation were formally addressed by the much maligned Truth and Reconciliation Commission (TRC), chaired by Archbishop Desmond Tutu, which first sat in 1995. The mission of the TRC was to bring the truth of apartheid abuse to light, but many rightly argued this was at the cost of justice. Firstly, some perpetrators of gross violations of human rights were effectively let off the hook through the Commission's processes of amnesty (however, amnesty could be, and often was, refused if the crimes were deemed non-political or exceeded even the definition of "gross violations") and, secondly, the systemic abuses of apartheid were not accounted for.

While the "new South Africa" is engaged with nation-building and with bearing witness to and reconciling itself with the past, the novels of the third phase work through the insurmountability of truth and reconciliation in the public, national sphere as well as in the sphere of the self. In these novels white writers experience and attempt to resolve a crisis of authority as they struggle to find their place during a time of seismic change. In other words, there is an acceptance, or at least a recognition, of the pitfalls writerly authority engenders.

Finally, in the fourth phase, Coetzee moves beyond a specifically postcolonialist paradigm. I focus on the quasi-novel *Elizabeth Costello* and *Diary of a Bad Year*, with brief reference to *Slow Man*, to explore the ways in which in these works Coetzee pares the problem of the author's authority via the radical defamiliarization of genre, or "genre acts". The end of apartheid has signalled new directions in South African literature, which inevitably had been overdetermined by apartheid, and has enabled writers to look inward, to the self, and outward and beyond to the global as well as the local. By defamiliarizing genre boundaries to reveal that really they were porous all along, these metafictions refigure Said's definition of the public intellectual as one who "speaks truth to power" and forgoes personal interests in favour of "secular rationality". Through acts of genre, Coetzee calls into question the process of obtaining intellectual truths, a critical activity that is for Said the very lifeblood of the public intellectual.

Whatever controversy Coetzee's oeuvre has sparked and perhaps even courted is the product of the tensions the paradox of postcolonial authorship generates, a paradox that drives all of Coetzee's novels and much of his non-fiction: that writing on others' behalf threatens the ethico-politics that go to the very heart of the postcolonial text. Coetzee's self-reflexivity on matters of authority and what Said calls the "permission to narrate" ("Permission"), on colonial and apartheid violence, on censorship and the censoring self and on the negotiation of truth and reconciliation in the context of national liberation, has variously baffled, infuriated, intrigued and captivated his readers. No doubt his writing will continue to influence new generations of South African and postcolonial writers for generations to come in its penetrating explorations into (post)colonial writerly practice. This book, in its detailed analysis of the writer figure in Coetzee's work, hopes to elucidate Coetzee's ideas on authorial authority so that they might be applied more widely to colonial and postcolonial literatures.

Chapter 1
"Father Makes Merry with Children": Madness and Mythology in *Dusklands*

In his first novel *Dusklands* (1974), J. M. Coetzee has baffled many of his readers by juxtaposing two apparently discrete narratives: "The Vietnam Project" narrated by Eugene Dawn, an American propagandist writing in the early 1970s, and "The Narrative of Jacobus Coetzee" narrated by a line of South African Coetzees. The most prominent of this line, Jacobus Coetzee, J. M. Coetzee claims as an ancestor (DP 52). (The other Coetzees in the text, including "Coetzee" in Dawn's narrative, are fictional.)[1] In *Doubling the Point* J. M. Coetzee indicates that the book is his response to the Vietnam War and to South African history (DP 27) – not only colonialism, informed by the author's reading of the "annals of the exploration of southern Africa", but also apartheid because Jacobus Coetzee's narrative is retold by Dr. S. J. Coetzee at the moment immediately preceding the election of the Afrikaner National Party into government in 1948. With many critics reading the work as two separate narratives, as Dominic Head observes, criticisms of the text have tended to focus on the "obliquity of the book's method", the most condemnatory of which have suggested that J. M. Coetzee is complicit in the very project he seeks to challenge, the "excitement of colonial self-aggrandizement". Head rightly argues, however, that "complicity is a theme of the novel, and is inevitably enacted in the sequence of first-person narratives, where each narrating subject is exposed as a product and perpetrator of colonial projects" (*J. M. Coetzee* 29).

Complicity is realized metaphorically in the psychic collapse of Dawn and Jacobus Coetzee, both of whom are authors in the service of imperialism and colonialism respectively, and who work to perpetuate the myths of these two ideologies (Jacobus is only an author of sorts because he is illiterate and his narrative has therefore been transcribed). It is only through our reading Dawn's report, prepared for the American Department of Defense on methods of propaganda, that Jacobus's colonial enterprise as myth is more obviously signalled. So reading the novel as a single piece composed of two corresponding parts, as Head suggests, rather than self-contained stories is therefore more fruitful, and is no doubt closer to J. M. Coetzee's intention in the novel's construction. The relation in the first section between author (Dawn), text (the report) and world (the military and the Vietnamese) is paralleled with the second, "The Narrative of Jacobus Coetzee" – Jacobus (author) is dictating his annals (text) of colonial exploration (world)

---

[1]   For clarity, the name of real-life author J. M. Coetzee will be referred to in full and without inverted commas throughout the chapter.

– a strategy that invites the reader to draw some obvious comparisons between the two main narrators or "author-functions", in Foucauldian terms ("What is an Author?" 148).

Both Dawn and Jacobus work at establishing and maintaining dominant mythologies, yet I will argue that what Roland Barthes calls the distorting effect of myth in his enduring work *Mythologies* (129) eventually fractures their own sense of self: ironically, as they descend into madness they become victims of the very ideologies they are busy promoting because they are unable properly to read the myths they produce. While Dawn, writing from a twentieth-century perspective, is driven insane by his morally dubious work as an American propagandist during the U.S. government's military intervention into Vietnam and Cambodia in the 1960s and 70s (that foretells the horrors of Abu Ghraib gaol and the contemporary "war on terror" [cf. Spencer, "Colonial Violence"]), Jacobus Coetzee's madness apparently stems from physical disease rather than a bad conscience: the delirium of fever and infection. Yet because he remains oblivious to the sociopathic and dehumanizing nature of his colonizing mission, the boil next to his anus and his wrath at being mocked and degraded by his Namaqua captors during his trek into their territory translate as metaphors for the madness of colonialism. In different ways Dawn and Jacobus's violent and depraved encounter with the other, in which they try to break the other down, works like a disease on their own consciousness (and in Dawn's case his conscience too). The pseudo-rational discourse that camouflages colonial and imperial conquest is undercut by the madness of these two myth-makers and of the ideologies they expound to reveal the madness of so-called civilization. "The Vietnam Project" serves as a lens or reading practice by which to read the more oblique mythologizing in "The Narrative of Jacobus Coetzee"; in other words, schematically, Jacobus Coetzee's more metaphorically realized madness is read through the terms of Dawn's overt myth-making and his experience of psychological collapse. The myths of imperial and colonial enterprise are exposed as a kind of madness because they register a willed misrecognition of their subject, the imperial and colonial other.

This sketch of the scheme and thematics of the novel tallies with J. M. Coetzee's often cited address "The Novel Today" (1988) at the *Weekly Mail* Book Week in Cape Town in 1987 in which he discusses the relation between the genre of the novel and the "historical present". He writes against the grain of the "dominant tendency" to contain the novel under the umbrella of history whereby fiction reproduces real historical event (NT 2). Through the notion of rivalling rather than supplementing history, he advocates:

> a novel that operates in terms of its own procedures and issues in its own conclusions, not one that operates in terms of the procedures of history and eventuates in conclusions that are checkable by history … In particular I mean a novel that evolves its own paradigms and myths, in the process (and here is the point at which true rivalry, even enmity, perhaps enters the picture)

perhaps going so far as to show up the mythic status of history – in other words, demythologising history. (NT 3)

J. M. Coetzee is careful to point out that he is not endorsing the literary at the expense of the political: the project of rivalry would call into question the very ideologies of historiographic practice, necessarily politicizing these modes of "anti-realist" fiction through their (textual) resistance (NT 4). Madness, I will argue, is the fulcrum of this deconstructive, demythologizing strategy.

Eugene Dawn works in the Mythography section of the Kennedy Institute in the United States. Through his (metatextual) account of his preparation of the "Vietnam Report", written in the basement of the Harry S. Truman Library, we learn of his troubled relation with his superior "Coetzee"; his sense of dis-ease with his vocation; his failing marriage to his wife Marilyn; his mental collapse culminating in his kidnapping and stabbing his son Martin; and finally, his committal to an asylum. In David Attwell's words, Dawn is a "disgraced" employee at the Institute because he "breaks ... [the] threshold of ['moral discretion'] repeatedly and explicitly", for instance, when he advocates a "program of assassination and of area bombing" (*J. M. Coetzee* 42). Even though the U.S. government comes close to or indeed crosses the moral threshold, it is not Dawn's place to provoke attention to this fact; ideological subterfuge is, after all, the function of mythology. In the second part, the first and most substantial section is narrated by the partially historical Jacobus Coetzee, a colonial explorer in South Africa in 1760, who details his three expeditions: the first "beyond the Great River" and the two journeys to "the land of the Great Namaqua" (D 61; 66; 100). On the second of the three journeys Jacobus falls ill and is nursed by the Namaquas, who effectively hold him captive. The third mission – the second to the Great Namaqua – led by Captain Hendrik Hop, is primarily to capture and punish Jacobus Coetzee's runaway servants. This mission is presented as a transcription written on Jacobus Coetzee's behalf, revised and retold in the 1930s and 1940s by S. J. Coetzee, a lecturer at the historically Afrikaner Stellenbosch University who is a distant relation of Jacobus Coetzee and father of the (fictional) translator "J. M. Coetzee", who also prefaces the book. The "Afterword" by S. J. Coetzee is part of a series of lectures given annually to the Van Plettenberg Society between 1934 and 1948, on the eve of the Afrikaner National Party's ascendency to power, and is followed by a deposition in the form of an appendix dictated by Jacobus Coetzee in 1760.

As a first instance of what I shall call Coetzee's "acts of genre", where "acts" imply performance, duplicity and self-consciousness, by placing himself as a character in his novel, J. M. Coetzee makes self-ironizing claims to authenticity (in this case via the genres of documentary, travelogue and historical document) and unsettles the reading process: the reader is encouraged to sift through the narrative for elements of truth. Not only does this involve the reader ethically in the life of the work, as Rosemary Jolly suggests, it also gestures J. M. Coetzee's own accountability to history (*Colonization* 121).

Myth, according to Barthes, is a *"metalanguage"* (*Mythologies* 115): it provides a form by which discourse can itself be naturalized (131). Myth seeks to naturalize not innate human behaviour (Nature) but History, via the social. Modern life is structured by myth, which sets about obscuring the *"what-goes-without-saying"* or, put more bluntly, "ideological abuse" (*Mythologies* 11). It is self-evident, therefore, why Barthes's theory of myth can be usefully applied to a colonial paradigm. Indeed, French colonialism is one of Barthes's key concerns. In "Myth Today", the essay that closes his aphoristic mythologies, Barthes describes how the image on the cover of the French magazine *Paris-Match* of the "Negro" soldier saluting the tricolour presents a "semiological system": it signifies multiply, most importantly here (note the ironic distance Barthes establishes between author and text), that "all [France's] sons, without any colour discrimination, faithfully serve under her flag, and that there is no better answer to the detractors of an alleged colonialism than the zeal shown by this Negro in serving his so-called oppressors" (*Mythologies* 116). The signifier, what the picture *presents* or its mode of presentation, is "already formed with a previous system (*a black soldier is giving the French salute*)". The signified, what the picture *represents* or "means", Barthes says, is a "purposeful mixture of Frenchness and militariness", but there is also a "presence of the signified through the signifier" (*Mythologies* 116) – mythological signifieds also can be multiple. This is the myth of benevolent colonialism: the "Negro" soldier is not a "symbol" or an "example" but a "gesture" (*Mythologies* 122) which naturalizes the principles and methods of the French empire. This is why myth is a kind of "language-robbery" (*Mythologies* 131) because it distorts first-order language by picking and choosing which meanings to emphasize and which to conceal. Barthes even wonders if there might be a "mythology of the mythologist" (*Mythologies* 12), hinting, I conjecture, that his own deployment of a structuralist approach to myth deflects attention from his leftist politics whilst allowing him to get his ideas heard.

In the manner of Barthes's mythologies, the repellent photographs that Dawn paws over are meant to reaffirm the invincibility of the U.S., which, as history has testified, was itself mythological: the first, a pornographic image of the child-woman and the American lieutenant, the second of American soldiers displaying their macabre trophies of shrunken Vietnamese heads and the third, a picture of a Vietnamese prisoner of war, his face pressed against the bars of his cage with the camera focused on one eye that glints in the sun. The first is a transparent display of patriarchal, colonialist triumph: the woman's body is a commodity in the system of patriarchal-colonialist exchange (theorists of anti-colonial nationalism have abundantly demonstrated that women were perceived in this way in the struggle between revolutionary nationalists and the colonizer [cf. Chatterjee *Nation*; Kandiyoti "Identity"; Yeğenoğlu *Colonial Fantasies*]). The second revises the myth of the colonial hunt (colonizer asserts his dominion by posing with leg rested jauntily upon the corpse of an animal). The heads of the corpses "are trophies: the Annamese tiger having been exterminated, there remain only men and certain hardy lesser mammals" (D 15). The association pervasive in racist ideology between the ethnic other and animals which reduces the other to less than human is re-emphasized in the third photograph of the caged soldier whose eye Dawn unconsciously wishes to gouge out as he strokes the surface of the print. Perhaps the eye represents a resisting consciousness that can return the gaze of its oppressor. The violence (or the implied violence in the first picture) portrayed in these images radically distances us as readers whilst paradoxically making us complicit through the act of looking.

Barthes identifies three modes of interpreting myth: firstly, myth read as empty signifier; secondly, myth read as full signifier and, thirdly, myth read as "an inextricable whole made of meaning and form". The first mode is "cynical": a literal reading is made whereby, in the example of the image of the French tricolour, the saluting "Negro" soldier becomes a symbol or example of French imperialism. The second is "demystifying" and distinguishes between meaning and form to read the "distortion" of the image/text: the "Negro" soldier is an "alibi of French imperiality". The third is "dynamic" in which the image is read holistically, as it was intended: the soldier manifests the "very *presence* of French imperiality" (*Mythologies* 128). In the first two modes myth loses its coherence and is destroyed, whereas in the third ideology comes into play and myth is "at once true and unreal" (*Mythologies* 128). As a mythographer, Dawn's objective is to produce myths that procure the third mode, but the text, by portraying Dawn as mad and therefore unreliable and by disrupting its own verisimilitude via parody and deconstruction, elicits both the first and second modes, both cynical and demystifying. This disjuncture between reading practices embodied in Dawn is the madness of his mythologizing project.

Dawn is unable to move beyond the "Western" discourse in which he is entrenched. Not unlike the implicit ideal writer presented by J. M. Coetzee in *White Writing* who would portray Africa in African terms (J. M. Coetzee identifies "a historical insecurity regarding the place of the artist of European heritage in the African landscape" [WW 62]), Dawn strives to represent the landscape in which he finds himself authentically, with "the air of a real world through the looking-glass" (D 37). Of course, the joke here is that Dawn's mythography has closer affinities with Alice's wonderland. In fact, he is the unwitting subject of his own mythography so consumed is he by his own mythologizing. Although he advances propaganda that takes account of Vietnamese culture, rather than a mode that operates within a "Western" discursive field, his thinking is itself deeply rooted in imperialist ideology and, as Attwell demonstrates, the Freudian myth of the "primal horde": indeed, the "parodic effect" in this part of the book "depends on Dawn's perspective coming from *within* imperialism and its traditions" (*J. M. Coetzee* 43–44).

Dawn confuses the nature of his vocation and is blind to the limits of the genre with which he works. His superior, "Coetzee", commenting upon Dawn's report, suggests he should be sympathetic to the needs of his reader (the American military) and self-conscious about the methodologies he employs. As it stands, the report is obscure and of an "*avant-garde* nature" (D 4) and appears to be written

FREUD.

for the benefit of "Coetzee". Observant of the prevailing tensions between the Mythography Department and the army, "Coetzee" cautions Dawn to make the report accessible to an army readership, "in words of one syllable", explaining "how myths operate in human society, how signs are exchanged, and so forth" (D 4). Dawn, on the other hand, wants to privilege the creative and explicitly links the writing of propaganda – an aggressive corruption of historical truths that is overtly ideological – with art. The ironic humour that surfaces in the later works reveals itself here with Dawn unconsciously absolving himself of responsibility by making such an association, whilst the narrative registers the unethical and demythologized nature of his myth-making (in Barthes, the second, "demystifying" mode that "destroys" myth). For a man who answers to the military, Dawn remarks unreflexively that he shuns conflict of any hue, having stated that he is fearful of angering "Coetzee", who "is now a failed creative person who lives vicariously off true creative people" (D1). Not only does Dawn perceive his current vocation as poetry of sorts, he convinces himself that mythography, his "present specialism", is "an open field like philosophy or criticism because it has not yet found a methodology to lose itself for ever in the mazes of" (D 31). Dawn's misapprehension of the rules of the game, where he likens philosophy or the pursuit of truth to its very antithesis, propaganda or manufactured "truths", underscores the distortions produced by ideology, here, the myths of imperialism. It is a symptom of his psychosis and in turn a metaphor for the madness upon which such ideologies are built. "I am a hero of resistance … no less than that, properly understood, in metaphor" (D 27), he says, and, "I see things and have a duty toward history that cannot wait" (D 29). Dawn unwittingly exposes himself as a failed writer with literary and heroic pretensions: in fact, he is simply a lackey of the American government. Ironically, this "hero of resistance", who is deeply suspicious of the U.S. government, has yet to set foot on Vietnamese soil.

Dawn's constant reassertion of self, like Jacobus Coetzee's, exposes his profound insecurity and psychic instability and, as I have argued, he becomes a victim of the imperialist project he serves. His work, the business of what he calls "psychological warfare", centres on the question, what psychic and psychological "factors" make the enemy "resistant to penetration"?: "Having answered this question we can go on to ask: how can we make our programs more penetrant"? (D 25–26). Note the Freudian linguistic register that is a feature of the book. The construction and deconstruction (or, literally, destruction) of the subject, the enemy Vietnamese, premises the introduction to Dawn's report. By drawing a picture of the myths and social norms of Vietnamese society (community, patrilineality and so on) in order that these might be undermined, propagandists like Dawn aim to "break down group morale" (D 24). Dawn's subsequent psychological breakdown, a metaphor for mimetic violence, reproduces the very aims of his report. Though Dawn writes of "the victim's preoccupation with taint" under the heading "Testimony of CT" (political assassination) (D 23), the text signals quite transparently that Dawn and Jacobus are each tainted by the mythologizing in which they are engaged. (Nowhere in the narrative is the meaning of the letters

FATHER-SON   HEGEL   JOLLY

"CT" elaborated: this is the dehumanizing, mythologizing language of war, where death and human suffering are traded.)

Jolly argues that both Jacobus and Dawn internalize their "repeated acts of violation" – Jacobus finds pleasure bursting his carbuncle and Dawn stabs his son, Martin. Dawn confuses his own identity with Martin's in what Jolly reads as a sadomasochistic impulse. The sadist feels his independence threatened by the other's recognition of dependence upon him and can therefore only truly feel independent by violating the other. This Jolly couches in terms of the mythological father: "since recognition of the self ... is the source of erotic pleasure, the sadist experiences sexual satisfaction in his violation of the role of the all-powerful father" (*Colonization* 113–14).

The father/son relationship of Dawn and Martin ironically mirrors the structure of Vietnamese society that Dawn is working to disable. His "tough-approach" to Martin ("How loud must I shout ... before [the child] will believe that all is for the best, that I love him with a father's love?" [D 38].) reflects the mythologized paternalism of his report. Under section 1.4 *"The father-voice"*, Dawn writes: "The father is authority, infallibility, ubiquity" (D 21). However, mimetically reproducing his relationship with Martin, under section 1.51, "Countermyths", he points out that the fallibility of the father-myth lies in the "portrayal of the father as vulnerable" (D 25). As Dawn plunges into the deepest recesses of insanity, "Martin" counter-intuitively metamorphoses in Dawn's sick mind into the father-voice as Dawn's grasp on reality is subsumed by wild fantasies. Since the external world of the sadist, Jolly argues, refuses to "offer the sadists the recognition [they] desire ... they turn upon themselves in what becomes a masochistic bid for self-recognition" (*Colonization* 118).

That the self is consolidated in its recognition of the other is readily apparent in J. M. Coetzee's portrayal of Jacobus Coetzee; as Attwell observes: "In the initial moments of the encounter Jacobus Coetzee sizes up the Namaqua leader and is condescendingly pleased with his self-assurance and humanity (this is the Hegelian pleasure of extracting self-validation from the recognition given by the Other)" (*J. M. Coetzee* 48). Jacobus Coetzee's condition reflects the Afrikaners' struggle as farmers against the decline of their cultural history that, as J. M. Coetzee explains in "The Farm Novels of C. M. van den Heever", necessitates such a reassertion of self: "We [ ] see efforts to buttress Afrikaner patriarchalism in order that a heightened significance should be attached to the acts of the founding fathers, to maintaining their legacy and perpetuating their values" (WW 83).

If we take as an example the case of Jacobus and "idleness", we might come to a better understanding of Jacobus's bid for self-recognition that as Attwell points out, is Hegelian rather than Manichean because it depends upon some form of cultural exchange (*J. M. Coetzee* 51–52). S. J. Coetzee's Afterword situates

Jacobus as a colonialist and a "Boer":[2] he is openly admiring of Jacobus Coetzee, naming him a hero who "is acknowledged by students of our early history as the discoverer of the Orange River and the giraffe" (D 108). He claims that his Afterword, however, serves to "present a more complete and therefore more just view of Jacobus Coetzee … To understand the life of this obscure farmer requires a positive act of the imagination" (D 108–09). This last comment, of course, throws all the preceding narrative into doubt, suggesting, as it does, that it is only through willed invention that Jacobus Coetzee's story can be uncovered at all. S. J. Coetzee, as mythographer, celebrates Jacobus as a hero of Boer history (as opposed to a European settler one), and gives credence to the racist stereotyping of the "Hottentots" (Khoisan) (D 114) that attributes "Hottentot" "idleness" to settler culture, to drinking liquor and smoking tobacco.

Jacobus Coetzee is blind to his own hypocrisy. He regards the Bushmen as "listless and unreliable", while on the other hand, "I progressed to an exposition of my career as tamer of the wild. In the wild I lose my sense of boundaries. This is the consequence of space and solitude" (D 78). Although it is acceptable for him to live outside colonial social norms in the veld, he expects the indigenous peoples to observe cultural and social practices alien to them. In the vast "emptiness" of the veld, where the boundaries of self and other are in suspension, he unwittingly becomes more akin to the Bushman, whose "idleness", J. M. Coetzee argues in "Idleness in South Africa", is early European travel writers' misrecognition of a recourse to reverie (WW 18). Such writers, who are duped by their own mythologies, lack the conceptual framework to properly understand (read) the other. The colonialist myth of "Hottentot" idleness is coeval, J. M. Coetzee suggests, with the emergence of the work ethic during the European Enlightenment. The "idle" "Hottentot", in the manner of the Hegelian master/slave dialectic, provides a convenient foil to the European in these early literary representations but also a threat: the "Hottentot" is "*under-developed*" but also scandalously not so different from the European (original emphasis; WW 22). "Hottentot" idleness, J. M. Coetzee argues, disproves the travel writer's preconceived "discourses about elemental man". Failing to correspond to the anthropological grid of differences drawn up by these early travellers brings about the potentially self-annihilating realization that they share more equivalences than differences (original emphasis; WW 23).

At the same time, S. J. Coetzee re-evaluates Jacobus Coetzee's (colonialist) historiography: Jacobus Coetzee is portrayed as an "obscure farmer" and as the little man of history; he records reciprocity between master and servant, whose children played together (but only to reaffirm the hegemony of the master) (D 115); "Hottentot" life is portrayed in harmony with the Boers and, like the Boers', is "capable of picturesqueness … The quiet farmhouse on the slopes, the quiet huts

---

[2]   In *White Writing* Coetzee explains that he uses terms like "Hottentot", "Bushman" and "Boer", which in the case of "Hottentot" and "Bushman" are deeply offensive, in line with "old-time usage" (WW 1n.).

in the hollow, the starlit sky" (D 115). Above all, S. J. Coetzee calls into question the colonialist myth of discovery: "The region was so vast, its explorers so few, that the historian may legitimately think of its features as unknown, and of each ask the question, Who discovered this?, or, to be more precise, Which European discovered this?" (D 115–16).[3] S. J. Coetzee's analysis in the Afterword conveys the conflictual relationship between Boer and European that, Attwell argues, conveniently supported the Afrikaner nationalist ideology of the 1940s (*J. M. Coetzee* 45; see also Gallagher, *Story* 28–30). S. J. Coetzee dismisses European botanists in the following terms: "The criteria for a new discovery employed by the gentlemen from Europe were surely parochial. They required that every specimen fill a hole in their European taxonomies" (D 116). He speaks of the "inward moment of discovery" which he credits to the Boer who draws not only from his own experiences and knowledge but from that of the Bushman as well (D 116). References to idleness also allude to the stereotypes that formed part of the case European travel writers, whom J. M. Coetzee refers to as "spokesmen of colonialism", were to build against the Boer frontiersmen in the nineteenth century (WW 29–30), thus making the Boer farmer and the "Hottentot" unlikely allies. As J. M. Coetzee argues in *White Writing*, the Boer threatened the purity and superiority of the European over the African: "The spokesmen of colonialism are dismayed by the squalor and sloth of Boer life because it affords sinister evidence of how European stock can regress after a few generations in Africa" (30).

The close proximity of self and other that the presence of the "Hottentot" threatens to expose leads Jacobus unconsciously to attempt to install more tangible boundaries between the peoples he encounters, appropriating, for instance, Zeno's Paradox and theories of infinity: "Under the Hottentot captivity I had not failed to keep the Zeno beetle in mind. There had been legs, metaphorical legs, and much else too, that I had been prepared to lose" (D 96). Under the Zenonian principle, the beetle is *seemingly* infinitely indestructible: "The fourth game was the most interesting one, the Zenonian case in which only an infinitely diminishing fraction of my self survived, the fictive echo of a tiny 'I' whispered across the void of eternity" (D 98; cf. Attwell, *J. M. Coetzee* 53; Dovey, *Novels* 111). Jacobus utilizes these principles to maintain his own increasingly fragile sense of self but, like Dawn's, this is ruptured when it becomes apparent that in the "wilderness", in colonialist terms, Jacobus enters the same psychological space inhabited by those he strives to other.

The lack of self-reflexivity or self-understanding in Dawn and Jacobus or a skewed self-reflexivity that we might call madness is usefully illuminated by J. M. Coetzee's argument in "Apartheid Thinking" that apartheid ideology was mad. J. M. Coetzee treats the writing of the progenitor of apartheid ideology, Geoffrey

---

[3] VanZanten Gallagher notes that the "Bantu" (Xhosa), according to white South African mythology, were only relatively recent immigrants to South Africa, arriving in the eighteenth century at the same time as the Boers on their "trek to the interior" (*Story* 25).

Cronjé, as a kind of crazed (secular) confession. By way of qualification, J. M. Coetzee perceives Cronjé's work,

> not as a repentant confession – far from it – but as a confession of belief, a credo all the more revealing for being full of ignorance and madness. In what now seems old-fashioned innocence, Cronjé falls into a delirium of writing with a lack of reserve, a lack of prudent self-censorship, quite foreign to his successors in the academic-bureaucratic castle he helped to build. In that delirium we catch glimpses of apartheid nakedly occupied in thinking itself out. But we can share these glimpses only if we read the texts, follow the ravings, from inside, if we inhabit with part of ourselves Cronjé's position as writing subject. (GO 165)

Searching for their own particular warped sense of "truth", both protagonists in *Dusklands*, in their short-sighted introspection and inflated assertion of self, present the reader with confessions not unlike Cronjé's; indeed, both display "a lack of prudent self-censorship". In this respect we are most likely to attain a kind of truthfulness: not the truth of their narratives, but of the unconscious workings of their minds and of the ideologies that motivate them.

The act of reading these two "confessions" necessarily encourages the reader to empathize with Dawn and Jacobus, and thus on a symbolic level the reader is made complicit in their abuse even though, paradoxically, the gratuitous nature of their violence marks a radical hiatus that refuses to allow the reader to enter fully the life of the text or, in fact, to empathize with its protagonists. Therefore, by disturbing the reader's sensibilities in this way, the text simulates madness in the experience of reading: the reader experiences the madness of "civilization" "from inside".

It is worth lingering here over the issues around confession and the lack of self-censorship raised by this novel that are also linked to the theme of complicity (issues treated in more depth in Chapters 6, 7 and 8 which are devoted to the third phase of Coetzee's writing). "The Vietnam Project", proving for an ethically minded white writer such as Coetzee thematically apt as the introduction to the oeuvre (cf. Attwell, *J. M. Coetzee* 57), opens with the ironized confession of a guilt-stricken white aggressor: "My name is Eugene Dawn. I cannot help that" (D 1). In a back-handed fashion, Dawn apologizes perhaps for the quaintness or ludicrousness of his name, and not for his unethical vocation. He works for the New Life Project and his name, the combination of "Eugene" ("eugenics", the scientific programme of selective breeding adopted by Hitler's Nazis) and "Dawn", which thus puns on the "dawn of a new race". He is involved in reconstructing the Vietnamese psyche under the auspices of a government that would dissociate itself from the sinister implications of a eugenicist programme, yet the tactics this government employs are themselves suspect. Jacobus Coetzee's narrative opens with a similarly ironic self-disclosure, though with different, racially supremacist ramifications: "Five years ago Adam Wijnand, a Bastard ["Coloured"], *no shame in that*, packed up and trekked to Korana country" (emphasis added; D 57). That which is defended by Jacobus Coetzee – racial alterity – is automatically thrown

NOT SURE
✳
?

Amy.

RACIAL ALTERITY.

into doubt by the portrayal of Jacobus that follows. Both these white writers therefore offer misplaced, and in Jacobus Coetzee's case, insincere, confessions: Dawn fails to recognize his culpability for American atrocities in Vietnam, and Jacobus Coetzee exposes his own racism, ironically, by his tacit denial of it.

Dawn gradually regresses into endless self-scrutiny, what he calls "the self reading the self to the self in all infinity" (D 38), echoed almost verbatim by J. M. Coetzee's analysis of confession in "Confession and Double Thoughts". If, as J. M. Coetzee claims in *Doubling the Point*, "all writing is autobiography" and autobiography is driven by the desire for self-knowledge (391; 105), we can deduce that writing necessarily involves self-knowledge. Subjected to the problem of endless confession, each confession requiring further confession, ad infinitum (DP 291), Dawn is prey to the tortuous breakdown of self; only by breaking this chain of self-analysis and self-doubt will he be able to retain his grasp on his sanity. Whereas in the later works the writer-protagonists self-critically and self-consciously grapple with existential questions about their place as writers, Dawn's misgiving about this role manifests itself psychically, through mental breakdown. On the other hand, guilt is *enacted upon* Jacobus Coetzee *as a character in a work of fiction*: the motifs of excavation and sickness configure a writerly dis-ease – J. M. Coetzee's – with colonialist violence. By juxtaposing the two narratives, J. M. Coetzee raises questions about guilt and responsibility, or, in Jacobus Coetzee's case, an absence of guilt and responsibility.

?MT
'SIKE

Typifying the Coetzean writer, Dawn is tormented by the demons of guilt as he struggles with his responsibilities as a writer, in this case of propaganda, and with the attendant ethics such a profession challenges. Guilt in the first narrative is explicitly identified as the cause of Dawn's breakdown. The doctors' diagnosis, Dawn says, is

> that intimate contact with the design of war made me callous to suffering and created in me a need for violent solutions to problems of living, infecting me at the same time with guilty feelings that showed themselves in nervous symptoms. (D 48)

also a gender aspect here – feminization

Dawn's "nervous symptoms" invert Jean-Paul Sartre's claim, in his preface to Frantz Fanon's *The Wretched of the Earth* (1961), that the "status of 'native' is a nervous condition" (17). Sartre is writing about the psychosis experienced by the "native" who internalizes an indignant response to colonial violence. In Dawn's case he internalizes guilt. Whether a response to anger or guilt, the resultant implosion of self reduces the subject to madness. Ironically, however, Dawn positions himself *as the victim* of guilty feelings: confined in a psychiatric institution, he displaces any sense of personal accountability for his morally dubious occupation by claiming, "The reason I am not ashamed [at finding myself in the hospital] is of course that I have a better case history than the long-term patients" (D 46). In accordance with the framing device of the novel, his crazed, misconceived sense of guilt refracts the monstrous Jacobus's myopia.

? straying into the territory of psychoanalysis, not sure how helpful that is to her cause.

The distinction between guilt and shame has preoccupied philosophers and critical thinkers, particularly in the field of postcolonial studies (see, for example, Bhabha, "Postcolonial Authority"; Gilroy, *Against Race*) given that it pivots on the ethical and sometimes political responses the ashamed or guilty subject experiences towards the other. Sartre famously picks up these ethical tensions in *Being and Nothingness* (1957), "*I* am ashamed of *myself* before the *Other*. If any one of these dimensions disappears, the shame disappears as well" (289–90). Walter Sinnott-Armstrong summarizes the distinction as follows: "the object of guilt is an individual act, whereas the object of shame is a whole self or a character trait. In short, people feel guilty for what they do, and they feel ashamed of what they are" ("Ashamed" 200). The ethical implications of this distinction are clear: shame is more attuned to accountability and responsibility and to an end product of self-reform. Guilt, typically experienced physiologically as a paling of the skin, and shame, which induces the blush of embarrassment, are symptoms of the subject's self-perception of the wrongdoing: the invisibility of guilt means it can go unaccounted for whilst shame ineluctably signals personal responsibility. To understand what kind of guilty experiences these are in the light of his psychosis, we must unravel Dawn's perceptions of his own actions and of his relationship to the other.

Dawn's guilt manifests itself unconsciously in his paranoiac delusions. Paranoia, suggests J. M. Coetzee in "Taking Offense", is the product of the belief that the "intention to offend is detected behind every action giving offense" (GO 20). Like Dostoevsky in *The Master of Petersburg* (1994) or, indeed, the Dostoevsky who penned *The Possessed* (1872), Dawn suffers from epilepsy, which historically was misconceived as "demon-possession" (which is how it is presented in *Dusklands*) and which in turn in all three texts, on one level, can be read as a metaphor for guilt. Demon-possession hovers behind Dawn's words: "If this inner face of mine, this vizor of muscle, had features, they would be the monstrous troglodyte features of a man who bunches his sleeping eyes and mouth as a totally unacceptable dream forces itself into him" (D 7). He refers to his wife's "novelettish reading of my plight" (D 10), saying that she believes his "human sympathies have been coarsened … [and that he has] become addicted to violent and perverse fantasies" (D 9). These fantasies about his work permeate his private, sexual life: his paranoia manifests the belief that Marilyn is indulging in casual, extramarital sex, though he has no evidence to substantiate this delusion save a sexually explicit photograph of his wife published in *Playboy Magazine*. In turn, sexual fantasies are linked to the writing process; ironically, Dawn's wild inventions mirror the inventiveness of his propaganda work. The perverted discourses of propaganda (a distortion of the truth for political purposes) and pornography (material soliciting an erotic rather than an aesthetic or emotional response) are juxtaposed to reveal that both are encoded by patriarchy and imperialism. Dawn thinks of the photograph of Marilyn in just these terms – "Meat for your master" (D 13) – and the three photographs he retains from the report, Head suggests, "offer a distillation of imperialist violence" (*J. M. Coetzee* 32).

Dawn must "exorcise [the demons of madness] while they are weak and [he] is strong" (D 49). He seeks absolution for stabbing his son but, nevertheless, refuses to accept culpability,

> because I know that if Martin understood the strain I was under he would forgive me; and because also I believe guilt to be a sterile disposition of the mind unlikely to further my cure. (D 44)

Since Dawn's response is directed towards the action of stabbing and not to his own sense of self, his response to the crime can be diagnosed as guilt rather than shame, ruling out the possibility of self-reform. Nonetheless, even his guilt is misdirected since, bizarrely, his criminal actions figure nowhere in this confession. He refuses to accept responsibility on two counts: firstly, taking advantage of the naïve, unconditional love of the child for its parent, he believes he would be forgiven by Martin, and secondly, self-interest tells him that guilt will not cure his psychic collapse. This is what we might call the postmodern subject's schizophrenic BAUMAN? response to reality: Dawn's understanding of his actions has detached itself entirely from the fact of the crime.

Fredric Jameson argues that postmodernism, characterized by the "waning of affect" (*Postmodernism* 10) whereby feelings "are now free-floating and impersonal and tend to be dominated by a peculiar kind of euphoria" (*Postmodernism* 16), is best represented by the schizophrenic condition. Modernism on the other hand embodies the experiences of alienation and isolation. Jameson turns to Jacques Lacan to define schizophrenia: "A breakdown in the signifying chain, that is, the interlocking syntagmatic series of signifiers which constitutes an utterance or meaning" (*Postmodernism* 26). Jameson chooses largely to skirt around the symbolically familial basis upon which Lacan's definition rests, but Lacan sits nicely with the analysis of Dawn made here because the rival of the schizophrenic is not the biological father of the Oedipal Complex but the "Name-of-the-Father" as a linguistic function of authority (*Postmodernism* 26). In postmodern culture the relationship between signifier and signified, between word or sound-image (form) and concept (content), is replaced, according to Jameson, by "that objective mirage of signification generated and projected by the relationship of signifiers among themselves" (*Postmodernism* 26). Schizophrenia manifests in the subject in whom the signifying chain "snaps". Jameson points out that his interest in schizophrenia is not clinical but cultural, as a "suggestive aesthetic model" (*Postmodernism* 26), as it is on one level in *Dusklands* if we read the protagonists' madness as a *metaphor* of imperial and colonial violence.

Not unlike the "depthlessness" of the postmodern condition, Dawn invites a superficial reading of his report. Dawn's treatment of the photographs corresponds with Jameson's analysis of postmodernity as a "waning of affect", which Jameson attributes to the "late capitalist" phase. Dawn's fetishization of the photographs betrays his disassociation from Vietnam, of being literally out of *touch* with reality: "I close my eyes and pass my fingertips over the cool, odorless surface

how do photographs function in
JNC — also HoE.

FRIEND.

of the print" (D 16). He struggles to rectify this by pressing on the image of the prisoner's eye. This is the postmodernist relation between reader and text. The photographs themselves in *Dusklands* cannot be described in terms of the depthlessness of which Jameson writes, "which confers its deathly quality" to the image (*Postmodernism* 9), because except for the ambiguous photograph of the child-woman, these are photographs of very real human suffering. Nevertheless, Dawn's response to these images is symptomatic of the "waning of affect" that Jameson theorizes:

> On mornings when my spirits have been low and nothing has come, I have always had the stabilizing knowledge that, unfolded from their wrappings and exposed, these pictures could be relied on to give my imagination the slight electric impulse that is all it needs to set it free again. (D 13)

The first picture, as referred to above, depicts an American lieutenant, a giant of a man, copulating with a woman so tiny she could be a child (D 13). The framing of the picture under the heading "Father Makes Merry" returns us to the patriarchal relations that structure Vietnamese society and hence, in turn, to U.S. mythography. Is the woman drugged, a prostitute, being raped; could the scene be staged? She is caught between two screens, the camera lens and the blank television that not only reflects the flashing bulb but also mirrors the blankness or depthlessness of the woman's expression, rendering her a readerless text. In the process she is simultaneously dehumanized by the "consumer" of the photograph. More positively, she figures a resisting text.

How? ||

If we consider Dawn's inability to process the mythologies about which he writes, illustrated in his perverse interest in the photographs that capture scenes of heinous abuse, and if we take into account his psychosis which reaches its nadir in his inability to comprehend the enormity of his crime when he stabs his son, we can readily see how he corresponds with the postmodern schizophrenic subject sketched by Jameson. Such an analysis, however, is complicated by the ethico-politics of J. M. Coetzee's project in conjuring protagonists like Dawn and Jacobus Coetzee, representations which jar with Jameson's model of depthlessness and a "weakening of historicity" (*Postmodernism* 6). From this we can deduce that the break Jameson identifies between high modernism and postmodernism is less pronounced than he implies. Indeed, Dawn bridges this divide: a character who is the subject of postmodern discourse but one moulded and shaped into a late modernist text that by definition will be ethical if not political as well.

J. M. Coetzee explains Freud's theory of paranoia in an essay on censorship in South Africa, "that part of paranoia is a general detachment of libido from the world" (GO 198). He goes on to argue that in the twilight years of apartheid, this detachment of libido in white South Africans took the form of the loss of an imaginative capacity to envisage the future (GO 198–99). In the political sphere paranoia manifested itself at the level of fear of "total onslaught" of enemy states against South Africa as well as "Western Christian civilization in Africa"

interesting ||

(GO 199).[4] Paranoia also exhibited itself in censorship. Applied to Dawn's case it becomes evident how the paranoiac state, here the U.S., projects its malaise on to the very envoy it charges with conveying its dark message. What J. M. Coetzee identifies as the "essential gesture of censorship" is the ability to judge what to admit into the consciousness and what to refuse. Clearly in the case of propaganda, writers are abundantly aware that their judgement functions on a different plane, that propaganda involves the embellishment of the facts. In Dawn this phenomenon manifests itself in his inability to judge what is real and what is not, what to admit and what to refuse.

Jacobus Coetzee, who lacks any such albeit pathological self-reflexivity, is portrayed as a foolishly egocentric and self-aggrandizing colonist: "Perhaps on my horse and with the sun over my right shoulder I looked like a god" to the Hottentots (D 71). This is myth and madness in the raw: Jacobus is the standard-bearer of colonial expansionism and the herald of its madness. His gun is the colonist's "mediator with the world" because it reminds him of his own mortality, just as it gives him the power to take a life (D 79). He perceives executing his renegade servants as a duty: a "sacrifice for myself and for my countrymen", having "taken it upon myself to be the one to pull the trigger", for "God's judgement is just" (D 106); he believes that a "world without me is inconceivable" (D 107). Read on a literal level, from Jacobus Coetzee's point of view, this last remark is tautological, allowing J. M. Coetzee to mock his protagonist's myopia. Jacobus Coetzee lacks the capacity to reform, his mission fails but he undergoes no ethical awakening, and in this respect he is unlike the later (white) narrator-authors, who at the very least are self-questioning and typically burdened by guilt.

According to J. M. Coetzee in "Apartheid Thinking", the Boers' paranoiac fear of miscegenation revealed in Cronjé's writing, which was based upon notions of "racial purity" (GO 166; 168–76), can only be exorcized from the collective South African consciousness by according madness its place in history (GO 164). To categorize madness ontologically as it has been in South Africa, J. M. Coetzee argues, is to dislocate it from history yet he concedes that to call apartheid thinking mad might be construed as political side-stepping and that white liberals used the diagnosis of madness to "distance[ ] themselves" from apartheid whilst doing nothing to end black oppression (GO 163–64). This argument highlights the problem of linking madness with criminality and imperial complicity in Dawn, who cannot be held fully accountable when he stabs his son because his insanity diminishes his responsibility (or he can only be held accountable as criminally insane). Nevertheless, because his madness is the consequence of his particular vocation, on these grounds his accountability – and therefore the ethics of the book – must stand. ? what does this mean?

---

    4   In response to the "total onslaught" of the 1980s insurrections in South Africa, P. W. Botha launched a policy of "total strategy" that was to bring a range of policies together in the fight against the revolutionaries (Beinart 245).

In its reflections on the madness of "civilization" *Dusklands* offers a damning critique of Enlightenment thinking and so-called rationality (cf. Attwell, *J. M. Coetzee* 37–40; Head, *J. M. Coetzee* 28–29) pivoting on the madness of "civilization". The quotation from Flaubert, "What is important is the philosophy of history" that prefaces "The Narrative of Jacobus Coetzee" transparently signals the book's parodic design, which in turn exposes the ideologies underpinning history. Flaubert's text is itself parodic, as Attwell reminds us (*J. M. Coetzee* 44–45). Placing the quotation before the second narrative exposes Jacobus Coetzee's monumental lack of self-reflexivity towards his colonialist agenda: "The one gulf that divides us from the Hottentots is our Christianity. We are Christians, a folk with a destiny. They become Christians too, but their Christianity is an empty word" (D 57-58). Jacobus Coetzee's excessive pronouncements are then juxtaposed with his unselfconscious revelations about his own brutalized and misogynistic notion of Christianity in his description of Bushmen women; irony lays bare Christianity as an "empty word". The figure of the "Christian" he parodically inhabits is violently imposed upon the other:

> [The Bushman girl] has seen you kill the men who represented power to her … .
> You have become Power itself now and she nothing, a rag you wipe yourself on
> and throw away. She is completely disposable. She is something for nothing,
> free. (D 61)

According to Jacobus, this is unlike Dutch women, who "carry an aura of property with them. They are first of all property themselves … You lose your freedom" (D 61). Sexual intercourse with Bushmen women carries no burden of responsibility: not unlike the women of Dawn's seedy imagination, such women are utterly objectifiable, existing, Jacobus Coetzee believes, merely to satisfy his pleasure.

Commentators on *Dusklands* are quick to call into question, on ethical grounds, the representation of violence. Yet violence, which is couched in terms of pseudo-rationality in the novel, is suggestive of the madness of oppressive ideologies, here, imperialism, colonialism and apartheid. Attwell alerts us to the negative response of some readers to this aspect of the book: "The violence of the Hop expedition in Jacobus Coetzee's narrative is so startling as to become a burden" (*J. M. Coetzee* 54). Knox-Shaw, for instance, argues that through such graphic violence, J. M. Coetzee "reenact[s] 'true savagery' and thereby further[s] its claims" (qtd. in Attwell, *J. M. Coetzee* 54; Knox-Shaw 33). Attwell counters these critics, however, by arguing that "Such writing [in *Dusklands*] is surely transgressive, not in a theoretical manner that enables one to explain it away, but in an *aggressive* mode that is aimed at readers' sensibilities" (*J. M. Coetzee* 55). The reader is defamiliarized from the text through its pornographic or obscene linguistic register, an effect that reproduces the gulf between self and other and between the writer and reader of which Jolly writes. In "Taking Offense" Coetzee is careful to distinguish between pornography and obscenity which are "not co-referential … a subject cannot react with unmixed pleasure to pornography yet at the same time call it obscene" if it induces what Joel Feinberg calls "disliked mental states" (Feinberg qtd. in GO 20). Dawn's photographs are obscene but he reads them pornographically – another indicator of his madness. The photographs are both titillating *and* violent (whereas Jacobus's sociopathic response to "Bushmen" women bears all the trademarks of colonial violence). By necessarily engaging with the pornographic in the novel, the reader is made complicit in this violence, which, as I have already discussed, would account for the violence being especially troubling. The reading experience of this particular novel is itself "mad" (destablizing) because as readers, we are both complicit with and revulsed from the text. Dawn's three photographs of his prisoners, which have a perverse stabilizing effect, he believes, on his sense of self (D 13), the sexual violence done to the young "Hottentot" girl in Jacobus Coetzee's narrative, and even the violence the latter enacts upon himself when he bursts the carbuncle, which is a means of re-establishing his sense of self, have recourse to the Zenonian myth of infinite infallibility and game-playing (D 98).

The violence meted out upon the other is, if in a minimal way, witnessed by the reader via the act of reading. We are alternatively encouraged to empathize with the other and, through witnessing, made complicit in the other's abuse, which, as I have explained, is the madness of this particular reading act. Reading is, at some level, to experience, and perhaps this is why J. M. Coetzee represents violence in such intimate, stomach-churning detail: entering Dawn's, Jacobus Coetzee's, or, indeed, Cronjé's subject position, for instance, the reader experiences (a simulation of) complicity and madness, what in other contexts J. M. Coetzee has called taint or contagion. The ethical inflections of such a move are therefore self-evident. Head confirms this argument when he suggests that, "To some extent, there is, in such passages, an enactment of the brutal pseudo-rationality that the novel would reject. Consequently, one is required to be a resisting reader, and this is signalled quite obviously" (*J. M. Coetzee* 34).

The work of demythologizing historical narrative, both history and the historical novel, leads J. M. Coetzee in *Dusklands* to peel away the processes of mythology and to inhabit inventively the mythographer's mind and in turn to expose the madness of so-called civilization. Dawn and Jacobus are deeply embroiled in the ideological work of imperialism and Empire, busy establishing the myths of the father. But, preparing the ground for J. M. Coetzee's next novels, *In the Heart of the Country* (1977) and *Waiting for the Barbarians* (1980), we see how the distorting effect of myth leads to madness which, as revealed in these servants of imperial and colonial powers who struggle to shore up the fragments of their shattered selves, is in part the somatic response to the acts of violence they have perpetrated against the other in the "father's" name.

Though *Dusklands* may prove too contrived for some readers, the juxtaposition of the two separate narratives reflects J. M. Coetzee's own dislocated identity: escaping apartheid South Africa in the late 1960s and early 70s to the U.S., the writer appears equally disillusioned with (the myth of) the free world that he portrays in *Dusklands*.

Chapter 2

Refusing to "Yield to the Spectre of Reason": The Madwoman in the Attic in *In the Heart of the Country*

Writing is not free expression.

J. M. Coetzee, *Doubling the Point* 65

Madness continues to take centre stage in J. M. Coetzee's second novel, *In the Heart of the Country* (1977) (hereafter referred to as *Heart of the Country*). This time, however, Coetzee enters the consciousness of a *female* narrator, Magda, who lives on the South African Karoo and is of Boer farming stock, and who therefore inhabits the psychically and textually precarious position of being both oppressor, as white colonial, and oppressed, as female. The preoccupation of this novel is the female colonial writer's psychic struggle with identity, achieved, as in the earlier novel *Dusklands* (1974), through the portrayal of an author-figure who descends into madness. Such a reading may strike some as contrary to Coetzee's intention because the protagonist only functions symbolically as author – of her life – but I will argue that it is the representation of Magda *as writer* that goes to the heart of the work. It is by resisting and then succumbing to writing that Magda battles against the "spectre of reason" that oppresses her (HC 150). Yielding to this spectre means submitting to the patriarchy and Afrikaner literary history that are her masters.

In Magda's search for self-understanding, her psychological stability is threatened by the colonial encounter, namely, her interaction with her servants, Hendrik and Klein-Anna, who in the politically inclusive sense are black. In "Beyond the Limit", Stephen Clingman traces the link between madness, colonialism and miscegenation in Southern African fiction, focusing on the effect on the other of repression. He argues that "in the colonial setting the analytical consideration of madness is intrinsically connected with a search for significant limits", those distinguishing the colonizer from the colonized (247), that without such limits "the colony falls apart" (248). "For those within the colony", he goes on, "it is no surprise that lines of symbolic demarcation form an integral part of [ ] other kinds of delineation", that is, living space, ownership of land, economic and political rights, social and cultural practices and behaviours (248). Madness is "beyond the limit", or, as Michel Foucault has argued in *Madness and Civilization* (1965), madness has long defined the limits (of reason and normalcy) both psychologically and literally (Clingman, "Beyond the Limit" 247; Foucault, *Madness* 8). Examples of this trope in Southern African fiction are plentiful: Olive Schreiner's *The Story of an African Farm* (1883), Sarah Gertrude Millin's *God's Stepchildren* (1924), William Plomer's *Turbott Wolfe* (1925), Peter Abraham's *The Path of Thunder* (1948), Doris Lessing's *The Grass is Singing* (1950), Bessie Head's *A Question of Power* (1974), Mongane Wally Serote's *To Every Birth Its Blood* (1981) and, post-apartheid, K. Sello Duiker's *The Quiet Violence of Dreams* (2001).

It is through the tensions generated by the confluence of gendered and raced oppression that Magda's insanity (her social condition) can be traced, yet she also functions as the "unstable" text or what Caroline Rody has called a "paper-thin literary trope" ("Daughter's Revolt" 161). As for Dawn in *Dusklands*, madness renders Magda an unreliable narrator. Coetzee, however, is skeptical about the usefulness of reading Magda as mad: "Magda is passionate in the way that one can be in fiction (I see no further point in calling her mad)" (DP 62). Although this affirms the book's experimental design, as Roland Barthes's "Death of the Author" warns us, we should not feel obliged as readers to the whims or will of the author nor to the effect the author intends. I therefore will argue that Magda is both mad literally and literarily, working on the principle that the categories of the real and the literary in this novel are irrevocably entangled, deriving meaning from each other. In her struggle to retain her sanity and her sense of self she is confronted with a Coetzean double bind: as a character in a book, she must represent herself through writing if she wants to assert her autonomy but to do so means being subject to discourse, which in this novel is always already patriarchal (as well as colonialist).

Shoshana Felman's concern in *Writing and Madness* (1985) with "modes and structures of *repression* within literary language" leads her to conclude that "Between literature and madness there exists an obscure but essential kinship: a kinship entailed, precisely, by *whatever blocks them off*, by that which destines them alike to repression and disavowal" (*Writing and Madness* 16). Felman, whose approach is deconstructive, advocates reading correlations between the literariness of madness and the madness of literature because, she argues, both literature and madness are premised upon repression or what Freud calls "a failure of translation" (qtd. in Felman, *Writing and Madness* 19), by what is left unsaid. The duality of madness in *Heart of the Country* is made available by reading the silences spoken in Magda's psychosis *and* the literary history in which she is placed. Perhaps it is here, however, that Coetzee's novel is compromised. As Clingman argues, Felman's deconstructive methodology, that neglects the social factors that induce madness, is weakened by its inherent essentialism; Felman reads all literary texts as "mad": "'writing' and 'madness' are nothing other than mutually referential" ("Beyond the Limit" 234). Coetzee's comment on the fruitlessness of reading Magda as mad points us in a similar direction, but, with Barthes in mind, on this point I would beg to differ.

The name 'Magda', which we learn only midway through the narrative, invokes the absurdist naming by Molloy of the mother-figure in Samuel Beckett's novel:

> I called her Mag, when I had to call her something … . For before you say mag, you say ma, inevitably. And da, in my part of the world, means father. Besides, for me the question did not arise, at the period I'm worming into now, I mean the question of whether to call her Ma, Mag or the Countess Caca. (*Molloy* 17–18)

So for Molloy, Mag-da is at once meaningless, or illustrative of the need to find meaning even where none exists, and represents the formative child-parent relationship in a child's development that is key to Coetzee's novel. This paradox of meaning and not-meaning is, moreover, indicative of Magda's unstable condition – both literal and literary – and it is partly her construction *as mad* that allows Coetzee to achieve this.

"Magda" also parodies the symbolism of the wife of the mythologized Great Trek leader, Piet Retief (Gallagher, *Story* 84): the heroine of Coetzee's novel doesn't fulfil the homely requirements of the celebrated Afrikaner women accorded to her namesake; Susan VanZanten Gallagher, invoking the title of the novel, notes that "Traditional discourse holds that a moral domesticity makes women the 'heart' of the country" (*Story* 94). Magda's spinsterhood serves only to exaggerate her marginality in what is a deeply patriarchal society with its expectations of women as wives and mothers (*vrou en moeder*), who are upheld as the custodians of racial purity and the morality of the tribe.

The experience of alienation, Clingman suggests (and Magda is the personification of alienation *par excellence*), "from the foreign land, the continent, and its peoples [ ] is the reality of the colonial enterprise" ("Beyond" 236). Magda feels alienated by the (sexual) relationships that she imagines have been built between her father and his new bride, between the black servants Hendrik and Klein-Anna, and between her father and Klein-Anna: "lines have been drawn, I am excluded from communion" (HC 57). She experiences both Electral fantasies – the daughter, here infantilized (HC 55; 77; 97), desiring the father and usurped by the "mother" – and colonialist fantasies of the fear of and desire for the black other. Magda conceives of Hendrik as a father-figure and the women with whom her father and Hendrik have relationships as mother-figures. Magda's own mother has apparently died. She is also alienated from the land, as Rita Barnard and Caroline Rody have amply discussed (Barnard, "Dream Topographies" 51; Rody, "Colonial Daughter's Revolt" 171).

Coetzee, in *White Writing* (1988), unravels the mythologizing work of early Afrikaner literature, particularly that propogating 1930s and 40s nationalism, which, as with all new nationalisms, designated culture as a weapon in its ideological armour. The *plaasroman*, he argues, bolsters the Afrikaner myth of the founding fathers, reifying in the process the Afrikaner's "natural right" to the land: "Thus we find the ancestors hagiographised as men and women of heroic strength, fortitude, and faith, and instituted as the originators of lineages" (WW 84; 83). The myth of the "natural right" of the Afrikaner to the land not only supports a "history of settlement" but also masks "one of *displacement*" of South Africa's black peoples, Rita Barnard argues ("Dream Topographies" 52), and this erasure constitutes a kind of madness embedded in Afrikaner mythology. Highlighting a passage in the novel in which Magda imagines a geography peopled by Hendrik's forebears who, "in the olden days crisscrossed the desert with their flocks and their chattels, heading from A to B or from X to Y" (HC 20) before the whites colonized the land, Barnard argues that Coetzee's utopianist ethics lie in his endeavour to repopulate this landscape ("Dream Topographies" 49).

So the novel, which appeared in a South African edition in 1978 with the dialogue in Afrikaans, unwrites the mythologizing of the *plaasroman* that relies upon the same kind of boundary-marking outlined above. Victoria Rosner, writing about the Southern African pastoral, argues that, "If the male settler was defined in relation to his mastery of the land, the female settler was defined in relation to the house, and that house was defined in relation to the body". Stepping over the boundaries of the "house-body", as Rosner calls it, meant transgressing not only gender but race and national boundaries too (Rosner 73). In other words, transgression in the context of Boer cultural history threatened the limits of Boer identity and was to be guarded against at all costs. The consequence of such transgression was not only punitive but psychological as well because the transgressive woman, by challenging the cultural identity imposed upon her, exercised what it meant to be Afrikaner and in so doing invited madness. Clingman suggests that miscegenation constitutes a "return of the repressed" ("Beyond the Limit" 240): once white South Africans' fantasies about black bodies become reality madness ensues as a consequence of such testing of the social limits. The novel also "unwrites" the South African tragedy, which, as Ian Glenn suggests, typically portrays a doomed romance between the mixed-race couple ("Game Hunting" 131–32) that threatens the preserve of white purity.

Since critiques of patriarchy and colonialism are implicitly paralleled and set in opposition in the text, understanding Magda's plight entails addressing a "hierarchy" of oppressions, those of women and of colonized peoples, as well as that of the lunatic as other. (I use the word lunatic in the context that as sentient beings we are all susceptible to madness.) The novel opens with Magda referring to herself, her father and her father's "new bride", who may be the figment of Magda's imagination, as the "antagonists" rather than the protagonists of the tale (HC 1), in this way, marking an Oedipal breakdown of familial relations and inviting a feminist critique. Later, Magda undermines this version of her story by stating that her father did not remarry. At stake is whether the text prioritizes feminist over anti-colonialist discourse. Stephen Watson even identifies traces of eurocentrism when he wonders "why Magda gives (among others) what is so obviously a Freudian explanation for her predicament … refer[ring] to the 'childhood rape' as if she were some glib psychology undergraduate" ("Colonialism" 29). The effect of Magda not only being oppressed by the structures of Afrikaner society, but also her attempts to *institute* oppression over her servants is one of displacement in the "equation" of injustices, that of gender/sexuality and race.

The problem of equating oppressions is revisited in two of the later works, published concurrently, *The Lives of Animals* (1999) and obliquely in *Disgrace* (1999). By means of what Laura Wright calls the protagonist Elizabeth Costello's feminist "rant" ("Feminist-Vegetarian" 196), <u>Lives</u> challenges commonly held assumptions about animal "versus" human rights. In this way, *Lives* addresses some of the problems raised by *Disgrace*, a novel that closes with its protagonist, Professor David Lurie, in an act suggestive of atonement for his abuse of a female student, giving up one of the sick dogs under his care for euthanasia. The implication here is that on the scales of justice, Lurie is able to balance the life of a suffering animal with that of a human, one who by South African designation, significantly, is "coloured". Frantz Fanon addresses the same problematic of equating oppressions in *Black Skin, White Masks* (1952). On the grounds of the interconnectedness of race and class difference, he challenges O. Mannoni's analysis of what Fanon glosses as the "so-called dependency complex of colonized peoples"; Mannoni "has not understood its real coordinates", and instead bases his thesis upon the confrontation between "civilized" and "primitive" (*Black Skin* 85). Fanon asserts that "All forms of exploitation resemble one another … . All forms of exploitation are identical because all of them are applied against the same "object": "man" (83; 88). Fanon's analysis is itself, of course, unwittingly hegemonic in its then conventional use of "man" to signify "people".

Foe (1986), Coetzee's fifth novel, grapples with this conundrum. Susan Barton's narrative, which constitutes the first three of four parts of the book, is subsumed symbolically (and, in ethico-political terms, only minimally) by that of Friday, the colonial other. In the fourth and final part Friday's "voice" is portrayed as a series of "o's" issuing from his mouth which are the "sounds of the island" (F 154). During the course of the narrative Barton comes to the realization that her attempts to give voice to Friday (F 118), as the silenced and silent other, are ethically ill-conceived, that speaking for him actually purloins Friday's right to self-determinism.

Like Friday, Magda imagines she is an "O", but while Friday's "o" suggests autonomy, in Magda's case it connotes femininity, realized only negatively:

> I am a hole crying to be whole … I am … not unaware that there is a hole between my legs that has never been filled, leading to another hole never filled either. If I am an O, I am sometimes persuaded, it must be because I am a woman. (HC 45)

The "O" or lack with which Magda identifies herself, her vagina, parodies Sigmund Freud's supposition in "Lecture XIII: Femininity" that female genitalia are the "atrophied" version of the male's, and that the girl-child is always initially homosexual, erotically desiring the body of the mother before bestowing her affection upon the father – Magda's daughter seduction fantasy. Not only does "O" signify the atrophied condition of femininity in Coetzee's novel, it also represents a double signification of unfulfilled desire since Magda is a virgin. With a perverse sense of logic, she even wonders if her (fantasy of) rape will have made her a woman (HC 117).

The novel arms itself with the French feminist challenge to Freud. Luce Irigaray, for instance, demands: "How can we accept the idea ['penis-envy'] that woman's entire sexual development is governed by her lack of, and thus by her longing for, jealousy of, and demand for, the male organ?" (*This Sex* 69). Magda's lack is not only gendered, as spinster, on a textual level, it represents the repressed female voice more generally: as in Irigaray's analysis, the Feminine Symbolic. However, whilst Irigaray, like Freud, has been challenged for essentializing femininity,[1] Magda's social alienation is specifically that of the Afrikaner spinster on the farm because she has failed to take her place at that hallowed table of *vrou en moeder*.

In her relationship with her servants, Magda is unable to reconcile her needs as a woman with her position as colonizer. What is more, this relation inverts Fanonian discourse. In "The Psychopathology of Blackness" Fanon writes: "When the Negro makes contact with the white world, a certain sensitizing action takes place. If his psychic structure is weak, one observes a collapse of the ego" (*Black Skin* 154). Fanon deconstructs the conceptually dubious notion that "race" is a biological category in "The Fact of Blackness", arguing that "blackness" can be historicized and is therefore socially constructed. Moreover, black people adopt the white masks bestowed by whites: blackness masquerades as whiteness. The essay details the effects of racism on the psyche of black people by tortuously staging a "drama of consciousness" (Parry, "Resistance Theory" 189). Fanon imagines this psychic confrontation with his own otherness: "I came into the world imbued with the will to find a meaning in things ... and then I found that I was an object in the midst of other objects" (*Black Skin* 109). In a similar way, Magda struggles to define the boundaries of her own self when she rejects Hendrik's remonstration that as racially marginalized he and Klein-Anna will be punished for the murder of Magda's father; ironically, Magda does this, in part, by distinguishing herself from other whites in her resistance to the other's objectifying gaze (here, Hendrik's): "Do you think I am too spineless to acknowledge my guilt? ... I am not simply one of the whites, I am *I*. I am I, not a people. Why have I to pay for other people's sins?" (HC 128).

"The Fact of Blackness" maps the painful transition from Fanon's self-perception of a non-raced identity, one informed by Enlightenment thinking, to one of alterity, subjected to "crushing objecthood" (109) and "overdetermined from without" (116). Although he goes on to embrace a celebratory Black Consciousness ("Now the fragments have been put together again by another self" [*Black Skin* 109]), even this stage is self-limiting and Fanon, the modernizer, is forced to question the foundations of Négritude: "Out of the necessities of my struggle I had chosen the method of regression ... I am made of the irrational ... And now how my voice vibrates!" (123). Fanon's sense of self is fractured alongside his faith in Enlightenment thinking: racism does not obey the laws of

---

[1]   Margaret Whitford, an exponent of Irigaray, briefly outlines these criticisms ("Introduction" 2; see also Felman, "Women and Madness" 119–20).

reason and is impossible to challenge based on reasoned or reasonable argument. Under these terms, racism is itself a kind of madness.

Through the deconstruction of "blackness" *Heart of the Country* tacitly critiques the obsessive racial categorization that went to the heart of apartheid thinking as well as the racism inherent in colonialist ideology, which served, in part, to obscure the economic motivations behind the will to colonize. "Blackness" in the novel is defamiliarized by its subversion as a biological category. "Black" typically describes everything *but* Hendrik's or Anna's black skin, destabilizing Magda's sense of self as white: Magda conceives of herself as "a miserable black virgin", a "black bored spinster", whose story is "a dull black blind stupid miserable story, ignorant of its meaning" (HC 5). She casts herself as the deadly black widow spider, spinning her tale around her, lamenting that "From wearing black too long I have grown into a black person" (HC 105). She imagines Hendrik "throwing his heavy black words" at her when she is unable to pay his wages (HC 114).

Magda's psychosis curbs the dominance that her whiteness accords her. Not only does madness by definition situate her as other alongside her femininity, and in particular alongside her spinsterhood, any authority she attempts to give her story is undermined because it is the product of psychosis. The two "deaths" of Magda's father (in her first account she claims she kills him with an axe, in the second with a gun, yet he reappears at the end of the narrative a decrepit old man), and of her "rape" by Hendrik (rehearsed five times and always subject to doubt), are just two inconsistencies in her story. The rape scene throws light on the double signification of madness in the text, on the state of Magda's mind as well as textual instability. Together these serve to expose what we might call the madness of "civilization". Critics are divided on the meaning of the rape. Attwell argues that the portrayal of different versions is suggestive of (colonialist) fantasy (*J. M. Coetzee* 62), whilst Head disputes Dick Penner's claim that, in Head's words, "in successive versions of the rape scene, the violence of perpetrator and victim diminishes, while the victim's acceptance increases, and this might also support the idea of a colonial fantasy". Head points out that the sense of Magda as victim is "surely reinforced by the repetition which … serves to intensify rather than ameliorate the impression of ordeal" (*J. M. Coetzee* 58–59). Rody interprets the scenes as rape but argues nevertheless that, by repeatedly restaging it, Magda loses credibility: her story may or may not be authentic yet the crisis that ensues "reverses the power relations of the black man and white woman" ("Colonial Daughter's Revolt" 175). Attridge, on the other hand, contends that the "rape" is presented in only two versions, the first constituting Magda's fear of sex with Hendrik (or with any man, for that matter), and the second the experience itself (*J. M. Coetzee* 28). What seems clear is that the narrative self-consciously *plays into* and *parodies* the colonialist fantasy of black-on-white-rape, which remains a pathological anxiety of white South Africans today. As the versions layer upon one another, which Head argues is symptomatic of the increasing conflict between violator and violated and Attridge argues is in fact the event of rape itself following Magda's fantasy, Hendrik's words translate improbably into those of a cheap bodice-ripper or bawdy farce: "Don't be afraid"; "Everyone likes it"; "Hold tight!". Hendrik's encouragements are thus suggestive of Magda's inexperience in and therefore of her wild imaginings of sex. On each occasion Magda wonders whether she is hallucinating these utterances, lending weight to the idea that they are the product of an unstable mind *and* constitute a text that self-reflexively re-constructs the colonial fantasy.

Fanon sheds light on this fantasy when he discredits O. Mannoni's "Prospero complex":

> It is defined as the sum of those unconscious neurotic tendencies that delineate at the same time the "picture" of the paternalist colonial and the portrait of "the racialist whose daughter has suffered an [imaginary] attempted rape at the hands of an inferior being. (added text Fanon's; *Black Skin* 107; Mannoni 70)

The colonial rape complex is a well-rehearsed trope in South African literature. André Brink's *Imaginings of Sand* (1996) and *Rights of Desire* (2000), Coetzee's *Disgrace* (1999), Dangor's *Bitter Fruit* (2001), Farida Karodia's *Other Secrets* (2000), Lewis Nkosi's *Mating Birds* (1987) and Jo-Anne Richards's *The Innocence of Roast Chicken* (1996) are just some examples. British-born Doris Lessing's first novel, *The Grass is Singing* (1949), set in Rhodesia (now Zimbabwe) from where Lessing had recently emigrated, explores such white sexual neuroses about black masculinity without staging rape. Meg Samuelson, writing about rape in the literature of the South African transition, pointedly warns that rape should not be read simply as a *metaphor* for racial division in South Africa because "It is an endemic – and proliferating – social disorder" (88). Nevertheless, as Lucy Graham shows in her critique of *Disgrace*, "sensationalized media accounts of white women raped by black men were symptoms of the 'black peril' hysteria of the early twentieth century and contributed to oppressive legislative measures against black people in South Africa". Such accounts, Graham warns, have been resurfacing in the transition period of the 1990s ("Reading the Unspeakable" 435; cf. Clingman, "Beyond the Limit" 250). The South African President, Thabo Mbeki, published a response to global media reports of the "epidemic" of rape in South Africa, claiming that it has become an issue of racism that feeds upon whites' fear of blacks: "In the end [whites] fear freedom from their psychosis, convinced that this would destroy their sense of identity" ("Good News" n. pag.). Note the association Mbeki makes between whites' inability to delimit identity and madness. Graham, who argues that Mbeki is, in part, responding to these entrenched white perceptions of black men, points out that in fact most rapes in contemporary South Africa are intraracial rather than interracial ("Unspeakable" 435–36).

Magda believes that Hendrik rapes her to seek retribution from her father, firstly, for entering into sexual relations with Klein-Anna, and, secondly, for subjecting him in the colonial relation. As delusional, Magda's narrative therefore has all the ingredients of Oedipal and colonialist fantasies of desire, fear and envy that are realized in actual rape in *Disgrace*. (Elizabeth Lowry suggests that *Disgrace* re-evaluates issues raised by *Heart of the Country*, of how blacks and whites can live peaceably alongside each other in the inceptive state ["Like a Dog" 13].)

Mirroring Magda's earlier account of the return of the newly remarried father to the farm, the imagined arrival of Hendrik with his new bride casts Hendrik as a father-figure to Magda and therefore not only maintains the daughter's desire for the father of psychoanalytic theory, but also inverts colonialist racist hierarchies by portraying the black servant subjugating the white master-figure. Enraged at being displaced by Klein-Anna, as surrogate (M)other, Magda pictures shooting her father and, when he supposedly dies of his wounds, entreating Hendrik, the spurned husband, to help her bury him. In due course, Magda's narrative records a shift in the dynamics of the master/servant relationship. Hendrik with the aid of Klein-Anna apparently gains "ownership" of both the farm and Magda. In Magda's case, this is achieved through rape, which always remains subject to doubt, and through (Magda's desire for) sexual intimacy. The white woman's body in this novel and *Disgrace* is perceived by the victim as both a commodity within a patriarchal system of exchange and as the site where (androcentric) master/slave relations are acted out, though as Graham points out, Lucy in *Disgrace* "remains resolutely silent about her experience" ("Unspeakable" 433). Women in these texts have been codified within a historically patriarchal system of retribution, revenge and reparations. In the eyes of Lurie in *Disgrace*, who is struggling to rationalize his daughter Lucy's rape, Lucy represents "Booty, war reparations; another incident in the great campaign of redistribution" (DIS 176). Graham strives to make the "unspeakable" silences around rape heard, based on the question, "who does *not* speak and why?" (Higgins and Silver qtd. in "Unspeakable" 434; see also Higgins and Silver 3). *Disgrace*, she argues, "dissolves [race] boundaries" between Lurie and Lucy's attackers ("Unspeakable" 433), allowing the ambivalence of rape's silences to "double[ ] back", so that Coetzee makes himself and his reader responsible in the dissemination of Lucy's story ("Unspeakable" 434). This pattern of deconstruction is adumbrated in the earlier work, *Heart of the Country*. Given that colonial masters frequently raped their female servants and slaves, the nature of the liaison between Magda's father and Klein-Anna, whom Hendrik sets about beating once the affair is made public, requires closer examination. At best it is probably coercive. Magda fails to enlighten us, evidenced in the prospective nature of her version of the union: "In a month's time, I can see it, I will be bringing my father and my maid breakfast in bed" (HC 54).

What distinguishes the portrayal of madness in this text from other examples from South African literature is Magda's self-consciousness, not as a psychotic character who lives out the colonial condition (there are plenty of these), but as a metatextual conceit, subject to the whims of her author. Whilst the materiality of Magda's story, which powerfully conveys her sense of dislocation, should not be neglected in any discussion of the work, the narrative tangibly announces its own fictionality *as text*: Magda is not only controlled literally, under patriarchal authority, just as she controls the colonial other; she is also controlled literarily

CONTROL

as a character in a text, both by her author and by literary history. Moreover, she struggles with her own authority as author:

> In a house shaped by destiny like an H I have lived all my life, in a theatre of stone and sun fenced in with miles of wire, spinning my trail from room to room … Then we have retired to sleep, to dream allegories of baulked desire such as we are blessedly unfitted to interpret[.] (HC 3)

Magda resists her role as colonial spinster and writer both in her dual function as "real" entity and literary trope, and ultimately both she and the text register the failure of this resistance. It is this tension between character and trope – Magda's awareness of her fictionality mires her deeper and deeper in madness – that has preoccupied critics of the novel. Glenn, for instance, suggests that: "The play between the I-as-narrator and the I-as-subject is one of the novel's many stylistic games. A failure to decode that game means a failure to grasp what Coetzee is doing in the novel" ("Game Hunting" 123). Rody recognizes the intricacy of Coetzee's construction, that Magda "is perhaps the best spokesperson we have for a person's – or a text's – entrapment in language" ("Mad Colonial Daughter's Revolt" 160–61). Felman in her study of madness and literature perceives the relation between character and trope rather differently, as resistance: madness, like literature, constitutes "an irreducible resistance to interpretation" (*Writing and Madness* 254).

Interviewed by Watson, Coetzee confoundingly argues that "Magda is not a colonial spinster" just as "Jacobus Coetzee is not a[n eighteenth-]century frontiersman"; they are "I-figures in books" (qtd. in Glenn, "Game Hunting" 122; Coetzee qtd. in Watson, "Speaking" 23), in line, Glenn suggests, with the semiotics of Jakobson and Benveniste ("Game Hunting" 124). Coetzee's retreat into the realms of textual play (Glenn aptly titles his essay "Game Hunting") might well allow him to prevaricate on the ethico-political issues the text raises – the condition of women in Afrikaner society, their place in a "hierarchy" of oppression, the difficulty in representing such women, are just three examples. At the same time, paradoxically, the novel's very textuality facilitates ethico-political debate by apportioning the reader interpretative autonomy through this very ambiguity: the reader must take responsibility for constructing a version of events and for making sense of Magda's story. Attridge addresses this readerly engagement in his discussion of the modernist aesthetics of the work, what he calls its "textual otherness" or "*textualterity*". The "formal strategies" modernism uses to foreground language and the device of genre should not be written off simply as textual play but an acknowledgement, despite what authors may think they are doing to the contrary, "that literature's distinctive power and *potential ethical force* reside in a *testing and unsettling of deeply held assumptions of transparency, instrumentality, and direct referentiality*". Attridge contends that such testing allows the reader to apprehend otherness "which those assumptions had silently excluded" (emphasis added; *J. M. Coetzee* 30).

?NARRATIVE IDENTITY.

An example of this strategy of fostering an agential reader is the division of the narrative into numbered paragraphs, what Coetzee calls a "montage" effect:

> *In the Heart of the Country* is … constructed out of quite brief sequences, which are numbered as a way of pointing to what is not there between them: the kind of scene-setting and connective tissue that the traditional novel used to find necessary – particularly the South African novel of rural life that *In the Heart of the Country* takes off from. (DP 59–60)

Such a strategy has a defamiliarizing effect: the reader must decipher the narrative but also must reconstruct what is left unsaid, in its silences. The numbering of paragraphs is suggestive of confessional diary writings, confirmed by Magda: "I am a spinster with a locked diary", she laments (HC 4); the truthfulness of her confession, of course, is thrown into doubt because her narrative suggests psychosis. She is compelled to give order to the seemingly sparse story of her life and, conceiving of herself as a mirror-image, believes she "will dwindle and expire here in the heart of the country unless she has at least a thin porridge of event to live on" (HC 25). The self-consciousness of the narrative intimates that writing breathes life into her (she is quite obviously "dying" of boredom), yet at the same time, as the subject of patriarchal, and indeed, colonialist, discourse, she is imprisoned by it. Working against the conventions of the (realist) novel, the numbers in fact point up a *lack of* order or rationality that their inclusion might imply. Magda herself experiences gaps in her memory: "A day must have intervened here. Where there is a blank there must have been a day during which my father sickened irrecoverably … I suspect that the day the day was missing I was not there" (HC 86–87). The passing of time must be broken down into smaller manageable or bearable chunks, both for Magda and, apparently, for the reader of the novel. It is ironic of course that the missing day is when something apparently actually *does* happen.

On a textual level, Magda is ensnared in a double bind for whilst she depends upon narrative for her substance, at the same time it girds her to the Law of the Father. On the one hand, she believes that she is unable to break free from the process of creating fictions or from becoming a fiction: "I make it all up in order that it shall make me up. I cannot stop now" (HC 79). On the other, the narrative implies she is the symbolic author of her text for she wonders if she has "inky violet" blood in her veins (HC 68); as a "poetess of interiority" (HC 38), she claims "lyric is my medium, not chronicle" (HC 77); she is the "black widow-spider" weaving her tale (HC 43; 6) who struggles for autonomy of her story, which should have "a beginning, a middle, and an end" (HC 46); she stresses that she "deal[s] in signs merely" (HC 29). Magda's divided self, as oppressor and oppressed, is figured in this author conceit, where authorship always already connotes mastery. But as a character in a story she is also its servant, both dominated and marginalized, self and other. This is her predicament. She struggles to free herself from writing and being written since, as Irigaray's speculations reveal, the act of writing makes her both complicit with yet subjected by phallogocentrism.

It is from her phallogocentric self and from Coetzee as emblematic patriarch and author (in the context of this novel, the terms are covalent) that she struggles to liberate herself whilst at the same time needing to assert her autonomy, "I am I" (HC 78). Self-consciously and unconsciously, through "writing" and madness respectively, she spins fictions around herself, very much as authors construct their tales. As the story draws to a close, supposedly abandoned by her servants, Magda imagines communicating with "machines in the sky": "Having failed to make my shouts heard … I turned to writing" (HC 144). She even flippantly toys with her reader by announcing in the opening passages of the book that her father arrived home with his new bride "in a dog-cart drawn by a horse with an ostrich-plume waving on its forehead", only to cast doubt upon this account: "Or perhaps they were drawn by two plumed donkeys, that is also possible … More detail I cannot give unless I begin to embroider, for I was not watching" (HC 1). Magda both weaves and unravels a tale, thereby functioning minimally as both the writer and reader of her text. Deranged and hearing voices conveyed by "machines that fly in the sky" (HC 137), she tries to make sense of them.

Gallagher argues that the time of the narrative loosely spans the period 1870 to 1960 because references are made to the use of horses and carts, bicycles, trains and aeroplanes, and to the demand for taxes from Magda for municipal services (*Story* 83). As Head points out, since the plot is presented unrealistically or *anti*-realistically, this representation requires that we suspend our disbelief (*J. M. Coetzee* 51). Magda may be presaging a future time, narrating from the late twentieth century whilst trapped psychologically in the colonial past, or, as a character-type in a book, may be struggling to dislodge herself from colonial literary history. We are not expected to historicize the work accurately: indeed, by defamiliarizing historical time, Coetzee carves a space to ask questions about colonial (literary) history, including the status of the text and its author within that history. Gone mad, and thus every account that she "writes" has to be conditional, she imagines "writing" messages to the "skygods" (HC 150) with stones, desperately announcing her self and her body in a last-ditch attempt to escape her psychological committal to the farm. She is forced, she believes, to turn to "writing" – which is subject to the Law of the Father – because her shouts go apparently unheard. Indeed, she advertises herself within a masculinized notion of femininity, as a sexualized body: "FEMM – AMOR POR TU" (HC 145). Ultimately marking the failure of her attempts to resist dominant modes of writing, and again negating the preceding events, the narrative draws to a close with the reappearance of the father, though now decrepit since he is deaf, blind and incontinent.

The voices Magda hears from the "flying machines" (HC 138) figure the crisis of the pathological space in which she resides:

> They accuse me, if I understand them, of turning my life into a fiction, out of boredom … as though I were reading myself like a book, and found the book dull, and put it aside and began to make myself up instead … when I could find no enemy outside, when hordes of brown horsemen would not pour out of the

hills waving their bows and ululating, I made an enemy out of myself. (HC 139–40)

Magda realizes that her psychic disease is turned inwards, that the fear of black bodies, "brown horsemen", is the projection of her own paranoia. This is the point from which Coetzee's third novel *Waiting for the Barbarians* (1980) begins, where the settlers wait in fear of the arrival of the enigmatic "barbarians". Like the society that populates Constantine P. Cavafy's poem (1904) to which the latter novel makes titular reference, without the "barbarians" to preoccupy her, who in Cavafy are "a kind of solution", Magda projects her neuroses back on herself. Nonetheless, she is also attributed insight into this complex and her psychological frailty. Her life is characterized by a lack of fulfilment and desire and, like the settlers in the poem, she finds herself in a perpetual state of waiting, trapped in the mythological and mythologizing colonial condition which, the novel suggests, is also a patriarchal domain.

The psychic interiority mapped by *Heart of the Country* recalls Marlow's psychological journey into the interior of the mind in Joseph Conrad's *Heart of Darkness* (1902). Critics such as Chinua Achebe have condemned Conrad's novel for its representation of the African as simply the foil against which Marlow's psyche is explored: "Can nobody see the preposterous and perverse arrogance in thus reducing Africa to the role of props for the break-up of one petty European mind?" (*Hopes and Impediments* 8). (Achebe's primary concern is the politics of canonization.) Similarly, in *Heart of the Country* Hendrik and Klein-Anna are objectified by Magda under colonialist discourse; Magda abusively seeks to feminize herself through their bodies, making no attempt to represent the other save the other side of herself. For instance, she imperiously prefixes the servant-girl Anna's name "Klein-Anna" – a hybrid of Anna Freud and Melanie Klein, both disciples of Freud who specialized in the psychoanalysis of children yet whose work brought them into conflict with each other. (Anna Freud developed the model of the Good Mother.)

However, in *Heart of Darkness* Conrad preserves an ironic distance from the imperialist discourse he presents through the formal device of the framed narrative: Marlow recounts his tale to an unnamed narrator on a ship docked in the Thames. In Conrad's defence, Edward Said argues that "Conrad's self-consciously circular narrative forms draw attention to themselves as artificial constructions, encouraging us to sense the potential of a reality that seemed inaccessible to imperialism, just beyond its control" (*Culture and Imperialism* 32) and confirmed by Benita Parry when she refers to the novella's "plural and contradictory discourses" ("Afterlife" n. pag.). Likewise, Coetzee distances himself from colonialist and Afrikaner nationalist discourse by portraying a character *en abyme*, laying bare the processes by which she is written. She is a character who, as insane *and* unreliable, is a paltry representative of the "great colonizing mission".

The slipperiness of Coetzee's critique can perhaps best be explained by Barnard's contention that "The capacity for changing the rules of the game is precisely what [Coetzee] values most in a work of art" ("Dream Topographies" 53), and this is no more evident than in his self-conscious manipulation of the *plaasroman* genre in this novel. Magda wonders whether it might be better to "give up the fiction of farming" (HC 126) and is all too aware when positioning herself, and being positioned by Coetzee, that she is a stock character of the genre: "I am *the one who*", she says. Her father is the archetypal head of the Boer household: "My father is *the one who* paces the floorboards back and forth" (emphasis added; HC 1). Where sexual passion in Coetzee is analogous to artistic production, in this novel Magda struggles with her sexual identity and analogously is oppressed by words and (literary) language. Finding herself in the genre of the *plaasroman*, albeit a highly ironized version, for Magda the written word signifies isolation and the denial of sexual and social intercourse. Language is isolating on two counts: firstly, its subject is the self always already constituted by the masculine symbolic from which Magda is striving to break free, and, secondly, her story, even though other-directed, is a monologue rather than a dialogue, connoting the struggle with words and speech of the socially alienated: as in Samuel Beckett's plays, the struggle to be heard (cf. Rody 161).

Magda's place in the novel is paradoxical since she is both entrapped by language (or "writes" about being trapped) whilst she presses against it, transgressing boundaries. Reified in madness, female repression and colonial anxiety are ineluctably bound to Magda as metafictional trope. She inhabits the space that Felman identifies as the bridge between madness and writing: "literature and madness are informed *by* each other … precisely linked by what attempts to shut them out" (*Writing and Madness* 16).

In an essay on Gerrit Achterberg's poem "Ballade van de Gasfitter", Coetzee locates a similar layering of signification in the use of the personal pronouns "I" and "you" ("shifters", according to Jakobson [qtd. in DP 71]), which is a relationship between the self and other as well as the self's relationship to language. The distance between the "I" and "You" of the poem, Coetzee argues, is not only that between the characters portrayed, the gasfitter and the woman, but also between a metaphysical being and the poem itself (DP 69). The Dutch word *dichten*, he points out, has no comparable homonym in English, and means both "plugging a hole", but also "to write poetry": thus the gasfitter in the poem is "sealing off leaks [but] is also the poet at work" (DP 73). In *Heart of the Country* Magda's recognition of herself as "lack" and as a hole or an "O" represents both her femininity, negatively constituted, and her ineffectuality as an artist. "O" represents an "empty" consciousness or the blank text. This hole may be the hole to which Sartre refers in *Being and Nothingness* (1956), which Coetzee in turn identifies with the hole in the Achterberg poem:

> Consciousness is presented [in Sartre] as a hole through which nothingness pours into the world. If we recognize Sartre as the darker spirit behind Achterberg, the quest of the *I* for the hole becomes an absurd quest for confrontation with the void[.] (DP 74)

Coetzee concludes that the "fate of the gasfitter is precisely self-annihilation, a dwindling away of selfhood" (DP 75).

Like Achterberg's gasfitter, as a character and "author" in and of her story, Magda occupies polarized positions of "You" and "I", a space she construes as her double signification in which she endeavours to preserve the remnants of a dissipated, subjected self (cf. Attwell, *J. M. Coetzee* 58–59). She states: "If I am an emblem then I am an emblem" (HC 10) and later that "This monologue of the self is a maze of words out of which I shall not find a way until someone else gives me a lead" (HC 17). Here, she is appealing both to the author and to an imagined sexual partner who will teach her through intercourse how to make herself a woman. And the two, author and lover, are inextricably linked:

> Aching to form the words that will translate me into the land of myth and hero ... I am not a happy peasant. I am a miserable black virgin, and my story is my story, even if it is a dull black blind stupid miserable story, ignorant of its meaning ... . I am I. (HC 5)

Alluding to her fictionality, she compares herself in her isolation, "like a good castaway", to the resourceful Robinson Crusoe and to the neglected archetypal victim Cinderella: "CINDRLA ES MI ... QUIERO UN AUTR ... SON ISOLADO" (HC 144). That the meaning of "AUTR" is left ambiguous registers Magda's dual "function": in French *l'autre* means "other" while *l'auteur* translates as "author". Of course, Magda mixes Spanish and French. The text offers two possible readings. Firstly, like Magda's desire to escape words and language (authorship in the service of patriarchy), the act of writing is presented as antifeminist: Magda adopts the stereotyped role of the objectified and subservient woman in her inscriptions in stones. Secondly, feminist and queer theories of performativity would suggest that she is minimally resistant because she self-consciously mimes womanhood, parody effecting critique (cf. Irigaray, *This Sex* 134; Butler, *Bodies* 230–33). However, her failure to resist, as in the first model of writing, is evidenced in the futility of her bid for freedom by laying messages in stones, a futility which is accentuated by her delusion that she is communicating in Spanish or her *idea* of Spanish, because it is a language she does not understand.

Believing intercourse, both sexual and social, would enable her to resist the masculinist notion of fathering stories (as a spinster, authorship for Magda engenders oppression), she struggles to embrace sexual love yet even these efforts are thwarted: "The law has gripped my throat, I say and do not say ... its one hand on my tongue, its other on my lips" (HC 91–92). Lips are interchangeably those of the mouth and female genitalia. Magda's conception of herself as both socially and sexually oppressed by the Father's will is reified somatically, represented by the mouth (speech) and genitalia (copulation) respectively. She is inhabited by the Father. In a desperate bid to communicate with others, she turns to sexual love because, she believes, this will bypass the written word. In the same manner that she imagines entering the body of Klein-Anna in order to experience "authentic" human feelings, she unwittingly inverts the motif of being entered by the body of the Father (her father) when she pictures climbing, like Hamlet, into his grave,[2] and, by occupying the grave in this way, signals self-affirmation. Despite Magda's pleas to stop, Hendrik later dresses up in her dead father's clothes to taunt her in a grotesque patriarchal masquerade (HC 106).

Sexual love for Magda, therefore, is the path to agency and resistance, whilst writing and reading, or being written or read, which signify entrapment and oppression, block this path off. In this respect Magda is anti-textual just as her madness renders her uninterpretable:

> What do I lack? … Is it mere passion? Is it merely a vision of a second existence passionate enough to carry me from the mundane of being into the doubleness of signification? … What automatism is this, what liberation is it going to bring me, and without liberation what is the point of my story? … Who is behind my oppression? (HC 4–5)

The light begins to dawn on Magda that she also is oppressed by her author, Coetzee: that she is an unwilling and unwitting participant in the system which oppresses her, one which she cannot escape. In her anguished quest for meaningful liberation she exposes the ethical residues of the text. Any ethico-politically minded work must offer some kind of resolution or alternative to the dilemmas it constructs and without future orientation or divergent perspectives this becomes untenable. In *Heart of the Country* this resolution is the metafictional quality of Magda's tale, the voicing of anxieties about language and authorship, and Magda's developing awareness of her predicament, as oppressor and oppressed. Paradoxically, her attempts to liberate herself through sexual love are inappropriate and simply reinstall another form of oppression, this time the racial oppression of Hendrik and Klein-Anna. The latter, according to Magda, is "oppressed particularly by my talk" (HC 123). Revealing the pathos of Magda's plight, these failed attempts at communion render the sincerity or authenticity of her lesson in loving invalid, and instead lay bare Magda's naïveté and repression. Moreover, Magda actively pursues the "real" experience that is encoded in the very discourse she resists. She takes it upon herself to reclaim a place for the "colonial daughters" who, like colonized indigenes, find themselves othered by colonial discourse: "I am not a principle, a rule of discourse … I need a history and a culture … I am alone again … in the historical present" (HC 130–31). Of course, Magda neglects to mention here that she is complicit in the act of othering as well.

Magda situates herself and is situated by the author Coetzee as the "madwoman in the attic" of feminist theory: "I am the one who stays in her room reading or

---

2   In Shakespeare's Oedipal tragedy, Hamlet throws himself into Ophelia's grave despairing: "Hold off the earth awhile/Till I have caught her once more in mine arms" (Act 5.1, 131–32).

writing or fighting migraines. The colonies are full of girls like that, but none, I
think, so extreme as I" (HC 1). The privilege of privacy signals only her isolation
and marginality, as she says: "Between four walls my rage is baffled. Reflected
from planes of plaster and tile and board and wallpaper, my outpourings rain back
on me" (HC 43), and that "In the cloister of my room I am the mad hag I am
destined to be" (HC 8). This motif has been widely read into women's texts like
Charlotte Perkins Gilman's *The Yellow Wallpaper* (1892), Charlotte Brontë's *Jane
Eyre* (1847) and Jean Rhys's *Wide Sargasso Sea* (1966), which all politicize the
marginalization of early women writers through the trope of the mad, incarcerated
and isolated female "neurotic".

Sandra Gilbert and Susan Gubar argue that the trope of the "mad woman in the
attic" in nineteenth-century women's texts constitutes the resisting female writer
and in this sense madness therefore signifies autonomy. Here, they read Bertha in
Jane Eyre as Jane's mad alter-ego:

> it is disturbingly clear from recurrent images in [*Jane Eyre*] that Bertha not
> only acts *for* Jane, she also acts *like* Jane. The imprisoned Bertha, running
> "backwards and forwards" on all fours in the attic, for instance, recalls not only
> Jane the governess, whose only relief from mental pain was to pace "backwards
> and forwards" in the third story, but also that "bad animal" who was ten-year-
> old Jane, imprisoned in the red-room, howling and mad … . At that point,
> significantly, when the Bertha in Jane falls from the ruined wall of Thornfield
> and is destroyed … the burden of her past will be lifted – and she will wake.

Not unlike Achebe's reading of Conrad and Clingman's reading of the limits that
bound identity, Gayatri Spivak has pointed up the eurocentrism of Gilbert and
Gubar's reading: Bertha Rochester, a white Caribbean Creole, merely serves as a
mirror against which to measure "plain Jane's progress" – the title of Gilbert and
Gubar's essay. As Edward Said demonstrates in *Culture and Imperialism* (1993),
the bones of novels like *Jane Eyre* are buried in colonial places. For Spivak *Jane
Eyre* is guilty of reproducing an imperialist concern for subject constitution based
on "childbearing and soul making" – in the latter case, imperialism was regarded as
a higher social mission and saw its duty as civilizing the "native". Jane establishes
her sense of self, therefore, through her romantic love for Rochester *and* through
evidence of her moral fortitude. By portraying Bertha Rochester, on the other
hand, as an indeterminate being, part-human, part-animal, as Brontë chooses
to, Bertha's entitlement to a "soul" in the novel is weakened. For Spivak, this
means that "Native" again serves as "self-consolidating Other" (Spivak, "Three
Women's Texts" 254). Indeed, in the economy of the novel Bertha *must* die for
Jane to achieve *her* place in it. The process of subject constitution is staged self-
consciously in *Heart of the Country* as Magda struggles to define herself in her
attempts at communicating with the other. The novel inverts Gilbert and Gubar's
thesis: madness and sexuality are set at odds with writing in the novel (because
writing is always already phallocentric), serving only to emphasize Magda's status

as symbolic yet resistant "author" of her story. When Magda eventually turns to writing (in stones) she is conscious that she has succumbed to the Law of the Father. She is born into a language which she uses to give birth to her frustration, anguish and psychosis (Head appropriately calls her invasion of other bodies "monstrous birth[s]" [*J. M. Coetzee* 55]).

Answering Attwell's question about a "history of self-cancelling literature" which centres on a "poetics of failure" and which Attwell identifies with *Heart of the Country*, Coetzee suggests that Magda is "an anomalous figure: her passion [for South Africa, its landscape and its people] doesn't belong in the genre [the pastoral] in which she finds herself" (DP 61–62). *Heart of the Country* asks questions about its genre, questions which for Attwell are based on a failure of reciprocity that undermines the colonial humanism that resides in the South African pastoral. Yet, returning us to the real/literary perception of reciprocity captured in the Achterberg essay, Coetzee says that he is more interested in the way that the postmodern novel treats a condition such as "falling in love" as "the *figure* of a relationship … rather than the relationship per se" (original emphasis; DP 62). This he puts down to a process of historicizing falling in love. Again, Magda inhabits a site of dislocation both literally and literarily: parodying the South African pastoral, she cannot authenticate her relationship with Hendrik and Klein-Anna though she attempts to do so, nor can she resolve her alienation from (literary) language.

Anticipating the later novels, *Life & Times of Michael K* (1983) and *Disgrace* (1999), Magda dreams up a utopianist pastoral closure to her story as a means of reconciling herself to the land and her lot. Ultimately, a happy ending is forestalled because this vision commits her to a life without companionship or agency. At every turn her desire to escape, or escapism, is frustrated: "am I going to yield to the spectre of reason and explain myself to myself in the only kind of confession we protestants know? To die an enigma with a full soul or to die emptied of my secrets" (HC 150). Modernity, therefore, is conceived only negatively. The arrival of the hallucinatory "skygods", temporally marking the dawning of the modern age, forces her to communicate *through writing,* and thus to bend to the Law of the Father having failed to realize a feminine symbolic. Rody argues that Magda's reveals "an extreme degree of alienation in language" through her "effusive, subversive *écriture feminine*" (Rody 160). I would put this rather differently: Magda's encounters with writing only *reinforce* her social and textual alienation. She also realises that she "writes", and is written, against the grain of Afrikaner mythology: "Perhaps my rage at my father is simply rage at the violations of the old language, the correct language", she says (HC 47). The "old" and "correct" language operate within the criss-crossing paradigms of patriarchy and colonialism (both denoted by the Law of the Father) but is also Afrikaans, a hybrid which has been used to administer oppression. Because Magda's father is also the symbolic Father, she believes that authentic commun(icat)ion between herself (white, female) and Hendrik (black, male) is only possible through sexual love, rather than the spoken or written word: "The language that should pass between myself and these people was subverted by my father and cannot be recovered. What passes between us now is a parody ... It was my father-tongue" (HC 106).

Discourse, according to Irigaray, itself can be read as a kind of "grammar" with "its syntactic laws or requirements, its imaginary configurations, its metaphoric networks, and also, of course, what it does not articulate at the level of utterance: *its silences*" (original emphasis; *This Sex* 75). As an Afrikaner spinster, Magda associates silence with a literary history that suppresses or occludes women's stories. Paradoxically, her monologue, which she recognizes as "spurious babble", is meaningless within such a system: "a history so tedious in the telling that it might as well be a history of silence. What I lack is the courage to stop talking, to die back into the silence I came from" (HC 65). That discourse is inherently masculinist, having the power in Irigaray's words to "reduce all others to the economy of the Same" (*This Sex* 74), means Magda's only refuge is silence and the refusal to participate within it.

As a character in a book, Magda self-consciously calls upon her author, Coetzee, to listen to the silences enshrouding women's histories. She wonders if "One day some as yet unborn scholar ... should study the kernel of the truth of this fancy [the childhood rape]" (HC 3–4). Not only does she allude to Coetzee, as an "unborn scholar" and champion of the antipastoral movement, ironically, she also engages in such a project as (minimal) author of her own story. Emotionally inept and unloved, Magda finally is excluded from the mythical tradition of both *plaasroman* and the South African tragedy. The duality of Coetzee's critique is suggested through irony and paradox in the title of the book, "heart" connoting a profoundly nationalist-rural community with the *vrou en moeder* as its figurehead, but also passion and empathy. Magda repeatedly refers to the farmstead as a "desert" (HC 20; 42; 50; 51; 53; 55; 140) and as the "heart of nowhere" (HC 120). She bemoans her lack of passion and agency, placing desire and authorship in opposition:

> A woman with *red blood* in her veins (what colour is mine? a watery pink? an *inky violet*?) would have pushed a hatchet into [Hendrik's] hands and bundled him into the house to search out vengeance. A woman determined to be the author of her own life would not have shrunk from hurling open the curtains and flooding the guilty deed with light[.] (emphasis added; HC 68)

For Magda, desire cannot be accommodated by phallocentric language. Her imagined dialogue with her racial other, Klein-Anna, reveals to her that "Words alienate. Language is no medium for desire.... . It is only by alienating the desired that language masters it" (HC 28–29). Paradoxically, Magda is an unreliable narrator who resists writing yet she is always obsessively "writing" her incessant diatribe which, given its philosophic and literary nature, is both not-mad and mad. Felman notes that "literature is ... in a position of excess, since it includes that which philosophy excludes by definition: madness. Madness thus becomes an overflow, that which remains of literature after philosophy has been subtracted from it" (*Writing and Madness* 51). The success of Magda's opposition to writing is ambiguous: madness, or her flights of fancy, provides her with a place to resist being figured in and by discourse and to combat her boredom as the archetypal colonial spinster, whilst her textual instability allows her to subvert dominant literary genres. Yet this "madness" also destabilizes all usable meaning the novel encodes (cf. Attwell, "Life and Times" 25), including its politicized discourse about Afrikaner women's writing and writing about such women.

Felman puts the question:

> Might it not be possible to define the very specificity of literature as that which *suspends the answer* to the question of knowing whether the madness literature speaks of is literal or figurative? The specific property of the thing called literature is such, in other words, that the rhetorical status of its madness can no longer be determined. (*Writing and Madness* 253)

Felman argues that literature's particular quality is its ability to "unsettle the boundary" between what she calls "psychosis" and "stereotype" (253), or between the clinical condition of madness and the ways that madness gets represented in writing, which always relies on preconceptions because madness resists language, the conduit of reason. Magda recognizes the radical potential of madness as resistance, as a means of remaining outside and beyond dominant forms of writing, but it is a challenge she is unable to meet. She is reduced to communicate via the symbolic order she rejects, yielding to the spectre of reason. Which leads me to conclude that what might be called the "poetics of reciprocity" in the novel, both Magda's attempts at communion with her servants and the relationship between the "You" and "I" of the text, might better be called, in Coetzee's words, the "poetics of failure" (DP 86).

Chapter 3
Madness and Civilization in
Waiting for the Barbarians

We have yet to write the history of that other form of madness, by which men, in an act of sovereign reason, confine their neighbors, and communicate and recognize each other through the merciless language of non-madness.

Michel Foucault, *Madness and Civilization* (1965), ix

And some who have just returned from the border say
there are no barbarians any longer.
And now, what's going to happen to us without barbarians?
They were, those people, a kind of solution.

Constantine P. Cavafy, "Waiting for the Barbarians" (1904)

J. M. Coetzee's third novel *Waiting for the Barbarians* (1980) (hereafter, *Barbarians*), which makes a titular allusion to the Greek modernist Constantine P. Cavafy's poem, stages the state of waiting of a colonizing people, who live in fear of attack by the elusive "barbarians". (The text renders the term "barbarian" an effect of imperial discourse.) The Magistrate, who narrates the story, is the administrator of a settler outpost of an indeterminate place and time and which thus constitutes a kind of temporal no-man's-land or "interregnum". This term, co-opted by Gordimer from the Italian Marxist Antonio Gramsci's reinterpretation, denotes a transitional period between regimes when, in Gramsci's words, "the old is dying, and the new cannot be born" (qtd. in Gordimer, *Essential Gesture* 263). The Magistrate's authority is usurped by Police Colonel Joll and his sidekick Mandel when they arrive with a relief battalion to protect the outpost. In the interim the Magistrate forms an obsessive relationship with an enigmatic barbarian girl who has been tortured at the hands of Joll (only consummated on the journey to return the girl to her people). As a result of this undertaking, which the Magistrate construes as a moral obligation, Joll accuses him of treason for supposedly colluding with the enemy and, like the captured barbarians, he is imprisoned and tortured.

At the same time, the Magistrate is aware of his shortcomings in his role as administrator: that his relationship with the barbarian girl and what he calls his "questionable desires" (WB 79) are not untouched by self-interest – *her* pain defines *his* guilty conscience – and, not unlike Magda's relationship with her servants in *In the Heart of the Country* (1977), is an abuse of power. He realizes that the distance between himself and the vile Joll is therefore not so great. Wounded bodies are texts subject to being read: this is the commonality that brings the Magistrate and his adversary together: "Though I cringe with shame … I must ask myself whether … I was not in my heart of hearts regretting that I could not engrave myself on [the barbarian girl] as deeply" as Joll, he says (WB 148). Preparing the ground for the protagonists in the later works, Dostoevsky in *The Master of Petersburg* (1994) and Professor David Lurie in *Disgrace* (1999), the Magistrate sees himself "sinking further and further into disgrace" (WB 105), just as the townspeople are disgraced by the spectacle of torture to which they are party (WB 118). The power of the novel lies in part in the Magistrate's realization that the boundaries between himself and the dehumanizing regime of Empire and the warped notions of reason it promotes are disturbingly unclear. Yet in his proximity to the likes of Joll on the one hand and in his imprisonment and torture at the hands of the latter on the other, the Magistrate's position of both oppressor and oppressed is experienced as a kind of double consciousness that can only lead to madness. *what does this mean*

Michel Foucault's historicizing in *Madness and Civilization* denaturalizes madness, which, he argues, is premised on boundaries, on what marks off reason that is always already bounded by systems of power from an unreason that resists. In Europe, civil society's relation to madness shifts during the course of the Medieval, "Classical" and Modern periods from the perception of madness outside society, threatening its limits (Foucault makes a lengthy discussion of the ship of fools of the Renaissance period which contained madness by driving it from society [*Madness*, 8]), to madness within and the fear of contagion. Finally, in the modern era madness is objectified as mental illness, regulated by the discourse of medical science: the mad were now subject to "reasonable" methods of treatment and control. Society's need for boundaries of self-definition necessitate constructing "the insane" as other, but this process is inherently self-revealing. In *Barbarians*, the binaries of reason/unreason and mad/not-mad, are exposed in the context of Enlightenment thinking as constructions that serve to maintain Empire's power.

Whilst madness is treated explicitly in Coetzee's first two novels, *Dusklands* (1974) and *In the Heart of the Country*, through the portrayal of psychically unstable narrator-authors, it is the colonialist fantasies and paranoia named in the latter by Magda as "hordes of brown horsemen" (HC 140) and Empire's own "barbarous" regime that constitute madness in this novel. Arif Dirlik has argued that those critics of the novel reading Empire as an allegory of the totalitarian state are "missing the point entirely" because "Coetzee's Empire does what it does to the barbarian not because it is totalitarian; rather it becomes totalitarian *in the process of dehumanizing the barbarian*" (emphasis added; Dirlik 333): this is the madness of "civilization". The narrative critiques Enlightenment thinking by demonstrating that it is in the interests of Empire to construct the "enemy" out of the barbarians. In this way, echoing Cavafy's poem in which the barbarians provide the Senate with "a kind of solution" (5–6), Empire maintains control over the colony and can pursue its uncompromising campaign. Recalling Magda's fantasy of rape and the one pervaded by O. Mannoni that Frantz Fanon so bitterly dismisses ("the racialist whose daughter has suffered an [imaginary] attempted rape at the hands of an inferior being" (added text Fanon's; *Black Skin* 107; Mannoni 70), the Magistrate observes:

> Once in every generation, without fail, there is an episode of hysteria about the barbarians. There is no woman living along the frontier who has not dreamed of a dark barbarian hand coming from under the bed to grip her ankle, no man who has not frightened himself with visions of the barbarians carousing in his home … raping his daughters. These dreams are the consequence of too much ease. (WB 9)

The colonial mind, festering upon the luxury of free time made possible by the indenture and enslavement of others, willfully confuses fantasies of rape with rape proper. Here we see a tension between (feminized) sexual desire for and (masculinized) fear and jealousy of the racial other: the verb "to dream of" meaning both "dreaming" in a literal sense and "lusting after", and "to frighten (oneself)" suggestive of both an unconscious fear of otherness and consciously willed fear in the form of obsessional jealousy.

The frontier people's anxiety about attack, however, is not wholly unfounded because the bodies of two dead soldiers on horseback are returned by the barbarians strapped to their horses in retaliation of the threat the soldiers' presence would present. Attwell observes that it is the manner in which Empire "*imagines*" the barbarian that is important (original emphasis; *J. M. Coetzee* 71), which would make the colonization of subjecthood the novel's central theme. To convey the limits of the discourses of reason, *Barbarians* stages an orientalizing process which therefore, as Edward Said argues, "has less to do with the 'Orient' than it does with 'our' world" (*Orientalism* 12) that, in the context of this novel, is Empire's colonial outpost. Here, the Occident is inserted *within* the Orient.

The madness of the protagonists in all three texts is realized in their breakdown of self (the Magistrate is constructed as mad when Mandel forces him to dress in a woman's frock and orders a mock hanging), but is also loosely analogous to the unreason of apartheid ideology outlined by Coetzee in his essay "Apartheid Thinking" (*Giving Offense*). (Robert Spencer is struck by the prescience of this novel in the context of the "West's" "war on terror" and its deployment of methods of torture ["Colonial Violence"], which, as the pictures from Abu Ghraib gaol reveal, might be read as a kind of madness.) Coetzee recognizes the pitfalls of calling apartheid mad:

> to call apartheid mad is by no means to imply that the liberal-capitalist segregationism that preceded it was sane. It makes sense of a kind, indeed, to argue that both were mad … How short-sighted does self-interest have to be before it ceases to be sane, and how much more short-sighted before it begins to be crazy? (GO 163)

In these words, upon which I suggest, *Barbarians* turns, the Magistrate surprises himself to find that he is the embodiment of this self-interest par excellence in his relationship with the barbarian girl.

Unlike most of Coetzee's narrators, the Magistrate only engages minimally with the project of writing; more accurately, he is an archaeologist, an archivist and, above all, a reader of texts and critic of Empire. Not only has he collected a series of excavated poplar slips bearing strange inscriptions, in the final passages of the book he struggles to prepare a record of the settler town, having gathered his "historical" resources, including the inscrutable barbarian girl with whom he becomes intimate. The passivity of the girl, who nonchalantly accepts his ritualistic bathing of her feet, renders her a resisting, unreadable "text" but the Magistrate, undeterred, promises himself that "until the marks on this girl's body are deciphered and understood I cannot let go of her" (WB 33). The Magistrate reads the girl as a blank page: "she is incomplete"; ironically distorting the "dark interior" of colonialist discourse, he believes "with this woman it is as if there is no interior". Looking upon the girl before they part, he unwittingly reveals that to understand her is to better understand himself: "This is the last time ... to scrutinize the motions of my heart, to understand who she really is... . There is only a blankness, and desolation that there has to be such blankness" (WB 45; 46; 79). The depraved Joll, who operates within a different moral code which I read as "mad", likewise presents the Magistrate with the problem of reading, for it is not until the end of the story that Joll removes his dark, mirrored glasses to reveal his eyes, the "window to the soul".

Just as he reacts to the girl as inscrutable text, the Magistrate's imagination stalls in front of the blank page as he tries to set down a record of the town: "what I find myself beginning to write is not the annals of an Imperial outpost or an account of how the people of that outpost spent their last year composing their souls as they waited for the barbarians" (WB 168). Such histories orientalize the other and are always already underwritten by power. Instead he turns to the "charm" of the natural world: to a nomadic symbiosis with the changing seasons, the harvests and the "migrations of waterbirds" (WB 169). Apart from this yearning for Nature and the pastoral, writing in the novel is couched consistently in negative terms: Joll's macabre inscriptions on the bodies of the barbarian prisoners; the Magistrate's unsuccessful attempts to write a history of the town; and earlier, his experience of writer's block that, in a familiar Coetzean conceit, links sexual potency with the flow of the pen: "It seems appropriate that a man who does not know what to do with the woman in his bed should not know how to write" (WB 63). Conscious of his obligations to the settlers in any account he sets down, the Magistrate realizes that not until he has been pushed to the limits of human suffering, as the text implies the barbarians have, "will [he] abandon the locutions of a civil servant with literary ambitions and begin to tell the truth" (WB 169). At the end of the novel he is confronted by the culmination of these problems of history and ethical understanding:

I wanted to live outside the history that Empire imposes on its subjects, even its lost subjects. I never wished it for the barbarians that they should have the history of Empire laid upon them. How can I believe that that is cause for shame? (WB 169–70)

In these penultimate passages the Magistrate struggles for closure, for the end of Empire and the relinquishing of authority: he "dreams of ends[,] dreams not of how to live but of how to die" (WB 146). The oppressive Empire, on the other hand, resists obscurity and its own demise through conquest, which is "A mad vision yet a virulent one" (WB 146).

As a cynical critic of Empire, the Magistrate even politicizes the act of reading. Mordantly, he pretends to decipher the poplar slips for Joll, first reading the scenes of torture in the opening passages of the novel:

Now let us see what the next one says. See, there is only a single character. It is the barbarian character *war*, but it has other senses too. It can stand for *vengeance*, and, if you turn it upside down like this, it can be made to read *justice*. There is no knowing which sense is intended. That is part of barbarian cunning… . [The slips] form an allegory. They can be read in many orders. Further, each single slip can be read in many ways. Together they can be read as a domestic journal, or they can be read as a plan of war, or they can be turned on their sides and read as a history of the last years of the Empire – the old Empire, I mean. (WB 122)

Not only does this act of reading allow the Magistrate to launch a covert attack on Joll, it also calls into question the Manichean allegory employed by Empire to police its authority. By offering alternative readings and alluding to the barbarians' just war – or the Magistrate's translation of "war", which can also mean "vengeance" and "justice" – the Magistrate satirizes the monolith of Empire's colonial history, suggesting that truth is far more malleable than such histories would allow. The Magistrate plays upon Empire's paranoia since the slips are most likely to be innocuous and certainly are not a secret code between him and the barbarians. We will never know their true meaning because the Magistrate simply mimes the act of reading ("I do not even know whether to read from right to left or from left to right" [WB 121]), providing with sharp-tongued irony the narratives of war that Joll and his cronies crave and which would bolster Empire's mission.

The novel self-consciously invites allegorical readings, not only here but in the representations of Empire and torture, in the girl and Joll as blank texts, in the Magistrate's attempts to write a history of the settlement, in the dream sequences. Paradoxically, these passages also alert the reader to the dangers allegory engenders (which is why one critic titles her essay "Allegory of Allegories" [Dovey]), primarily, the forestalling of imaginative, and thus critical, enquiry. What is more, as I have explained above, the Magistrate makes associations between this kind of reading practice and the work of Empire, which disguises its desire to subject *how? needs to unpack this further.*

the barbarian prisoners by professing a desire to "read" them. It achieves this end through torture.

That the novel is set in an unspecifiable place and time leads some critics to suggest that it offers a universal ethical message. Susan VanZanten Gallagher agrees with Anthony Burgess in his review that the novel is about nowhere and therefore about everywhere ("Torture and the Novel" 281-82; Burgess 88). Commenting on the use of "Empire" in the text, Dominic Head suggests that "The omission of the definite article helps to widen the connotations of 'Empire', which becomes available as an emblem of imperialism through history" (*J. M. Coetzee* 72–73; see also Attwell, *J. M. Coetzee* 71). Abdul R. JanMohamed is critical of the novel's political opacity on the grounds that it espouses the universalism of colonialist literature. The novel,

> a deliberate allegory, epitomizes the dehistoricizing, desocializing tendency of colonialist fiction … [It] refuses to acknowledge its historical sources or to make allusions to the specific barbarism of the apartheid regime. The novel thus implies that we are all somehow equally guilty and that fascism is endemic to all societies. ("Economy" 73)

Attwell makes a case for "history-as-myth" being the "fulcrum" of the works up to and including *Age of Iron* (1990), but in *Barbarians* the focus is history "as discursive field" and "an object in itself" (*J. M. Coetzee* 72), which would seem to corroborate JanMohamed's point. We should question whether Coetzee is guilty, as JanMohamed claims Homi Bhabha in "The Other Question" is, of skirting the material reality of colonial conflict to prioritize colonial discourse "as if it existed in a vacuum" (JanMohamed, "Economy" 60). We might ask whether *Barbarians* employs the very madness ("blindness" to the other) that it means to critique. This is implied in JanMohamed's words: "In its studied refusal to accept historical responsibility, this novel, like all 'imaginary' colonialist texts, attempts to mystify the imperial endeavour by representing the relation between self and Other in metaphysical terms" ("Economy" 73). I return to this debate below.

Given that the novel, which portrays torture and police brutality in the most graphic terms, was published in 1980, soon after the Soweto uprisings and the murder of the student leader Steve Biko whilst in police custody, as critics have abundantly commented, the intention to critique the contemporary milieu in South Africa is clear. Indeed, many of these critics link the torture of the old man at the beginning of the novel with the death of Biko. Attwell rightly contends that the reading of "ethical universalism" is not wholly accurate of a novel that utilizes a "strategic refusal of specificity" (*J. M. Coetzee* 73). Peter D. McDonald has recently discovered that *Barbarians* was put before the censors, which would suggest that, with its allusions to the contemporary situation, it offended the apartheid regime. The novel was subsequently passed by the censorship board, the Directorate of Publications, because of its apparently universal scope (McDonald "Not Undesirable"; "The Writer" 45–51).

ALLEGORY   ATTRIDGE

By ridiculing Joll and parodying the processes by which Empire knows its subjects, the Magistrate exposes the "truths" of Empire and, simultaneously, calls into question overdetermined reading practices. Attridge points out, however, that it is not surprising that South African writers like Coetzee have deconstructed the allegorizing process in this way, "[g]iven the extensive suffering caused in South Africa by dehumanizing codifications" (*J. M. Coetzee* 62). Yet Attridge also takes a stand "against allegory" in his reading of Coetzee; though he states that he isn't "against allegory" as such, he is "*for* reading as an event, for restraining the urge to leave the text, or rather the experience of the text, behind … for opening oneself to the text's forays beyond the doxa" (*J. M. Coetzee* 64). This is just the kind of reading that the Magistrate is unable to make in his relationship with the girl.

Whereas Attwell argues that history as discourse is the fulcrum of this text, my sense is that acts of misreading and misrepresentation as symptoms of colonial violence (madness) are closer to the mark. The narrative, for instance, provides a transparently bogus police record of the old man's murder at the hands of Joll and his cronies which parodies just such accounts given credence by apartheid law.[1] The South African poet Christopher van Wyk's poem, "In Detention" (1979), highlights the shamelessness of such reports. The poem begins:

unoriginal

> He fell from the ninth floor
> He hanged himself
> He slipped on a piece of soap while washing
> He hanged himself
> He slipped on a piece of soap while washing
> He fell from the ninth floor
> He hanged himself while washing
> He slipped from the ninth floor
> He hung from the ninth floor (Brink and Coetzee, *A Land Apart* 50)

The heavy irony through wordplay makes nonsense of "factual" evidence submitted by the police. Madness manifests itself in the audacity of the lying to reveal, paradoxically, the truth of apartheid rule. In a similar fashion, the Magistrate mocks Joll in Joll's language of xenophobic state ideology: "Can you tell us whether we have anything to fear [from the barbarians]? Can we rest securely at night?" (WB 25). Acts of misreading and misrepresentation such as this therefore convey the, often state-orchestrated, wilful confusion of reason and unreason that is symptomatic of the madness of "civilization".

In Foucault, Coetzee writes, madness and reason are

---

[1]   See also Alex la Guma's *In the Fog of the Season's End* (1972) and Mongane Wally Serote's *To Every Birth Its Blood* (1981) for other examples of novels that portray such accounts.

reduc[ed] … to the status of warring twins. In this perspective, each of the twins sees the other as possessing an overmastering prestige … which it must at all costs have for itself. This in turn may help us to see why it is that the actions of reason come to look more and more like madness, just as madness, and particularly the madness of paranoia, looks like an excess of reason: because each is imitating the other. (GO 91)

unethical ?!

Madness is a lack of self-knowledge, but here, paradoxically, it is the post-Cartesian model of reason that tries to distinguish itself from madness. Coetzee glosses Foucault: "It does not know itself in that it claims to be based on full self-knowledge, on knowledge of itself as the voice of transcendent reason, whereas it is in fact only the voice of a certain power" (GO 85). Foucault is interested, not in the medical definition of madness, but in the relation between state authority and the subject: madness is defined by authority as unreason, in conflict with the reasonable discourse of modernity (*Madness and Civilization* 212). Paradoxically, *because* madness is conceptualized as unreason, it is already placed, albeit negatively, within a system of knowledge. In the final analysis, reason is collapsed as mad or unreasonable: "madness and non-madness, *reason and non-reason are inextricably involved: inseparable at the moment when they do not yet exist, and existing for each other, in relation to each other, in the exchange which separates them*" (emphasis added; *Madness and Civilization* xii).

The Magistrate's desire for the barbarian girl also should be read as mad given that it is based on a lack of reciprocity, self-interest and an irrational neglect of truth justified through the Magistrate's wavering belief in his altruistic motivations for taking her in. Here, the fetishistic desire in colonial discourse to which JanMohamed refers, the desire to be recognized by the other in order to clarify one's sense of self, emerges in the Magistrate's concern for the girl ("Economy" 66–67). She is finally returned to her people in his words, "a stranger; a visitor from strange parts now on her way home after a less than happy visit" (WB 79). The Magistrate's self-interest is clearly signalled when he makes use of her tortured body to satisfy his own desires, not unlike Magda's misuse, real or imagined, of the bodies of Hendrik and Klein-Anna in *In Heart of the Country*. (Here, any comparison with Magda ends because the Magistrate, unlike Magda, is increasingly conscious of the dubious motives that drive the charity he shows the girl.) Each night, uninvited, the Magistrate ritually bathes and oils her broken feet and in the process is lulled into a trance-like sleep, ironically oblivious of the presence of the girl herself. The Magistrate's somnambulistic state is symptomatic of his lack of ethical vision. Representing his fixation with the girl's victimhood (which Attwell is right to attribute to a South African liberal consciousness [*J. M. Coetzee* 80]), each time he partakes in the ritual he is satiated by her woundedness and is overtaken by sleep. He is fixated with her *as maimed victim* and is driven to find out the truth about her torture at the hands of Joll: "pain is truth; all else is subject to doubt. That is what I bear away from my conversation with Colonel Joll" (WB 5). The Magistrate's endeavour to understand the girl, or more properly to understand himself, through her pain, though continually undermined by his *WHAT ?!* desire, paradoxically, to obliterate it, ultimately objectifies her, serving only to *?!* perpetuate her oppression begun at the hands of her torturers. The madness figured in washing therefore resonates with ethnic cleansing. Laura Wright suggests that, figured in the metaphor of his washing the girl's body, the Magistrate attempts to wash himself clean from his sense of complicity with Empire "through the intellectualization of his ambivalent position as a champion of an anachronistic imperialism" (*Writing* 74).

In "Wounded Attachments" Wendy Brown identifies a paradox in liberal identity politics: that in its attempt to empower, identity work serves the forces of marginalization ("the triumph of the weak as weak" [William Connolly qtd. in Brown 400]). Brown explains that:

> In its emergence as a protest against marginalization or subordination, politicized
> identity … becomes attached to its own exclusion both because it is premised
> on this exclusion for its very existence as identity and because the formation of
> identity at the site of exclusion, as exclusion, augments or "alters the direction
> of the suffering" entailed in subordination or marginalization by finding a site of
> blame for it. But in so doing, it installs its pain over its unredeemed history in the
> foundation of its political claim, in its demand for recognition as identity. (406)

not explained— lacking context

In other words, the foundations of identity politics intended to bolster marginal identities are built upon wounded attachments. In *Barbarians* the girl's is a "narcissistic wound" (Brown 405) *by proxy*. The Magistrate admits, however, that whilst he can only know her body as wounded, how the girl perceives her wounds is likely to be different: "she has perhaps by now grown into and become that new deficient body, feeling no more deformed than a cat feels deformed for having claws instead of fingers" (WB 61). Brown challenges identity politics which are predicated on the regulation of otherness between "particularistic 'I's' and a universal 'we'" (391). She turns to Nietzsche to find a way out of this impasse, to the "'virtues of forgetting', for if identity structured in part by ressentiment *?!* resubjugates itself through its investment in its own pain... memory is the house of this activity and this refusal". However, she quickly abandons Nietzsche; erasure through forgetting is unviable given that marginalized identities are typically already "inscribed" by erasure (Brown 406). Moreover, in geopolitical paradigms such as Empire, erasure and forgetting are not only inappropriate but should be actively challenged. Brown's solution is "to configure a radically democratic political culture that can sustain such a project in its midst without being overtaken by it", and part of this reconfiguration would be premised upon expressing "desires". The Magistrate glimpses a different kind of barbarian girl when he witnesses her easy interaction and garrulousness with the young men enlisted to make the trip back to her home. Notably, two of these are conscripts (the other is a local) so the Magistrate witnesses an inter-racial interaction, and one that is not based upon the Manichaean paradigm.

The reciprocity between the girl and the Magistrate is consolidated in the motif of eyes and blindness: not only is the barbarian girl blind – blindness typically symbolizing philosophical vision – Joll's dark eye glasses, as a "new invention", are linked implicitly to the dawning of modernity (WB 1). Moreover, the Magistrate describes Joll's henchman Mandel as looking through those "lovely blue eyes … as an actor from behind a mask" (WB 84). As texts to be read, the girl and these servants of Empire are inscrutable: the Magistrate misreads the girl's impenetrability for blankness, and the face in Joll's glasses, one imagines, is the Magistrate's own staring back at him. These acts of "reading" suggest that it is the process of reading (the self) that Coetzee holds up for scrutiny rather than the "texts" themselves.

Foucault quotes the *Encylopédie*'s definition of madness: "to depart from reason 'with confidence and in the firm conviction that one is following it'". The obscuring of truth results in madness, Foucault elaborates. Blindness constitutes a lack of moral, rather than physical, truth and hence a kind of madness. Blindness "refers also to ill-founded beliefs, mistaken judgements, to the whole background of errors inseparable from the madness" (Foucault, *Madness and Civilization* 104–106). Foucault distinguishes between physical and moral truth by quoting from an article on mania in the *Encyclopédie*:

> "Physical truth consists of the accurate relation of our sensations with physical objects"; there will be a form of madness determined by the impossibility of acceding to this form of truth … "Moral truth," on the other hand, "consists in the exactitude of the relations we discern either between moral objects, or between those objects and ourselves". (Foucault, *Madness and Civilization* 105)

The blindness to reading observed here by Foucault in *Barbarians* manifests itself not in the barbarian girl but in the Magistrate and Colonel Joll. Blindness to physical truth in Foucault's analysis is psychosis; blindness to its moral counterpart is the "madness of civilization", in the thrall of which both Joll and the Magistrate are held. Though Joll is a proponent of "physical truth" – "pain is truth", he so cruelly proclaims (WB 5) – he is patently delusional in moral terms and the Magistrate, despite championing moral truths, is morally suspect in his wounded attachment to the girl's broken body. Madness lurks in his inability to read her outside the imperious mindset. Nevertheless, the Magistrate is partially redeemed by his awareness of the self-interested motives behind his decision to house the girl.

Not only is the Magistrate fixated with the girl in her pain, he is tormented by a series of dreams in which he struggles to resolve (to interpret) his ambivalent relationship with her, but which, in actuality, reinforces the failure of reciprocity that colours their relationship. Symbolically loaded, as Foucault suggests, "dreams, madness, the unreasonable can … slip into [an] *excess of meaning*" (emphasis added; *Madness* 19) which all require interpreting. Colonialist notions of subject formation, of which the recurring image of the snowman is a metaphor, are realized in the illusory space of dreams and parody the fictional status of the other constructed by colonialist discourse. (Snow not only connotes inhospitability but also impermanence.) The first dream looks forward to the appearance of the barbarian girl in the narrative: the face of the girl in the dream is blank, suggesting the impossibility of authentic communication with or reading of the other. In a later dream the girl's face becomes an embryo; in another, the Magistrate's attempts to communicate with the children that populate it through speech and touch are thwarted because ice covers both his mouth and hands. The narrative thus presses the lack of reciprocity between the Magistrate and his others, which in the dreams are children. Likewise, the snow fort is always unpeopled, emphasizing the lack of communion. The Magistrate then dreams of "the girl", whom he first mistakenly believes to be "digging away in the bowels of the castle" (WB 119), only to realize that she is baking bread, which she offers to him in an act of fellowship, cast in Christian mythology. In one dream the girl's feet become abstracted from her body, suggestive of the fetishistic nature of the Magistrate's interest in her. In general, read as allegories of the Manichaean struggle, the dreams show how colonialism, with the Magistrate as its reluctant representative, attempts to construct the colonial other as a means of clarifying and maintaining notions of the self. As Attwell points out, "continuity and reciprocity [which] ultimately depend on the idea of human community" are absent from the dream sequence (*J. M. Coetzee*, 81), just as they are absent in the Magistrate's waking self.

Arrested by Joll for supposedly "treasonably consorting with the enemy" (WB 85), dressed in a woman's frock and gibbeted on a tree, the Magistrate is reduced to what Mandel, Joll's henchman, calls a "clown, a madman" (WB 124). Mandel scapegoats the Magistrate by constructing him as the fool; finally deeming it unnecessary, as the result of this construction, to imprison him, Mandel allows him to roam freely, half-mad, through the town. The construction of the Magistrate by Mandel as insane corresponds with Foucault's thesis in *Discipline and Punish* of the birth of the criminal subject during the Enlightenment. As Foucault writes, "From being an art of unbearable sensations punishment has become an economy of suspended rights" (*Discipline* 11). Modern penal methods, such as Jeremy Bentham's Panopticon, shifted the object of punishment from the physical body to the soul, to the self-regulation and consciousness-raising of the prisoner who, kept alive, is given the opportunity to experience guilt, remorse and to reform. The Magistrate declares that Mandel "deals with my soul" (WB 129). Of course, in *Barbarians* both the soul and the physical body are disciplined, pointing up, inadvertently perhaps, Foucault's prematurely optimistic claim that torture is no longer practised by the "West".

Foucault's epistemic critique in *Madness and Civilization* demonstrates that madness, or more accurately, social conceptions of madness, can be historicized to be read politically, rendering madness "not mad". In literary representations of the fool madness typically symbolizes sagacity. In this vein Coetzee turns in "Erasmus: Madness and Rivalry" to Erasmus's *Praise of Folly* (1509), which maps "the possibility of a position for the critic of the scene of political rivalry", a response which, he says, was surprisingly prescient given the rivalry that would unfold a decade later between the Pope and Luther (GO 84). Erasmus adopts the well-known political position, or more properly the "*non*position" (GO 84), of the fool, which allows him to challenge opposing sides without reprisal but that often brings together such rivals in their efforts to overcome him. As both fool and not-fool, this split self corresponds with of the dialectic of unreason and reason. Fool in this context functions as empowered mediator. This constitutes a position not wholly unlike that of non-partisanship outlined by Edward Said in his model of the public intellectual, who should be "independent, autonomously functioning" (*Representations* 67), except that Said's intellectual will act despite the threat of reprisal and rejects outright nonpositionality (*Representations* 100).

For Erasmus, the apparently uncommitted position of "mad-but-not-really-mad" (uncommitted because of its retreat into madness) in fact functions at the level of ethical representation: Coetzee alerts us to "a highly self-aware reflection [in Erasmus] on the limitations on any project speaking on behalf of madness" (GO 84). For Jacques Derrida, writing about Foucault, here lies the impasse: speaking responsibly on behalf of madness, representing its silences, necessarily means passing over to enemy lines, to order and the voice of reason (*Writing*, 36; GO 87). Hence central to Foucault's analysis is a discourse that reads madness on its own terms and this, Derrida argues, "is the most audacious and seductive aspect of [Foucault's] venture … But it is also, with all seriousness, the *maddest* aspect of his project" (*Writing* 34; qtd. in GO 86).

From the outset the Magistrate is conscious of the mechanics of Empire's (discursive) power; he and Joll "pause, savouring from our different positions the ironies of the word ['civilization']" (WB 13). His torturers show him "the meaning of humanity" (WB 126): Empire's henchmen, he says, are the "new barbarians" (WB 85). The novel suggests that nurturing the *fear of* the threat of the barbarians is Empire's means of defining the "civilized" self. Of course, the settler community's own paranoiac xenophobia is instead exposed. Through a Foucauldian lens, ambivalence in *Barbarians*, including the ambivalent discourse of colonialism and a Janus-faced modernity, lays bare the madness of reason and the "civilizing" mission.

The madness of civilization is no more starkly apparent than in the torture chamber, Coetzee's subject in "Into the Dark Chamber": "Relations in the torture room provide a metaphor, bare and extreme, for relations between authoritarianism and its victims. In the torture room unlimited force is exerted upon the physical being of an individual in a twilight of *legal illegality*" (emphasis added; DP 363). The gratuitous nature of the violence enacted upon the Magistrate in his mock execution exposes the madness of his torturer Mandel. This is the Hegelian dialectic rather than the Manichaean allegory that JanMohamed theorizes: tortured and torturer are figured around a kind of ironic doubling or *doppelgänger* effect. The Magistrate is paired variously with Joll, Mandel and the barbarian girl, and these pairings function as "dark twins" or "schizophrenic" discourse. As the Magistrate confesses, "who am I to assert my distance from [Joll]? I drink with

SELF SCRUTINY.   *OBSCURE MADNESS*

him, I eat with him, I show him the sights" (WB 6). Referring to the most explicit scene of torture in the novel, when the barbarian prisoners are beaten mercilessly under the watchful eye of Joll, the morally sickened Magistrate inverts the object of Joll's vile game from prisoner to Joll himself. Courageously putting his own freedom in jeopardy in the name of justice, he rails: "*You* are the enemy, *you* have made the war, and *you* have given them [the barbarians] all the martyrs they need – starting not now but a year ago when you committed your first filthy barbarities here!" He even invokes History in his defence: "History will bear me out!" (WB 125). Yet the text always returns us to the Magistrate's own irrationality in his relationship with the girl and to his effectively turning a blind eye to the atrocities of Empire, including the murder of the old man in custody.

The Magistrate's desire for the girl, which at first is only the desire to know the truth of her pain, fills him with the madness of tortuous self-doubt. Coetzee implicitly links desire with madness in the Erasmus essay:

> Desire ... does not know itself. It proceeds from a lack. What the desiring subject lacks, and ultimately desires, is fullness of being. The model is adopted as model because it appears endowed with superior being. Imitating the desires of the model is a way of gaining being ... . It is loss of difference rather than difference itself that leads to conflict ... . From loss of difference emerges rivalry ... . As differences dwindle and mimetic violence mounts, there is ultimately nothing done or felt by one protagonist that is not done or felt by the other. There is no way of differentiating them: the protagonists become doubles. (GO 92)

The tortured girl in the Magistrate's eyes distils the truth of Empire and of the Magistrate's rival Joll: "There is nothing to link me with torturers ... I must assert my distance from Colonel Joll! I will not suffer for his crimes!", he says (WB 48). However, the Magistrate comes to an awareness that he is not so different from his rival Joll after all, conscious that "an interrogator can wear two masks, speak with two voices, one harsh, one seductive" (WB 8), and later that the "distance between myself and [the girl's] torturers ... is negligible" (WB 29). With great effort, the Magistrate, who has remarked upon his own unattractiveness, calls to mind the girl's "ugliness" (until this moment she has remained "featureless" [50]), which is mirrored by the settlers' collective imagining of the barbarian accused of raping one of their children: "[the girl's] friends claim a barbarian did it ... . They recognised him as a barbarian by his ugliness" (WB 134). The narcissistic Joll wears sunglasses to maintain a youthful appearance, and Mandel is described by the Magistrate as "vain" and one who might "flex[ ] his muscles for [his girlfriend], feeding on her admiration" (WB 84). This preoccupation with the aesthetics of the body (and conversely, the abhorrence of physical imperfection) recalls the sinister promotion of the athletic physique in fascist discourse. The Magistrate's attempts to understand the girl, as mirrored surface (to touch her "is like caressing an urn or a ball, something which is all surface" [WB 52]), in fact constitute a means of casting light upon his own identity. The ugliness of the barbarians recalls the often

?(really.

cited passage in Joseph Conrad's *Heart of Darkness*, when Marlow, observing the natives leap and turn, recognizes their humanity, or more properly, his *own* lack of civility: "What thrilled you was just the thought of their humanity – like yours … Ugly" (105–06).

The scene in *Barbarians* referred to above depicting the spectacle of torture of the barbarian prisoners alludes not only to Foucault's construction of criminality but also to Franz Kafka's "In the Penal Colony" (1914) in which a European traveller to an unspecified island is invited by the Commandant to witness the cruel methods of punishment employed by the old regime. Coetzee and Kafka depict the taint induced in witnesses of torture. Coetzee's Joll draws the word "ENEMY" on each prisoner's dirt-covered back and they are whipped until the words are washed away by their own blood. In Kafka's story the officer administering the old method of torture rationalizes acts of seemingly gratuitous violence in the following terms: on the brink of death, the "condemned man" under torture experiences an "enlightenment" that "begins around the eyes" as the window to the soul. Like Kafka's explorer, the Magistrate is forced to question his conscience when made party to the spectacle of torture: ultimately, both characters feel morally impelled to speak out against the barbarity they witness. Both, however, are portrayed as ethically ambivalent: just as the Magistrate's relationship to the barbarian girl reveals his moral turpitude, so the explorer, as he quits the island, drives back two prisoners as they attempt to board his departing boat. The explorer leaves the colony apparently having learnt nothing from his journey, which is also a journey of conscience. Similarly, the explorer reveals a perverse sense of morality when the officer's implement of torture, the "Harrow", malfunctions after the officer places himself beneath it and is quickly killed. In rational terms, the officer suffers a merciful death yet the explorer construes the execution differently: "this was no exquisite torture such as the officer had desired, this was plain murder" (165). While the officer is overtly fascinated by the torture chamber (as South African writers were, according to Coetzee, during apartheid [DP 363]), the protagonist's very identification in the story as explorer and alien to the colony suggests that he is an explorer into the depths of human depravity, including his own. Kafka even contextualizes the tale within a postcolonial paradigm: the officer anticipates the explorer's criticisms of his methods with statements such as: "In our country we have a different criminal procedure," or, "We haven't used torture since the Middle Ages" (155–56). Evidenced in this dark satire of the modern state, Kafka doesn't suffer from the myopia of Foucault.

In both Coetzee's and Kafka's stories the prisoner is reduced by his torturer to animalistic behaviour. In *Barbarians* the barbarian prisoners, joined by a wire cord through their mouths and hands are, according to their captors, pacified "meek as lambs" (WB 113); the Magistrate denounces Joll's intention to kill the barbarians with a heavy hammer: "You would not use a hammer on a beast" (WB 117); Kafka's condemned man is shackled to a guard, "so like a submissive dog that one might have thought he could be left to run free … and would only need to be whistled for when the execution was due to begin" (PC 141). Serving

Empire's dark project, the animal metaphors render the other less than human. The prisoners in both narratives function as texts upon which their torturers inscribe their macabre writing. Indeed, both stories take account of the oppression behind the will to colonize, including the act of writing the colonial subject, through the parodic treatment of "writing" and "archaeology" in the narratives, illustrated in the Magistrate's interest in the slips and his anthropological fascination for the girl. Nonetheless, and undermining JanMohamed's Manichean reading, as Foucault suggests, "Impossible animals, issuing from a demented imagination, become the secret nature of man" (*Madness* 21), just as the demented imagination of Joll and the officer project their own bestiality on to their prey.[2]

"Imaginary" literatures like *Barbarians*, according to JanMohamed, not only fail to illuminate the condition of the racial other, they reaffirm their own "ethnocentric assumptions": "instead of actually depicting the outer limits of 'civilization', ['imaginary' literature] codifies and preserves structures of its own mentality ... instead of seeing the native as a bridge towards syncretic possibility, it uses him as a mirror that reflects the colonialist's self-image" ("Economy" 65–66). However, Coetzee self-reflexively stages this process, even employing the motif of the mirrored surface – Joll's glasses, the girl as mirrored ball – to express the ethnocentric impulse. Dividing colonial literature into two categories, the "imaginary" mentioned above, which objectifies the other, and the "symbolic", which strives to break down the Manichean divide, JanMohamed goes on to argue that Joseph Conrad successfully occupies the latter. *Heart of Darkness*, JanMohamed writes, is a "'symbolic' novella that *deliberately thematizes* the libidinal economy of the 'imaginary'" (emphasis added; 70). Yet, as I have shown, this is a strategy that Coetzee employs. As JanMohamed stipulates, in the "'imaginary' text, the subject is eclipsed by his fixation on and fetishisation of the Other" (67). In *Barbarians* this is deliberately and self-consciously orchestrated through the girl as urn and mirrored surface and through the Magistrate's ritualistic bathing of her feet. The author of the "symbolic" work, JanMohamed argues, fruitfully resists the urge to represent the other and "this decision is based on an understanding that differences between self and Other cannot be adequately transcended within the colonial context." Instead, such an author will focus on the "subjugating process and on the mentality of the conqueror" ("Economy" 81–82). Again, we see Coetzee at work. JanMohamed then goes on to celebrate Gordimer as an author of "symbolic" works that from *July's People* onwards "focus on the bankruptcy of the liberal ideology, on the effects of South African fascism on the liberal consciousness of her white protagonists, and on their progressive radicalization" (82). Missing from this formulation in *Barbarians*, I suggest, is the Magistrate's "radicalization", though he does speak out on behalf of the

---

[2]   While in these scenes Coetzee is faithful to his source, there are a number of clear departures, most significantly in Kafka's story the condemned man is himself portrayed as morally depraved, for when he is freed from the Harrow he is as fascinated by torture as the officer and is happy to see his persecutor suffer even more than he has.

persecuted. Yet *Barbarians* leaves us with the possibility of the Magistrate's "ethical awakening" – the title of Dominic Head's chapter on the novel (*J. M. Coetzee*, 72–92). I would go further: Coetzee's novel always calls into question its own procedures and encourages an agential reader who engages actively, and thus critically, in the life of the text. Perhaps this is where its radicality lies. In fact, Coetzee breaks down the Manichaean allegories he employs – barbarian/ civilized, mad/not-mad, reason/unreason, self/other – which leads me to conclude that, whilst the servants of Empire struggle to maintain boundaries that can only be described as Manichean, Hegel's dialectical relationship, which is "mutually damaging" (Head, *J. M. Coetzee* 6), more accurately describes the patterning of the text and the Magistrate's own self-doubt.

The efforts of the children, representing future generations, in the closing dream sequence to build what the Magistrate evaluates as "not a bad snowman" offer only the barest hope of redemption for the settler community. As Mrs. Curren in *Age of Iron* (1990) is aware, "We embrace our children to be folded into the arms of the future, to pass ourselves on beyond death, to be transported" (AI 5). While *Barbarians* tacitly assigns children such value, its message is profoundly bleak for the Magistrate notes that "somewhere, always, a child is being beaten" (WB 88), a phrase lifted from Freud's essay "A Child is Being Beaten: A Contribution to the Study of the Origin of Sexual Perversion". The inconclusiveness of the novel – the Magistrate confesses that "There has been something staring me in the face, and still I do not see it" (WB 170) – is suggestive of a blindness to history. After all, the "texts" that together form a colonial history – the slips, the girl, Joll – continue to confound him. However, that *he has learnt that he has learnt nothing* amounts to an ethical awakening to the madness that engulfs him.

Chapter 4
Cultivating the Margins
in the Trial of Michael K:
"Strategies in the Service of Skepticism"

[handwritten: see 73,75 etc. But, how is she using this? remains unclear.]

> Rousseau was right, in his particular confessional economy, to point out *what is held back* (money, the truth) as being key to freedom.
>
> J. M. Coetzee, "Truth in Autobiography" 6

> But in the smallest and greatest happiness there is always one thing that makes it happiness: the power of forgetting, or, in more learned phrase, the capacity of feeling "unhistorically" throughout its duration.
>
> Fredrich Nietzsche, *The Use and Abuse of History* 6

The tone of J. M. Coetzee's fourth novel *Life & Times of Michael K* (1983) is set in the opening sentence: "The *first thing* the midwife noticed about Michael K when she helped him out of his mother into the world was that he had a *hare lip*" (emphasis added; MK 3). Since his earliest memory, the protagonist Michael K passively accepts his marginality: "Year after year Michael K sat on a blanket watching his mother polish other people's floors, learning to be quiet" (MK 3–4). His life is characterized by a series of rejections, the response his disfigurement elicits from those he encounters representing a more general alienation (MK 48; 50; 76). It is ironic that the first woman in the novel who doesn't shun him is a prostitute he encounters near the end of the narrative who, when encouraged by her pimp to have oral sex with him, then kisses him full on the mouth (MK 179). Michael K is marginalized not only by his physical appearance but by race, by his socio-economic status as a disenfranchised "Cape coloured" and a vagrant ("On the charge sheet he was listed 'Michael Visagie – CM [Coloured Male] – 40 – NFA [No Fixed Abode] – Unemployed'" [MK 70]), by his position as a fatherless child and by his simpleness and otherworldliness. Significantly for the argument I am forwarding here, in these words Coetzee makes only veiled reference to racial identity and in doing so refuses to endorse the obsessive categorization instituted by the apartheid regime.

Michael K is the epitome of alienation and cultivates his isolation as a means of resisting the tumult of the "now", an imagined future South Africa in which the iron-hard rule of apartheid persists. A life dominated by institutions has instilled a dread of state regulation, regulation that he struggles to evade: raised in an orphanage, Huis Norenius, as an adult he is incarcerated in the Jakkalsdrif

[handwritten: ↓ what does this mean?]

labour camp and the Kenilworth rehabilitation camp. Yet Michael K is not actively resistant – and this is the source of much of the criticism of the novel, as I go on to explain – but one way to resist apartheid's system of classification and segregation is not to recognize it at all. In this chapter I will argue that Michael K attempts to stand outside this system by resisting the regime's regulation of the body by means of time, space and the land. Writing the body and writing the land are common topoi in postcolonial literature because it was the colonial state's regulation of bodies and land that stoked the colonial mission. To explore Michael K's resistance, Coetzee appropriates the parables of Franz Kafka and unwrites Daniel Defoe's classic fable *Robinson Crusoe* (1719) in the way they pertain to the regulated body.[1] In turn, Michael K resists being figured in discourse: as the unreaderly text, he also resists genre and the allegorizing process. The allegories of gardening/ farming, food and so on, are organized around him, inviting yet blocking exegesis. What is more, he refuses to yield his story despite being repeatedly pressed to do so (MK 121, 122, 138). He even resists what Coetzee calls the attempts of the author to put a "stranglehold" on him (DP 206): whilst the title of the work, *Life & Times*, promises biography, Michael K, who thinks "unhistorically" (to borrow from Nietzsche), passively resists the laws of genre – in the case of biography, the intimate knowledge of personality and the personal and public life of the subject. This manoeuvre allows Coetzee to create a tension between himself, as author, and a character who resists his will, signalling in other words Coetzee questioning his own authority. This is the authority of the white South African writer (cf. Attwell, *J. M. Coetzee* 89) and, I will argue, the authority of the writer of "postcolonial" fiction. Although at the time of writing, the early 1980s, postcolonial studies was in its infancy, Coetzee issues a prescient warning about the problems of systematizing the (post)colonial subject within its own discourse.

Nonetheless, critics have been vociferous in what they regard as Coetzee's obfuscation of black resistance in South Africa at the time the novel was penned. Coetzee's compatriot Nadine Gordimer is skeptical of the novel's achievements and of the contexts in which it is set. In *Life & Times*, with its bleak prediction of a future South Africa, "Hope is a seed. That's all. That's everything. It's better to live [like Michael K] on your knees, planting something" ("Idea" 6). Similarly, one critic writing in the *African Communist* and known only as Z. N. is frustrated

---

[1]   Patricia Merivale summarizes Kafkan readings of *Life & Times* as follows: "Whether to be slighted (Ward, Gallagher), parenthetically refuted (Gordimer), taken for granted (Steiner, Zamora, Lazarus, and Attwell), criticized (Lehmann-Haupt: the Kafkan "tributes" and "borrowings" "are overdone and call an unnecessary amount of attention to themselves"), inflated (Brink: "[Michael K] combin[es] the figures of Christ and Kafka's K"), or alternately evaded and grudgingly conceded by Coetzee himself … differences or … specific echoes and general resemblances (Olson, Post, or Sévry)" ("Audible" 152–53). On a number of counts, however, Merivale is somewhat misleading: Attwell gives a relatively detailed treatment of Kafka, for instance, and, regarding Merivale's summation of Brink, Coetzee does make associations between Christ and Michael K.

by the novel's apparent lack of a committed political vision: "The absence of any meaningful relationship between Michael K and anybody else ... means that in fact we are dealing not with a human spirit but an amoeba, from whose life we can draw neither example nor warning" (qtd. in Attwell, *J. M. Coetzee* 92). What unites all these critics is the need to extract the novel's allegorical meaning. Indeed, grappling with the wider significance of a text, sometimes through allegory, is a need that goes to the heart of all reading and that includes an understanding of the *condition humaine*.

For Gordimer, the use of allegory in the text, Michael K as the "little man of history" and gardener, falls woefully short of her call for the protesting writer's "essential gesture": to "declare himself positively as answerable to the order struggling to be born" (*Essential Gesture* 278). She argues,

> The unique and controversial aspect of this work is that while it is implicitly and highly political, Coetzee's heroes are those who ignore history, not make it. ... The presentation of the truth and meaning of what white has done to black stands out on every page; yet it denies the energy of the will to resist evil. ("Idea" 3–6)

Gordimer argues that what Georg Lukács identifies "as the integral relation between private and social destiny" in the novel is skewed in favour of the private, threatening "the work's unity of art and life" ("Idea" 6).

Lukács's theory of the syncretization of private and public is taken up in a different fashion by Fredric Jameson in his notorious summation of "Third-World literatures in the era of multi-national capitalism" in which, admitting that he is making a "sweeping hypothesis", he proclaims that "all third-world literatures are necessarily ... allegorical, and in a very specific way: they are to be read as ... *national allegories*" ("Third-World Literatures" 69). He identifies a radical split in the Western realist and modernist novel (unlike Lukács he brackets the two) between the political and the private, because, he argues, sexuality and the unconscious – the libidinal, private sphere – on the one hand, and economics, class and politics – the public – on the other are thought incommensurable. In the "Third World" context such a distinction cannot be made for "*the story of the private individual destiny is always an allegory of the embattled situation of the public third-world culture and society*". There exists in "Third-World" literatures a "different ratio of the political to the personal" and, accordingly, "libidinal investment[ ] is to be read in primarily political and social terms" (original emphasis; 69–72).

The "cultural revolution" to which "Third World" texts inevitably ally themselves, Jameson contends, rests upon the Marxist Antonio Gramsci's notion of subalternity, "namely the feelings of mental inferiority and habits of subservience and obedience which necessarily and structurally develop in situations of domination" (76). (What Gordimer would make of this aspect of Jameson's analysis is, I think, self-evident.) Importantly, a sense of inferiority projected in such works isn't a psychological issue but one of an "objective and collective spirit", a "psychic structure" that is materially and economically determined (Jameson 76). "National allegories" can therefore usefully open up a "concrete perspective on the real future" (77). Jameson has been useful in demonstrating how, in postcolonial literatures, the private can carry the full weight of the political, yet he has also rightly been challenged, most prominently by Aijaz Ahmad, for his "rhetoric of Otherness" that is guilty of essentializing the "Third World" subject (Ahmad 3). Ahmad disputes the very notion of a "Third-World literature" "which can be constructed as an internally coherent object of theoretical knowledge. There are fundamental issues … which cannot be resolved at this level of generality without an altogether positivist reductionism" (Ahmad 4). Ahmad joins that cohort in postcolonial studies that is prudently suspicious of the Western-centrism of postcolonial discourse itself. In the light of Jameson, what is at stake in *Life & Times* is the way in which Coetzee engages or, indeed, *disengages*, with the idea of the national allegory attributed to the work, in other words, the way in which the novel encodes the relationship between privacy and the political, and, more importantly, what the purpose and effect of such a strategy might be.

Coetzee tacitly acknowledges the urgency of committed literature during apartheid in "The Novel Today" (1987) by stating that he doesn't advocate curling up with a good read over and above "revolutionary art" (4), but is left cold by political language of any hue. Accepting David Attwell's label of "late-modernist" (DP 200) and thereby placing himself on the margins of South African progressives who during apartheid typically aligned themselves with realism, he identifies Lukács's appeal to realism against "modernist decadence" (DP 202) as central to the movement for committed literature. Lukács argues that in the modernist work, which he believes is pathological and narcissistic, "Man is reduced to a sequence of unrelated experimental fragments; he is as inexplicable to others as to himself" (26). The "ideology of modernism" (which is the title of Lukács's essay) has important ethico-political implications: "Every human action is based on a presupposition of its inherent meaningfulness, at least to the subject. Absence of meaning [as in the modernist work] makes a mockery of action and reduces art to naturalistic description" (Lukács 36).

Yet in the modernist *Life & Times*, that encodes a radical disruption of linear time and self-reflexivity, as I am arguing, "meaninglessness" – or, more properly, meaning that is encrypted in texts – itself bears meaning. As critics like Neil Lazarus have shown, it would be wrong to disregard modernist works on the grounds that they lack radical potentiality. Such writing, Lazarus argues, is oppositional in the way that it "enters into history, or more precisely *refuses to be encoded seamlessly into history*" in its status as literary text (emphasis added; "Modernism and Modernity" 135). Criticisms levelled against *Life & Times* – the elusiveness and obscurity of the protagonist, who the Medical Officer describes as the "obscurest of the obscure" (MK 142), and the opacity of the allegories it employs – have centred on its apparently questionable postcoloniality. Nonetheless, the text's autocritical mode established by its self-diminishing allegories chimes with the appeal of a number of progressive South African intellectuals during apartheid,

ALIENATION   SELF-SCRUTINY

→ about author's self, no?!

including Gordimer, for a self-scrutinizing and thus more ethico-politically
effective kind of writing than what they regarded as the politically debased forms
of some committed texts (Ndebele, *Rediscovery* 50). It must be said that South
African literature of a traditionally committed mode, work by Alex La Guma and
Mongane Wally Serote, for instance, is also capable of such self-scrutiny. are?

Coetzee admits in *Doubling the Point* (1992) to a difficulty with "stating
positions, taking positions" (DP 205). The parallels this "nonposition" elicits
between his own marginality and his elusive protagonist hinge upon the subversive
potential of alienation. Coetzee tacitly acknowledges his own sense of alienation
when he comments with some irony, "What is left of Michael K after he has been
explained in terms of my marginality in Africa?" (DP 199). Of course, with two
Booker prizes and the Nobel Laureate behind him, with the commercial success of
Disgrace (1999) and the intense global interest in his work, it would be difficult to
speak about Coetzee as marginal today. Coetzee picks up the theme of alienation
when he refers to Kafka's influence on his writing in *Doubling the Point*:
"alienation is … a strategy in the service of skepticism" (DP 203). However, his
recoil from the idea that alienation is a "*state*, a state of being" and the idea that
"art [can] become[ ] the alienated artist's private means, his private vice even, for
turning lack and woe into gain" in the same interview are palpable. For Coetzee,
we might surmise, this attributes too much subversive energy to alienation. Rather,
he concedes that alienation is not only a "position" but a "practice" (DP 203).

This is the crux of a novel in which, though its unloved and loveless protagonist
is not only racially oppressed but is the exemplar of *social* alienation, Michael
K *practices* alienation by transgressing the very foundations of apartheid law:
namely, classification and segregation. On his journey to his mother's childhood
farm, he quests for meaning but, trapped in a nightmarish Kafkan world of state
oppression, the world of the camp and the prison, this meaning must exist beyond
the camps (MK 182). In the struggle to make sense of his life,

> Michael K knew that he would not crawl out and stand up and cross from the
> darkness into firelight to announce himself. He even knew the reason why:
> because enough men had gone off to war saying the time for gardening was
> when the war was over; whereas there must be men to stay behind and keep
> gardening alive, or at least the idea of gardening[.] (MK 109)

If we equate gardening with a desire for aesthetic pleasure and a state of
contemplation, the light that burns at the heart of this work, it seems, is what
Dominic Head in a different context has called Coetzee's "enduring belief in
fiction" ("Belief in Frogs" 115). This belief is founded on the ways that fiction,
operating within an autonomous discursive universe, can unsettle other modes of
discourse, history, for example, or apartheid ideology.

In a familiar Coetzean device, this transgression of apartheid law is also figured
textually by the work's (and Michael K's) resistance to allegorical readings, even
though as a number of critics have commented, the work is structured, paradoxically,

by allegory (cf. Attridge, *J. M. Coetzee* 64; Head, *J. M. Coetzee* 23–24; Slemon, "Post-Colonial Allegory" 163). This is one way that the novel borrows from the principle of Kafka's *Parables and Paradoxes* (1946), which as the title suggests is also framed on paradox. This self-diminishing allegorical device is signalled most transparently in the Medical Officer's words to Michael K:

> Your stay in the camp was merely an allegory, if you know that word. It was an allegory – speaking at the highest level – of how scandalously, how outrageously a meaning can take residence in a system without becoming a term in it. Did you notice how, whenever I tried to pin you down, you slipped away? (MK 166)

So Michael K resists not only state oppression but, as a character in a book, he resists interpretation.

David I. Grossvogel, writing about Kafka, identifies a problem in the fabric of the parable, which is a kind of moral allegory, in that it "acknowledges intellectual slippage, a failure of the mind to apprehend its object … it means both *same* and *resembling* – that is to say, identical and different". Allegory is also a kind of substitute, both the "same and resembling", "evidenc[ing] the perplexity of knowing" (Grossvogel 191). Indeed, the capacity for strategies of skepticism Coetzee ascribes the parable, which lies in this perplexity, could equally be attributed to the Coetzean allegory. The parable, Coetzee argues, is "a mode favoured by marginal groups – groups that don't have a place in the mainstream, in the main plot of history – because it is hard to pin down unequivocally what the point is" (NT 4).

What is instantly striking in *Life & Times* is that graphically "Michael K" lacks the full stop of Kafka's protagonist, both heightening the sense of elusiveness he embodies and signalling the incompleteness of his story. (The ending of K.'s story in *The Trial* [1925] is absolute because he is executed "Like a dog!") This is borne out by Coetzee's comments on the inconclusiveness of the title of the work: "To my ear, 'The Life' implies that the life is over, whereas 'Life' does not commit itself" (Morphet, "Two Interviews" 454). Like his namesake, Coetzee's K is characterized by a lack of agency: things *happen to* him, he *allows* them to happen; his resistance, to the State and its players, to his mother, to the war, to history, to being authored and to writing, is passive, taking the form of elusiveness, both real and textual (as a character functioning within the pages of a book), towards those who would confine him.

Kafka has been a major influence on contemporary South African writers because Kafkan themes, including the distrustful, fearful interpreter and skeptical reading practices, readily capture the paranoiac and brutalizing apartheid mindset. Coetzee finds that Kafka endures because of the silence that his fiction speaks: "Is it not what Kafka does *not* speak, refuses to speak, under that interrogation, that will continue to fuel our desire for him (I hope forever)?" (DP 199–200). Through the vehicle of the elusive and reticent Michael K, Coetzee cultivates a reader who reads between the lines, attentive to what is left unsaid. In *White Writing* Coetzee traces a contemporary affinity for silence which he yokes to a modernist project:

> Our ears today are finely attuned to modes of silence. We have been brought up on the music of Webern: substantial silence structured by tracings of sound. Our craft is all in reading *the other*: gaps, inverses, undersides; the veiled; the dark, the buried, the feminine; alterities. (original emphasis; WW 81)

Yet Coetzee warns that even this kind of reading "is in peril" because "like all triumphant subversion", it is in danger of being incorporated into dominant modes (WW 81), which is why for Coetzee the skepticism of Kafka is so appealing.

Perhaps surprisingly, though Michael K is obscure and frustrates interpretation, the novel utilizes one of the most recognizably South African settings in the oeuvre, even if in what Attwell calls a "future projection" of civil war as a response to the National Party's proposals for a new constitution in the early 1980s and foretelling the South African States of Emergency of 1985–1990 (*J. M. Coetzee* 91). The novel engages with contemporary mass resistance to apartheid which had included nation-wide strikes, student protests and civil unrest, especially in the years 1979–80, which saw the peak of "rural removals and displaced urbanization" (Beinart xvi; see also Beinart 225–35). Michael K struggles to resist the relentless momentum of history but as a "Cape coloured" is firmly rooted within it and by the end of the narrative, having been drawn reluctantly into the war, is wrongly accused of being partisan to a band of guerrillas who have ensconced themselves on the Visagie farm.

Since *Life & Times* exactingly establishes a counter-reading to the allegorical one it promotes, it alerts the reader to the dangers of allegory, or the reductiveness that can result from reading allegorically (a criticism levelled at Jameson's theory of national allegory); indeed, in the context of apartheid it *politicizes* this very problem. Grossvogel's comments on the use of the parable – a kind of moral allegory – in Kafka are enlightening:

> Long before Kafka turns formally to the parable, he has already constructed a fiction that proves, in the multiple instances of its own slippage, to be more than a mere fiction. And in this endeavour, he is seconded by an ironic fate: none of his major fiction is complete in the form we have of it … It is on this shifting ground that contrives the deceptive revelation of a parable whose magnitude is equal to the totality of the fiction that Kafka establishes a central parable that his fiction treats as a problematic text – a parable whose lesson is the doubtful nature of parables. (192)

If Kafka's fiction is meta-parabolic, Coetzee's is meta-allegorical: an allegory "whose lesson is the doubtful nature" of allegories as they conform to *systems of meaning*. Notably, Coetzee chooses to appropriate unfinished or incomplete texts, adding to this sense of slippage, not only here with *The Trial, The Castle* (1926)

DERRIDA.

[handwritten: this is close to Derek's argument w.r.t. "informally innovative text"]

and "The Burrow" (1923–24), but also in *Waiting for the Barbarians* (1980) with Kafka's "In the Penal Colony" (1914) and in *The Master of Petersburg* (1994) with Fyodor Dostoevsky's *The Possessed* (1872). In so doing, *Barbarians* and *Life & Times* gesture towards the inscrutable and resistant other as "text", and *The Master of Petersburg* resonates with debates on censorship.

Like Kafka's protagonist, Michael K is repeatedly misrepresented and misunderstood (misread) by those whose path he crosses on his journey to the Visagie farm, most notably the Medical Officer who, like Captain Oosthuizen (MK 124), misnames him "Michaels". At first the Medical Officer fails to recognize the innate sagacity and meaning of Michael K and only later reappraises his perception, adopting him as both his literal and spiritual guide to beyond the camps ("I have chosen you to show me the way" [MK 163]). Grossvogel fleshes out the consequences misreading has for the reader, linking Kafka's fiction to what he calls the "Borgesian" or "reflecting" surface: a text that, like a "mirror", "keeps his reader out even as it talks to that reader about him and his problematic world" (183). The consequence of this kind of text is a self-conscious, agential reader, aware of the "desire to penetrate the Borgesian surface" (183). It therefore is plausible that the only credible readings of Kafka *and* Coetzee, confoundingly, would be misreadings.

[handwritten left margin: By Derrida's own? [illegible]]

Joseph K.'s situation, as a reader impelled to interpret his surroundings, is reproduced in the embedded parable "Before the Law" at the end of *The Trial*, recounted to him by the priest. If, as Jacques Derrida has suggested, the "law" is a metaphor for literature (*Acts* 186–87), the novel stages its own artifice. Awaiting his death sentence, for instance, the ill-fortuned Joseph K. curses the "Law": "Tenth-rate old actors they send for me ... They want to finish me off cheaply" (249). The drive to interpret is all the more exigent because K. stands trial for a crime punishable by death but one that, in the manner of totalitarian authority, remains a mystery to him. Each reading K. makes of the priest's story is frustrated, the priest instructs him, by an incompleteness or lack of clarity, just as *Life & Times* and Michael K (as text) block interpretation.

[handwritten left margin: or really not Derrida's surprise?]

Although its allusions to totalitarianism credit Kafka with a Saidian "worldliness" (Said, "Text"), Derrida claims that "Before the Law" "does not tell or describe anything but itself as text". Even though to my mind this reading is overdetermined, Derrida is useful when he points out that the parable "guards itself, maintains itself ... It is the law, makes the law and leaves the reader before the law" (*Acts* 210–11). If the priest's parable "guards itself", so *The Trial* frustrates interpretation both by Joseph K., as reader, and by the reader of Kafka's story. The parallels with *Life & Times* are therefore self-evident. However, Derrida is not reading the "law" or "literature" in terms of fiction, allegory, myth, symbol or parable (*Acts* 186), but in the French sense of *la loi*, equating it with the taxonomic qualities that characterize genre. Nonetheless, Michael K is a paragon of the resistant text because he eludes codification, both real (that of the state) and textual (by refuting the allegorical readings that his characterization invites).

Grossvogel suggests that, like the Oedipus myth, Kafka's *The Trial* pivots upon misreading: "The gods know that, one way or another, Oedipus is fated not to understand. His quick wit and impetuousness notwithstanding, Oedipus is turned into a plodding and awkward interpreter" (183). For Maurice Blanchot this problem of interpretation in Kafka is transferred to the reader:

> Whoever stays with the story penetrates into something opaque that he does not understand, while whoever holds the meaning cannot get back to the darkness of which it is the tellable light. The two readers can never meet; we are one, then the other, we understand always more or always less than is necessary. True readings remain impossible. (*Work of Fire* 4)

Joseph K.'s action of reading the world and the law mirrors the act of reading *The Trial*. K. is confounded by the law and, ensnared in the labyrinthine nightmare of the fiction, he is trapped "before the law". Embedded in the larger text, Kafka's parable reproduces the impossibility of K.'s situation and of "correct" or definitive readings.

Coetzee's novel is framed around the Oedipus myth: Michael K's Oedipal relation to the Father (the law, the state, the police, the war [MK 105]) is one of suspicion and avoidance and he nurtures the maternal bond, both with his mother and his crop – his pumpkins and melons which he perceives as his children. The Medical Officer even warns Michael K away from his mother who "sounds like … the very embodiment of great Mother Death" (MK 150). In his quest for meaning, Michael K is another "plodding and awkward interpreter" and the text hinges upon "incorrect" readings. Dominic Head identifies Coetzee's novel as, in part, a *Bildungsroman* (*J. M. Coetzee* 93) and Grossvogel points out that in German "trial" – *der Prozess* – also translates as "process" (194). As a reader in and of the text, Michael K negotiates himself through the trials of life. His naivety, like K.'s, leaves him bewildered by the world in which he finds himself and he wrestles ontologically with his sense of purpose. As a reader of the text and a sign of textual practice, he is incorporated into the reading process:

> it seemed to him that scene after scene of life was playing itself out before him and that the scenes all cohered. He had a presentiment of a single meaning upon which they were converging or threatening to converge, though he did not know yet what that might be. (MK 89)

Life & Times installs what Grossvogel would call a "Borgesian surface" and a text and reader – Michael K – who is aware of himself as sign battling to comprehend his signification.

A pattern of misreading is established by the text that encourages, indeed *directs*, the reader down a similar path. The Medical Officer misrecognizes Michael K as a "poor simpleton" (MK 155); yet Michael K, realizing that his life has been systematized by apartheid, in fact displays an innate wisdom by *affecting* simple-

FORM.   SILENCE   ADORNO.

mindedness when quizzed at a roadblock by the police: "If I look very stupid, he thought, perhaps they will let me through" (MK 40). It is this apparent stupidity, he believes, that will save him: "At least, he thought, at least I have not been clever … I was mute and stupid at the beginning, I will be mute and stupid at the end" (MK 182). As it is elsewhere in the narrative, the question "who speaks?" is masked by ambiguity: is this the consciousness of Michael K or that of an omniscient narrator who would hold authority over him? Michael K's speech and thought are only ever presented by report in the first and third sections of the novel – "he thought", "he found", "he said" (Parry, "Speech and Silence" 154) – and in the second section his story rests in the hands of the Medical Officer.

Indeed, it is for his adumbration of the other *as silent* that Coetzee has met his fiercest criticism. Whilst Gordimer, for instance, reproves Coetzee's failure to represent the manifest organized black resistance to apartheid, Benita Parry argues that Michael K is "written as a being without an identity … an exemplar of the mind turned inward" from a authorial position that is always already that of authority and privilege, "grounded in the cognitive systems of the West" ("Speech and Silence" 154; 150). But whilst such a strategy might suggest Michael K's lack of autonomy, reversing this dynamic reveals it might equally signal that the Medical Officer, as Michael K's self-elected spokesperson, and even Coetzee, as author, don't properly *know* him. This ambiguity that hovers around Michael K's subjectivity, coupled with the overt inconsistencies in his characterization outlined above, also leave the reader not knowing him and, therefore, through processes of interpretation and critical analysis, the reader is implicated in his "trial". The consequences of this narrative strategy are clear: as readers we are obliged to experience the discursive process that has structured Michael K's life, a process that mirrors not only the classification instituted by apartheid, but also a discourse of postcolonial criticism. In this way we are encouraged to recognize the limitations and ideological problems that encumber such a role.

The reader approaches a text, according to Grossvogel, with a "desire for his text to have meaning (that is to say an *end*)", a desire which, as he rightly points out, *The Trial* withstands as it is a text "that adroitly confuses critics and other readers" (185). Theodor Adorno articulates this relationship between reader and text in Kafka's fiction in a similar fashion, but adds that the reader must also take responsibility for any reading made:

> Among Kafka's presuppositions, not least is that the contemplative relation between text and reader is shaken to its very roots. His texts are designed not to sustain a constant distance between themselves and their victim but rather to agitate his feelings to a point where he fears that the narrative will shoot towards him like a locomotive in a three-dimensional film. Such aggressive physical proximity undermines the reader's habit of identifying himself with the figures in the novel…. As long as the word has not been found, the reader must be held accountable. ("Notes on Kafka" 96)

For Adorno, this complex relation is an ethico-political strategy. The idea of responsible reading, however, is complicated in *Life & Times* by its allusions to white South African liberalism and white guilt configured in the Medical Officer, who, becoming exasperated with Michael K, presses him to "yield" his meaning. He claims that he is the only one who can properly "read" Michael K: "I alone see you as ... a human soul above and beneath classification, a soul blessedly untouched by doctrine, untouched by history" (MK 151).

The term "liberal", of course, has very specific connotations in South Africa because, whilst on a fundamental level disagreeing with apartheid ideology, liberals were perceived by some to be willing to turn a blind eye to apartheid abuse, making them complicit.[2] In *I Write What I Like* (published posthumously in 1978), the student leader Steve Biko is disparaging of "that curious bunch of [white] nonconformists", "liberals, leftists", who "argue that they are not responsible for white racism and the country's 'inhumanity to the black man'" (20); "A game at which the liberals have become masters is that of deliberate evasiveness", he goes on (*I Write* 22). The Medical Officer concludes that, if the "meaning" of Michael K "were no more than a lack in [him]self [the Medical Officer] ... of something to believe in", he might as well put "a bullet through [his own] head" (MK 165). Yet if *this* realization (that otherness simply defines the self) merely serves to prove *his* sincerity, the Medical Officer fails once again.

In perpetually eluding meaning Michael K goes some way to shape his own destiny. Though the Medical Officer believes Michael K is "not a hero and did not pretend to be, not even a hero of fasting" (MK 163), he does outwit his gaolers, including the author and the reader of the text, in a number of important ways. Firstly, he evades history, a place in which he would be accorded heroic status; and secondly, by association, he evades time, which he equates with camp regulation. This is a story in which little actually happens, where Michael K struggles to stand outside history and forgets the passing of time. Yet problematically a slowing or even stopping of time is, for Coetzee, symptomatic of the apartheid condition which was characterized by reactionary conservatism. Responding to Attwell's comment that his fiction "allow[s] the narrators to reflect directly on their experience of temporality" (DP 208), Coetzee explains:

> The party of Afrikaner Christian nationalism ... set about stopping or even turning back the clock. Its programs involved a radically discontinuous intervention into time, in that it tried to stop dead or turn around a range of developments normal (in the sense of being the norm) in colonial societies. It also aimed at instituting a sluggish no-time in which an already anachronistic order of patriarchal clans and tribal despotisms would be frozen in place. (DP 209)

---

[2]   For a brief discussion of liberal politics and its oppositional objectives see Beinart, 179–180.

not sure about this?

So Coetzee links the forward movement of time with progress, which was not in the interests of Afrikaner nationalism on matters of race.

A temporally inflected mood characterizes *Life & Times* through what Coetzee identifies as its "pace of narration", which, he suggests, is the novel's overriding technique (DP 142). Paradoxically, this mood, which is most apparent in the burrow scenes when Michael K retreats from the world in his impulsion towards obscurity, corresponds to the "slow time" of apartheid and therefore would apparently confirm Gordimer's point about the inefficacy of Michael K's resistance.

In his detailed analysis of the treatment of time in Kafka's story, "Time, Tense and Aspect in Kafka's 'The Burrow' (1981)", one of several intertexts of *Life & Times*, Coetzee argues that the presentation of time mystifies the reader through defamiliarization. Just as Michael K endeavours to exist beyond time, the meaning of "The Burrow" turns upon

> the experience of a break-down of time, of the time-sense: one moment does
> not flow into the next – on the contrary, each moment has the threat or promise
> of being (not becoming) a timeless forever, unconnected to, ungenerated by, the
> past. (DP 203)

By severing himself from history, Michael K refuses to be moulded by the slow time of apartheid. He passively resists apartheid's system of time.

This can be better understood by closer inspection of Kafka. The presentation of time in "The Burrow" is, Coetzee says, "baffling" because habitual time must be reconciled with time that is plottable on a continuum. Time in the story disrupts not only the conventions of realist fiction, which rests, Coetzee points out, on the laws of Newtonian physics, it also subverts the German tense system used by Kafka (DP 211). While challenging much of Dorrit Cohn's analysis of time and tense in "The Burrow", arguing that they cannot be schematized in the way that Cohn suggests, Coetzee agrees the structuring of time in the story is, in Cohn's words, "paradoxical [and] … based on a denial of the distinction between repetitious and singular events" (qtd. in DP 219). Similarly, Coetzee also affirms Cohn's "identif[ication of] the ambiguities of present-tense verb forms as the formal field whose exploitation makes the higher-level paradoxes of 'The Burrow' possible" (DP 219), and with her overall analysis that the narrative is framed primarily around "a constantly repeated present" (qtd. in DP 220), or as Coetzee puts it, "time experienced as continual crisis" (DP 230; cf. Attwell, *J. M. Coetzee* 102).

In the burrow scenes in *Life & Times* Michael K, his body racked by illness, becomes disconnected from the passing of time: for the moment, time becomes irrelevant. By escaping incarceration, withdrawing from the "now" of apartheid and from the constraints of history, he lives outside time. As he grows weaker, he "los[es] track of time":

> Sometimes, waking stifled … he knew that it was day. There were long periods
> when he lay in a grey stupor too tired to kick himself free of sleep. He could feel

the processes of his body slowing down. You are forgetting to breathe, he would say to himself, and yet lie without breathing. He raised a hand heavy as lead and put it over his heart: far away, as if in another country, he felt a languid stretching and closing. Through whole cycles of the heavens he slept… . Sometimes he would emerge into wakefulness unsure whether he had slept a day or a week or a month. It occurred to him that he might not be fully in possession of himself. You must eat, he would say, and struggle to get up and look for a pumpkin. But then he would relax again, and stretch his legs and yawn in sensual pleasure so sweet that he wished for nothing but to lie and let it ripple through him… . Then step by step his sleep grew to be lighter and the periods of wakefulness more frequent. He began to be visited by trains of images so rapid and unconnected that he could not follow them. He tossed and turned, unsatisfied by sleep but too drained of strength to rise… . There was a thunderstorm. (MK 118–19)

In this passage Coetzee ruptures a linear, forward-moving sense of time in a non-schematic way, time in "continual crisis". The burrow scenes and his withdrawal into solitude represent a crisis point for Michael K, who increasingly forgets to eat, mirrored by time sequences which themselves are in crisis: ever-shifting, time slows, quickens pace a little, almost stands still. Just as Michael K experiences time, the reader is disorientated and defamiliarized from it.

In the burrow scenes a disruption of linear time is realized primarily through a peculiar and varied verb scheme and temporal clauses that emphasize a change in pace, for instance, marking iterative duration as in "there were *long periods* when he *lay*", or frequency – "*sometimes … he knew*": "sometimes" being non-specific and therefore vague, and marking an incongruity with the state of knowing. The modal auxiliary *would*, signalling reported action, is used in the iterative past ("he *would begin*", "he *would come out*"), frequently indicated by temporal adverbs ("*sometimes* he would emerge") and denoting a continuous, or habitual action-in-the-past. Modal auxiliaries are used in the past tense to present free indirect speech ("*You must eat*, he *would say*"), connoting iterative habitual action over an extended period of time (emphasized here by the subjunctive *would*, which is again suggestive of uncertainty). Clauses such as "*Then step by step* his sleep *grew to be lighter and* the *periods* of wakefulness *more frequent*" express a forward movement of time – "event" time. Events that are finite, marked by a beginning and an end, in this instance, "*periods of wakefulness*", are qualified by temporal clauses expressing repeated and durative action ("*grew to be … more frequent*"). Tense shifts from past ("He *lost track* of time", *lost* connoting a finite state of being), to a habitual past ("*sometimes, waking stifled … he knew*"). The burrow sequence is punctuated by the thunderstorm ("There *was* a thunderstorm"), the event of the storm being marked by the simple past tense. Similarly, these passages are themselves set apart from the rest of the narrative by the use of the simple past tense: Michael K "lost track of time". A period of contemplation is represented through a general slowing of pace. Though already detached from the world outside because of his physical weakness, he now enters a space of lost time that signals the nadir of his illness. Gestured by the simple past tense, the storm marks Michael K's re-emergence from the burrow into the tumult of the present: the soldiers arrive and he is returned to the camps. Part Two of the novel, following this interlude and the arrival of the soldiers, is narrated in the first person by the Medical Officer, who symbolically takes authority of Michael K's story, taking it upon himself to speak on Michael K's behalf. This section is marked by a quickening of time and pace, highlighting the shift into the consciousness of a man who notes that Michael K is not "wholly of our world" (MK 130).

Marking his freedom from the world of the camp and the prison, Michael K withdraws from society because a solitary life is easier to endure; his island of isolation is, in part, self-imposed: "He had kept no tally of the days nor recorded the changes of the moon. He was not a prisoner or a castaway, his life by the dam was not a sentence that he had to serve out" (MK 114–15). So not only does *Life & Times* invoke a Kafkan deconstruction of time, it also inverts time as it structures Defoe's *Robinson Crusoe*. As Jameson points out, allegory has the "capacity … to generate a range of distinct meanings or messages, simultaneously, as the allegorical tenor and vehicle change place" ("Third-World Literature" 74). Penned during the zenith of European mercantile expansion and a move by the "West" to colonize other places, *Robinson Crusoe* is framed on the myths of Calvinistic individualism and colonialism: the castaway Crusoe diligently works the land and takes it upon himself to provide the moral and spiritual guidance of Friday, whom he enslaves. Imperiously and unselfconsciously, he instructs Friday in Christianity: "and thus by degrees I opened his eyes" (*Robinson Crusoe* 194). On arriving on the island, Crusoe experiences a sense of urgency to rein in time as he retrieves stock from the sunken vessel and struggles to build his makeshift home which, tellingly, he names "my Castle": "I had no time to lose", "without losing time"; "I had lost no time"; "if I had had more time" and "This cost me a great deal of time" (*Robinson Crusoe* 42; 44; 50; 50; 52). Crusoe, the epitome of the modern, self-made man who lives by the principles of Enlightenment and a Calvinistic work ethic, next sets about organizing and rationalizing his days cast away to allay his fear of losing track of time and by association his powers of reason: "in general it may be observed that I was very seldom idle … having regularly divided my time, according to the several daily employments that were before me" (*Robinson Crusoe* 102). While for Crusoe the charting of the passage of time is not simply a means of keeping a tally of the days but will also contribute to his legacy (he meticulously records his days on the island in his journal), Michael K, who loses track of time, resists committing himself to history or to a collective consciousness and stands outside apartheid law.

Michael K's pathetic ruminations are an attempt to pre-empt racist discourse and the suffering it engenders:

> I am not building a house … to pass on to other generations. What I make ought
> to be careless, makeshift … So that if ever they find this place … and say to each

other: What shiftless creatures, how little pride they took in their work!, it will not matter. (MK 101)

Cast adrift in the veld, he realizes that, unlike Crusoe, he must *learn* the habit of "idleness", a loaded term in South Africa since it was appropriated by early colonizers, by the apartheid state and by racists generally as a means of stereotyping and thereby regulating racial difference. He "was learning to love idleness, idleness no longer as stretches of freedom reclaimed by stealth here and there from involuntary labour … but as a yielding up of himself to time" (MK 115).

In *White Writing* Coetzee argues that in early white South African literature "relapse into sloth is a betrayal of the high pastoral impulse" (WW 75). "[N]either pleased nor displeased when there was work to do" (MK 115), Michael K is not challenging a work ethic; rather, he yearns unconsciously to stand outside the time of the camps, of apartheid and of South Africa's bleak history-in-the-making. Here, because Michael K cultivates his social alienation, we are reminded of Gordimer's criticism of the novel quoted above, that Coetzee weights what Lukács defines as the textual symbiosis between the private and public – in Gordimer's words, "private and social destiny" – in favour of the private. Michael K's status as "resisting text" also works at the level of resisting the normative modes of postcolonial theory, in which, in the case of Jameson, the public-political *always* takes centre stage via the private, libidinal sphere. For Jameson, the private translates as national allegory. Michael K's private resistance highlights the very politics the text presses against, drawing the work, nonetheless and paradoxically, into the realms of political critique.

Coetzee argues that early European travel writers neglected to draw parallels between the "idle Hottentot" (Khoisan) and the "pastoral platitude of the wandering shepherd, with his meager possessions and his easily satisfied wants [who reveals a] way of escaping from the cares of civilization" (WW 19). Indeed, making the appropriation of Defoe's fable all the more incisive, Coetzee contextualizes misreadings of "idleness" in the novel (myopic since they fail to connect ideas of contemplation with physical quietude) as a "war on social parasitism" ongoing in Europe during the Reformation, the Renaissance and the Enlightenment, largely through the doctrine of Calvinism and, during the Enlightenment, the evolution of the concept "work" (WW 20–21). "Leisure" in early travel writing about South Africa, on the other hand, is the preserve of the bourgeoisie during this period: "Leisure holds the promise of the generation of all those differences that constitute culture and make man Anthropological Man; idleness holds no promise save that of stasis" (WW 25). The rhetoric of idleness propagated during the European Enlightenment is uncritically mapped in the Discourse of the Cape of early travel writing so that the indigenous people's active refusal to enter the colonial employment system is overlooked (WW 21). Importantly, Coetzee argues, "old conceptual frameworks" were inadequate for this new situation (WW 24). Michael Moses draws on Rousseau's *Reveries* to compare Michael K to Rousseau's "solitary walker". This leads Moses to read "idleness" as a period of reverie rather than

PLAASROMAN

sloth: "Like Rousseau, Michael K finds that his existential submersion in the cycle of the days and seasons, his sense of an endlessly repeating present, produces in him a feeling of utter contentment" ("Solitary Walkers" 146).

Michael K's retreat to the veld which, like Kafka's Hunger Artist, invokes Jesus's forty days in the wilderness, brings him close to death and to an enlightenment ("A Hunger Artist" 270),[3] albeit of failure: his eremitic life, unlike Crusoe's, is not a time of mastery (of space) for he realizes dolefully that "I let myself believe that this was one of those islands without an owner. Now I am learning the truth. Now I am learning my lesson" (MK 61).

Michael K sets about writing the land, not only through the inversion of Crusoe's conquest of time and space, but also through the inversion of the ideology underpinning the Afrikaner *plaasroman* or farm novel. In the *plaasroman*, rather than turning to the African "wilderness" or nature, the writer focuses on a nostalgic return to the "childhood farm" (WW 175) with its implied claim on the land. For the Afrikaner, Coetzee observes, the "farm, rather than nature, however regionally defined, is conceived as the sacral place where the soul can expand in freedom" (WW 175). The farm is typically the "source of meaning" to which the narrative progresses (WW 88) (the source to which Michael K is journeying). In Uys Krige's poem "Plaashek" (farm gate),[4] for instance, Coetzee argues,

> The wanderer return[s] to the farm where he was born and experienc[es] in the act of opening the farm gate the same intimation of a return to the true self and primitive moral sources that Wordsworth feels in returning to the dales and fells. (WW 175)

In his quest for meaning, experiencing such an epiphany, Michael K writes upon the land by gardening rather than farming his seeds (MK 109) and relishes subsisting off the land (MK 46). (He fails fully to realize his vision, however, since he eats from a trough on "crushed mealies and bonemeal" [MK 46].) Gardening evokes "the Judaeo-Christian myth of Eden" (WW 3), but this is the Garden that, in European eyes, has degenerated into what Coetzee calls an "anti-Garden", "where the wilderness takes root once again in men's hearts" (WW 3).

Although Michael K symbolically reclaims the Visagie farmland, he prefers to eke out a feral existence in his burrow rather than in the derelict farmhouse abandoned by its former owners. During the course of his journey (which is both physical and metaphysical), he learns to appreciate the South African landscape in African terms rather than in the mode which his employment as a gardener has tutored him. Coetzee's device is one of counterpoint and inversion: the land as figured in early white South African literature, which is presented in a narrative or chronological form, is revised spatially into scenes which capture description. What

---

[3]   In Kafka's parable "A Hunger Artist" the protagonist makes a profession of fasting. His fasts, which render his body spectacular, always last forty days (270).

[4]   My thanks to Kai Easton for this translation.

Coetzee calls the "Discourse of the Cape", which as with all discourse is inherently normative, not surprisingly creates "Eurocentric conceptual schemes in favour of a scheme based on native conceptual categories" and becomes "mere *narrative* rather than a comprehensive *description*" (WW 15). Coetzee elaborates, "The crippling weakness of anthropological narrative as compared with anthropological description is that, in reverting to chronological sequence, it forgoes access to the achronological, spatial, God's-eye organization of categorical description" (WW 15). The appropriation of Kafka's use of tense to disrupt linear time overcomes this problem as Michael K inserts himself into the ecology of the land. In the veld Michael K displays an affinity for his environment when he likens himself to "a termite boring its way through a rock" (MK 66), a "speck upon the surface of an earth too deeply asleep to notice the scratch of ant-feet, the rasp of butterfly teeth, the tumbling of dust" (MK 97), "like a flower" (MK 99), a "parasite dozing in the gut", a "lizard under a stone" (MK 116). Rejecting the colonizer's project of land acquisition ("he could not imagine himself spending his life driving stakes into the ground, erecting fences, dividing up the land" [MK 97]), he becomes hyper-aware of his habitat, and exists, if only temporarily, in symbiosis with it.

Coetzee effects an anti-pastoral moment in *Life & Times* when, alone in the wilderness of the veld, Michael K realizes that Wynberg Park where he had been employed (land "tamed" by the colonizer) is "more vegetal than mineral … I have lost my love for that kind of earth … It is no longer the greens and the brown that I want but the yellow and the red". Michael K's days in the veld teach him to read the landscape in a different way, beyond the Eurocentric schema to which his eye has been trained: "I am becoming a different kind of man" (MK 68). This reading is lent weight by Moses's comparison of Michael K to Rousseau's solitary walker in contemplative mood, which nonetheless implicitly yokes Michael K to the image of the Noble Savage: "In [an] atemporal state, the solitary walker finds that he can enjoy a *primordial experience* which is covered over and hidden from him when he lives in society: the pure and rarefied sensation of merely existing" (emphasis added; "Solitary Walkers" 146).

On a secondary allegorical level, the garden is an antidote to the prescriptive requirements of culture during the apartheid era. Michael K envisages the guerrilla soldiers who pass through the farm telling him that the time has come when energies should be channelled into war work not prettifying the landscape. Analogously, art was expected to show "relevance and commitment", though Gordimer, to whom this mantra is ascribed, was herself opposed to conforming to orthodoxies of conformity, even in anti-apartheid writing (*Essential Gesture*, 106). The Medical Officer, in his fruitless attempts to persuade Michael K to "yield his story", offers an alternative meaning:

> The garden for which you are presently heading is nowhere and everywhere except in the camps. It is another name for the only place where you belong … where you do not feel homeless. It is off every map, no road leads to it that is merely a road, and only you know the way.

v. important figure in the novel.

For the Medical Officer, Michael K's "sacred and alluring" garden "produces the food of life", namely, freedom (MK 166). His words recall Kafka's parable "My Destination" whose protagonist sets out on a journey to reach "Away-From-Here, that is my destination", suggestive of a spiritual quest for self ("My Destination" 189).

The motifs of gardening and farming are therefore inflected by those of food and hunger, configured in the postcolonial topos of writing the body. When Michael K spreads the ashes of his mother, fertilizing the ground where he will plant his pumpkin seeds, he "begins his life as a cultivator" (MK 59) and it is from this point that he begins to resist the authoring of his body:

> It is because I am a gardener, he thought, because that is my nature … The impulse to plant had been re-awoken in him; now … he found his waking life bound tightly to the patch of earth he had begun to cultivate and the seeds he had planted there. (MK 59)

From severing the maternal bond through death springs Michael K's inscription on the land (his progeny of fruits), reclaimed as an African Eden of the kind Pauline Smith depicts in *The Beadle* (1926) and that Coetzee labels utopian and an unattainable ideal (WW 66–67). Akin to Michael K's relation to his mother, this bond must be severed. The "text" – here, Michael K's crop – is thus released from the bonds of authorship, configured in Michael K: "There was a cord of tenderness that stretched from him to the patch of earth beside the dam that must be cut" (MK 66). Inevitably Michael K will eat his "children", just as the presence of his mother consumed him. Overriding the patriarchal notion of fathering stories, Michael K is mother to his text: while he is enthralled with eating the flesh of the fruits of his labour and of Mother Earth, he rejects the food of the Father represented in the war, the law, the State, the institution and authorship.   KAFKA.

needs more explanation

freudian

It is in Coetzee's intertexts "A Hunger Artist" and "The Hunger Strike", recalled in the burrow scenes, that the motifs of writing, food and fasting converge. Michael K expresses autonomy by means of his physicality. Indeed, he cultivates his position of alterity: his body becomes increasingly insubstantial as he forgets or, more properly, loses the will to eat. Kafka's "The Hunger Strike" opens with the words: "The most insatiable people are certain ascetics, who go on hunger-strike in all spheres of life, thinking that in this way they will simultaneously achieve the following" (187). "The Hunger Strike" counsels that it is the *will* to starve – a philosophy of fasting – that is paramount in the *desire* to fast, rather than the act of fasting itself. Michael K, the Medical Officer believes, hungers "for a different kind of food, food that no camp could supply" and, signified by the crop of melons and pumpkins Michael K has nurtured, this is the "bread of freedom" (MK 163–64; 146). Kafka's "My Destination" sheds light on Michael K's spiritual sustenance:

"You have no provisions with you," [the servant] said. "I need none," I [the Master] said, "the journey is so long that I must die of hunger if I don't get anything on the way. No provisions can save me. For it is, fortunately, a truly immense journey." ("My Destination" 189)

The Master understands his journey in literal terms as an eternal journey (temporally and spatially), and therefore, his skewed sense of logic tells him, no amount of food could possibly sustain him. Of course, "here" always travels with us, so it is an infinite, metaphysical journey and perhaps it will take as long for the Master to realize it.

Kafka's hunger artist, like Michael K, "withdraw[s] deep into himself, paying no attention to anyone or anything, not even to the all-important striking of the clock" ("Hunger Artist" 268). Like Michael K under the Medical Officer's watchful gaze, the hunger artist is objectified as a spectacle of fasting and he eventually dies unnoticed. His withered corpse is replaced by a panther whose vital, "noble body, furnished almost to the bursting point with all that it needed, seemed to carry freedom around with it too" (277). His death is brought about, ironically, because his body is no longer spectacular, though he is on display in his cage for all to see. As in the flawed premise of liberal identity politics (Brown, "Wounded Attachments" 406), he is pathologically defined, nurtured and subjected by his own oppression.

While Attwell suggests that Coetzee turns to Kafka's "A Hunger Artist" for Michael K's "prodigious capacity for survival" (DP 198), paradoxically, as Merivale contends, as a "'Hunger Artist', Michael K shapes his being by negating it, by living minimally, by accepting no food" ("Audible Palimpsests" 161). As Michael K sets to work "with the business of making a dwelling" (MK 99–100), at the same time he begins to lose his sense of hunger: "Hunger was a sensation he did not feel and barely remembered. If he ate, eating what he could find, it was because he had not yet shaken off the belief that bodies that do not eat die" (MK 101). Michael K's loss of hunger rather than of appetite is indicative of his lack of *will* to starve himself, to strike. Paradoxically, his very resistance to eating figures a minimal level of autonomy, even if only negatively: firstly, by forgetting to eat when living on the veld (where he also loses track of time) and, secondly, by refusing food in the prison hospital. The Medical Officer imagines warning Michael K: "The laws are made of iron, Michaels, I hope you are learning that. No matter how thin you make yourself, they will not relax. There is no home left for universal souls" (MK 151). It might not be too far-fetched to suggest that in this appeal to universalism through the representation of a liberal character who is so obviously critiqued, Coetzee anticipates those critics who condemn him for a lack of political vision. INTERESTING POINT.

In Freudian terms, the Father – the iron laws, the institution, authorship – is abjected by Michael K through his rejection of food, or the food of the State. Instead, he aspires to live off the land, eating only the food of Mother Nature. Hunger, which symbolizes his insubstantiality, is a state Michael K has known

really? or insubstantiality?
not sure?

since childhood; his will has acquiesced to passivity: "Then he had grown older and stopped wanting. Whatever the nature of the beast that had howled inside him, it was starved into stillness" (MK 68). Eating is explicitly invested with power in the text since it is employed as an analogue for the colonial relation: the inmates at Jakkalsdrif are compared by a police captain to a "nest of parasites hanging from the neat sunlit town, eating its substance". Michael K, on the other hand, "lying idle in his bed", sees beyond the racism implied in the captain's words because "it was no longer obvious which was host and which parasite, camp or town" (MK 116).

Writing, death, the abjection of food and resistance to time are equivalences in Michael K's resistance to classification for, as the Medical Officer warns him,

> You are going to die, and your story is going to die too, forever and ever, unless you come to your senses and listen to me… . We have all tumbled over the lip into the cauldron of history … only you … have managed to live in the old way, drifting through time … no more trying to change the course of history than a grain of sand does… The truth is that you are going to perish in obscurity … and no one is going to remember you but me, unless you yield and at last open your mouth. I appeal to you Michaels: *yield*! (MK 151–52)

By the various means sketched above, Michael K authors his own body, a body that colonial and apartheid discourse have sought to inscribe, define and regulate. For Michael K to have meaning, implores the Medical Officer, he must relinquish his story, otherwise he will die forgotten (for he will surely die). Michael K represents both the absences in the text, as the "hole in the narrative" (MK 109–110; F 121), and its very existence, as text. Michael K's silence might be explained by Laura Wright's suggestion that language is "the medium of communication that cannot be trusted as it problematizes access to the narrative of suffering whose text is the body" (*Writing* 94).

It is from the authority suffering bestows, claims Coetzee, that the body in pain derives its power for the pain of the body cannot be disputed (DP 248). Michael K's resistance to time, to the food of the State and to the land, all regulated by apartheid and apartheid discourse, also constitutes his resistance to writing, even if apartheid's metaphorical writing the body. Michael K therefore not only resists being read, he also resists writing his story under the conditions of apartheid, which always until now was the story penned by the oppressor. Unlike Crusoe in Defoe's novel, he has no desire to leave his story to posterity, just as he has no desire to remember his days in the veld because, according to this logic, writing would entail bending to the very ideology that oppresses him: "There will be not a grain left bearing my marks" (MK 124). What is more, Michael K is conscious of the "lack" he embodies: "Always, when he tried to explain himself to himself, there remained a gap, a hole … His was always a story with a hole in it: a wrong story, always wrong" (MK 109–10). Although Michael K signifies absence and atrophy, paradoxically, this lack, like Webern's silences, is itself substantial. Michael K's hunger – a kind of atrophy – is the hunger for ontological meaning, for a sense of purpose in a time of historical crisis. It is the silences enjoyed by the privileged, who can extricate themselves from the chaos of the "now" by "fence[ing] themselves in with miles and miles of silence", that he envisages bequeathing to his progeny (MK 47).

It dawns upon the Medical Officer that he has been misreading Michael K all along. He

> began to see the originality of the resistance you [Michael K] offered. You were not a hero and did not pretend to be, not even a hero of fasting. In fact you did not resist at all … you had failed because you had exhausted your resources of obeying us. (MK 163)

Fixated on uncovering the truth about Michael K, the Medical Officer pursues "truths": "Michaels means something, and the meaning he has is not private to me". With a growing ethical awareness, however, he acknowledges that the meaning of Michael K should not illuminate his own shortcomings or his "hunger for belief" (MK 165).

Without offering narrative closure, Coetzee chooses to end the novel with a parable: imagining a homecoming to the war-torn farm, Michael K envisages subsisting using a teaspoon to draw water from a well. He "would lower it down the shaft deep into the earth, and when he brought it up there would be water in the bowl of the spoon; and in that way, he would say, one can live" (MK 183–84). Thus he contemplates living in a minimalist fashion, taking from the earth only that which he requires to subsist. By small deeds come the will to expansive gestures. As Head points out, the narrative is drawn full-circle with this motif, "since it was a teaspoon with which the infant hare-lipped Michael K was fed, again by way of improvisation", enforcing Michael K's resistance merely through *being* (*J. M. Coetzee* 109). Presented as a future-in-the-past, the passage refuses to disclose Michael K's end, his probable death.

Although critics like Gordimer are right to argue that *Life & Times* privileges private destiny over political endeavour in the figure of Michael K, such critics on another level are also missing the point. In a book that "adroitly confuses" its reader through its self-diminishing allegories, the powerful achievement of *Life & Times* is its prescient auto-critique, work that is necessary if oppositional discourses, ones that are truly interventionist, are to remain credible. Ahmad, in his challenging analysis of Jameson's national allegory, comes to the painful realization that, on reading Jameson's "All third-world texts are necessarily …", "what was being theorized was, among other things, myself" ("Jameson's Rhetoric" 3–4). In *Life & Times*, attempts are self-consciously staged to theorize Michael K as "Third World" subject. His belief that "Perhaps the truth is that it is enough to be out of the camps … [p]erhaps that is enough of an achievement for the time being" signals not only an exigent resistance to state regulation, but also to the discourses in which, as the embodiment of social alienation, he inevitably finds himself written. His resistance is credible if, as Coetzee, writing about Jacques Rousseau's Confessions, says, *"what is held back* … [is] key to freedom" ("Truth" 6). Why *this* activity of withholding is important for theorizing the "Third World" which, according to Jameson, is built upon the crippling dynamic of subalternity (inferiority, marginality, subordination), is, I believe, manifest.

but maybe not for others?
no harm in
unpacking

Chapter 5
Bodying Forth the Other:
Friday and the "Discursive Situation" in *Foe*

In "The Text, the World, the Critic" Edward Said puts forward the audacious proposition that:

> Texts are fundamentally facts of power, not of democratic exchange. They compel attention away from the world even as their beginning intention as texts, coupled with the inherent authoritarianism of the authorial authority (the repetition in this phrase is a deliberate emphasis on some tautology within all texts since all texts are in some way self-confirmatory), makes for sustained power. (178–79)

J. M. Coetzee's fifth novel, *Foe* (1986), one of his most metafictional to date, deconstructs this "discursive situation" which, as Said clarifies, "far from being a type of idyllic conversation between equals [as Ricoeur would have it], is more usually of a kind typified by the relation between colonizer and colonized, the oppressor and the oppressed" ("Text" 181–82). In this vein the reader of *Foe* is called upon to be mistrustfully mindful of the relationship between author and text. As Coetzee puts it, "'the nature and processes of fiction' may also be called the question of *who writes*? Who takes up the position of power, pen in hand?" (qtd. in Kossew 161). This "discursive situation" is realized in *Foe*, as I will argue, in the figure of Friday, a character borrowed from Daniel Defoe's classic fable, *Robinson Crusoe* (1719); yet, paradoxically, Friday also resists being figured in discourse. He is a substantial body not simply the substance of a story. (For the purposes of my argument substance will connote discursive "worldliness" and substantiality will connote bodily materiality.) Cruso (the "e" disappears in Coetzee's version) also features and the name of a third protagonist, Susan Barton, is derived from the heroine, Roxana, in another of Defoe's works, *Roxana* (1724), whose real name is Susan. Roxana's daughter is also named Susan. In Coetzee's Robinsonade, Cruso struggles to mould Friday as colonial subject (he is seemingly utterly subjected), whereas Barton sets herself the task of releasing him from his bonds. Yet, crucially, she misconstrues his bodily substantiality for his substance as story: he is nothing, she believes, until his is fashioned in discourse.[1]

---

[1]   Barbara Eckstein makes a reading of "substance" in *Foe*, but reads a substance/ subject dialectic into the text, collapsing substance with substantiality. She writes: "Isolated with Foe's writing tools, Barton fears that as storyteller she is part of the story and not

Key to unlocking the secret silences in *Foe*, including the silence of authorial erasure, is an understanding of how Coetzee, in the tradition of postcolonial writing, "unwrites" his colonial intertexts, but also how these texts impinge upon each other. Of course, there is a danger in "unwritings" such as this, as John Marx points out, that they will "tend to reinforce the centrality of Western writing by default", and this is a problem that a number of critics have picked up on in their readings of *Foe*. Marx concludes, nevertheless, that "treating canonical texts as a source of raw material could not help but transform them" ("Postcolonial Literature" 89).

Shipwrecked on a desolate and unidentified island inhabited only by Cruso and Friday, Barton is designated the main narrator of *Foe* (she narrates the first three of four parts), whilst Cruso, the essential colonizer in *Robinson Crusoe*, is relegated to the margins of Coetzee's story: not only is he supplanted by Barton as narrator and author of the adventure, he also dies in the early stages of the narrative, never making the ideologically all-important journey home. If the island motif provides what Peter Hulme calls "a simplifying crucible in which complexities can be reduced to their essential components", a place to "compose" the self (*Colonial Encounters* 186; 189), it is Crusoe's reconstituted self that *must* return home to England to fulfil the colonizing promise. (Crusoe, of course, will go on to have further colonial adventures in far-flung places.) In *Foe* not only is Cruso implicated in this identity work, but Barton and Friday – who in Defoe serves the Enlightenment project of offsetting the eponymous "modern" Crusoe – are too. (It is therefore unsurprising then that *Foe* has invited a number of feminist as well as postcolonialist readings.) Not unlike the structure of the story favoured by Coetzee's author Foe (Defoe, minus the pretentious prefix), which is the story of Barton's lost daughter, in *Robinson Crusoe* the story of the island is merely one part of the larger narrative. As Benita Parry points out, "Crusoe [in Defoe's novel] … has a life before and after his years on the island, and the story of this rehearses the stages of colonialism prior to formal empire" characterized by an "aggressive mercantilism" virulently supported by the slave trade and colonial outposts in Asia and Latin America ("*Robinson Crusoe*" n. pag.).

As in Defoe's version, Friday is Cruso's slave, but the nature of this colonial encounter departs from its source in a number of important ways. *Robinson Crusoe* provides us with the colonial encounter which is the stuff of the "mythic beginning" (Hulme 190): Friday famously subjects himself by placing his head under Crusoe's foot. When Barton arrives on the island in *Foe* Friday is by now enslaved, colonial violence already done, with the effect, problematically, of essentializing Friday as slave because we know nothing of his life before. Choosing to do away with

---

a being with *substance*. Closing her eyes she tries to send to Foe a vision of the island which is 'a *substantial* body' (F 53) and entreats him to return her *substance* to her (F 51). In her struggle, she retains her distinction between silence and story – 'a storing-place of memories' (F 59) – and adds to it this distinction between *substance* and *story*" (emphasis added; "Iconicity" n. pag.).

the myth of beginnings, Coetzee refocuses the story on the silences that envelop Friday. Perhaps most crucially, the Friday of *Robinson Crusoe* not only can speak (Coetzee's Friday is mute because his tongue has been ripped out), he also quickly gains a workable grasp of English by which, ironically, as *Foe* so pointedly demonstrates, he can be shaped by his master: in *Robinson Crusoe* Crusoe teaches Friday to say "Master" (*Robinson* 185) and in *Foe* Cruso admits to teaching Friday only the words that Cruso believes will equip him in his role as slave.

In *Foe* it is the silence of Friday's tongue that gradually overwhelms the narrative. The novel was penned at the height of apartheid oppression, in the years of the States of Emergency, beginning in 1985, so Friday's muteness readily associates itself with the silencing of South Africa's black peoples who not least were denied the rights of free citizens and a voice in matters of the state. For Neville Alexander, *Foe* is testimony to this oppression: "The apparent inaccessibility of Friday's world to the Europeans in this story is an artist's devastating judgement of the crippling anti-humanist consequences of colonialism and racism on the self-confident white world" (qtd. in Attwell, *J. M. Coetzee* 108; *Plea* 38). Friday in *Foe* is probably a black African slave, a "Negro with a head of fuzzy wool" (F 5), whilst in its intertext Friday is Amerindian, and specifically *not* a "negro". Defoe's Crusoe describes him as a "comely, handsome fellow … he had all the sweetness and softness of an European … His hair was long and black, not curled like wool … his nose small, not flat like the Negroes" (*Robinson* 184). That Friday in *Robinson Crusoe* is perceived as facially similar to a European, and pointedly not African, has the effect of lessening the threat to Crusoe's psycho-social integrity; indeed, there are brief interludes in the narrative when Crusoe recognizes a common humanity between himself and "his man". By distinguishing Friday in this way in *Foe*, Coetzee designates him a slave, shipwrecked en route on the Middle Passage, from Africa to the Americas. By this means, Coetzee unravels the ways in which Friday, as character, is constituted by colonialist discourse. One aspect of the narrative that often gets overlooked in readings of *Foe* is that like Cruso and Barton, Friday is also a castaway. As Barton at least has the perspicacity to realize, "Shipwreck is a great leveller" (F 70). In *Foe* it is Friday and Barton, rather than Friday and his master, who travel to England after the island adventure and it is in England that Barton will have her epiphany about her own role in Friday's "education" and that Friday will take a stand against being incorporated into the imperialist-colonialist system of representation.

Nevertheless, it is the story of Robinson Crusoe's island, rather than the return to England, that for today's audiences has endured, evidenced in the plethora of Robinsonades that Defoe's novel has spawned (in literature, William Golding's *Lord of the Flies* [1954] and Michel Tournier's *Friday and Robinson* [1977] and in film Nicolas Roeg's *Castaway* [1987] and Robert Zemeckis's *Cast Away* [2000]).[2] As discussed above, Hulme argues that in *Robinson Crusoe* this framing

---

[2]   For a discussion of "neo-liberal" global subject-formation in *Cast Away*, see Li, Victor, "Globalization's Robinsonade".

device figures the "mythic" genesis of colonialist ideology (176). Lewis Nkosi
in "*Robinson Crusoe*: Call Me Master" draws on this mythic quality by claiming
that English readers "cannot read *Robinson Crusoe* properly, just as they cannot
read *The Tempest* for what it is, because they cannot read themselves into the
book" (*Home and Exile* 154); in other words, they lack the ethical vantage point
that empathizing properly with the "native" requires and are blinded to correct
readings of *colonial* myth because they are always already embedded within it.

Said extends the idea of the "worldliness" of texts in his later work *Culture
and Imperialism* (1993), in which he argues that the "facts of empire" provide the
"structure of attitude and reference" in novels like Jane Austen's *Mansfield Park*
(1814), Charlotte Brontë's *Jane Eyre* (1847) and, of course, Defoe's *Robinson
Crusoe*. In Said's words, *Robinson Crusoe* is the "prototypical modern realistic
novel [that] certainly not accidentally … is about a European who creates a fiefdom
for himself on a distant, non-European island" (*Culture* xiii). The colonialist
contexts of these works, Said observes, provide the social and moral fabric for the
imperial state (*Culture*, 100–16; 73), and this can be brought to light by reading
contrapuntally. The task of the "contrapuntal" reader is not to lose sight of either
the worldly or literary aspects of the analysis, to scrutinize the contexts of the work
whilst keeping in mind its narrative pleasures, in the case of Austen's *Mansfield
Park*, for instance, a deftly crafted comedy of manners.[3] In *Mansfield Park* the
fortune of Sir Thomas Bertram, gentleman-father to Tom and Edmund, is built on
the back of slavery: the novel hyper-discreetly, in a very Austenian way, references
the family's slave plantation in Antigua. Said suggests that from our modern
perspective, Sir Thomas's successes and failures in the colonies derive from "the
muted national experience of individual identity, behaviour, and 'ordination'"
(*Culture* 116).

Preferring to focus on the island adventure (F 121), the secret of which Friday
doggedly guards, Barton inadvertently chooses the myth of the colonial encounter
as the framing device of her story. By staging the process of the privileging, the text
traces her gradual realization that the project she has engaged Foe to write simply
reproduces colonialist doxa: "If [Friday] was not a slave, was he nevertheless not
the helpless captive of my desire to have our story told?" (F 150).

As I have suggested in my discussion of *In the Heart of the Country* (1977)
in Chapter 2, Western-centric feminism in Coetzee's fiction risks subsuming the
politics of racial otherness, an otherness figured here in perhaps its most stark
form, the mute slave. Barton, who at the outset believes it is her voice that has
been suppressed, likens herself in the scene of writing to a slave (F 87) and to a
newborn (F 126), as she has likened Friday to an "unborn" (F 122). Yet her lack
is quickly supplanted by that of Friday: it is the substance of his "voice" (that is,
his agency) that ultimately is not heard. Retracing Coetzee's steps, we see that

---

[3]   Director Patricia Rozema's adaptation of *Mansfield Park* (1999) makes a daring,
if to my mind heavy-handed, Saidian reading of the text by foregrounding its colonialist
substructure.

in *Foe* the colonialist discourse of *Robinson Crusoe* is offset by the "feminism" ✓✓
of *Roxana*, the two realized as competing discourses. Barton not only rejects the
daughter-figure whom Foe has tried to foist upon her and whom she utterly rejects
as her own, but also inverts the femininity attributed to her as Muse by becoming
both "goddess and begetter" of her tale (F 126). Despite enlisting Foe to fashion her
account, she maintains the "father's" right to its control (F 123) and symbolically
gestures this authority when she mounts Foe as she has sex with him, reducing him
to "feminine" submission. As Attwell suggests, both Roxana and Barton wish to
be "author of [their] li[ves] … control[ling their] destiny" (*J. M. Coetzee* 110). || ᵂ BAKHTIN

The protagonist of *Roxana*, whose real name is Susan and who, like Barton,
lives as a self-styled mistress or "whore" to a string of wealthy men, advocates
what today would be considered a feminist attitude towards marriage, surprisingly
predating the works of Mary Wollstonecraft (b. 1759) to whose Maria of *Maria,
or, the Wrongs of Woman* (published posthumously in 1798) she fruitfully might
be compared. "Roxana" shuns Sir Robert Clayton's marriage proposal in terms the
latter refers to as "amazonian":

> My heart was bent upon an independency of fortune, and I told him I knew no
> state of matrimony but what was at best a state of inferiority, if not of bondage; …
> I would be a man-woman; for as I was born free, I would die so. (*Roxana* 165)

However, not unlike Wollstonecraft's polemical novel, *Roxana* reinstalls
a patriarchal moral code since it is framed around Roxana's "fall" and her
subsequent return to piety when she gives up her dissolute life for marriage.
Nevertheless, Roxana's moral failings are tempered by self-scrutiny, and the
reader is encouraged through the first-person narrative to empathize with her
in her disgrace which, as in the case of Barton, is induced by dire economic
circumstance. Barton, however, who the text implies *may* have been a prostitute,
doesn't suffer the same anxieties about her femininity and is not afraid to || ✳
challenge both Foe's authorial and sexual authority.

In Defoe's novel Crusoe is meticulous in his attention to the minutiae of
his colonial adventure, which he religiously sets down in his journals, whereas
for *this* Cruso it is enough to have built his terraces. (Barton is perplexed, she
explains in her letters to Foe, by Cruso's apparent apathy towards recording his
time on the island.) Yet even the terraces, in Barton's eyes, display "a foolish
kind of agriculture" because, not only does Cruso lack the seeds to produce a
crop, he seems content to labour on them to fill his interminable days on the
island (F 34). Therefore, whilst Crusoe diligently works the land in *Robinson
Crusoe*, which typically is read as an allegory of economic individualism (Watt
62), in *Foe* Cruso's act of "writing the land" hones the colonialist acquisition of
space: fruitlessly staking out his territory, Cruso asserts his dominion rather than
productivity. Barton perceptively draws an analogy between the blood of slaves
spent in building the Egyptian tombs and the building of the terraces, which in
these terms yoke land to colonialist violence. Addressing the unresponsive Friday,

Barton imparts: "The further I journey from [Cruso's] terraces, the less they seem to me like fields waiting to be planted, the more like tombs" (F 83–84). Similarly, on the island, where the tools of writing have been rejected, Friday's body has been "written upon" by colonialism and colonialist discourse since not only has he been enslaved and his tongue cut out, he may also have been castrated. In Coetzee, where sexual potency is aligned with writerly production, this last act would signify not only Friday's inability to sire children, therefore removing one threat to colonial authority, but also the attempt to divest him of the power to author his own life.

But perhaps the most radical departure from its intertext is the mode in which *Foe* is delivered. The lyrical opening, at Barton's point of entry into the story and the island adventure – "With a sigh, making barely a splash, I slipped overboard" (F 5) – haunts the narrative (F 131; 133; 155–56) and returns us repeatedly to the site of trauma, the sunken slave ship, which lies buried at the bottom of the sea. Whilst Coetzee pays homage to Defoe's verisimilitude through an archaic syntax and through the epistle-style writings (this time Barton's letters to Foe rather than in *Robinson Crusoe* Crusoe's journal to posterity), here the stylistic comparison ends. Defoe's novel, Hulme contends, puts the constituents of "formal realism" together "but to an almost embarrassing degree": *Robinson Crusoe* is *so* authentic that the narrative "threatens" to depart from being literature at all, which, Hulme points out, is most obviously characterized by plot (177). Crusoe records the minutest detail of his adventure on the island in his journal, in part, to keep track of time. It was to be expected, given the novel's hyper-realism, that contemporary readers would be duped into believing they were reading a travelogue. Even recent analyses of the work, as Hulme notes, have tended to argue that "*Robinson Crusoe* mimes the texture of daily experience so accurately that", Hulme suggests, "only the most careful rereadings will perceive the underlying spiritual patterns that gives the narrative its true significance" (178). Hulme and other postcolonialists prefer to read Defoe's realism as adventure and, in turn, colonial romance. "Adventure" confers dual meaning: firstly, in its "pure" form as the stuff of heroic endeavour typically centring on the quest for treasure; secondly, as in financial venture ("merchant adventurer – anyone investing overseas" to "adventure capitalism, the asset stripper"). These two kinds of adventure, personal and financial, are coterminous in the colonial narrative. At the end of his escapade on the island, Crusoe finds he has amassed land and financial investments in the Brazils of some considerable amount (Hulme 182). Nevertheless, though Defoe's narrative is seemingly realistic, Crusoe's island is not. As Hulme points out, "the Amerindians would certainly not have ignored Crusoe's remarkably fertile island unless they had been driven off by the European competition for Caribbean land which was in full swing by 1659" (186).

Hulme argues that the "realistic detail" of the narrative:

> obscures elements of the narrative that ... would have to be called mythic [Crusoe is left "to live out alone his repetition of colonial beginnings"], in the

[margin annotation: Does she over-emphasise this?]

[margin annotation: ?]

sense that they have demonstrably less to do with the historic world of the mid-seventeenth-century Caribbean than they do with the primary stuff of colonialist ideology – the European hero's lonely first steps into the void of savagery. (186)

Hulme identifies points of "radical textual disturbance" around the colonial "beginning" in the narrative (particularly around the fear of being eaten by cannibals) that rupture the conventions of realism and that in turn point to the problems of "composing Crusoe's self" (*Colonial* 193). Importantly for Hulme, Crusoe arrives on the island equipped with a set of "ideological and cultural presuppositions" (*Colonial* 186), thus making him not the raw, unformed self of "natural man", nor the "initial unit of a market economy interacting" (*Colonial* 186), but a figure who will reproduce England's colonial mission in "miniature" (*Colonial* 194).

Whilst honouring Defoe's literary achievements (cf. DP 146), Coetzee's narrative mode sets about deconstructing the colonial "truths" of this earlier text, a text which, according to Hulme, hovers around Crusoe's "benevolent despotism" (186). It achieves this by circling the question, "what is truth?" Barton persistently talks about preserving the "truth" of her account [F 40; 121; 126] which she believes can only be achieved by unleashing the silenced story of Friday's tongue (F118). According to Attwell, the narrative forms the "endless chain" of confession Coetzee identifies in "Confession and Double Thoughts". As Attwell elaborates, "Each new section gets behind the preceding one until, at the point of closure, we have an unnamed narrator who seems to stand for the narrative function per se". The "constant" not subject to this endless re-evaluation and reappraisal, Attwell suggests, "marking the limit of self-knowledge in Susan's case and overwhelming the narrator at the novel's close, is Friday" (DP 247). Friday's substantiality might be constant but, as I am arguing here, his substance, or the ways he is perceived by others (that is, constructed in discourse), certainly is not. If *Robinson Crusoe* bequeathed the mantle of "father" of the English novel on Defoe, Coetzee's text works to unpack the colonial ideology that frames its intertext by delegitimating the authority of the colonialist author-figure – here, not only Defoe and Cruso, but also Barton and Coetzee himself – through this endless chain.

Foe typically is read as postmodernist, but this has been a thorny subject for some postcolonial critics who have questioned the propriety of utilizing a postmodern mode to address postcolonial problematics because postmodernism, through its apparent preoccupation with surface and by destabilizing meaning, is premised supposedly on a refusal to engage politically. For Graham Pechey, Coetzee appropriates a postmodern *mode* to convey postcolonial *issues*: "the ethically charged postmodern knowledge which [Coetzee's fiction] yields has less to do with some generalized 'postmodernist' textuality than with its highly self-conscious postcoloniality" ("Post-apartheid" 67). Helen Tiffin picks up the question of authority and form when discussing the Nigerian author Chinua

Achebe's *Things Fall Apart* (1958). Despite characteristics of postmodern form manifesting themselves in *Things Fall Apart*, she argues, "this [novel] is very different from, indeed, is antithetical to, many of the intellectual titillations of formal experiments in fragmentation that are symptomatic of the post-modern crisis of European authority, a 'crisis' whose own terms betray its motivation" ("Post-colonialism, Post-modernism" 175). Attwell, on the other hand, in conversation with Coetzee, identifies ethical tendencies such as these which might be read as "*continuing* some of the concerns of modernism … into new situations". A new kind of postmodern literature would release itself from "the taint of Eurocentric indulgence", he contends. Importantly, like Tiffin, Attwell distinguishes between Anglo-American and postcolonial strands, though Coetzee, in response, is not so dismissive of the former. (Attwell is referring to a "majority opinion" that regards Anglo-American postmodernism as "only feebly anticanonical" [DP 201].) I prefer to align myself to those critics like Attridge and Lazarus who read Coetzee's self-conscious ethicality as a sign of the modernist inflection in his writing (Attridge, *J. M. Coetzee* 2–6; Lazarus 148).

   The metafictional aspects of the work are brought together in the substance/ substantiality dialectic. As figures on the margins, Barton and Friday lack substance in discourse because their powers of self-representation are impeded. Yet they are substantial somatically in their suffering: Barton as a prostitute and Friday as a slave; "pain is truth", the Magistrate in *Waiting for the Barbarians* (1980) takes from his conversations with the torturer Colonel Joll (WB 5). Barton is preoccupied with the substance of her adventure in the hands of the author, Foe. In one of the letters she addresses to him, she writes,

> When I reflect on my story I seem to exist only as the one who came, the one who witnessed, the one who longed to be gone: a being without substance, a ghost beside the true body of Cruso. Is that the fate of all storytellers? Yet I was as much a body as Cruso. I ate and drank, I woke and slept, I longed.

Here, substance refers to a kind of verisimilitude and a faithfulness to her story. She asks Foe to "Return to me the substance I have lost … For though my story gives the truth, it does not give the substance of the truth" (F 51). In the letter of the following day she imagines "send[ing] out a vision of the island to hang before [Foe] *like* a substantial body" (emphasis added; F 53), and later of making the "air around [Friday] thick with words". Note here that Barton speaks about only a *representation* of the island, one that is only *like* a substantial body. Barton convinces herself that through the stories she tells him, Friday might construct an island that isn't a "barren and a silent place" (F 59). She confuses bodily substantiality with the substance of a story, misguided in the notion that through stories and words she can body forth Friday, as other. She recognizes that she lacks the art of storytelling, which is the reason she turns to Foe, in whose hands, she now believes, the kernel of the story will be forever lost. The "true story" is the story of Friday's silence, of which she remains ignorant. For Barton, her substantiality has been the chains of her oppression from which she is trying to break free: "I could return in every aspect to the life of a substantial body, the life you [Foe] recommend. But such a life is abject. It is the life of a thing. A whore used by men is used as a substantial body" (F 125–26). With the island serving as a space for subject *re*-constitution, Barton stresses her need to take control of her story and to reject the story of her past, which is one constructed by society (Barton as prostitute). Attridge argues that Barton realizes she is "determined not by herself but by the culture within which she seeks an identity" (*J. M. Coetzee* 79). She even conflates bodily substantiality with textual substance: "I am a *substantial being* with a *substantial history* in the world … for I am a free woman who asserts her freedom by telling her story according to her own story" (emphasis added; F 131). Foe reminds her, however, that she has omitted Friday from her account: Friday cannot be substantial, in the eyes of Barton, because he lacks the tools of language to assert or authorize his story. The book will try to refute this supposition, as I go on to explain: Friday, in his pain, is a substantial body, yet he resists being reduced to a story or being defined/confined by (Western-centric) discourse.

Grappling for control of the narrative, Barton and Foe debate the role of stories and of storytellers. To Barton's annoyance, who has turned to Foe as ghost-writer to craft her tale into a marketable narrative, Foe suggests that the story of the island be relegated to a minor role within a larger plot, which, he asserts, should focus on the search of a mother (Barton) for her lost daughter (F117). Whilst the author-figure Foe, emblem of the "Western" canon, would marginalize the story of Friday, it is this story that the liberal-minded Barton endeavours to exhume in order that the legacy of colonialism might be properly confronted. Foe sets sentiment against reason when he quickly dispels his desire for a story that emotes – he initially speaks about the "heart of the story" – and identifies its kernel instead with a watchful eye (F 141) that might be associated with rationality and which he links to the site of mourning and the act of witnessing: the sunken slave ship with its "eye staring up at [Friday] from the bottom of the sea" (F 141). Barton, on the other hand, perceives it as a mouth (F 141), and determinedly draws it back to the matter of Friday's tongue and the question of agency: "if the story seems stupid, that is only because it so doggedly holds its silence. The shadow whose lack you feel is there: it is the loss of Friday's tongue" (F 117). Although she acknowledges that it is Friday alone who can reveal the truth of his story, she believes she is morally obligated to teach Friday to communicate this: "The true story will not be heard till by art we have found a means of giving voice to Friday" (F 118). The postcolonial endeavour to portray and, problematically, even seek out otherness is captured in the pun on "art", connoting invention as well as writerly stealth. Barton guards what she construes as the essence of the story, her adventure on the island. She admonishes Foe,

> You err most tellingly in failing to distinguish between *my silences* and *the silences of a being such as Friday*. Friday has *no command of words and therefore no defence against being re-shaped* day by day in conformity with the

> desires of others. I say he is a cannibal and he becomes a cannibal; I say he is
> a laundryman and he becomes a laundryman. What is the truth of Friday? You
> will respond: he is neither cannibal nor laundryman, they are mere names, they
> do not touch his essence, *he is a substantial body*, he is himself, Friday is Friday.
> But that is not so. No matter what he is to himself (is he anything to himself?
> – how can he tell us?), *what he is to the world is what I make of him.* Therefore
> the silence of Friday is a helpless silence. He is the child of his silence, a child
> unborn, a child waiting to be born that cannot be born. Whereas the silence I
> keep regarding Bahia and other matters is chosen and purposeful: it is my own
> silence. (emphasis added; F 121–22)

In these words Barton states her commitment to the power of discourse and, in
fact, Enlightenment: Friday's substantiality is meaningless unless it has substance,
which Barton hopes to achieve by giving him access to language and learning.

    Barton is wrong on two counts: firstly, she intends imposing the language of
the colonizer on Friday. William Shakespeare's Caliban in *The Tempest*, one of
Foe's intertexts, is all too aware of the oppressive mechanisms at work in such a
manoeuvre because language serves only to "enlighten" him on his enslavement:
"You taught me language and my profit on't/ Is I know how to curse" (Act 1, Scene
2). Secondly, as the novel later reveals, Friday actively *chooses* silence when he
refuses to be tutored in reading and writing by Barton. She imperiously assumes
Friday has no language, perceiving him as unformed, "only a turmoil of feelings
and urges" (F 143). As the "child waiting to be born that cannot be born", Friday's
silence – his story – is metaphorically bodied forth in the corpse of the dead baby
which he and Barton discover at the edge of a road on their travels from London
to Bristol. This chimes with the "lost daughter" narrative that preoccupies Foe.
Nonetheless, as female other, Barton also deems herself "ignorant as a newborn
babe" [F 126], unformed and lacking substance, in this way inadvertently alluding
to hers and Friday's shared humanity that has been excluded from the discourses
the novel presses against.

    Foe recounts two parables to Barton that illustrate his investment in
authorship; Susan's reinterpretation of them situates hers within a postcolonial
paradigm. According to Foe, the moral of the first, that tells of a woman wishing
to confess to a crime, is "that there comes a time when we must give reckoning of
ourselves to the world, and then forever after be content to hold our peace". The
second parable is about a condemned woman finding solace in the knowledge
that her memory will live on in her child, whom she places in the safe hands of
a sympathetic gaoler (F 124–25). In sum, the parables address the problems of
(narrative) closure and of drawing the quest for (self-)truths to an end. According
to Coetzee in "Confession and Double Thoughts", this sense of an ending risks
being unattainable in confession's cycle of "self-recognition and self-abasement"
(DP 282), just as Foe surmises that Barton is unable to relinquish her quest for
the truth of Friday's tongue (which actually supersedes her own loss of autonomy
since Friday's speechlessness marks *her* voice) and just as the narrative of *Foe*,

with its repeated dives into the wreck, seeks but denies closure too. What Foe regards as Barton's futile quest for truth is her attempt, albeit misguided and thus self-deceiving, to establish an ethical relation to her story, to be accountable to it. Whilst Barton's conscience is troubled by the ethics of literary embellishment, Foe's concern remains steadfastly with his fiction.

In her quest to learn the truth about Friday's tongue Barton draws two sketches, inviting Friday through pointing to disclose which represents the truth of the matter. However, by providing two versions she imagines may hold the key to his secret, she inadvertently reimposes the very silences she is trying to unlock. She is confounded by her realization that the picture itself could be misinterpreted, that the portrayal of Cruso cutting away Friday's tongue, from a different perspective, could resemble "a beneficent father putting a lump of fish into the mouth of child Friday" (F 68–69). Barton's pictures are exposed as a series of contextually and ideologically inscribed signs. In a familiar Coetzean conceit, the process of allegorical reading is itself parodied and the reductiveness that allegorical reading can induce laid bare.

It is the silences *Foe* guards that have most troubled critics of the novel. In her groundbreaking article "Speech and Silence in the Fictions of J. M. Coetzee", Benita Parry, for example:

> put[s] forward the polemical proposition that despite the fictions' disruptions of colonialist modes, the social authority on which the rhetoric relies and which it exerts is grounded in the cognitive systems of the West. Furthermore … the consequence of writing the silence attributed to the subjugated as a liberation from the constraints of subjectivity … can be read as re-enacting the received disposal of narrative authority. (150)

Parry contends that in *Foe* Coetzee fails not only to move beyond a Eurocentric stage, but inadvertently reimposes the very authority he endeavours to critique. She wonders "whether the reverberations of Coetzee's intertextual transpositions, as well as the logic and trajectory of his narrative strategies, do not inadvertently repeat the exclusionary colonialist gestures which the novels also criticize" (150). This has the effect, she argues, of "sustaining the West as the culture of reference" (151). What Parry calls for, recruiting Tzvetan Todorov, is heterology which "makes the difference of voices heard" (Todorov qtd. in Parry, "Speech and Silence" 152). Parry calls to task those critics like Gayatri Spivak who read Friday's silence as resistant. Spivak argues that "'The native', whatever that might mean, is not only a victim, he or she is also an agent. He or she is the curious guardian at the margin" ("Theory in the Margin" 172). This position is revised from Spivak's notorious and emphatic claim that in literature subalterns cannot speak because they are always already caught between the discourse of imperialist and nationalist elites. A subsequent version of "Can the Subaltern Speak?" appeared in *A Critique of Postcolonial Reason* (1999) in which Spivak

SELF-SILENCING/SELF-CENSORSHIP

is less unequivocal (309). Nevertheless, Parry is adamant that though Coetzee may well attempt to refuse

> to exercise the authority of the dominant culture to represent other and subjugated cultures … the fictions do just this, because of which European textual power, reinscribed in the formal syntax required of Literature, survives the attempted subversion of its dominion. ("Speech and Silence" 151)

GOOD

This exercise of authority is a move of which Barton is guilty, suggesting, therefore, that Coetzee may well be second-guessing his critics.

In *Doubling the Point* Coetzee makes clear that he utterly distrusts positionality (DP 205). Writing from a site of privilege as white South African and male, he self-consciously effects his own authorial silence in *Foe*, which is imperative in the debates the novel stages. His silence on matters of politics is not dissimilar to Albert Memmi's argument in *The Colonizer and the Colonized* (1965) that, in recognition of the hegemony of the colonizer, the colonialist intellectual "who refuses" faces the moral choice of quitting the colonies or remaining silent. The colonizer who quits "will put an end to his contradiction and uneasiness" (Memmi 43–44). Sheila Roberts notices parallels between the story of Friday's tongue and Memmi's grievance that his mother tongue (which metonymically also represents culture) has been suppressed by the colonizer: "In the linguistic conflict within the colonized, his mother tongue is that which is crushed. He himself sets about discarding this infirm language, hiding it from the sight of strangers" (Memmi 107; qtd. in Roberts, "House of Friday" 90). In *Foe* silence is Janus-faced for it not only signals Friday's oppression but also his autonomy. Occupying the metaphoric "hole in the narrative" (F 121), Friday, as mute, not only represents the oppressed voice of the colonial other, conversely, he is also autonomous in his refusals to disclose his "self" when bidden. That he is *accorded* this right by his author, as Parry's analysis shows, signals the complexity of adequate, that is to say ethico-political, representation.

Moreover, Friday is triply silenced because not only is he silent as mute and silenced by colonial discourse, he is also misread by Cruso, Barton and Foe, who, themselves subject to discourse, fail to recognize his resistance to the imperial mindset. Ironically, therefore, he is effectively silenced by those – primarily Barton but also Foe – who undertake to give him voice. On the island Barton surreptitiously observes him casting petals over the sea, which she construes as an exotic religious rite only for it later to transpire that he is performing an act of remembrance at the site of the sunken slave ship on which, we assume, he was cargo (F 31–32; 140–41). (Barton later deciphers this ritual as a memorial to the lost family or friends on such a ship [F 87].) Like Cruso and Foe, Barton is also susceptible to racist fantasies since she has suspicions that Friday practises cannibalism. Her prejudice comes to the fore when, travelling across England with Friday, she encounters the body of the dead baby girl wrapped in swaddling at the side of the road; she fears that left alone with the tiny corpse Friday might revert to his savagery. As in *Robinson Crusoe*, these fantasies are apparently unfounded, though Defoe's Crusoe does come upon human remains that purportedly have been eaten by natives. Crusoe clings to the belief that through his efforts Friday has been saved from his barbarousness (*Robinson Crusoe* 186). Indeed, Hulme suggests that this lack of proof in *Robinson Crusoe*, that "the ungrounded fear of cannibals always outweighs Crusoe's actual experiences", reveals a "psychosis at the heart of the European perceptions of Amerindian culture in the Caribbean" (193–94). What is more, in the schema of Enlightenment-thinking mapped earlier, this pathological fear of being eaten by cannibals is in fact a fear of the loss of "corporeal integrity" (Hulme 194). As Hulme observes, Friday's account in *Robinson Crusoe* of the practice of cannibalism is in fact very different from Crusoe's fantasy: "The Caribs, according to Friday, do eat human flesh but only the flesh of those that offer aggression: it seems that something like the Law of Nations operates in the native Caribbean" (195). In this respect *Foe* stages not only the colonialist fantasies about black bodies that appear in its intertext, but also those explored in the earlier novels, *In the Heart of the Country* and *Waiting for the Barbarians*.

The island motif prepares the ground for Barton's desire to construct Friday as subject, and certainly Barton's efforts are a means of her finding self-knowledge since otherness is defined in its relation to the self, as "always *perspectival* ... always *produced*" (Attridge, "Trusting the Other" 65). Firstly, Barton teaches Friday to write "Africa", which can only be the Africa of Barton's invention, the substance of myth, since she has never set foot on African soil. Yet she has the presumption to teach Friday, for whom the inscription "Africa" holds no meaning, about it. According to Spivak the idea of Africa is mythological and an "effort rich in meaning and its limits ... *Africa* is only a time-bound naming; like all proper names it is a mark with an arbitrary connection to its referent, a catachresis" ("Theory in the Margin" 170). Of his own volition, Friday then draws a series of "o's", which Foe prematurely believes is the "beginning" of his education: "Tomorrow you must teach him *a*" (F 152). Foe is wrong because "o" in fact represents Friday's resistance; as Spivak points out, the letter "o" in *Robinson Crusoe* is pidgin for "prayer" and therefore signifies a remembering of precolonial culture, itself a gesture of anti-colonial resistance ("Theory in the Margin" 171). "O" also signals Friday's unreason, Spivak claims, and is proof that, just as Barton admits her failure to teach Friday, Crusoe fails in his religious instruction ("Theory in the Margin" 171). At the end of *Foe* "o" is the "sound" that issues from Friday's mouth and washes over the island in a gestural recuperation of colonial territory and the oppressed voice.

If we compare the "o" produced by Friday with the "O" that configures Magda's lack in *In the Heart of the Country*, we can see an emergent resistance in Friday, who holds the author and reader – Cruso, Barton, Foe, Coetzee, us as readers – out. Hitherto simply mimetically reproducing Barton's efforts, Friday freely takes up the chalk and draws "row upon row of eyes upon feet: walking eyes". Refusing Barton's demands to give up the drawing board, he wipes the slate clean, both literally and metaphorically (F 146–47). In the vein of Frantz Fanon's *tabula raza* in *The Wretched of the Earth* (1961), this act calls for entirely new beginnings: the blank slate that prefigures texts as "facts of power". This is a Fanonian model of decolonization whereby "the proof of success lies in a whole social structure being changed *from the bottom up*" (emphasis added; *Wretched* 27).

Deciphering Friday's inscriptions proves exacting. As subaltern he is not only silenced by the colonial oppressor, but refuses the demands made of him to divulge his core, his subjectivity. Perhaps the eyes represent his watchfulness but also his freedom to "read" his environment for, as the sadistic Colonel Joll in *Waiting for the Barbarians* says, "Only the eyes have power. The eyes are free, they reach out to the horizon all around. Nothing is hidden from the eyes" (D 79). What Foe calls the "eye" of the story, in the fourth and final section of the novel, is presided over by the mute Friday. The feet Friday draws might represent his ability to escape, the foot, according to Attwell, being the signature of Friday in *Robinson Crusoe* (*J. M. Coetzee* 114). Barbara Eckstein, on the other hand, persuasively suggests that the rows of eyes upon feet represent the "literal vantage point of slaves in a hold … beneath the sailors' feet" ("Iconicity" 8). Spivak wonders if the eyes' "secret [is] that they hold no secret at all" ("Theory" 171), and is therefore another kind of withholding. Should the eyes be equated with reason, as I have already suggested, then Friday in wiping the slate clean gestures the repudiation of the Enlightenment discourses that have sanctioned his enslavement.

As Marcus Wood points out, "Muteness and blindness are dominant metaphors in Coetzee's rendering of Friday, and the final muteness and blindness are placed within the Western consciousness" (304) in its inability to fully comprehend or "read" the slave other. Under the subheading "What are we looking at, what can we see?", Wood draws attention to the unquestioning way the "Western" eye has regarded slavery:

> Looking, as opposed to reading, has not, in the context of slavery, been described as an exceptionally problematic activity … Maybe this is because there is still an irrational belief that pictures speak for themselves in a way that words do not. (6)

In Barton's attempts to know Friday through looking upon his body, Friday is objectified so that the master/slave dialectic that Barton thinks she is dismantling is simply reproduced in the colonizing effect of the gaze. Earlier, Barton comes upon Friday spinning in a dervish-like frenzy dressed in Foe's robes of authorship. Just as she is morbidly fascinated with Friday's tongue, she is intrigued by the possibility that he has been castrated: "In the dance nothing was still and yet everything was still…. . What had been hidden from me was revealed. I saw, or, I should say, my eyes were open to what was present to them" (F 119). Barton thus convinces herself that she still has failed to unearth the truth of Friday because, though she is presented with the corporeal substantiality of Friday's body, she is not presented with the story (the substance) this body holds. In the context of the customary analogy between artistic production and sexual potency, ambiguity shrouds Friday's emasculation, which is both literal and figurative. By choosing not to disclose Friday's genital mutilation, Coetzee refuses to engage with the same sexualized fantasies about black bodies in which his character Barton participates. It is only through Barton's lurid imagination when she draws pictures of the missing tongue that this story is graphically depicted.

Wood refocuses the impetus of looking by questioning the residual effects of aestheticizing the tortured body. Representation is both artistically and often institutionally problematic, he argues: assuming the authority to represent the slave's body is to declare authenticity and access to "a memory which lies outside the obvious resources of Western aesthetics" (219). The idiosyncratic Elizabeth Costello in Coetzee's "The Problem of Evil" (republished as one of the eight "lessons" in *Elizabeth Costello* [2003]) argues that we are tainted by our contact with evil: representing acts of evil degrades artist and reader alike. Problematically, the graphic scenes of torture and violence in *Dusklands* (1974) and *Waiting for the Barbarians*, as well as the contentious depiction of Lucy Lurie's rape in *Disgrace* (1999) (though the reader is only party to the attack on her father David), converse with the very devils that Costello reviles. ✓ TRUE.

Defining committed art as the expression of a certain ethos rather than tendentiousness, Theodor Adorno addresses the problem of evil from a different perspective: all art, even committed forms, is produced to satiate the senses, to bring beauty and pleasure into the world; hence, his famous maxim that "to write lyric poetry after Auschwitz is barbaric" ("Commitment" 78). Adorno asserts that "The so-called artistic representation of the sheer physical pain of people beaten to the ground by rifle-butts contains, however remotely, the power to elicit enjoyment out of it" ("Commitment" 84). Yet, reminding us of the paradox of postcolonial authorship with which Coetzee's fiction consistently engages, this presents us, Adorno maintains, with a conundrum because "This suffering ... also demands the continued existence of art while it prohibits it; it is in art alone that suffering can still find its own voice, consolation, without immediately being betrayed by it" ("Commitment" 85). Representing the other through "looking", even in the context of looking at cultural artefacts on display, therefore necessarily falls back on the double bind that delineates postcolonial authorship. ⭐ CORE FORMS OF BEING.

Pain signifies physical being (substantiality), as Coetzee eloquently observes in *Doubling the Point*:

> Whatever else, the body is not "that which is not," and the proof that it *is* is in the pain that it feels. The body with its pain becomes a counter to the endless trials of doubt.... it is not that one *grants* the authority of the suffering body: the suffering *takes* this authority: that is its power. (DP 248)

Elleke Boehmer argues, nevertheless, that colonialism inscribes meaning upon the body of the other and reads this body within its own ideological parameters:

> In colonial representation, exclusion or suppression can often literally be seen as "embodied" ... the Other is cast as corporeal, carnal, untamed, instinctual, raw, and therefore also open to mastery, available for use, for husbandry, for numbering, branding, cataloguing, description or possession ... . The body of the Other can represent only its own physicality, its own strangeness. ("Transfiguring" 269–70)

The paradox of any literary representation of the enslaved or indentured other – which, Boehmer suggests, is "made to advertise its own unknownness and savagery" – is that it will both "distance and ... sanitize" the other ("Transfiguring" 271). Yet, like Coetzee, Boehmer identifies the possibility of the colonized "recuperate[ing]" their subjected bodies through this (objectifying) physicality, thus enabling "self-articulation". In Boehmer's words, "Refus[ing] to mean within the oppressor's symbolic system", ("Transfiguring" 272), Friday dances, plays the flute and scribes hieroglyphics which are all strange to the colonizer – Cruso, Susan, Foe and, indeed, Coetzee.

In *The Body in Pain* (1985) Elaine Scarry claims that "Physical pain does not simply resist language but actively destroys it, bringing about an immediate reversion to a state anterior to language, to the sounds and cries a human being makes before language is learned" (4). For Scarry, silence, which is "the inexpressibility of pain", assumes only its repressive or oppressive qualities; pain's

> Resistance to language is not simply one of its incidental attributes but is essential to what it is ... for physical pain – unlike any other state of consciousness – has no referential content. It is not *of* or *for* anything. It is precisely because it takes no object that it, more than any other phenomenon, resists objectification in language. (Scarry 5)

Scarry asserts that to suffer pain is to "have certainty" whilst "hearing about pain [is] to have doubt" (4). What she describes as pain's "lack of referential content" is realized metaphorically as well as physically in Friday's obscurity and resistance to being written or read. In the context of the Friday of *Foe*, however, Scarry's thesis is fraught with ideological difficulties, not least that troublingly, theorized in this way, pain is analogous to Barton's perception of Friday as unmoulded and untutored.

As Scarry observes, the occlusions and silences which pain induces lead witnesses of the body in pain to speak on its behalf. This has ethico-political implications, for although the notion of "speaking for" another's pain is problematic (and there are many motivations for doing so), it usefully resituates the discourse of pain from private sphere to public (Scarry 6). Not speaking about pain, neither objectifying its "attributes" nor establishing the link between these attributes and their source, the human body "will always work to allow its appropriation and conflation with debased forms of power; conversely, the successful expression of pain will always work to expose and make impossible that appropriation and conflation" (Scarry 14). Nevertheless, despite offering useful insights into the relationship between pain and language and into the ethico-political ramifications of the silences pain engenders, *The Body in Pain*, purporting to be empirically grounded, is overly reliant upon easy rhetoric and "evidence" drawn from literature (cf. Singer's review of Scarry, "Unspeakable Acts" 29). Though Scarry's work is therefore useful for reading the figurative language of literature, its integrity applied to the material world is exercised.

The final, fantastical section of *Foe*, with its alternative, metafictional endings, throws the truth of the preceding narrative into question. Not only is the reader, like Barton and Foe, "lost in the maze of doubting", such an ending threatens to undermine the modicum of autonomy that Friday *does* achieve. Of course, that this autonomy is conferred by Coetzee always risks diminishing its ethico-political achievements. Foe's house is entered twice by an unnamed narrator – a number of critics have speculated that this might be Coetzee (see, for example, Petersen 251; Head, *J. M. Coetzee* 124; Begam 125), or perhaps it is simply the generic author. On both occasions Susan and Foe, side by side, lie dead on Foe's bed and Friday lies nearby. In the first instance, the narrator attempts to prise Friday's teeth apart, to extract meaning, as Barton has attempted to give him voice. Echoing Caliban – "Be not afeard, the isle is full of noises" (*The Tempest*, Act 3 Scene 2) – Friday is tied, emotionally, culturally, perhaps spiritually, to the (colonial) island: "From his mouth … issue the sounds of the island" (F 154).

Having already been positioned as interrogative readers who question the authority of the text and its author, we recognize that Friday's attachment to the island must be approached with caution: perhaps it signifies a place of bondage, as the final passage of the novel intimates through reference to the sunken slave ship. Friday, the African slave and castaway, in Coetzee's Robinsonade is as out of place on the island as he is in metropolitan London (unlike Defoe's character who, from the island, weather permitting, can see his home). As a castaway, Friday is subject to the conventions of the genre, the remoteness of the island providing the necessary conditions for distilling the self. If Crusoe's return to England in *Robinson Crusoe* is necessary for him to reaffirm the myths of colonial enterprise, Friday's time in London in *Foe* anticipates the end of Empire and atonement for the atrocities committed in its name. As emblem of the slave trade, he is bringing its dirty message home.

The unnamed narrator enters the house for a second time, tacitly acknowledging, as Head suggests, the "inadequacy of the first attempt" because the "association of Friday merely with the sounds of the island can be seen as a continuing marginalization, a stereotypical identification of the 'native' with 'native culture'" (*J. M. Coetzee* 124). This time the narrator observes a plaque bearing the inscription "*Daniel Defoe, Author*" on the wall, a (metafictional) sign, Attwell argues, that positions us in the world of the original Crusoe story, in the realm of the literary history we knew before the appearance of *Foe* (*J. M. Coetzee* 115). All three figures lie dead, Foe and Susan in a casual embrace, and a scar now visible around Friday's neck, "like a necklace, left by a rope or chain" (F 155).

This mark not only recalls the two pouches Friday has worn – the first holding the petals, the second the letter that grants his freedom – but also the chains of slavery. The narrator discovers Barton's crumbling narrative in a dispatch box which has never been published, thereby forcefully rejecting the "truth" of the preceding text once again.

In the third ending, diving into the opaque realms of metafiction, the unnamed narrator swims into the wreckage of a ship and comes upon the swollen, bloated bodies of Barton and the captain, then Friday. With a chain around his neck, Friday is marked emphatically as cargo on a slave ship, a revelation which again repositions the whole of the preceding narrative and Barton's place as narrator within it. In the light of the fact that it is not only Barton but Friday, too, who has been cast away, the story of the island is claimed, not reclaimed (because the Middle Passage renders Friday displaced), as his. Like Barton's efforts to teach Friday to "speak", the narrator's question, "what ship is this?", proves futile for, as the narrator quickly realizes, "this is not a place of words ... This is a place where bodies are their own signs. It is the home of Friday" (F 157). Again, the narrator tries to exert authority over Friday, "trying to find a way in" to his mouth. It opens; his breath "flows up through his body and out upon me ... it runs northward and southward to the ends of the earth" (F 157). If Friday's autonomy is limited, the symbolic resonance of this scene, as Friday's voice lyrically embraces the world, is not. Reading blindness as a metaphor for insight, Wood imagines: "what that water tells us, as it beats on the eyelids, is that the memory of slavery belongs to all of us, and requires our acknowledgement, if only we dare to look" (305). Nevertheless, this illusory place is consigned to the peripheral and destabilizing world of textual play and as a gesture of the other's resistance, is therefore moot. As Sue Kossew suggests, these closing passages might simply confirm that the text itself tries to extract meaning from Friday "in the name of interests that are not his own" (*Pen* 115) and Spivak concludes: "Friday is affirmed to be there, the margin caught in the empire of signs". Like Kossew, Spivak advises vigilance in interpreting this ending for, she suggests, "we also know that Coetzee's book warns that Friday's body is not its own sign" ("Theory in the Margin" 174).

If *Foe* is a novel about the writing of a colonialist book and the power imbued therein and Friday metaphorically realizes Said's "discursive situation", the problem of interpretation is integral to them both. Coetzee has set himself the insuperable task of disclosing whilst not disclosing the taboo of Friday's tongue and through it the question of subaltern agency. Parry is right that Coetzee objectifies Friday within the same parameters he brings to bear on the colonizing mission. Although Coetzee displays a responsibility for the other, he takes a theological category into the social realm without really contemplating the problems of the transfer. But above all, is Coetzee not concerned with the limitations of the author in representing others' stories, with the problems that this activity occasions, all the time acutely aware that, in Said's words, "texts are fundamentally facts of power"? Barton realizes this when it dawns upon her that all the while she has been driven to seek out Friday's substance, neglecting the fact that his substantiality prefigures any (colonialist) story that might be told about him.

✓ GOOD CHAPTER.

Chapter 6

Writing in the Face of Death:
"False Etymologies" and "Home Truths"
in the *Age of Iron*

Death is the only truth left.

J. M. Coetzee, *Age of Iron* 23

If the white writer is to break out of his double alienation, he too [like his black counterpart] has to recognize a false consciousness within himself, he too has to discard a white-based value-system which it is fashionable to say "no longer" corresponds to the real entities of South African life but which in fact never did.

Nadine Gordimer, *The Essential Gesture* 138–39

Mrs Curren's letter or the novel?

The protagonist Mrs Curren of J. M. Coetzee's sixth novel *Age of Iron* (1990) is dying of cancer and the text notionally constitutes the letter she is writing to her daughter who, in a symbolic stand against apartheid, has quit South Africa for the U.S. The letter includes dialogue and description and is written over a period of three years from the mid to late 1980s, the waning but most virulent years of apartheid, making it, as Dominic Head observes, an improbable communication to her daughter (*J. M. Coetzee* 129). The epistolary conceit represents a confession of sorts by which Mrs Curren bares her soul: hers is the confessant's struggle for endings. Her monologue (although it contains *dialogue*, it represents a letter from one person to another) is addressed to both her daughter and to the unresponsive and aloof vagrant Vercueil who has taken residence, uninvited, in her house and whom she requests to act as her "messenger" (AI 44). Vercueil is required to post the letter *after* her death ("That is the important part", she says [AI 28]), in order she implies that the gesture is not construed as self-interested and an attempt to persuade her daughter to return to home. However, what is initiated as a token of affection simultaneously serves as a revisioning of Mrs Curren's own ethico-political consciousness in which she articulates her profound anxiety at her unwilling complicity, as white, in apartheid oppression. The letter gives her the opportunity to expiate and find absolution from her sense of guilt and shame for "staying on": "Though [colonialism] was not a crime I asked to be committed, it was committed in my name", she says (AI 149).

Mrs Curren is striving for truths, both private and political ones. Through the process of writing and linguistic fashioning, she struggles to get her voice publically heard. As Edward Said has suggested in the context of the public intellectual,

CANCER: illness as metaphor.

112   *J. M. Coetzee and the Paradox of Postcolonial Authorship*   chauvinist!

"Knowing how to use language well and knowing when to intervene in language are two essential features of intellectual action" (*Representations* 20). By means of a scrupulous regard for language not unlike Coetzee's (she is an etymologist by only profession), she not only voices her distrust of orthodox belief by challenging the weak forces of state oppression and militant resistance that she sees as running amok in 1980s Cape Town, but ultimately is forced by her personal experience of these violent times to rethink her own ethico-political worldview. It is my contention that through this language work, Mrs. Curren comes to the realization that her political belief is compromised by her private anguish, rendering the public pronouncements that she does make untenable in the "age of iron".

Through the motif of last words, the text requires us to ask whether Mrs. Curren's state of near-death facilitates a truthful, what Coetzee would call "heartfelt", rendering of the context from which she speaks. Does writing in the face of death alter her positioning towards the black revolutionaries the novel portrays? She is resolutely and entirely anti-violence and her ethics are humanist. (Her visceral response to violence, including the violence of revolutionary struggle, would also be Coetzee's, who is ready to admit he is "unable to, or refuse[s] to, conceive of a liberating violence" [DP 337].) Is this simply liberal posturing with its specific South African connotations of ineffectuality and of turning a blind eye or can death provide a space for Mrs. Curren to speak her mind? She imagines the boy revolutionary John goading her: "What is the point of consuming yourself in shame and loathing? ... why don't you *do* something?" (AI 132). Does the novel imply that political commitment sanctions the expression of the self in ways that echo the policing of society and culture by apartheid, namely through modes of "censorship", both of the self and the state? (A direct comparison of these two modes would be grossly misplaced given the severe consequences of state-instituted censorship practiced by the Afrikaner National Party during this period.)

Mrs. Curren learns of her personal tragedy on the day that Vercueil arrives in her life. Vercueil, as emblem of a national malaise, is therefore indelibly linked to Mrs. Curren's disease. Mrs. Curren tells John that her cancer is the birthing of a personal and collective crisis of conscience about apartheid oppression: "I have cancer from the accumulation of shame I have endured in my life. That is how cancer comes about: from self-loathing the body turns malignant and begins to eat away at itself" (AI 132). While she mourns the loss of her relationship with her daughter – there is no communication between them during the time of the narrative as the letter has not yet been posted – she conceives the news of her tumour as a kind of macabre homecoming with a newborn: "It was for me to take in my arms and fold to my chest and take home, without headshaking, without tears" (AI 3). Later, as she holds in her hands the bleeding head of John, who has been run off his bicycle by the police, she is tortured by the image of this terrible birth: "Monstrous growths, misbirths: a sign that one is beyond one's term" (AI 59). Cancer therefore signals not only Mrs. Curren's imminent death but also the impossible birth of an afflicted nation.

The narrative maps a tension between public and private entirely relevant to its contexts, the interregnum of late 1980s' South Africa: that period of uncertainty between regimes. The policy of "total strategy", a term coined by the French general Beaufré who, according to William Beinart, "emphasized that in modern warfare the whole society should be involved in a 'dialectic of two opposing wills'", was during the time of the narrative initiated by the government in a last-ditch attempt to shore up its rapidly diminishing power (Beinart 245; 246). Both Florence, mother of child-revolutionary Bheki, and the Afrikaner police insist the domain of the private is over, and that Mrs. Curren, writing her "private papers" (AI 28; 157), is thus out of sync with the times. Rifling through her letters, the detective searching her house is uncompromising: "This is not private, Mrs. Curren. You know that. Nothing is private any more" (AI 157). Similarly, challenged by Mrs. Curren for losing authority of her child, Florence retorts: "It is all changed today. There are no more mothers and fathers" (AI 36). Indeed, Mrs. Curren's outspokenness on matters of politics, her aversion to political dogma of any hue, is undercut by personal anxiety. Although the letter is her final communication to an absent daughter, it becomes a conduit for getting her voice heard on what she regards as the wanton violence not only of the state but of the revolutionaries as well. Yet as her drama of consciousness unfolds through the letter, she questions her right to speak out on matters of politics from a position – liberalism – that has been denigrated by the South African left as political quietism. Moreover, as her efforts to distinguish the political from her cocoon of privacy become more obviously futile and inept, she recognizes that her public protestations are marred by personal self-interest and an abject fear of death. I disagree, she comes to not fear death in the unconventional sense.

Coetzee notes that his novels often stage a "contest of interpretations" between the ethical and the political (DP 338). Identifying a proclivity for the ethical in his fiction, he argues, nonetheless, that "the last thing I want to do is to *defiantly* embrace the ethical as against the political. I don't want to contribute, in that way, toward marking the ethical pole with the lack" (DP 200). Put another way, Coetzee espouses the ethical as a *corrective* to the political (Attridge, "Trusting" 70). Derek Attridge defines the terms as they are assigned in the oeuvre: "the ethical involves an always contextualized responsiveness and responsibility to the other (as unique) and to the future (as unknowable), while the political is the realm of generalizations, programs, and predictions" ("Trusting" 70–71). It is Mrs. Curren's struggle to apply her ethical code to correct the political, a struggle that on a political level fails, upon which in this novel Coetzee's "contest of interpretations" self-consciously turns.

So whilst the narrative lays bare the stark intimacies of death, it is also deeply rooted in the public disgrace of apartheid. That the novel accurately portrays the gangs of Witdoeke, agitated by the security forces, burning down the informal shanties of the Cape Flats (AI 83), for instance, and that the daughter's decision to quit South Africa in 1976 coincides with the Soweto protests means that the novel can be readily historicized.[1] It would not be improbable to imagine that in *Age of Iron* Coetzee answers Gordimer's criticisms that the earlier *Life & Times of Michael K* (1983) "denies the energy of the will to resist evil" and that Coetzee fails to recognize the very real achievements of "the victims, who no longer see themselves as victims" (Gordimer, "Idea" 3–6). *Age of Iron* explicitly and powerfully engages with the political and, what is more, for the first time in the oeuvre black voices are portrayed with tangible (political) agency. As black resistance to apartheid gathers strength in response, for instance, to the States of Emergency of 1985–90 and opposition to apartheid internationally grows more effective (cf. Beinart 214), Coetzee's critique shifts focus to the manner and mode of political commitment itself.

The political intractability Mrs. Curren finds so disquieting goes to the heart of the novel, captured in its title: "age of iron" refers variously to the iron will of the black child-revolutionaries, to the daughter's iron resolve not to return to South Africa while the National Party holds power, to Mrs. Curren's doggedness both in not persuading her daughter to return and her own political will, and to the iron laws of parenting to which both Mrs. Curren and Florence are party (AI 46; 114; 115; 68; 67). Most obviously, the age of iron is also the unbending law of the regime and state oppression (AI 47), and expresses the sense of arrested development that characterized apartheid's reactionary nationalism. In a novel that portrays the conflict between the state and the insurgents who are black, as well as so-called black-on-black violence, "white" is identified by Mrs. Curren as "the colour of limbo" (AI 85).

Mrs. Curren is haunted by the silenced black voices in South Africa's history of colonial and apartheid rule. Recalling the resurfacing black corpse in Nadine Gordimer's *The Conservationist* (1974), she writes:

> when I walk upon ... this South Africa, I have a gathering feeling of walking upon black faces ... Millions of figures of pig-iron floating under the skin of the earth. The age of iron waiting to return. (AI 115)

South Africa's oppressed yet irrepressible black presence is allegorized as waiting for its moment of return. By imagining that she walks "upon" the faces of the dead and the ground imbibed by the legacy of apartheid, Mrs. Curren acknowledges her privilege and power and in turn her complicity in black oppression. That this is a "gathering feeling" is indicative of a consciousness in transition. Dominic Head identifies an inconsistency, however, between this novel and Coetzee's argument

---

[1]   In 1986 the pass laws were rescinded in response to the exponential rise in illegal squatter settlements: by the end of the decade the Cape Flats extending from Cape Town that were virtually uninhabited at the beginning of the decade were populated by an estimated three-quarters of a million settlers (Beinart xvi; 238; 244). The Witdoeke, named after its white headbands, was one of a number of black vigilante groups that operated between May and June 1986, burning down these squatter camps (Head, *J. M. Coetzee* 131–34).

in *White Writing* (1988) about *The Conservationist* that, in Head's words, "casts doubt on the validity of the symbol of ownership of the land, contained in the motif of the resurfacing corpse" (*J. M. Coetzee* 133; WW 81). Nevertheless, Head goes on, Coetzee puts the motif to the same purpose in this novel "in a steely image which redoubles a sense of white complicity" (*J. M. Coetzee* 133).

The South Africa Coetzee portrays is apocalyptic and, like a scene from Bosch, is peopled by the insane and characterized by images of disease, fire and damnation. Indeed, Hell in Mrs. Curren's narrative emanates from South Africa's pervasive ideologies: "Hades, Hell: the domain of ideas" (AI 101). It is ghoulishly fitting that Mrs. Curren intends to protest against the regime by setting fire to herself, though she later reneges on this decision. Caught up in the violence of the Witdoeke vigilantes, she is incensed and confounded by the intransigence of the Afrikaner police which she construes as a kind of insanity: "All of us running mad, possessed by devils. When madness climbs the throne, who in the land escapes the contagion?" (AI 97). What Coetzee writes about the scene in Gordimer's novel *Burger's Daughter* (1979) in which the protagonist Rosa Burger witnesses a man beating his donkey resonates here: "The spectacle comes from the inner reaches of Dante's hell, beyond the scope of morality" (DP 367–68).

Mrs. Curren joins the ranks of Coetzee's conscience-stricken writers for her letter is a confession of sorts in its pursuit of personal and political truths. (It is clear that she also understands that there can be a moral value in lying because, for altruistic ends, she lies on three occasions: to save Vercueil's dignity, she lies to the neighbour who informs her that a vagrant has been seen on her property; she lies to the police in order that she might go in search of Bheki, and she claims ownership of John's gun to protect him from the police. Mrs. Curren also lies when she explains the meaning of charity to Vercueil, a point that I elaborate below.) Through her interactions with Vercueil and John, Mrs. Curren realizes that what she calls her "resurrection" (AI 115), in a familiar Coetzean trope, will only come through "loving the unlovable" since selflessly investing in the other ensures the most ethically pure actions:

> That is my first word, my first confession … I want to be saved. How shall I be saved? By doing what I do not want to do … I must love, first of all, the unlovable. [John] is here for a reason. He is part of my salvation. I must love him. (AI 124–25)

Up until this point Mrs. Curren has been unable to garner the inner resources to act out of love, though she has shown charity. She lies to protect John from the police and is unafraid to speak out in his defence, getting her disgust at his treatment at the hands of the police heard – he is "just a child", she remonstrates with them (AI 139; 140). Likewise, through the bond of trust with Vercueil that slowly evolves, she believes she will find sanctuary (self-forgiveness) within herself. Her circular sense of logic tells her:

VERCUEIL   *DOSTOEVSKY*   *ETHICS*

DEATH

> Because I cannot trust Vercueil I must trust him … I give my life to Vercueil to carry over. I trust Vercueil because I do not love Vercueil. I love him because I do not love him. Because he is the weak reed I lean upon him. (AI 119–20)

Mrs. Curren has not even been sure of Vercueil's name; she tells Florence: "His name is Mr. Vercueil … Vercueil, Verkuil, Verskuil. That's what he says" (AI 34). In Afrikaans "verkul" means "to cheat" and "verskuil" means to hide or conceal, emphasizing the inscrutability otherness such as Vercueil's vagrancy and racial identity encodes (Attwell, "Dialogue" 176; Head, *J. M. Coetzee* 140).[2]

Mrs. Curren thus seeks redemption through her relationships with John and the derelict Vercueil, whom David Attwell names her "Angel of Death" because in the closing sequence Vercueil squeezes the life-force from her body (DP 250; see also Attwell, "Dialogue" 175–76). Not only does the care she shows these two fill the gap left by her self-exiled daughter, it leads her to reassess her perception of those from whom she felt alienated, including the political activists. In this way private experience shapes and defines her conception of the political. Under apartheid, politico-historical truths were actively suppressed and distorted yet, Mrs. Curren believes, the forces of opposition are also purveyors of untruths: "Calvin victorious, reborn in the dogmatists and witch-hunters of both armies" (AI 47). Her own quest for truth, however, both her soul-searching and questioning of political orthodoxies, leads to a political epiphany, to the realization following the discovery of Bheki's body: "Now [her] eyes are open and [she] can never close them again" (AI 95).

Mrs. Curren is the antithesis of the Dostoevskian confessant who, according to Coetzee, is characterized by gratuitous "self-unmasking" (DP 280) because, from the outset, Mrs. Curren has a profound sense of the ethical. Her sincerity, or rather her *self-belief*, is not in doubt, and, within Coetzee's model of confession, the truthfulness of her outpourings is lent weight by her imminent death. Referring to Dostoevsky's Ippolit in *The Idiot* (1868), Coetzee argues that the confessant on the point of death will most reliably render a truthful confession because "The sincerity of the motive behind last confessions cannot be impugned … because that sincerity is guaranteed by the death of the confessant" (DP 284). (Of course, even the dying confessant can be self-deceiving.) Writing about Tolstoy in the same essay, Coetzee defines the sincerity of the dying:

> The sense of urgency that the crisis [the "confrontation with his own death"] brings about, the relentlessness of the process in which the self is stripped of its comforting fictions, the single-mindedness of the quest for truth: all these qualities enter into the term *sincerity*. (DP 262)

This is not yet clearly defined. Is she using Attridge as in the [?] on 113

---

2   Although Vercueil's racial identity is not disclosed, since John admonishes him for his alcoholism in deictic terms – "*They* are making *you* into a dog" (emphasis added; AI 42) – it is likely, as Attridge suggests, that he is black ("Trusting" 72).

? coloured… GREEN EYES.

Attridge points out that because Mrs. Curren's letter is posthumous it is given "without thought of return" ("Trusting" 61). The letter apparently breaks off as Vercueil squeezes out her last breath. In one interpretation, the narrative is brought to a close by an unnamed narrator whom we might surmise is Coetzee; an alternative might suggest that Mrs. Curren is writing at the point of death as in Samuel Beckett's *Malone Dies* (1956) in which the story of Malone ends with his words petering out on the page (*Molloy* 289). However, that the letter is given without constraint does not guarantee, as Attridge claims, a fuller expression of love; Mrs. Curren's self-disclosures reveal that the letter is not as selfless an act of love as she intended, as I explain below.

At the heart of the problem of endings, Coetzee argues in *Doubling the Point*, is "the debate … between cynicism and grace. Cynicism: the denial of any ultimate basis for values. Grace: a condition in which the truth can be told clearly, without blindness" (DP 392). Anticipating death, Mrs. Curren grapples with this dilemma, which is marked by the historical condition in which she finds herself. During the course of her story she vacillates between the poles, searching for transparent truths but always frustrated by the impasse of political dogma, as she sees it, of both apartheid ideology and revolutionary activism. It is in the dilemma of being caught between cynicism and grace that the political and the ethical are liable to converge. Living in the "age of iron", the age of political resolve on one side and the unbending law of the state on the other, and against her personal beliefs, Mrs. Curren is reduced to a position of cynicism. The narrative even moots the devastating possibility that in a place such as this grace, or truth, is no longer attainable. Mrs. Curren's predicament is echoed in Coetzee's analysis of the protagonist in Marcellus Emants's *A Posthumous Confession* (1894): "such pain becomes most acute when we recognize how unbridgeably vast the gap is between the ideal and the true self" (SS 43). The locus of Mrs. Curren's confessional writings is the incompatibility of her ideal self (grace) and her true self (cynicism), which she is always struggling to reconcile.

Mrs. Curren is what William C. Spengemann might call the "converted narrator" (qtd. in DP 260), whose life, Coetzee argues, falls into a before and after and whose "knowing, converted, narrating self stands invisibly beside the experiencing, acting self [such a narrator] tells about" (DP 260), overseeing the process of conversion. (The ending of *Age of Iron* lays bare its device because as Mrs. Curren draws her last breath in the present of the narrative, the two narrating selves apparently fuse into one.) Mrs. Curren believes that "Death is the only truth left" (AI 23), yet comes to realize that her planned protest to set herself alight in front of the "House of Lies" – what Coetzee would call a "philosophical suicide" (DP 285) – would prove futile. She believes that in the eyes of the young she lacks political credibility in as much as her death would simply end her own (private) pain. She realizes the self-interest inherent in the suicide bid, that her motives are not generated by public duty but by personal pain, and so, in turn, it dawns upon her that as a gesture of political protest it lacks purchase: "The truth is, there was always something false about that impulse, deeply false, no matter what rage or despair it answered… . Will the lies stop because a sick old woman kills herself?" (AI 129). Mrs. Curren undergoes a *political* enlightenment only in the sense that she is confronted with the realities of oppression which will harden her *ethical* resolve. but no ref. to Baler or Yeoh fries

It is via Mrs. Curren's engagement with ethics of care, trust, love and so on, that she makes interventions into the political. The letter is primarily a gift and is intended as an act of love – "my daughter's inheritance. They are all I can give her, all she will accept, coming from this country" (AI 28). Yet Mrs. Curren is cautious of her own motives in writing it and she comes to an awareness through its preparation – "I begin to understand" (AI 5) – that, like her intention to kill herself, her writing is imbued with self-interest. In his theory of the categorical imperative Immanuel Kant argues that morality is premised on duty: an act is only morally good if it stems from a sense of duty, untainted by ulterior motives ("The Noble Descent of Duty" 39–41; see also Kant, "Categorical Imperative" 274–279; Kant, *The Moral Law* 59–65). The letter violates the ethics of gift-giving because, rather than simply conveying mother-love, it is her means of uncovering self-truths. The mother-daughter bond is not a wholly unselfish one, as Mrs. Curren so guilelessly reveals: "To whom this writing then? The answer: to you but not to you; to me; to you in me" (AI 5). She even admits that raising children is a way of outwitting her own death:

> We embrace our children to be folded in the arms of the future, to pass ourselves on beyond death … We bear children in order to be mothered by them. Home truths, a mother's truth: from now to the end that is all you will hear from me. (AI 5)

The letter, "a baring of something else, but not of my heart" (AI 13), is not intended to recount the story of her wasting body, from which, the text implies, her writing is a release (AI 170). Even so, it provides little solace. We wonder whether Mrs. Curren meant to post the letter at all for she assures its reader: "*I will not show to you what you will not be able to bear*", only to do just that, describing herself as "a woman in a burning house running from window to window, calling through the bars for help" (emphasis added; AI 170). This calls into question the truth value of her letter and suggests that, rather than a gift of love, it is a means of venting her anguish about her lost daughter and her illness. Mrs. Curren admits that the letter places her daughter under moral obligation and, affirming language's oppressive quality, promises to set her free from "this rope of words" (AI 181). Her letter has become, metaphorically, both a lifeline by which to save herself and the bonds from which she promises to cut her daughter loose, and therefore violates the ethics of gift-giving and bequest – the latter by its very nature *cannot* be reciprocated.

Invoking Émile Zola's open "*Lettre au Président de la République*" (1898),[3] Mrs. Curren realizes that the letter is, in part, an accusation: "*J'accuse*. I accuse you of abandoning me… . I fling my pain at you" (AI 127). Zola, in defence of

(margin note: What are these? Not linked to Kant?)

---

3   Zola's letter, "J'Accuse!", addressed to the French President, was published in the French newspaper *L'Aurore* in 1898. Supporting the civil liberties of Dreyfus, who had been

Dreyfus against the railings of the anti-Semitic Right in Republican France, calls upon universal notions of truth, justice and liberty: "Truth and justice, so ardently longed for! How terrible it is to see them trampled, unrecognized and ignored! … My fiery protest is simply the cry of my very soul" (Zola n. pag.). Zola's letter is subsequently alluded to in *Disgrace* (1999) when the disgraced academic Professor David Lurie imagines the father of the young female student with whom Lurie has been conducting an affair signing a formal letter of complaint of sexual harassment against him – "*J'accuse*" (DIS 40). Mrs. Curren's self-disclosures betray her feelings of resentment towards her daughter, couched in terms of honesty and plain-speaking. Loading blame upon her, Mrs. Curren even divulges her planned suicide and names Vercueil her "husband": "Forgive me if the picture offends you … One must love what is to hand, as a dog loves" (AI 174). Mrs. Curren identifies her own neediness, as she inventories Vercueil's needs, which in sum are "Too much to give: too much for someone who longs, if the truth be told, *to creep into her own mother's lap and be comforted*" (emphasis added; AI 17). What is supposed to be a bequest and a token of mother-love is revealed therefore to be both self-interested and self-deceiving. Lurie and Mrs. Curren's invocation of Zola is ill-conceived: Lurie is mired in self-pity over the repercussions of his exploitative relationship and Mrs. Curren is expressing the anguish of a neglected mother. Both thus fail to meet the standards of public intellectualism to which Zola's letter pertains, though Mrs. Curren's efforts far outweigh those of Lurie. What she believes is her conviction in public truths, she recognizes, is self-interested and bound up with her response to her fast-approaching death.

Coetzee argues in *Doubling the Point* that Mrs. Curren's story is "about having a say … What matters is that the contest is staged" (DP 250). Despite the very private nature of Mrs. Curren's letter and her disavowal of political rhetoric per se, Mrs. Curren resolves to "speak truth to power" (Said, *Representations* 85). Although unlike Said's intellectual she doesn't get her voice heard in public forums, her outspokenness resonates with his analysis; the public intellectual is

> someone whose whole being is staked on a critical sense, a sense of being unwilling to accept easy formulas, or ready-made clichés, or the smooth, ever-so-accommodating confirmations of what the powerful or conventional have to say, and what they do. Not just passively unwilling, but actively willing to say so in public. (Said, *Representations* 23)

less significant than Poyner seems to indicate.

Mrs. Curren achieves a critical edge through her relentless self-questioning and through her challenge to the political ideologues by daring to speak out. Addressing her daughter (but also the reader of the text), she even appeals for critical reading: "attend to the writing, not to me. If lies and pleas and excuses weave among the words, listen for them. Do not pass them over, do not forgive them easily. Read all,

---

court-martialled and imprisoned, Zola called upon *Le Déclaration des Droits de l'Homme et du Citoyen* (Declaration of Human and Civil Rights) in Dreyfus's defence.

Ok so Poyner is concerned w politics here, but not much rel. to Attwell!

even this adjuration, with a cold eye" (AI 95–96). Trained as an etymologist and Classics lecturer, she hones language to suit her needs, and in so doing becomes a thorn in the side of the purveyors of political dogma.

Citing the linguist Benjamin Whorf's claim that Indo-European syntax results in a "mechanistic way of thinking", Coetzee identifies that quality of language which generates uncritical thinking: "one can unconsciously project the structure of one's language out on to the stars and then believe that the resulting map is a true picture of the universe" (DP 184). The British intellectual George Orwell presses this argument further in "Politics and the English Language" in his contention that the state of English is in decline, the significance of which, he says, should not be underestimated. Slack, unschooled language produces slack, unschooled thought, which in turn leads to bad politics. Orwell even contends that "if thought corrupts language, language can also corrupt thought" (407). Meaningless words, for instance, can be "used in a consciously dishonest way" to disguise political untruths. "Democracy", to take one example, can be invoked by any regime that wants to be looked upon favourably (Orwell, 403). As J. C. in Coetzee's *Diary of a Bad Year* (2007) provocatively opines "on democracy" in his collection of "strong opinions", "Democracy does not allow for politics outside the democratic system. In this sense, democracy is totalitarian" (DBY 15). The language of euphemism has its own sinister ends, Orwell suggests, covering up gross injustices and the atrocities of war: "pacification", "rectification of frontiers" and "elimination of unreliable elements" all clinically disguise the reality of human suffering. This process, however, "is reversible". If these bad habits are remedied, "one can think more clearly, and to think clearly is a necessary first step toward political regeneration: so that the fight against bad English is not frivolous and is not the exclusive concern of professional writers" (Orwell 398). Whilst Orwell is writing about the decline of English in 1940s Britain, his position can be mapped readily on to the ill-use of political language more generally.

Like Orwell and Said (with his suspicion of "easy formulas or ready-made clichés"), Mrs. Curren is mistrustful of the inexact shapes into which the language of contemporary politics has been squeezed. Language has become tired and meaningless but, more importantly, it has also become corrupt. Mrs. Curren's insights into the use and abuse of language catalyzes her own self-scrutiny. Her scrupulous regard for language therefore is her private, ethical means of challenging the iron-hard rules not only of the state but also, in her eyes, of anti-apartheid militancy. In keeping with Orwell, whilst her singular intellectualism structures her sensitivity to language, her language also self-consciously structures her intellectualism. Words function as the catalyst of empathetic understanding with the other, bringing Mrs. Curren to her revised position. When she offers him work as a gardener, Vercueil provides her with a stark lesson in the meaning of charity. She advises him that they "can't proceed on a basis of charity" (AI 19), a covert kindness on her part since she is trying to spare him the humiliation of accepting handouts. He demands an explanation why, as she has suggested, he does not merit

? moral reading not really

her support: "Deserve ... Who deserves anything?" he asks (AI 19). If she expects gratitude for her philanthropy, Vercueil is not forthcoming.

Mrs. Curren is exasperated that her words fall on deaf ears. Rather than being receptive to her ideas, which would make him the "ideal confessor",[4] Vercueil seems indifferent since he often fails to respond and at times appears not even to listen. Mrs. Curren regards John as emblematic of the "new puritans" (AI 75) and is quick to pass judgement on him: ✓ her statement/advice "Be slow to judge"

> There is something stupid about him, something deliberately stupid, obstructive, intractable ... Though his eyes were open, he did not see; what I said he did not hear ... . The words of a woman, therefore negligible; of an old woman, therefore doubly negligible; but above all of a white. (AI 71–72)

Mrs. Curren pointedly links John's "stupidity" not only to gender and age difference but also to questions of race: he does not see or hear the truth (Mrs. Curren's truth, that is) because "above all" she is "a white" (AI 71–72). She imagines John's indignation at what he perceives as an empty rhetoric that resonates with South African liberalism:

> Talk, talk! Talk had weighed down the generation of his grandparents and the generation of his parents. Lies, promises, blandishments, threats: they had walked stooped under the weight of all the talk. Not he. He threw off talk. (AI 132)

She believes she sees (racial and gendered) hatred in his eyes, yet it might equally be the expression of a frightened child since this is, after all, only Mrs. Curren's *reading* of him. His political intransigence – what Mrs. Curren calls his calculated "stupidity" – anticipates the portrayal of the nihilist leader Nechaev in Coetzee's next novel *The Master of Petersburg* (1994), whose political beliefs are premised on the notion that "everything is permitted" and that "we don't endlessly think *on the one hand* and *on the other hand*, we just *do!*" (MP 114; 104). The political intractability of South Africa's militant youth, Mrs. Curren believes, is not unlike the National Party's iron-hard rule. In response to John's condemnation of Vercueil's alcoholism, she laments: "The new puritans, holding to the rule, holding up the rule. Abhorring alcohol, that softens the rule, dissolves iron ... Suspicious of devious discourse, like this" (AI 75). John's convictions are in fact a carefully formulated and orchestrated political position and a historically accurate representation of the contemporary milieu: student protesters during the 1980s were opposed to drinking because it was thought to stymie learning, sociality and activism (cf. Beinart 220–21). Mrs. Curren, not surprisingly, offers a different,

so what?

---

[4]   As Coetzee explains in "Confession and Double Thoughts", the humane yet stupid Prince Myshkin in Fyodor Dostoevsky's *The Idiot* (1868) is, according to his confessants, the "ideal confessor-figure" because he readily accepts human fallibility and his understanding of "truth" isn't vested in self-interest (DP 283).

humane perspective favouring the ethical over the political: she advocates making allowances for Vercueil's vice. Reciprocity is skewed because though the ethos, or more accurately the apathy, of Vercueil accommodates Mrs. Curren's voice, for the likes of John and Bheki, "the rising generation, who do not drink, I cannot speak, can only lecture" (AI 75).

Centring on the word "comradeship", a heated debate between Mrs. Curren and Mr. Thabane ensues about commitment and the place of children in war framed in the polarized terms of ethics (Mrs. Curren) "versus" politics (Mr. Thabane). Mrs. Curren is emphatic in her rejection of violence in whatever name, that "as for this killing, this bloodletting in the name of *comradeship*, I detest it with all my heart and soul. I think it is barbarous" (AI 136). Inflamed by Mr. Thabane's retort that she does not "understand very much about comradeship", she draws parallels with oppressive regimes, including the Nazis: "Comradeship is nothing but a mystique of death, of killing and dying, masquerading as what you call a bond (a bond of what? Love? I doubt it)" (AI 137). Mr. Thabane, of course, is also talking about a kind of friendship based on absolute trust which, as Beinart observes, was a moral imperative in the resistance struggle and in the very notion of "comradeship" (213).

Suggestive of Said, Orwell and Coetzee's critique of ill-formulated language, Mrs. Curren regards Mr. Thabane's attempts to tutor her in the effects of apartheid oppression as a kind of "Ventriloquism, the legacy of Socrates, as oppressive in Africa as it was in Athens" (AI 91). In her own quest for truth she remains perspicacious: "These are terrible sights … But I cannot denounce them in other people's words. I must find my own words, from myself. Otherwise it is not the truth" (AI 91). To Mrs. Curren's ears even the dissonance of the Afrikaans language, with its heavy cadences that she can only associate with the atrocities of the apartheid regime, denotes intransigence and oppression. Hearing it spoken on the television elicits her impassioned response: "the slow, truculent Afrikaans rhythms with their deadening closes, like a hammer beating a post into the ground. Together, blow after blow, we listened. The disgrace of the life one lives under them" (AI 9). Afrikaans dialogue is used at moments of open hostility in the text, as a marker of unequal power relations. Mrs. Curren perceives a change in tone when the detective questioning her switches to Afrikaans (AI 157); Vercueil calls upon Afrikaans to curse Florence who has dismissed him as "rubbish" (AI 44) and Mrs. Curren employs Afrikaans to tell the police "I stand on the other side" (AI 140). Afrikaans is the language of last resort when dialogue breaks down. Except in this last example, in order to emphasize a communicative impasse Coetzee does not offer translations. (The South African edition of *In the Heart of the Country*, published in 1978, presented all dialogue in Afrikaans. Although this would not have been a problem for South African readers, as Attridge has noted, this device would nevertheless have defamiliarized them from the text [Attridge, *J. M. Coetzee* 22]. The struggle to communicate – authentic communication is always found wanting in the novel – is marked in this way by the language associated with the apartheid regime and Afrikaner nationalism.)

Mrs. Curren struggles to articulate, to find a language that expresses her ethical vision authentically and truthfully. She is once more shouted down, this time by a man in the crowd who retorts, "This woman talks shit" (AI 91). Her eloquent response counterpoints his vulgar linguistic register which threatens to stall intellectual debate: "'But what do you expect? ... To speak of this' – I waved a hand over the bush, the smoke, the filth littering the path – 'you would need the tongue of a god'" (AI 91). A stand against apartheid and the possibility of (political) transformation, she reasons, necessitates dialogue and imagining a common humanity. She attempts to demonstrate her position through the verbal challenges she makes to her (political) adversaries and through her letter. Here, she reflects on the power of words:

> [Words] may only be air but they come from my heart, from my womb. They are not Yes, they are not No. What is living inside me is something else, another word. And I am fighting for it, in my manner, fighting for it not to be stifled. (AI 133)

So OPEN-ENDED? see BREZINER

However, rather than offer solutions, the novel stages the debate about the efficacy of privileging the ethical over the political. It asks whether Mrs. Curren's voice is tenable in the "age of iron", and the self-doubt it expresses in response seems to be both hers and that of her author, Coetzee.

At every turn Mrs. Curren's right to voice her opinion is contested and, indeed, dismissed. Her understanding of the concept "charity" is challenged verbally by Vercueil and the boys. Bheki asks sardonically if they must bring passes when they visit the house; Florence and Mr. Thabane challenge her about her notion of commitment. She whispers her complaint to the television when she watches "one of those speeches" (AI 9) delivered by government ministers. Vercueil scorns her intention to set fire to herself in protest, just as she anticipates it would be scorned by Florence (AI 128–29), whom she challenged earlier for not enforcing Bheki's attendance at school. Of course, Mrs. Curren does speak out against the victimization of Bheki and John, lies about the gun, and vehemently condemns face-to-face the police who murder them. She is left feeling disgraced by the actions of the police after the bicycle incident (AI 78) and believes that the murder of Bheki will eat away at the policemen's souls (AI 98). She even attempts to warn Mr. Thabane, whose political activities she opposes, that he is in grave danger of becoming the next victim of the state.

In a key passage, Mrs. Curren identifies the importance of finding a voice, all too aware of the ethical problems this engenders. *By what right*, she asks, does she speak about and on behalf of others? She believes that hers is "the true voice of wisdom" but concedes with some irony that her right to speak out is compromised by white privilege:

who am I, *who am I* to have a voice at all? … I have no voice; I lost it long
ago; perhaps I have never had one … The rest should be silence. But with this
– whatever it is – this voice that is no voice, I go on. On and on. (AI 149)

Mrs. Curren musters the problem of authority that resurfaces in each of Coetzee's
fictions, and recognizes that it is contingent with South African colonial and
apartheid history: "a crime was committed long ago … it is part of my inheritance"
(AI 149).

Mrs. Curren has conviction in the power of words and (intellectual) discourse.
Writing and language are her private means of demonstrating her love for her
daughter: "in this world, in this time, I must reach out to you in words" (AI 8).
Later she intones, "I am *feeling* my way toward you; with each word I *feel* my
way" (emphasis added; AI 120). Here, emphasized through repetition and punning,
"feeling" connotes sentiment and empathy and, where blindness is typically
associated with philosophical insight, is suggestive of the intellectually blind
"feeling their way". Yet, though "feeling" also connotes political naïveté, with Mrs.
Curren feeling her way through a political labyrinth, empathy cuts across what
Mrs. Curren perceives as the dogma of political activism. She recognizes Vercueil's
lack in his inability to emote – ironically making him her ideal confessor (this is
what draws her to him): "'There is something that won't come, isn't there? … Why
don't you just speak and see where the words take you?' But he was at a threshold
he could not cross. He stood baulked, wordless" (AI 177). Although Mrs. Curren
speaks – indeed, like Magda in *In the Heart of the Country*, she goes "on and on"
– she is not heard. The withholding of speech by the racial others in Coetzee's
early works, on the other hand, is extolled: denied autonomy or a "voice", the texts
imply, withholding is the only means of resistance open to them.

Coetzee has suggested that.

> Elizabeth Curren brings to bear against the voices of history and historical
> judgement that resound around her two kinds of authority: the authority of the
> dying and the authority of the classics. Both these authorities are denied and
> even derided in her world: the first because hers is a private death, the second
> because it speaks from long ago and far away. (DP 250)

Mrs. Curren is a practitioner of words by training, though Latin, she instructs
Vercueil, is a "dead language … a language spoken by the dead" (AI 176). Having
tacitly conceded with these words that Latin lacks relevance in the context of
apartheid, she repeatedly and self-consciously draws attention to words that
etymologically are assigned ethical value: comradeship, charity, gratitude,
resolve, trust, love, confession, heroism, honour, shame, stupidity. Similarly, she
reflects upon the ethics of justice, truth, lies, comradeship, honour, heroism, and
on ethical contracts such as vows, bequests and wagers. She attempts to tutor
Vercueil in the idea of charity but misleads him with her "false etymologies".
The root of "charity" comes from the Latin for heart, she tells him, and, reversing

the theological adage, claims that receiving is as taxing as giving: "A lie: charity, *caritas*, has nothing to do with the heart. But what does it matter if my sermons rest on false etymologies? He barely listens when I speak to him" (AI 20). Deliberately falsifying the Latin in her appeal to the heart, she calls on reason's other, feeling. She ruminates on "stupid", construing the political dogma of both parties as a kind of stupidity. The National Party politicians, delivering "one of those speeches", are stupid in their intractability and immutability and their "feat, after years of etymological meditation on the word, to have raised stupidity to a virtue... . A gradient from *stupid* to *stunned* to *astonished*, to be turned to stone. The message: that the message never changes" (AI 26).

An attentiveness to language, to searching meaning out, constitutes Mrs. Curren's challenge to the ideologues. As the crux of her ethico-political position, language is ascribed historicity, and is thus necessarily future-directed because historical perspective looks to the possibility of change. She confesses to Vercueil, for instance, that until now she had avoided using the term "heroism": "The times call for heroism. A word that, as I speak it, sounds foreign to my lips. I doubt that I have ever used it before, even in a lecture. Why not? Perhaps out of respect. Perhaps out of shame" (AI 151). What her recent experiences teach her, especially the deaths of the two boys, is that there still exists a place in the world for the word "heroism" in its proper sense. On her intention to immolate herself, she writes: "I meant to go through with it: is that the truth? Yes. No. Yes-no. There is such a word, but it has never been allowed into the dictionaries. Yes-no: every woman knows what it means as it defeats every man" (A106). Connoting indecision, ambivalence, withholding and a condition of political limbo, for Mrs. Curren "Yes-no", which is a South African colloquialism, even is incorporated into the vocabulary of the interregnum. She also assigns "Yes-no" to her (lack of) personal resolve to speak the truth to her daughter, not beg her to break her vow and return to South Africa to her mother's deathbed.

But Mrs. Curren's pursuit of truth and authentic language becomes self-parodying: as she moves closer towards death and suggestive of a drug-induced delirium, she tries to unravel the meanings of words that she imagines as anagrams: "Borodino" – the nineteenth-century Russian battle she compares to contemporary South Africa; "Diconal" – her medication; even her own name. Her struggle to make sense of the world through language, through her "false etymologies", is presented in the stock Coetzean motif of the labyrinth:

> This letter has become a maze, and I a dog in the maze ... Why do I not call for help, call to God? ... God is another dog in another maze ... he is lost as I am lost. (AI 126)

This is a place where, in Harry Mulisch's words, "Heaven was impossible, only hell might perhaps exist", for even God has lost his way (qtd. in Coetzee, *Stranger Shores* 50). She even reads her experience of the world allegorically when, in the desperate search for Bheki in the townships, she comments on Florence's two young girls: "Hope and Beauty. It was like living an allegory" (AI 84). Of course, given Mrs. Curren's negative predisposition towards rules and orthodoxies, allegory is itself a mode with which she would hold no truck.

In "What Is a Classic?", in a titular reference to T. S. Eliot's lecture, Coetzee argues that the classic is based on the "criterion of testing and survival... The classic defines itself by surviving. *Therefore the interrogation of the classic, no matter how hostile, is part of the history of the classic, inevitable and even to be welcomed*" (emphasis added; SS 18–19). Mrs. Curren lives out this process of testing and survival if on an ethical rather than aesthetic level: she tests etymologies, reworking them according to her needs and refusing to accept meaning uncritically. Mrs. Curren's letter, which she puts before her readers as critics, is submitted to this process, as indeed is Mrs. Curren, given that writing is her means of outwitting death. She talks about "passing the test" in her "wager" with Vercueil (and with death) (AI 128; 119) and of bequeathing her letter. Like *Age of Iron*, the letter is future-directed since Mrs. Curren and Coetzee anticipate an audience reading and re-reading it. The test Coetzee sets his character is, will her account be interpreted as speaking truth to power or simply as the rantings of an infirm eccentric? As her sense of being haunted by the resurfacing black corpse illustrates, she treats her responsibility to history with gravity, that from the past we might learn to set right the present for the sake of the future. Coetzee's comments on historical understanding in "What is a Classic?" are apposite: it is "that part of our present – namely the part that belongs to history – that we cannot fully understand, since it requires us to understand ourselves not only as objects of historical forces but as subjects of our own historical self-understanding" (SS 15). Despite Mrs. Curren's classical knowledge of Thucydides, which teaches her, she says, what can happen to our humanity in time of war" (AI 73), her classical learning, nevertheless, is so remote from the present in which she finds herself that her words inevitably fall on deaf ears. As Said stipulates, a prerequisite of public intellectualism is that you get your voice *heard* (emphasis added; *Representations*, 100). Where Mrs. Curren's opinions *do* get disseminated, ironically, is amongst reading communities who are always already communities of elites.

In *Age of Iron*, physical pain, which signals Mrs. Curren's imminent death, gives her the courage to have her say, where other avenues, not least her dialogue with her daughter, have been shut down. Elaine Scarry, discussed in Chapter 5, argues that the silence engendered by pain "resists objectification in language" (5), whereas for Mrs. Curren, pain, both physical and emotional, facilitates free speech or, in her own words, enables her to go "On and on". Suffering her pain, she is not unlike Coetzee's other maimed or disfigured protagonists – the barbarian girl in *Waiting for the Barbarians* (1980), Michael K in *Life & Times* (1983), Friday in *Foe* (1986) – whose autonomy, problematically, is figured in their woundedness. (The white Paul Rayment in *Slow Man* [2005], who loses his leg in a bicycle accident, is maimed *and* autonomous, indicating that physical disability in Coetzee signifies racial or gendered oppression.) In a nation whose government has denied basic human rights of almost 9/10 of its population, the suffering body lends certainty. As Coetzee argues; "The body with its pain becomes a counter to the endless trials of doubt … . Not grace, then, but at least the body" (DP 248). Nevertheless, though feeling her way in the public domain through her private rope of words, Mrs. Curren's personal struggle against cancer prevails and she concedes: "The country smoulders, yet with the best will in the world I can only half-attend. My true attention is all inward, *upon the thing, the word, the word for the thing* inching through my body" (emphasis added; AI 36). Her pain has reduced language to signs that *cannot* be moulded.

Attwell suggests to Coetzee that the ending of *Age of Iron* holds the possibility of absolution on both the personal and national plane. Coetzee, however, is hesitant: "the end of the novel seems to me more troubled (in the sense the sea can be troubled) than you imply" (DP 250). In the final reckoning, Mrs. Curren finds redemption through death, which for the secular reader promises no sense of hope for the future. Her letter, on the other hand, through which she will immortalize herself but, paradoxically, that may never be delivered and its "message" lost, provides only testimony to the age of iron: it may serve as an example of how *not* to live, yet offers no solutions for the "now". Mrs. Curren is forceful in her ethical resolve and in getting herself heard, yet a poverty resides in her notions of charity, trust and so on, indicated by the helplessness and hopelessness of her actions to which Coetzee self-consciously alerts us. Her intellectual authority is weakened by her preference for the introspection that her home truths import.

Chapter 7

Evading the Censor/Censoring the Self in
The Master of Petersburg

I choose the crooked road and take children into dark places. I follow the dance of
the pen.

J. M. Coetzee, *The Master of Petersburg* 236

There is more to the sorry business, however, than just the shame of it. He has come
to London to do what is impossible in South Africa: to explore the depths. Without
descending into the depths one cannot be an artist.

J. M. Coetzee, *Youth* 131

The writer-protagonist Fyodor Dostoevsky of J. M. Coetzee's seventh novel *The Master of Petersburg* (1994) is tormented by the same dilemma that troubles the young John in Coetzee's quasi-fictional memoir *Youth* (2002). The at once pretentious and gauche John is torn between the demands of his ambition to pursue the life of a writer and those of self-censorship: to what extent can he give himself up to free expression without violating the bounds of the ethical? *The Master of Petersburg* explores the writer's intimate relation to his work through a fictionalized Dostoevsky, the Russian master who in real life, as Stephen Watson notes, was described by a contemporary as a "cruel talent", and by fellow literary master and adversary Ivan Turgenev as a "Russian de Sade" (qtd. in Watson, "Writer and the Devil" 48).

Coetzee divulges his investment in the problem of self-censorship in *Doubling the Point* (1992) when he invokes Nadine Gordimer's idea of the "essential gesture" of engaged writing: "What is a writer's freedom? … The most obvious threat is official censorship. But [quoting Gordimer] a 'more insidious' threat comes from the writer's 'very awareness of what is expected of him': 'conformity to an orthodoxy of opposition'" (DP 382; see also Gordimer, *Essential Gesture* 106). Whilst self-censorship can be necessary on ethical and political grounds, it has the potential to stymie not only the ethical and political force of a literary work but also its aesthetics. Evidenced in the ongoing cultural debates about writerly commitment, such a problem had particular resonance in apartheid South Africa when certain requirements were often self-imposed by the writer who resisted the forces of the state. Coetzee argues that writing is always autobiographical (DP 391) and that "the only sure truth in autobiography is that one's self-interest will be located at one's blind spot" (DP 391; 392). Whilst, as I will argue, this blindspot is self-consciously constructed by Coetzee in the figure of Dostoevsky, it might usefully be tested against Coetzee's own writerly practice. The choice of unwriting a novel like *The Possessed* with its particular political baggage at a transformative moment in South African history such as this – 1994, the transition from apartheid to democracy – is telling and begs the question, what does Coetzee reveal and, conversely, what does he censor of himself?

The analysis that follows will show that, through the interplay of the dialectical motifs of evading the censor and censoring the self, *The Master of Petersburg* endeavours to cultivate a critical and self-reflexive reading community. Coetzee is all too aware this is vital at a historical juncture of such magnitude, a time when South Africa for the first time becomes a fully postcolonial state. As Frantz Fanon presciently warned, all new postcolonial states are susceptible to the "pitfalls of national consciousness" (neo-colonialism) whereby the new regime promises change but which in reality harbours the interests of the old. Quickly forgetting the needs of the people once independence is declared, "the leader will reveal his inner purpose: to become the general president of that company of profiteers impatient for their returns which constitutes the national bourgeoisie" (*Wretched* 133). Fostering the critical faculty in the way that I argue *The Master of Petersburg* does, a faculty which Edward Said argues is the lynchpin of public intellectualism (*Representations* 23), is one measure that can militate against the problem of neo-colonialism.

The work of the reader encountering a censored or self-censored text is, in the manner of the forensic scientist, to piece together its illicit or hidden subtexts: elision, ambiguity, omission, allegory, parable and metaphor all exercise the reader in the work of interpretation. This is the reason, Coetzee points out in "The Novel Today" (1987), that the parable is favoured by marginalized communities who stand outside history because its message is obscure (NT 1). Setting anti-realist fiction against history and the historical novel which reaffirm the status quo, Coetzee argues that the ineffectiveness of censorship has been its failure to "recognise that the offensiveness of stories" doesn't lie in their capacity to transgress rules imposed by others, but to make and change these rules at will (NT 3). Yet Coetzee is also suspicious of genre rules if they force particular readings; in colonial and apartheid contexts such rules are analogous to processes of systematization, codification and control that have been intimately bound up with power and oppression (cf. Attridge's comments on allegory [*J. M. Coetzee* 62]).

Fredric Jameson argues that the act of interpretation should itself be subject to scrutiny: "every commentary must be at the same time a metacommentary" ("Metacommentary" 10). Jameson likens metacommentary to the "Freudian hermeneutic" which distinguishes between the manifest and latent workings of a text, between the concealment and the message concealed. "This initial distinction", he goes on, "already answers our basic question: Why does the work require interpretation in the first place? by posing it forthrightly from the outset, by implying the presence of some type of Censor which the message must slip past" ("Metacommentary" 15). For Jameson, the act of interpretation is not to discover a "resolution" to the conundrum of a text's meaning, "but a commentary on the very conditions of existence of the problem itself" ("Metacommentary" 10). Jameson's argument distils the "message" of Coetzee's novel: that as readers, we must always question our role within the life of the text. How do we read a text that self-censors? How do we read the unsaid? And, above all, *why* are we required to do so?

The self-exiled Dostoevsky in *The Master of Petersburg* has returned incognito from Dresden to St. Petersburg to discover the truth about the death of his stepson Pavel, to mourn his loss, to lay his ghost to rest and to resolve his own ambivalence about his relationship as father to his stepson. Both as a writer and father (evoking the fathering of stories), Dostoevsky feels duty-bound to recover and record his stepson's memory: "A gate has closed behind his son … To open that gate is the labour laid upon him" (MP 19). Nevertheless, Dostoevsky imagines an Oedipal struggle between them, heightened by a self-awareness that, as a novelist, he is always casting his writerly eye over the life and death of his stepson in the name of his craft: though grieving Pavel, he is already scrutinizing the boy's past for the seeds of a good story. Moreover, as Derek Attridge suggests, his residence in St. Petersburg far outlasts its apparent function of putting the dead boy's belongings in order: Dostoevsky appears to be waiting the arrival of something he has yet to articulate (Attridge, "Expecting" 26–27).

The novel stages Fyodor Dostoevsky's process of creative thinking that would beget *The Possessed* (1872) (also known as *The Devils*), Coetzee's primary intertext (Pechey, "Post-Apartheid" 71; Attridge, "Expecting" 35). It is the idea of this book in *The Master of Petersburg* that the fictional Dostoevsky awaits. The real-life Dostoevsky initially perceived *The Possessed* a "pamphlet-novel" and had "high hopes for the piece, but in a tendentious, rather than artistic sense[;] I want to utter a few ideas, even if my artistry is destroyed in the process" [qtd. in Leatherbarrow 24; 27). What began as propaganda was only later transformed into a work of literary merit, as W. J. Leatherbarrow argues, as the novel shifted focus from political nihilism to nihilism in its social and moral form (Leatherbarrow 25; 27–28) based on Dostoevsky's newly found commitment to Orthodox Christianity.

The final chapter in Coetzee's novel titled "Stavrogin" specifically imagines the genesis of the "At Tihon's" chapter in *The Possessed*, originally suppressed by the editor of *The Russian Herald* where it first appeared in serialized form who deemed Nikolay Stavrogin Vsyevolodovitch's confession of the abuse of the girl Matryosha obscene and therefore unfit for publication. Curiously, Dostoevsky himself later withheld the chapter when the book went to print but a copy has survived as an appendix to the edition translated by Constance Garnett (the edition referred to here). Avrahm Yarmolinsky, who prepared the Foreword to this edition, notes that he is unable to enlighten the reader on this point (ix), whilst Leatherbarrow argues that Dostoevsky simply couldn't fulfil the requirements of the magazine and so decided to omit the chapter altogether (43).

In his confession Stavrogin experiences the conflicting emotions, both remorse and "a pleasurable sensation", that typify the confessions of the Dostoevskian hero identified by Coetzee in "Confession and Double Thoughts" (DP 275).

Absolution, as the goal of confession attained by questing for "truth about the self", is overridden in Dostoevsky's confessants as they begin to take gratuitous pleasure in the act of confessing and, consequently, fail to find closure (DP 252). Stavrogin conceals his part in the "penknife affair" for which the girl Matryosha is wrongly accused and neglects to intervene in her public shaming even though he believes she may be suicidal. He becomes self-consciously enamoured of his story, embellishing his confession: "I note this", he writes, "because it is important for the story" (*The Possessed* 704). In Coetzee's novel Dostoevsky, like Stavrogin, admits to a "voluptuous urge to confess" to his young wife in Dresden, his confessions "bedevilling their marriage far more than the infidelities themselves" (MP 62). Of course, that Coetzee's Dostoevsky *thinks about* abusing the girl Matryosha, imagining her laid out naked on the bed, is very different from his acting upon these thoughts. As D. H. Lawrence, writing in defence of his censored novel *Lady Chatterley's Lover* (1928), observes: "culture and civilization have taught us … [that] the act does not necessarily follow on the thought" (qtd. in GO 49; see also Lawrence, *Propos* 9–10). Nevertheless, Dostoevsky *is* culpable in that he is subtly corrupting the child and effaces Pavel's diaries based on this experience. This will become the story of Stavrogin seducing Matryosha in *The Possessed*: "this is a passage he will not forget and may even one day rework into his writing" (MP 24).

Attridge and Zinovy Zinik comprehensively draw comparisons between the author Dostoevsky and Coetzee's character, noting that both are living in Dresden in 1869, observed by the Russian secret police and unable to return freely to Petersburg because they are being pursued by their creditors – the real-life Dostoevsky, like his fictional counterpart, was afflicted with a dangerous penchant for gambling. Dostoevsky began writing *The Possessed* in December 1869, a month after Coetzee sets the denouement of *The Master of Petersburg*. Like his counterpart, the real-life Dostoevsky has a stepson called Pavel whom he offers financial support. Both Dostoevskys suffer from epilepsy, previously thought of as a kind of possession and, as Attridge observes, "the tortured spirals of self-doubt, self-denigration, and self-exculpation that occupy so much of the protagonist's mental world are familiar from Dostoevsky's fiction and letters" ("Expecting" 24). In *The Master of Petersburg* Dostoevsky unburdens his grief to his "confessors" Anna and Matryosha. Pavel can be loosely equated with Stavrogin who confesses to his abuse of the girl-child Matryosha in Dostoevsky's novel. Sergei Nechaev is a historical figure who infamously was implicated in the murder of a student member of the nihilists, I. I. Ivanov, who Nechaev believed might betray the organization (Offord 68). Whilst Dostoevsky obscures representations in *The Possessed* of both Nechaev, as Peter Verkhovensky, and Ivanov, as Ivan Shatov, Coetzee takes the liberty of unmasking them in his novel. Coetzee, however, also makes significant departures from historical truths, notably, that in real life Pavel outlived Dostoevsky (Attridge, "Expecting" 24–25; see also Zinik 19).

Coetzee's novel therefore assumes that the reader has knowledge of what is a complex and difficult work and is versed in the dominant, European canon.

Whilst in Coetzee's earlier "radical metafiction" (DP 86) *Foe*, allusions to Daniel Defoe's *Robinson Crusoe* (1719) are transparent, familiarity with *The Possessed*, particularly the suppressed chapter, as Attridge observes, is less likely ("Expecting" 32). Nonetheless, by engaging with a novel that effectively has been censored, Coetzee notionally enacts an evasion of the censor and situates the reader of *The Master of Petersburg* as this censor-figure or critic who must fill in the gaps of the "missing" (inter)text, just as in *Foe*, the reader is challengingly positioned as critic or "foe" of the work.

Coetzee's novel also brings together Dostoevsky and his long-term rival Ivan Turgenev and Turgenev's *Fathers and Sons* (1862) that charts the same moment in Russian history. (Coetzee borrows the names Pavel and Anna Sergeyevna from *Fathers and Sons*.) The conflict between the two Russian authors has been well documented; as D.C. Offord points out, Turgenev is "viciously lampooned in the character of Karmazinov" in *The Possessed* (82). Both Turgenev and Dostoevsky recognized the responsibility of the older "liberal" generation, with its ties to Western Europe that so rankled with Dostoevsky, for the revolutionary fervour of the younger, 1860s generation (Offord 78; see also Peace 142). It was with Turgenev's "liberalism", his courting of young radicals and his lack of nationalism associated with his liking of Western Europe that Dostoevsky took issue and it was not until shortly before Dostoevsky's death that the two resolved their differences (Leatherbarrow 13). All three works, *Fathers and Sons*, *The Possessed* and *The Master of Petersburg*, draw upon this generational conflict and are, accordingly, structured around the father-son relationship. In nihilist ideology the "father" (authority) must be regularly rooted out for, as Nechaev in *The Master of Petersburg* says, "Revolution is the end of everything old, including fathers and sons... . With each generation the old revolution is overturned and history starts again. *Carte blanche*" (MP 189). "Father" also signifies the writerly authority of Coetzee's Dostoevsky, who is the "master of Petersburg".

This is the first of Coetzee's novels to be published post-apartheid and, set in St. Petersburg, Tsarist Russia, ironically, it is the first in which he most obviously withdraws from geopolitical contexts that can be said to be (post)colonial. Writing for *The Master of Petersburg* began in the transitional period marked in 1990 by the ANC leader Nelson Mandela's release from his 27-year incarceration and when negotiating the winding down of apartheid was set in motion. Parallels between Tsarist Russia and apartheid South Africa are transparent: both are oppressive societies which have subjected their citizens to censorship, imprisonment, torture and exile; both nations are undergoing seismic change, characterized by Nechaev's remark in the novel that "We are on the brink of a new age where we are free to think any thought" (MP 201). In the 1860s, when both novels are set, Russia was under the new, "reformist" regime of Nicholas II which, following Russia's defeat in the Crimean War of 1853–56, introduced a series of reforms including the abolition of the institution of serfdom. Nevertheless, what Offord calls this "reforming ardor" quickly dissolved in response to the build-up of militant activity amongst the intelligentsia (Offord 65; 66). In both Russia and

CONFESSION   MADNESS

134   *J. M. Coetzee and the Paradox of Postcolonial Authorship*

So what? not entirely
proved, but not forms of move

South Africa the disparity between rich and poor was (and still is) vast, a fact of
which, problematically, Coetzee's novel takes little account. The issue of poverty
is only addressed explicitly when a blindfolded Dostoevsky is led to the depths
of the metropolis to meet Nechaev. Finally, of course, both Russia and South
Africa spawned effective revolutionary movements that targeted state oppression.
Continuing themes begun in *Age of Iron* (1990), this particular writer, Dostoevsky,
is disturbed by what he perceives as the demon-possession of revolutionary zeal.

Published two years prior to the inauguration of the Truth and Reconciliation
Commission in 1995 and in the year of South Africa's first democratic elections, the
novel, like its intertext, anticipates pertinent questions about absolution – justice,
truth, sincerity, redemption, reparation, vengeance and forgiveness – configured in
the novel's singular confessional mode which Watson argues is "literally freighted
with an emotion which can only be described as religious" ("Writer" 57). Watson
suggests that *The Master of Petersburg* "becomes … an involuntary confession",
the meaning of which resides in a Christian ethic ("Writer" 59). This chimes with
the real-life Dostoevsky's own preoccupation with spiritual conversion in his later
work from the 1860s onwards, *Crime and Punishment*, *The Possessed* and *The
Brothers Karamzov* (1880), which, Alexandra F. Rudicina argues, are patterned by
the "archetypal scheme of rebirth through transgression followed by suffering, or
expiation, which informs the central myth of Christianity, the Fall of Man and his
Redemption" (Rudicina 1065). *The Possessed* expresses not only Dostoevsky's
disavowal of radical and liberal politics and his distaste for Western influence
on Russia but also his profound concern for a lack of Christian morality figured
in its principle character, Stavrogin (Leatherbarrow 28). Demons symbolize this
political, moral and religious turpitude.

Demons are the impetus of Coetzee's novel, including Dostoevsky's demons
of grief for his stepson Pavel (who died in suspicious circumstances) and his guilt
at the series of betrayals he enacts – of Pavel and Matryosha and her mother. In
his attempts to reconcile himself to his stepson's death, Dostoevsky realizes it
is by consorting with the demons of a guilty conscience that his imagination is
unleashed and he is enabled to write. Possession in *The Master of Petersburg*
is betokened by Dostoevsky's epilepsy (a historical fact), the "energy" behind
Nechaev's political activism (MP 113) and sexual ecstasy (Anna almost inaudibly
whispers "devil" as she climaxes during intercourse with Dostoevsky [MP 230]).
Madness is the effect of and crucible for Dostoevsky's imaginative writing, the
idea of *The Possessed*. B. M. Engelhardt argues that, in general, the Dostoevsky
hero "becomes a 'person of the idea,' a person possessed by an idea". This idea is
all-consuming and defines yet distorts both the hero's life and consciousness, until
"The idea leads an independent life in the hero's consciousness: in fact it is not he
but the idea that lives, and the novelist describes not the life of the hero but the life
of the idea in him" (Engelhardt qtd. in Bakhtin 22). Antonio Gramsci's definition of
the interregnum, coined by Gordimer writing about the transitional zone between
regimes in South Africa, captures the historical resonance of possession here: the
interregnum is a time when "the old is dying and the new cannot be born; in this

interregnum there arises a great diversity of morbid symptoms" (qtd. in Gordimer, *Essential Gesture* 263). Political transition manifests itself physically on the body: possessed by "morbid symptoms", just as Nechaev is possessed, Dostoevsky is the embodiment of a time when, in Coetzee's words, "literary standards, like everything else, are confused" (DP 384).

Post-apartheid, the problem of self-censorship plaguing the fictional Dostoevsky continues to encumber contemporary South African writers. Whilst a form of self-censorship under apartheid – *art engagé* – was perceived by some who felt bound by the principles of "relevance and commitment" (Gordimer, *The Essential Gesture*) to be a moral obligation, South African writers today, no longer forcibly constrained and regulated by the state, have been enabled to turn their critical gaze inward to the self, to self-reflection and self-questioning (though this is not to claim that such reflection was absent in writing of the apartheid era). Regime change has made this increasingly inward turn possible, yet we should not too hastily suppose that the responsibility and accountability many writers previously felt obligated to express – forms of self-censorship – have miraculously melted away. The sheer volume of literary works that critically engage with the "new South Africa", with the failures of the neo-liberal government and the Truth and Reconciliation Commission, the housing crisis, homelessness and xenophobia as consequences of widespread immigration and the catastrophe of AIDS, are testimony to this.

That Coetzee chooses to write about the uncompromising politics of nihilist revolutionaries who live by the motto "Everything is permitted for the sake of the future" (MP 200) at a time when South Africa is preoccupied with the discourses of forgiveness and reconciliation and expectantly awaits the birth of the "new South Africa" is troubling but will not surprise those acquainted with Coetzee's typically uncompromising vision. Attridge celebrates the work for this very quality, arguing that fiction that is able to unsettle the reader is fundamental to the practice of ethical writing and reading ("Expecting" 37). In "The Post-apartheid Sublime" Graham Pechey argues that the heady days of 1994 saw South Africa entering a period of "arrested neo-colonialism" and identifies a new moment in writing also present in *The Master of Petersburg* that is morally obliged to call itself to account. Yet Rob Nixon argues that the freedoms that the end of apartheid brought about also signalled constraints, for without the crisis of apartheid to fire the imagination, what was left to fuel the writer's imagination ("Aftermaths" 64)? Pechey takes this point further when he invokes the spectre of neo-colonialism in his contention that "The danger of the post-apartheid condition is that writing will appear to be aligned with the beneficent moves of the state, seeming to have nothing to do after the end of repression" ("Post-apartheid" 62–63).

If part of the work of postcolonial studies is to call into question heretofore normalized modes of discourse and ideology (history, the Enlightenment, colonialism and so on), we can see that the failure to apply the same critical principles to postcolonialism would be remiss. In this respect Coetzee's novel is prescient; indeed, echoes of the "pitfalls of national consciousness" identified by

Fanon rebound. Smuggled into Nechaev's hideout Dostoevsky asks, what will be different once the "people's vengeance has done its work and everyone has been levelled? Will you still be free to be whom you wish? Will each of us be free to be whom we wish, at last?" (MP 184). We should not forget, however, that the man challenging the idea of revolutionary utopia, Dostoevsky, both in real-life and in this work of fiction, becomes increasingly conservative with age. Even so, Attridge and Michael Marais suggest it is not important, as some early reviewers of the novel have done, to ask with whom Coetzee might align himself politically ("Expecting the Unexpected" 31; Marais, "Places of Pigs" 84–85). The novel offers important insights into the process and hazards of regime-change which certainly spoke to the political contexts of 1990s South Africa when the book was penned. Although the politics behind the book are not only intriguing but important, its political contexts function as a catalyst for the debate about censorship, which in turn catalyzes questions about the censoring self. Reading the Coetzee oeuvre can be characterized as an exercise in reading between the lines, filling in the gaps and Coetzee apparently endorses this activity in *White Writing* (1988) when he suggests that modernism teaches us to read the "gaps, inverses, undersides; the veiled; the dark, the buried, the feminine; alterities". But even modes of reading silence can become normalized, he argues, because once familiar these kinds of silence risk "becoming dominant in turn" (WW 81).

Not unlike Mrs. Curren in *Age of Iron*, Coetzee states that he has little interest in the debate about censorship per se since it "fail[s] to rise above the level of the political in the worst sense. It remains stalled at the level of (to use a good Flaubertian word) *bêtise*, stupidity" (DP 299). Rather than explicitly engaging with the politics of censorship, Coetzee suggests that his earlier novels, *Waiting for the Barbarians* (1980) and *Life & Times of Michael K* (1983), express a more visceral, what he calls "*pathological* response … to the ban on representing what went on in police cells" in South Africa (DP 300). Nevertheless, he concedes a certain admiration for fellow writers who have faced the censor's blue pencil and candidly anticipates, even accepts, the charge of evasion that so often has been laid at his feet because, he admits, his books are too oblique and esoteric to warrant the censor's attention: "I regard it as a badge of honour", he admits, "to have had a book banned in South Africa, and even more of an honor to have been acted against punitively … This honor I have never achieved nor, to be frank, merited" (DP 298).

Coetzee identifies a genealogy of conflict between writers and authority, including conflict between writers, the state and the state censor. Writers typically attributed to themselves a social role that hinges upon moral obligation:

> Hostility between the two sides, which soon became settled and institutional, was exacerbated by the tendency of artists from the late eighteenth century onward to assume it as their social role, and sometimes indeed as their vocation and destiny, to test the limits (that is to say, the weak points) of thought and

FANON

feeling, of representation, of the law, and of opposition itself, in ways that those in power were bound to find uncomfortable and even offensive. (GO 9)

so a pro?

The idea of being impelled to adopt a social role, I am arguing, would fly in the face of Coetzee's assertion that he writes the books he "wants to write" (DP 207). Nevertheless, his fiction "tests the limits" of acceptable discourse, illustrated not only by a sustained and ghoulishly intimate representation of violence and perverted sexual desire, but also by the shifting portrayal of racial alterity, from subjection and silence in the early works to agency and political intransigence in *Age of Iron* and *The Master of Petersburg*. *Disgrace*, of course, tests the limits with its controversial portrayal of black-on-white rape. Racial alterity in the most recent novels, *Elizabeth Costello* (2003), *Slow Man* (2005) and *Diary of a Bad Year* (2007), is figured in characters who, for the most part, are psychologically robust and often outspoken.

Not only does Coetzee corroborate his critics' charge that he is politically evasive by claiming a position of "nonposition" and explaining his discomfort at being "asked to answer for … my novels" (DP 205), he goes as far as self-consciously staging this evasion in *The Master of Petersburg*. Dostoevsky, Nechaev claims, is not incapable of comprehending the idea of revolution but wishes to circumvent it: "The idea is so tremendous that you cannot understand it, you and your generation. Or rather, you understand it only too well, and want to stifle it in the cradle" (MP 189). Evasiveness is not simply bloody-mindedness on Coetzee's part: his fiction expresses the ethico-political imperative of guarding the author's right to free expression, even if, during the years of apartheid, this compromised the principles of literary commitment. That *The Master of Petersburg* is written in the waning years of the apartheid regime, if we are mindful of Fanon, the critique of the practices of revolutionary politics are all the more timely. Before this transitional moment the move to challenge the forces of opposition on the part of Coetzee, a move representing the gaze turned inward of post-apartheid writing, would have been regarded justifiably with suspicion.

The Master of Petersburg alludes to the loss of privacy engendered by apartheid that in turn was to become detrimental to the cultural sphere, where culture was perceived a "weapon of the struggle" and protest literature, according to Lewis Nkosi, was debased by "journalistic fact parading outrageously as imaginative literature" (*Home and Exile* 126). In the hide-out where Dostoevsky and Nechaev thrash out the principles of commitment, Dostoevsky is pressed to write propaganda for Nechaev's revolutionary circle. Nechaev is giving him the opportunity, he says, to "awaken the world" (MP 181). A man in the crowd, invoking debates about censorship and free expression, comes to Dostoevsky's defence: "Writers have their own rules. They can't work with people looking over their shoulders" (MP 198). Ironically, Dostoevsky will feel an other self watching over his shoulder as he struggles to conceive *The Possessed*. Nechaev wishes to channel the energy of the crowd to political ends and with this in mind would override writers' authority over their work: "A crowd isn't interested in the fine points of authorship. A crowd has no intellect, only passions" (MP 200). Professing to have no time for intellection (despite the fact that nihilism was a philosophical doctrine), Nechaev's agenda is action through political violence: "History isn't thoughts, history isn't made in people's minds. History is made in the streets" (MP 200). Recalling the intransigence of both the black revolutionaries and the state's henchmen as well as the diminution of privacy in *Age of Iron*, Nechaev's position is unrelentingly materialist, placing writing firmly in the public sphere. The people "should learn new rules. Privacy is a luxury we can do without. People don't need privacy" (DP 198). Likewise, mocking Dostoevsky about Pavel's papers, the police investigator Maximov asks: "Is a story a private matter, would you say?" (MP 39). Having lost faith in Dostoevsky as a writer of conscience, Nechaev cannot fathom how he could have crafted so convincingly a character like the radical Raskolnikov in *Crime and Punishment* (1866), whom Nechaev had taken as a standard. Tacitly acknowledging the real-life Dostoevsky's political turnabout, Nechaev recognizes the desire in Dostoevsky as an artist to create a good story, that even the desperate poverty the novelist witnesses in Nechaev's hide-out might prove to be the stuff of fiction (MP 186).

In *The Master of Petersburg* Coetzee implicitly renounces the idea of committed literature through these dialogues between Dostoevsky and Nechaev and between Dostoevsky and Maximov. Dostoevsky condemns Nechaev, "You're mad, you don't know how to read" (MP 201), in response to Nechaev's use of Raskolnikov, a character from the real-life Dostoevsky's *Crime and Punishment*, as an exemplar of nihilism on which to model his life. Yet Coetzee's Dostoevsky recognizes a certain level of justice in Nechaev that exceeds his own when the revolutionary shows outrage at Dostoevsky's "depraved parable" of the poor prostituting their children to improve their lot (MP 184).

Even so, the ambivalence of Coetzee's portrayal of nihilism leads Marais to caution that "It is misguided to conclude … that since Dostoevsky implies 'that the [nihilists] are possessed by the devil, pervaded by evil', Coetzee simply shares this conviction". Marais bases his reading on the biblical parable of the Gadarene swine appropriated by Dostoevsky in *The Possessed* and in turn by Coetzee in *The Master of Petersburg* to convey the dangers of political fervour (the story of devils exorcised by Jesus from a sick man which then possess a herd of swine that stampedes into the sea). Where in *The Possessed* the possessed man represents liberal Russia and the inhabited swine the nihilists, Marais points out that Coetzee "applies the story of the Gadarene swine not only to Russia and the phenomenon of revolutionary nihilism, but also to Dostoevsky himself and his literary response to this phenomenon" ("Places of Pigs" 84–85). The novel therefore functions on multiple layers of signification. Nevertheless, in "Dostoevsky: The Miraculous Years", suggesting that Coetzee was not as neutral as Marais allows, Coetzee launches a vilifying attack on what he understands as the failures of nihilism, which was not only a "puerile" ideology, but one that:

> barely deserved the name of a philosophical doctrine … it seemed to Dostoevsky
> not just a heretical divergence from the utopian communitarianism of the 1840s
> but a malignant mutation of it – or, to use the master metaphor of *The Devils*,
> an evil spirit – taking over the minds of a rising generation of half-educated
> Russian youth. (SS 141)

Offord and Leatherbarrow are similarly outspoken but draw quite different
conclusions, both acknowledging the vulgar characterization of nihilism in
The Possessed, and Dostoevsky's visceral reaction against both revolutionary
politics *and* Russian liberalism (Offord 87; Leatherbarrow 11). As Leatherbarrow
comments, Dostoevsky's "political grotesques" are "unarguably" exaggerated;
Dostoevsky is the "'realist in a higher sense', sacrificing verisimilitude to
mythography" (35–36). A. V. Lunacharsky observes that Dostoevsky "exposes
the contradictory nature and duality of Dostoevsky's own social personality, his
oscillations between a revolutionary materialistic socialism and a conservative
religious world view – oscillations that never led to any decisive resolution" (qtd.
in Bakhtin 34). Choosing characters of such ambivalent ideology, or, alternatively,
who have been so ambivalently received by the reading public, chimes with the
schema of Coetzee's book, the nurturing of an "esoteric reading community" (Leo
Strauss qtd. in GO 169) that can read between the lines, filling in the gaps.

The ambivalence of the narrative, taking its lead from Dostoevsky, discourages
readers from aligning their sympathies with either figure. That Coetzee admires
such a strategy is evident when he refers to Gordimer's lauding in *The Essential
Gesture* of Turgenev as, in Coetzee's words, the "exemplary realist" (DP 383);
Turgenev, Coetzee agrees, "was able to subordinate his personal political beliefs
to the demands of his art to such a degree that his readers could not tell whether
his sympathies lay with the progressive characters in his novels or with the
reactionaries" (DP 383). Although Dostoevsky and Turgenev are both able to
unsettle any easy connection their readers might make between character and
author in terms of the politics each professes, today the two authors' incompatible
politics are common knowledge, and can be read as competing narratives in
Coetzee's novel. By appropriating both Turgenev and Dostoevsky, Coetzee effects
a form of "censorship", characterized by erasure and unwriting. In this respect,
diminishing the authority of authorship, the novel captures Roland Barthes's
thesis in "Death of the Author": "We know now that a text is not a line of words
releasing a single 'theological' meaning (the 'message' of the Author-God) but
a multi-dimensional space in which a variety of writings, none of them original,
blend and clash" ("Death" 116).

A concern in the novel for the right to free expression and, conversely, with
the self-censoring limits such free expression warrants exposes an anxiety about
authorship and the authority authorship engenders. The narrative self-consciously
undermines Dostoevsky's authority as author. Just as Coetzee borrows from
Turgenev as well as Dostoevsky, by pawing over Pavel's diaries Dostoevsky
conjures a palimpsest of influences for the idea of his book that depletes his

authority as "Author-God". His guilt is not only induced by effacing the private diaries but also by transgressing the boundaries of self-censorship and using the entries to feed his plot. Dostoevsky's interrogator Maximov returns Pavel's papers to Dostoevsky with the words: "There is no reason why you should not tell yourself that I have ceased to exist, in the same way that a character in a book can be said to cease to exist as soon as the book is closed" (MP 147). Here, Maximov confusingly conflates character with his own role as censor or reader, suggesting that it is the reader who chooses whether a character will live or die in the memory. For Barthes, the reader's authority takes precedence over that of the author: "The reader is the space on which all the quotations that make up a writing are inscribed without any of them being lost; a text's unity lies not in its origin but in its destination" ("Death" 118). Coetzee's novel asks us, as critical readers, to be skeptical of the writer's authority, implied in the naming of Dostoevsky as the "*master* of Petersburg" – a title that will come to taunt Dostoevsky – but like Barthes, it also asks us to reflect upon our own accountability within the life of the work. Although the reader, like the censor, has the means to divest the author of authorial authority, the motivations for doing so certainly diverge and are therefore difficult to compare.

Like the parable, which is subversive because, as Coetzee argues, it is difficult to pin down its meaning (NT 4), Dostoevsky's fiction subversively evades because it incorporates, in Coetzee's words, "*hidden polemic* and *hidden dialogue*" (original emphasis; GO 223). According to Mikhail Bakhtin in his celebrated *Problems in Dostoevsky's Poetics* (1984), Dostoevsky assigns his characters a double consciousness *and* autonomy: they simultaneously are independent from, yet constitute, the author's voice whilst they merge with the equally significant consciousnesses of the other characters (Bakhtin 7). South African authors like Breyten Breytenbach, whose writing was blue-pencilled by the censor, have employed just such a strategy (GO 224): Coetzee argues that in the early lines of Breytenbach's poem "The Conquerors", for example, "there is a rudimentary dialogue as the words of the other ('human', 'humanity') creep in" (GO 225).[1]

---

[1]   The poem reads:
> because we would not acknowledge them as human
>   beings
> everything human in us dried up
> and we cannot grieve over our dying
>   because we wanted nothing more than fear and
>   hatred
> we did not recognize the human uprising of
>   humanity
> and tried to find rough solutions but too late
> the flowers in the fire
> no one is interested in our solutions—

Polyphonm)   Þᴛᴜᴎᴋᴜᴎᴄ

Further exploring the subterfuge of polyphony, Pechey contends that Coetzee turns to Dostoevsky because the latter:

> keeps faith with modernity's promise of freedom whilst resisting its will to totality. The polyphonic novel is a space in which cynical and ironic voices are given full weight, where heroes sound like (but are not) authors and the author sounds like (but is not) just one hero among others. ("Post-Apartheid" 70)

Polyphony is the author's covert means of masking the authorial voice, in this way signalling a renunciation of authority. Coetzee sets such a critique in process, Dominic Head argues, by constructing Dostoevsky as both "master" and "not-master" (*J. M. Coetzee* 157). Dostoevsky associates the "master" titled conferred upon him with the "master blacksmith" and the "casting of bells" but names himself a "cracked bell" for "There is a crack running through" him (MP 141).

Doubling is not only realized in the representation of censorship in *The Master of Petersburg* but is a framing device sustained throughout the narrative. The shadowy presence Dostoevsky feels watching over him as he reads through and effaces Pavel's diary is Dostoevsky's other self and the "idea" of Dostoevsky's *The Possessed*: "This presence, so grey without feature – is this what he must father, give blood to, flesh, life? … Is the thing before him … the one that does the fathering, and must he give himself to being fathered by it?" (MP 240–41). (Stavrogin in *The Possessed* is plagued by the demons of a guilty conscience for his abuse of Matryosha but simultaneously draws sadistic pleasure from the child's distress; he wishes to confess but at first feels no remorse for his actions, or for his complicity in the girl's death.) Dostoevsky is driven by his inner demons (of creativity) to efface his son's diary, whilst reviling himself for doing so; his lust for Matryosha repels yet thrills him, as his fascination for nihilism and for Nechaev does – a fascination which Nechaev reciprocates.

With morbid, necrophilic associations Dostoevsky obsessively dons Pavel's white suit and the figure in the mirror that presents itself, who is his other self, becomes a monstrous parody of his son: "looking in the mirror, he sees only a seedy imposter and, beyond that, something surreptitious and obscene" (MP 71). Boundaries between father and son, between "he" and "I", are weakened and transmute into each other. The narrative implies Dostoevsky suffers an epileptic seizure (Matryosha asks him if he is sick). Dostoevsky imagines himself falling as his son fell from the tower: "When he comes back he has again lost all sense of who he is. He knows the *I*, but as he stares at it it becomes enigmatic as a rock in the middle of the desert" (MP 71). Blocking off the memory of his grief, however,

we are past understanding
we are of another kind
we are the children of Cain (Breytenbach qtd. in GO 225; see also Breytenbach, *Buffalo Bill* 115)

he uses/misuses the white suit – Pavel's story – to seduce Matryosha in the manner of the storyteller weaving fictions.

Bakhtin extrapolates the notion of doubling in terms of voice to suggest "that out of every contradiction within a single person Dostoevsky tries to create two persons, in order to dramatize the contradiction and develop it extensively" (28). In general, the divergence between Dostoevsky and his contemporaries can be characterized, according to Bakhtin, by the former's rejection of the "monologic world of the author's consciousness … that which had been all of reality here becomes only one of the aspects of reality … what appears – metaphorically speaking – is *novelistic counterpoint*" (emphasis added; *Problems* 43). Polyphony is one means of outsmarting the censor but is also a means of refusing to conform to societal expectations or to produce tendentious literature. Polyphony allows authors to withdraw from identifying with particular characters, to conceal their own point of view behind multiple consciousnesses and ironic voices, whilst it undermines any stable or coherent meaning. Coetzee's use of allegory, which serves, in part, to mask politicized discourse, self-consciously displays these aporias: typically his novels negate the very allegorical readings they solicit, illustrated by the frequent recourse to the motifs of the labyrinth and the anagram, and in the process highlight the limitations reading allegorically entails. In the debate between Dostoevsky and Nechaev about writerly commitment, Dostoevsky acerbically points out to the nihilist leader, Nechaev, that "Stories [rather than parables] can be about other people: you are not obliged to find a place for yourself in them" (MP 184). The reader, like Coetzee's author figures, is lost in a "maze of self-doubt" (F 135).

This split consciousness, expressed through polyphony, manifests itself in the relationship between the censor and the writer: the close proximity of the censor and censored writer is experienced in the writer as inner conflict or contagion. Coetzee's essay, "Taking Offense", identifies a perverse fascination of the writer for the censor, which leads to "humiliation, self-disgust and shame", and finally to madness:

> At an individual level, the contest with the censor is all too likely to assume an importance in the inner life of the writer that at the very least diverts him from his proper occupation and at its worst fascinates and even perverts the imagination. (GO 10)

The censor-figure becomes "involuntarily incorporated into the interior, psychic life" of the writer. "In willing fantasies of this kind", Coetzee goes on, "the censor is typically experienced as a parasite, a pathological invader of the body-self, repudiated with visceral intensity but never wholly expelled" (GO 10).

The Master of Petersburg lays bare the close proximity of Dostoevsky to his interrogator/censor manifested in disease or possession. Problematically, however, Dostoevsky conflates the position of reader with censor *and* censored when he quizzes his interrogator, Maximov, about his victims:

> What is the truth: do you suffer with him, or do you secretly exult being the arm
> that swings the axe? … reading is being the arm and being the axe *and* being the
> skull [of the interrogated]; reading is giving yourself up, not holding yourself at
> a distance and jeering. (MP 47)

According to Dostoevsky, who accuses Maximov of being unable to read properly,
reading like writing requires thinking oneself into multiple subject positions. In this
way one fully engages with the work. Maximov retorts that Dostoevsky, "speak[s]
of reading as though it were demon-possession" (MP 47) and sardonically asks
Dostoevsky, who believes Maximov is out for vengeance on Nechaev rather than
justice, to "teach him how to read", to "Explain to me these ideas that are not
ideas" (MP 48). Maximov's role as interrogator-censor is to determine a definitive
(and sanctioned) text, and this Dostoevsky cannot and will not provide.

The relationship between writer and censor is traduced into the rupture of self
and other in the self-censoring writer who struggles with the apparently conflicting
demands of conscience and art, a struggle which taken to its conclusion results
in psychic collapse. Dostoevsky implicates himself in the act of censorship by
conflating these roles of censor and reader in the quotation above, and realizes that
he is not altruistically pursuing truth or performing a moral duty by altering Pavel's
diary; quite the contrary, in fact: possessed, he has abandoned himself (and Pavel) to
his fiction. Self-censorship is therefore symptomatic of both the external pressures
imposed by society – state censorship or society's expectations of its writers –
and the inner conflict of the conflicted conscience. Of course, it also signifies the
necessary, ethico-political repression on which a free society depends.

The third-person, present-tense narration which presents Dostoevsky as
focalizer suggests confession, but this device also uncannily hints that Dostoevsky
has been incorporated as a character within his own fiction. Corroborated by the
scene in which Dostoevsky senses the apparition shadowing him as he writes,
we imagine Dostoevsky the author watching over the shoulder of his fictional
alter-ego, gleaning all available experience for his next work, *The Possessed*.
Alternatively, this may of course be his censoring superego, policing his thoughts:
"The pen does not move. Intermittently the stick-figure returns, the crumpled, old-
man travesty of himself. He is blocked, he is in prison" (MP 237).

Breytenbach's autobiographical *The True Confessions of an Albino Terrorist*
(1984) anticipates this demon-apparition, though in Breytenbach it is the censor
monitoring the output of writing: "A bizarre situation … when you write knowing
that the enemy is reading over your shoulder" (*Confessions* 159). The censor of
Breytenbach's prison-writings metamorphoses into the censoring self, which in
turn in Coetzee is manifested in Dostoevsky's guilty conscience. Breytenbach
experiences this as complicity. Unravelling the motif of the mirror/page in
Breytenbach's writing in which Breytenbach collapses the prison interrogator with
the censor or interrogator within as the "dark mirror-brother" (*True Confessions*
260), Coetzee observes the surfaces of the mirror and the blank page converge.
Just as censors call upon the censored to redouble their efforts to produce and

reproduce the required confession, so writers embody a "counter-self" which mocks the efforts of self-expression (GO 227). Indeed, Coetzee suggests, "the posture of the writer before the mirror/page is assimilated with the attitude of the co-operative prisoner under interrogation" (GO 228) and the interrogator becomes, in the context of writing, both the self-censor and the "self that writes itself" (GO 228), or, in *The Master of Petersburg*, the ghostly figure watching over Dostoevsky as he pens *The Possessed*.

Until Breytenbach turns his attention to his "black mirror-brother", Coetzee warns, however, all that is offered is "another ingenious poststructuralist figure of textual self-production" (GO 228). Put another way, metafiction is insubstantial if it fails to be grounded in the ethical. Coetzee's confessional mode in *The Master of Petersburg*, which is internalized and self-denunciatory, as Pechey explains, illustrates that the author "clearly regards the novel's scepticism-to-the-second-power as a valuable resource, not to be turned to partisan ends but equally not to be mistaken for non-engagement" ("Post-Apartheid" 70; 66). Theodor Adorno's definition of commitment is apposite given that the committed text would prioritize an estranging form that encourages the reader's critical engagement over tendentiousness or the projection of the author's own philosophical ideas that limits the text's ethico-political potential ("Commitment" 78-79).

The representation of Dostoevsky's psychic conflict, expressed in the polyphonous voices he himself embodies, raises questions about complicity and accountability because this black "mirror-brother" is "not Other but other/self, 'brother/I'" (GO 228). Coetzee identifies a process of confrontation and self-accusation reminiscent of the patterning of unresolved confession. Here, he is referring to Breytenbach's *End Papers* (1986) and wonders whether this relationship can ever be productive. That which Coetzee in a different context calls "warring twins" (GO 91), the white policeman and the black revolutionary, are:

> enemies brought together in the mirror. Is the mirror the place, then, where history is transcended? … Can dialogue with the mirror be trusted to proceed peaceably, or will it degenerate into hysterical confrontation … hysterical self-accusation, a spiralling descent into "the bottomless pit of deprecation and disgust"? (GO 229; Breytenbach, *End Papers* 33–34)

Breytenbach describes the passing of the self through a labyrinth: "it is a continuation of the looking for the Minotaur, that dark centre which is the I (eye), that Mister I" (mystery) (qtd. in GO 229; see also Breytenbach, *Confessions* 87). In Breytenbach's *Mouroir* (1983), which incorporates the spectre of impossible endings, the surface of mirror and page, Coetzee argues, are impassable and the search for the labyrinth's core thwarted: "Instead, a new surface recurs at every turn, leading into yet another corridor of the labyrinth… . Text becomes coextensive with life: text will not end till writing ends; writing will not end till breath ends" (GO 229–30). The pressures bearing down upon the writer which result in self-censorship in both its conscious and unconscious forms are configured in a dialogue between the writer's moral and artistic selves. Indeed, typically in Coetzee, writers' uncertainty about their artistic worth leads and in turn becomes ineluctably anchored to an uncertainty about their ethico-political integrity (the brutalizing Jacobus Coetzee in *Dusklands* [1974] being the obvious exception).

In *The Master of Petersburg* the tormented Dostoevsky finds himself lost in a literal labyrinth when he is taken to meet Nechaev (MP 105), whilst at the denouement, as Dostoevsky struggles to reconcile himself to his position as author, he recognizes that he "is in the old labyrinth". Not dissimilar to Mrs. Curren in *Age of Iron*, he is locked in a dangerous wager with God, at stake his art and his moral integrity: "It is the story of his gambling in another guise. He gambles because God does not speak. He gambles to make God speak. But to make God speak in the turn of a card is blasphemy" (MP 237). Thus Dostoevsky enters the bowels of writerly practice when he is taken to Nechaev's hideout. This place is a metaphor for the labyrinth of both censorship and confession – because here, as with Pavel's diaries and Dostoevsky's corruption of Matryosha, he will find inspiration for his book – and which in apartheid South Africa connotes the experience of writing under the strong-arm of apartheid law. A young man reading a newspaper, cryptically referred to as "the reader" and speaking French, the language associated with the Westernization which the real-life Dostoevsky so detested, mockingly offers the disorientated Dostoevsky directions out of the maze: "*Tout droit, tout droit!*" (MP 105) (straight ahead, straight ahead). In the eyes of these men who, in keeping with the generational conflict in the real-life Dostoevsky's Russia, are distinguished by their youth, Dostoevsky's loss of bearing denotes his loss of moral and political direction. The unnamed reader, representing the generic reader, is pushing the writer in a certain ideological direction.

Bakhtin analyzes the suppressed "At Tihon" chapter in *The Possessed* in terms of the other; what emerges in Stavrogin's confession, he argues, is Stavrogin's split consciousness, self/other. Importantly, not unlike the model of interrogator/ interrogated outlined above, the confessor-priest Tihon is drawn into this conflictual consciousness:

> Stavrogin's dialogue with Tihon is a maximally pure model of the confessional dialogue. The entire orientation of Stavrogin in this dialogue is determined by his dual attitude toward the "other person": by the impossibility of managing without his judgement and forgiveness, and at the same time by a hostility toward him and resistance to his judgement and forgiveness … It is as if two persons were speaking with Tihon, merged interruptedly into one. Tihon is confronted with two voices, into whose internal struggle he is drawn as a participant. (Bakhtin 262)

Stavrogin is able both to assimilate and to resist the "other person's" oppositional consciousnesses. Head links this "censor/writer confrontation" to a transitional moment in Coetzee's writing: not only does it constitute an important stage in the decolonizing process when the colonized subject recognizes the porousness of the boundaries that separate colonizer from colonized, more troublingly this recognition may result in "a disabling self-accusation" (*J. M. Coetzee* 149) which in certain contexts, I would interpose, should be read more positively as the necessary task of autocritique.

Dostoevsky realizes that it is to the other that he must turn as the path to absolution and redemption for his transgressions. The other, a "least thing", is signified, as in *Disgrace* and *Age of Iron* respectively, by a dog or a drunken beggar (MP 82). A decrepit dog or the unlovable "beggar", who is in fact a cleverly disguised police spy, will help Dostoevsky, he initially believes, to resolve his feelings about his stepson's death and about the betrayal, committed in the name of writing, that he feels he has enacted of Pavel's memory. He chances upon the animal chained to a drainpipe and senses its overwhelming terror akin, he imagines, to that his son must have experienced as he fell from the tower: "Pavel will not be saved till he has freed the dog and brought it into his bed, brought *the least thing*" (original emphasis; MP 82). In a last self-conscious twist, plunging into the realms of meta-textuality, Dostoevsky recognizes the pitfalls of self-revelation:

> He is waiting for a sign, and he is betting (there is no grander word he dare use) that the dog is not the sign, is not a sign at all, is just a dog among many dogs howling in the night. But he knows too that as long as he tries by cunning to distinguish things that are things from things that are signs he will not be saved. (MP 83)

Acknowledging the fallibility of identifying the other (the dog) with spiritual release and in the process testing his spiritual conviction – *The Possessed*, you will remember, is in part an expression of Dostoevsky's reawakened religiosity – Coetzee's Dostoevsky enters the world of signs (like that lyrically inhabited by Friday at the end of *Foe*) and tries to make sense of, to "read", his experiences. That the dog of Vladimir's poem in Samuel Beckett's *Waiting for Godot* (1952) is read as an inversion of "god" and thus an affirmation of the apocalyptic, absurdist nature of the play, makes Coetzee's nod towards Beckett all the more apt (apartheid is frequently associated with the absurd). Dostoevsky elides the otherness of dogs and beggars with that of Nechaev who, amongst others, he suspects is the apparition watching over his shoulder. It dawns on him that to bring the grieving process to an end he must accept his son's alliance and friendship with Nechaev; indeed, he must learn to love Nechaev, whom he regards as an "imitator; a pretender; a blasphemer" (MP 103), as he would his son. In part, this is about relinquishing his (fatherly and authorial) authority: "As Nechaev hates the fathers and makes implacable war on them, so must Pavel be allowed to follow him?", he wonders (MP 239).

Responding to a period of seismic transition in South Africa, *The Master of Petersburg* is a novel about the writer taking stock: censorship is no longer an immediate threat yet writers continue to be exercised by external pressures, as well as by their own demons of conscience. The cusp of regime change in contexts as extreme as apartheid is not the moment for writers to forget the task of testing the limits of acceptable discourse lest the consequences of neo-colonialism run their course. The heads of the new governments, Fanon warns, "are the true traitors in Africa, for they sell their country to the most terrifying of all its enemies: stupidity" (*Wretched* 148). In Coetzee's first novel published post-apartheid, Dostoevsky guards the sanctity of "art for art's sake", for he not only advocates the release of writers from social obligations to society, but also that readers should not be confined to their own limiting experiences. Signalling a new phase in South African writing, this is not a position the novel fully endorses, but rather, by nurturing the "esoteric reading community" that can read between the lines, it insists our engagement with texts should remain critical, attentive all the while to the fallibility of "correct" readings.

In *Doubling the Point* Coetzee likens the activity of criticism to the "act of triumphantly tearing the clothes off its subject and displaying the nakedness beneath – 'Behold the truth!'" In this, he argues, criticism "exposes a naïveté of its own" (DP 106). He warns of criticism becoming "lazy (and every orthodoxy grows lazy)", that in its role of demystification criticism "privileges mystifications" (DP 106). Criticism implies constraint, he suggests, for, whereas "The *feel* of writing fiction is one of freedom, of irresponsibility, or better, of responsibility toward something that has not yet emerged", criticism implies a responsibility towards an imagined goal (DP 246). Nurturing a deeper critical practice, *The Master of Petersburg* alerts the reader to the problems of the author's authority, encouraging a suspicion of authorial attempts to "master" the text. Yet the novel also cautions that this activity should be self-reflexive: as Jameson argues, every commentary should also be a metacommentary.

Chapter 8
Truth and Reconciliation in *Disgrace*[1]

Lizalise Idinga Lakho
                    "The forgiveness of sins makes a person whole" (Xhosa hymn)[2]

J. M. Coetzee returns to a South African setting in his second Booker Prize-winning novel *Disgrace* (1999) which, through the "trial" of its protagonist Professor David Lurie for his affair with one of his female students and his subsequent crisis of authority, tacitly calls into question the processes of the much maligned Truth and Reconciliation Commission (TRC) within the context of a nation in transition. The novel asks, what kind of truths can be legitimately told in public? Brought before a disciplinary committee at the university at which he is employed, Lurie is required to confess his guilt for his affair with Melanie, who, by South African designation is "coloured", the text implies, since Lurie inwardly renames her "Meláni", or "dark one" (DIS 18). This renaming, though unspoken, establishes a historical loop whereby the past is brought to bear on the present by alluding to the obsessive categorization of "race" under apartheid that lamentably continues to structure South African society today. The yoking of past and present in the narrative not only calls to mind the 1949 Prohibition of Mixed Marriages Act and the 1950 Immorality Act through Lurie's affair, for instance, but also the question of land distribution through the ownership of Lurie's daughter Lucy's smallholding and Lucy's perception of her rape by the three men as reparations. These historical resonances point to much larger questions than Lurie's tawdry affair, questions of accountability, responsibility and dispossession in the post-apartheid state. Thus the "trial" scene functions, firstly, as a catalyst that sets in motion a process of self-reflection and self-abnegation on Lurie's part, who rejects confession in the public sphere yet nevertheless unconsciously strives for self-forgiveness in the private, and, secondly, by analogy, as a vehicle to call into question the politicization by the TRC of the discourses of truth-telling, reparations and reconciliation in the public-national domain. *Disgrace* joins the genre of "TRC narratives" that has proliferated in recent years in South Africa that, in general, call into question the viability of the TRC: Nadine Gordimer's *The House Gun* (1998), Achmat Dangor's *Bitter Fruit* (2001) and Ndebele

---

[1]   An early version of this Chapter appeared in *Scrutiny2* 5.2 (2000).
[2]   Quoted by Commissioner Bongani Finca, this hymn opened the first Truth Commission hearing. Antjie Krog, in *Country of My Skull* (1998), suggests that the sentiment it expresses demonstrates that ideas of reconciliation, or redemption, are not confined to Christian culture (*Country* 17; 26).

Njabulo's *The Cry of Winnie Mandela* (2003) are just a few examples. Typically, such narratives point up a key flaw of the processes of the TRC: that discourses of truth and reconciliation are premised upon a Christianized, private ethics of confession and are therefore inequitable in the public sphere of the TRC.

A major problem facing the "new South Africa" following the demise of apartheid has been how blacks and whites (of the old regime) can now live peaceably together. The objective of the TRC, which was inaugurated in 1995 and covered the period 1 May 1960 to 10 May 1994, was national unity through reconciliation with, rather than recrimination of, the former oppressor. This was to be achieved through truth-telling, reparations and amnesty, by alleviating the victim of the burden of memory, making financial recompense and bringing the abuses of perpetrators to light. (The reparations operation of the TRC was, as Tutu conceded, found wanting because it failed to pay out anywhere near the sum to victims originally mooted ["Foreword", *TRC* 6:1].) In the context of the TRC, we should ask, firstly, how do truth-telling and amnesty impinge upon justice? And, secondly, from this, how do we measure truth?

Most commentators have noted that the TRC uncovered truth at the cost of justice (resources such as land, for instance, have not been redistributed under the new constitution), leading Mahmood Mamdani to conclude that the TRC was "born of political compromise" (Truth and Reconciliation Commission, "Transforming Society" n. pag.). Mamdani points out that under the TRC's auspices, "Reconciliation is a code word for a diminished truth" ("Truth" 182) – because at least one party in the contract of reconciliation will always be compromised. Yet compromise should always be regarded as transitory, he contends, enabling progression through an impasse. When in *Disgrace* Lurie tells his daughter Lucy, "I was offered a compromise, which I wouldn't accept", she counsels him that compromise has its place: "You shouldn't be so unbending, David. It isn't heroic to be unbending. Is there time to reconsider?" (DIS 66).

Mamdani asks, "what kind of truth did the TRC produce"? Truth, he suggests, can be thought of in two ways, individual and institutional. Individual truth, originating from the Old Testament, sets truth against power and is the opposite of lies. Institutional truth, theorized by critics of the Enlightenment from Marx onwards, produces partial, ideological truths which protect the interests of the institution. Mamdani argues that the truth of the TRC should be understood as institutional,

> as the outcome of a process of truth-seeking, one whose boundaries were so
> narrowly defined by power and whose search was so committed to reinforcing
> the new power, that it turned the political boundaries of a compromise into
> analytical boundaries of truth-seeking. By reinforcing a political compromise
> with a compromised truth ... the TRC has turned a political into a moral
> compromise and obscured the larger truth.

Whilst political compromise may be necessary to facilitate change, moral (individual, intellectual) compromise is not and may, indeed, undermine the political compromise that it was intended to support (Mamdani, "Truth" 177–78). In her autobiographical account of the TRC hearings, *Country of My Skull* (1998), the poet and journalist Antjie Krog recognizes the problem of reconciling truth and justice at the hearings: "If [the Commission's] interest in truth is linked only to amnesty and compensation, then it will have chosen not truth, but justice". In order to be inclusive, she claims, the TRC was right to give precedence to truth over justice: "If [the Commission] sees truth as the widest possible compilation of people's perceptions, stories, myths and experiences, it will have chosen to restore memory and foster a new humanity, and perhaps that is justice in its deepest sense" (Krog 16). However, truths such as this obscure what Mamdani calls the "banal reality" – itself a kind of truth – of apartheid that wasn't accounted for at the hearings ("Transforming Society" n. pag.).

The fact that the TRC, chaired by Tutu, was founded upon what some have called a Christian ethics has led many of its critics to point up the debasement in the process of the transposition to the public sphere of the hearings of the kinds of truth-telling, forgiveness and reconciliation usually reserved for the private sphere and derived from religious confession. Benita Parry, for instance, comments upon the "atmosphere of euphoric Christian revivalism" that tainted the hearings (*Postcolonial Studies* 188), whilst Jacques Derrida suggests that, "when Desmond Tutu was named president of the Truth and Reconciliation Commission, he Christianized the language uniquely destined to treat 'politically' motivated crimes (an enormous problem …)" ("On Forgiveness" 42). Derrida demarcates the realms of judgement, falling within the remit of the state and the public sphere, and forgiveness, which only the individual can grant ("On Forgiveness" 44). In the ethical economy of forgiveness the state "has neither the right nor the power" to forgive, Derrida claims, because "forgiveness has nothing to do with judgement", which *does* fall within the state's remit ("On Forgiveness" 43). Anthony Holiday, who picks up these anxieties about the religious inflections of the TRC's constitution, is troubled by the inadequacies of the conceptual categories of justice and truth at the hearings, arguing that "the conception of *justice* that informed the TRC's proceedings could scarcely be called 'Christian'" (emphasis added). The religious conception of forgiveness, he argues, is concerned with an "inner moral life" which cannot, by its very nature, be regulated by public bodies: "forgiveness, by reason of its conceptual dependence on remorse, must be an intensely personal, even a private matter" ("Forgiving" 55–56).

Nevertheless, the same critics of the TRC have tended to agree on what it *did* achieve, even if in a limited fashion. Mamdani suggests that the TRC's only real power has been to instigate debate ("Transforming Society" n. pag.) and Neville Alexander grants that indirectly it catalyzed "raising historical consciousness" through public debate about the past (qtd. in Parry, *Postcolonial* 189; see also Alexander, *Ordinary* 127). In a more celebratory tone, Ndebele welcomes the restorative function of the submissions to the TRC to suggest, "it is [the] reflective capacity, experienced as a shared social consciousness, that will be that lasting legacy of the stories of the TRC" ("Memory, Metaphor" 20).

Disgrace traces Lurie's faltering steps towards reconciliation not only with those directly touched by his actions but also with himself and with his own sense of place – recently, he has found himself *out of place* – in South African history and the "new South Africa". In the new Department of Communications he feels "more out of place than ever" (DIS 4) and on escaping to Lucy's farm thinks, "This is not what he came for – to be stuck in the back of beyond ... If he came for anything, it was to gather himself, gather his forces. Here he is losing himself day by day" (DIS 121). Rather than satisfy the Disciplinary Committee's requirement that his apology be made sincerely, Lurie departs the city for the sanctuary of his daughter's farm. The farm is burgled and Lucy is raped by the three black men, an event which forces Lurie to reassess his own relationship with women. Nonetheless, at the outset he is even "outraged at being treated like an outsider" – because he is a man – in the story of Lucy's rape (DIS 141). Even though, as Derek Attridge contends, "there is little to suggest ... that [Lurie] is *consciously* and *deliberately* embarking on a complete reinvention of his way of living" (emphasis added; "Age of Bronze" 103), some kind of reinvention occurs nevertheless.

Lurie holds the position of Adjunct Professor of Communications at a third-rate university, Cape Technical University, formerly Cape Town University College, his former department having been disbanded "as part of the great rationalization" programme and evidence of the continuing global devaluation of the Arts. Attridge goes as far as arguing that the loss of privacy felt by Lurie when he is required to confess to the committee is not merely a mapping of the transitional period within South Africa, post-apartheid, but looks beyond, to the global economy and the increasing influence of the United States ("Age of Bronze" 102–03). Attridge contends that "This narrative ... is not an attack on the new nation that emerged from the elections of 1994 and expresses no yearnings for the system of apartheid. Rather it portrays with immense distaste a new global age" ("Age of Bronze" 105). However, whilst *Disgrace* does look beyond its local contexts, it remains deeply rooted in local concerns, most strikingly the problems of the TRC that are parodied through the self-conscious staging of Lurie's trial as global spectacle, as Lurie says, "a TV show, in fact" (DIS 66). It also raises the land question and the question of rape. Moreover, it would be wrong to suggest that a critique of the new nation necessarily implies nostalgia for the old. As Frantz Fanon has warned, though we deplore the egregious abuses of the old regime, we should not ignore the pitfalls of the new.

To untangle the problem of truth-telling in the public sphere, we must first consider what truth means in the private and Coetzee's essay "Confession and Double Thoughts" (1985) provides a fitting starting point. In this essay Coetzee reads the confessional writing of Tolstoy, Rousseau and Dostoevsky to reveal the ways in which truth in the private sphere can be compromised. Secular confession, Coetzee argues, is characterized by the desire to "tell an essential truth about the self" (DP 252). Here Coetzee apologizes for a certain slippage between secular and religious confession: the first is directed towards an auditor or audience and the second to a confessor who holds the authority to grant absolution (DP 253). Coetzee also confines his discussion to voluntary confession and not to violent forms elicited through coercion, like those favoured by Colonel Joll in *Waiting for the Barbarians* (1980), who takes sadistic pleasure in extracting confessions through torture, claiming he is able to recognize the "tone of truth" which is only possible in a "special situation": "First I get lies, you see – this is what happens – first lies, then pressure, then more lies, then more pressure, then the break, then more pressure, then the truth. That is how you get the truth" (WB 5). Nevertheless, voluntary confessions also can be unreliable because understanding the truth about the self is problematized by questions of deception, self-deception and the problem of closure: how to end the cycle of self-analysis and self-doubt into which the confessant is liable to fall.

Reading Tolstoy, Coetzee identifies three elements of truth in the protagonist's confession: firstly, the facts of the event under scrutiny, secondly, the discovery of the truth about the self attained through confessing, and thirdly, what Coetzee calls the "unconscious" truth which "slips out in strange associations, false rationalisations, gaps, contradictions". Unconscious truths, in part, account for ironic confessions, where confessants believe they are confessing to one thing, but are in fact confessing to something entirely different (DP 257), yet in spite of which, these kinds of truth are likely to be the most reliable.

The experience of conversion, where the confessant sees the light, conventionally distinguishes between "true" and "false" selves, "the false self being rational and socially conditioned", writes Coetzee, "the true self instinctual and individual". The true/false binary can be mapped on to the private/public one, though in line with Coetzee "false" does not necessarily mean morally wrong. Rather, publicity requires maintaining face which is clearly a distortion of the "true" self. Coetzee argues that Tolstoy's writing, which calls into question the very idea of truth, moves beyond this polarization of "true" and "false" selves (DP 261). For Tolstoy, as in the case of Lurie, the confessant is *unconsciously* driven towards the truth, which Tolstoy conceives as "truth-directedness" or an "impulse toward God" (DP 261). The confessant undergoes a life-changing crisis, "a confrontation with his own death", according him a self-knowledge "that makes it absurd for him to continue in a self-deceived mode of existence" (DP 262). In *Disgrace* Lurie plumbs the depths of such a crisis in the aftermath of his affair with Melanie. In general, it is the experience of the urgency of this crisis, the unstoppable process to which confessants are subjected, their false selves laid bare, and the dogged questing for truth, which, in sum, constitute sincerity (DP 262).

At the disciplinary hearing Lurie is expected to express remorse as Farodia Rassool, sitting on the Disciplinary Committee, explains, "The statement should come from [Lurie], in his own words. Then we can see if it comes from his heart" (DIS 54). Applied to the TRC hearings, the question of sincerity in confession, particularly in relation to those applying for amnesty, is a particularly thorny one and on a political level is untenable. (Although the TRC never required those applying for amnesty to make public apologies, its Chairperson, the Reverend Tutu, at times did.) Questions of sincerity such as those expressed here have been realized in their most abstract form at the hearings in amnesty applications expressing guilt for failure to join the struggle. The problem of sincerity is isolated in the trial scene in its allusion to the misplaced religiosity of the public hearings. Lurie realizes that what is demanded of him is an apology "in the spirit of repentance" which, he believes, "belongs to … another universe of discourse" (DIS 55; 58). His refusal to validate the University's version of the truth calls into question the efficacy of confession in the public sphere (without offering any easy solutions): he is prepared to admit regret but refuses in doing so to confirm his sincerity which is "beyond the scope of the law" (DIS 55).

Writing about Rousseau's confession of the ribbon story in *Confessions*,[3] Paul de Man argues that authentic truths are only apparent when the confessant, in Coetzee's words, "lapses into the language of the Other". Such language is marked by an uncharacteristic style: "Rousseau is not speaking (for) himself; someone else is speaking through him" (DP 269). It is only through unconscious self-revelation that "deeper" truths are exposed. Rousseau's "language of the Other" is key to my understanding of Lurie's "epiphany", which I turn to below, in which processes of identification with and sympathy for the other are at work (cf. Attridge, *J. M. Coetzee* 183–85; Holland 403).

Whilst Lurie may simply be nursing his wounded pride, the larger, historical implications of the "trial" and his refusal to confess (ostensibly because he recognizes the weak points of the Committee's procedures) should not be overlooked. Inviting comparisons with the fetishized nature of reconciliation and forgiveness, both locally and in the "West", he explains to Lucy, "They wanted a spectacle" (DIS 66). Nonetheless Lurie laments the emerging prurience that has beset the "new South Africa" where "Private life is public business" (DIS 66). The novel suggests the loss of the private in the apartheid era is replaced by privacy that is made public, post-apartheid. Attridge is reminded of the Clinton-Lewinsky affair which revealed a paradox of societal attitudes towards sexuality: where sexuality is brought into the public sphere, as a matter for public dissection, according to Attridge, this generates "an increase in puritanical surveillance and moralistic denunciation" ("Age of Bronze" 102).

Lurie is introduced as a "disgraced disciple" of Wordsworth (DIS 46) who now, nearing the end of his unremarkable career, has immersed himself in the life and work of the sensualist Byron, "celebrant", according to Laura Claridge, "of the material world" (216). Wordsworth, on the other hand, Richard Bourke claims, "never overtly prescribed a 'decadent' Romantic aestheticism in his prose writings" (40); in *Poems in Two Volumes* (1807) Wordsworth declares that his

---

[3]   The story, according to Coetzee, which appears in both *Confessions* and *Rêveries*, tells how, employed as a manservant, Rousseau is found in the possession of a ribbon he has stolen. He blames a maidservant for the theft, making the accusation in her presence. The incident apparently troubles Rousseau for many years (DP 265).

[handwritten: INTERTEXTS]

[handwritten top: PTLO   PECHEY]

[handwritten: So: narrative as vehicle for normative morality]

poetry sets out "to teach the young and the gracious of any age [to become] more actively and securely virtuous" (qtd. in Bourke 41). Lurie is struggling to write his opera *Byron in Italy*, which tells the story of Byron fleeing to Italy to avoid "a scandal" (his incestuous relationship with his half-sister Augusta) and of his "last big love-affair", with Contessa Teresa Guiccioli (DIS 15). It is not insignificant that Lurie is presented as a mediocre academic and artist – *Byron in Italy*, he concedes, was "misconceived" (DIS 181) – whose experience of writer's block coincides with anxieties about his waning sexuality. The "conception" of the opera – derivatives of "to conceive" appear four times on the two pages describing Lurie's attempts to overcome this blockage – is set against the literal conception of Lucy's child in the text, who, as a child of rape, offers a bleak prediction of South Africa's future (DIS 180–81).

In broad terms, the Romantic tradition is characterized by a "crisis of authority" (Bourke 47), a crisis which in *Disgrace* is ironically inflected under the tenets of postcolonialism by the Romantics' apparent elitism, bestowed posthumously, as archetypes of the "Western" canon. Yet Romanticism speaks to Lurie's predicament as a disaffected and dislocated white writer in other ways too, as Graham Pechey points out:

> South Africa's British colonization coincides with a movement in the home country of counter-Enlightenment, which harnesses poetry as the vehicle of struggle against a reason seen as oppressive … Lurie's identification with [the Romantics] develops into a sharing of their fate, an exile that in his case is internal. ("Purgatorial Africa" 380) *[handwritten: interesting]*

Even so, this identification will be tested during the course of the narrative. Lurie has written three poorly received books, including *Wordsworth and the Burden of the Past*, which constitutes an ironic, titular reference to Lurie's own struggle for selfhood in the nascent state. As Pieter Vermeulen points out (182), there is a need both in Wordsworth's *The Prelude* and for Lurie as undistinguished tutor of the Romantics, to harmonize the imagination and what Lurie calls "the onslaughts of reality" (DIS 22).[4] Suggestive of a liberal consciousness that always until now has managed to keep the reality of apartheid at bay, Lurie's burden of guilt also expresses the guilt experienced by white liberals for their albeit unwilling complicity in South Africa's past. Vermeulen glosses an early scene in *Disgrace* in which Lurie ventures to enthuse his indifferent students in Wordsworth's "failed encounter with Mont Blanc in *Book 6* of *The Prelude*" (Vermeulen 182). Yet the two passages Lurie reads from which he intends to show how the imagination and reality might "coexist" (DIS 22), Vermeulen argues, "do not happen to add up to a harmonious situation", a point that, as Vermeulen notes (182–83), Lurie himself realizes: "The [second] passage is difficult, perhaps it even contradicts the Mont Blanc moment".

---

4   For further discussion of the Romantic intertexts in *Disgrace* see Easton, "Coetzee's *Disgrace*" and Marais, "J. M. Coetzee's *Disgrace*".

Lurie believes that, "Nevertheless, Wordsworth seems to be feeling his way toward a balance" (DIS 22). Mike Marais confirms this contradiction when he argues that an "ambiguity" resides at the "heart of Romanticism", "the fact that its aesthetic confidence is accompanied by a sense of inevitable failure" brought about by an anxiety in Romantic nature poetry about authentic imitation rather than empty copy ("Task" 85–86).[5] This failure of the imagination is evident in Lurie in his failure to resolve the needs of his art with his place in the "new South Africa". Yet like Wordsworth he "feels his way" towards a synthesis of the two.

Lurie reimagines his Byron text – the original concept for the opera failed because it did not "come from the heart" (DIS 181) – whilst revising his reading of the landscape (Lucy's homestead) within a Wordsworthian schema, which reworks the pastoral as an expression of the imagination. In *White Writing* (1988) Coetzee has located what he calls the "Wordsworthian question": "In what ways have I been moulded by the landscape in which I have lived?" (WW 171). Early European travellers in South Africa, who were able only to conceptualize the African landscape through a European lens, typically inverted this problem (WW 39). Failing to make the lesson on Wordsworth relevant to his students, of whom he despairs, Lurie locates just such a moment but, he implies, this can only be understood by turning "toward the great archetypes of the imagination we carry within us" (DIS 23). Whilst on first sight Lurie describes Lucy's farm as "poor land, poor soil … Exhausted. Good only for goats" (DIS 64), he subsequently reassesses this desolate vision to conjure a pastoral idyll. He catches sight of his daughter:

> at the centre of the picture a young woman, *das ewig Weibliche*,[6] lightly pregnant, in a straw sunhat. A scene ready-made for a Sargent or a Bonnard. City boys like him; but even city boys can recognize beauty when they see it, can have their breath taken away. (DIS 218)

Lurie's reaffirmation of a Wordsworthian ethic in the economy of confession sketched here chimes with Bourke's claim that Wordsworth is a figure who "poetically assuages, reconciles and redeems" (41), or Stephen Prickett's suggestion that Wordsworth practised the "healing art" (qtd. in Bourke 42). Lurie, who makes a symbolic return to the land as Lucy has before him, has become reconciled to the beauty of the ordinary.

Lucy is the very antithesis of Lurie's ideal woman. She resembles her father's mental picture of Byron's middle-aged Teresa: plain, dumpy and, what is more, to Lurie's chagrin she is gay. Whilst Lurie, like Byron, perceives himself to be the rakish "man of the city" (DIS 6), Lucy embraces the pastoral. Yet she rejects

---

[5]   Marais draws upon Tilottama Rajan's *Dark Interpreter: The Discourse of Romanticism* (1980) in making his argument.

[6]   "*Das ewig Weibliche*", meaning "the eternal feminine", are the opening words to the final line in Goethe's *Faust*.

the mastering of the land that is the primal stuff of the Afrikaner *plaasroman* or "farm novel" by refusing to call the homestead a farm: "it's just a piece of land where I grow things", she says (DIS 200). The dialectic between metropolis and rural in *Disgrace*, that also patterns the Byron/Wordsworth narrative, inverts the *plaasroman* which, Coetzee writes in *White Writing*, "harks back … to a lost ideal economic independence, to the idea of the farm as a 'koninkrykie' (little kingdom), where a man can be his own master" (WW 175). Between 1920 and 1940 the plaasroman "almost exclusively" concerned itself with the Afrikaner's "painful transition from farmer to townsman … [with] a renewal of the peasant order based on the myth of the return to the earth" (WW 63–79). The anti-pastoral, on the other hand, dominated by "English" South Africans, writes against this tradition. Humankind and nature no longer exist in harmony: the land is barren and hostile, the farming community its adversary. Stephen Gray, in his study of Southern African literature, argues that

> Landscape, in South African realist fiction, never merely sustains and magnifies man; it dwarfs and overwhelms, it remains unyielding and destructive. … worst of all [the land] disallows them from achieving man's most sacred desire, the desire to take root in the land and belong. … its characters do not – cannot – belong. (*Southern African Literature* 150–51)

Gray is referring specifically to the liberal Anglophone tradition of the antipastoral which "goes hand in hand with realism" and which is perhaps best illustrated by Olive Schreiner's *The Story of an African Farm* (1883) (Gray 136).

Lurie wavers between disdain and admiration (DIS 217) as he notices that Lucy is becoming a peasant, a "throwback", a *boervrou* (DIS 61; 60). He perceives historical continuity in his daughter's synthesis of nature and land that was lacking in her parents: "perhaps it was not [her parents] who produced her: perhaps history had the larger share … Perhaps history had learned a lesson" (DIS 61–62). Lurie reflects, "She talks easily about these matters. A frontier farmer of the new breed. In the old days, cattle and maize. Today, dogs and daffodils. The more things change the more they remain the same" (DIS 61).

James Graham, writing about the farm novel of Rhodesia/Zimbabwe, argues that stringent legislation of racial difference was used by the government of Rhodesia to support and maintain a specifically *Rhodesian* identity, rather than one that was simply "European" or British. This in turn demanded "a fastidious regime of self-discipline [in which a] supposedly inviolable boundary was drawn between the farmhouse and the surrounding land" (Graham, "Abject Land" n. pag.).[7] This all led to "a gendered as well as racialized spatial opposition". In other words, white Rhodesian women were figured differently in this relation from

---

[7]   This paper has now been published in *English Studies in Africa* as "An Abject Land? Remembering Women Differently in Doris Lessing's *The Grass is Singing* and Chenjerai Hove's *Bones*'."

white Rhodesian men: "As master of his African farm the white farmer could cross this boundary at will, but as the vulnerable custodian of racial purity, middle-class manners, Englishness and, encompassing all of these, domesticity, his wife could not" (Graham, "Abject Land" n. pag.). The white woman in the Southern African farm novel, overburdened with symbolism, is upheld as the guardian of white national identity, including the "purity" of the race. This explains why Lucy and her father, in a context of black dispossession from the land, come to perceive her as a commodity in the patriarchal system of exchange.

The dissipation of white ownership in the novel converges in the rape of Lucy by the black men who raid her home, and whom Lurie caustically names the holy trinity, "three fathers in one" (DIS 199). Expressing notions of what has become known in South Africa simply as white guilt, Lurie rationalizes the attack as symbolic reparation for a history of oppression: for Lurie, the rape signifies "the day of testing", Judgement Day (DIS 94); it

> was history speaking through them … A history of wrong … It may have seemed personal, but it wasn't. It came down from the ancestors … Booty, war reparations; another incident in the great campaign of redistribution. (DIS 156; 176)

When Lurie confronts Pollux, child-rapist and relative of Petrus, he imagines that the boy's challenging demeanour demands, *"By what right are you here?"* (original emphasis; DIS 132), a sentiment that questions the presence of whites in the post-apartheid state by alluding to the historical land issue. In an article on the South African pastoral in "the era of land reform", Jennifer Wenzel bridges past and present by linking the issue of land in the *plaasroman* with the (then) imminent and far-reaching 1998 Land Reform programme in post-apartheid South Africa:

> The cycle of anti-apartheid protest and state repression that began in the 1940s and climaxed in the 1980s challenged the logic of the *plaasroman*: the pastoral promise of the return to the land was countered by the political imperative of the return of the land. The 1994 elections represented one culmination of the struggle against apartheid, and the moment of political transition brought with it the possibility of a reconfiguration of land ownership through land reform: the possibility, for white commercial farmers, of losing the farm ("Pastoral Promise" 95).

Property describes and maintains the colonial and apartheid relation or, as James Ferguson puts it, "property … is not a relation between people and things … [but] a relation between people, concerning things" (qtd. in Wenzel 96; Ferguson n. pag.). This dynamic between people and land is clearly what Lurie has in mind. Lucy, like her father, wonders if the attack is retribution for the abuses of apartheid, including dispossession from the land: "the price one has to pay for staying on

PRIVACY

... They see me as owing something. They see themselves as debt collectors, tax collectors" (DIS 158).

Whilst Lurie anticipates the publicizing of Lucy's story of her rape across the district, suggesting that she has lost autonomy over her story – it is "Not her story to spread but theirs: they are its owners[; h]ow they put her in her place, how they showed her what a woman was for" (DIS 115) – Lucy purposefully moves it from the public to the private sphere: the attack "is a purely private matter. In another time, in another place it might be held to be a public matter. But in this place, at this time, it is not. It is my business and mine alone" (DIS 112). We should not miss the irony that Lucy makes the same claims to privacy rights as her father at the disciplinary hearing nor the fact that the crime committed against her will never go to court. If the effect of guarding the right to privacy in Lucy's case is seemingly to protect her attackers from the law, in Lurie's the reverse is true: his obdurate refusal to express remorse only mires him deeper in his disgrace.

Such resistance to public confession or testimony disavows the prevailing belief that the post-apartheid era heralds a return to the private. Privacy in the context of Lucy's refusal to "testify" is a last-ditch attempt to resist racist discourses of "black peril" resurfacing during this time, as I explain below, that hark back to apartheid. The claim to privacy in the context of Lucy's rape also ushers in a kind of levelling for Lucy who, "prepared to do anything, make any sacrifice, for the sake of peace" (DIS 208), acknowledges that the rape "is humiliating. But perhaps that is a good point to start from again" (DIS 204).

For Lucy, rape signifies a leveller of racial injustice that can be traced directly back to land. Pregnant, she confounds her father with her decision, firstly, to keep the child and, secondly, to accept Petrus's marriage proposal in return for his protection. Historically, in the economy of the farm novel, Lucy's acceptance of Petrus's proposal of marriage (a business arrangement rather than an affair of the heart) and his proposal to co-manage the farm violates the sanctity of the Afrikaner *vrou en moeder* (wife and mother) and the taboo of miscegenation by transgressing boundaries of gender and race. Warning Lucy she is on the "brink of a dangerous error" by choosing such a path via a loveless marriage to a kind of historical reconciliation, Lurie suggests, "You wish to humble yourself before history" (DIS 160).

The representation of rape in the text, disquietingly equated with the trope of the "rape of the land" through the metaphors of debt collection and reparation, is highly problematic in a country in which rape is endemic, though of course reviled across the political spectrum. Violence afflicts the "Rainbow Nation" which has failed to deliver the promises of social transformation and economic prosperity it seemed to offer. Coetzee chooses to write about a criminal class of South African society with which Petrus is in connivance. Knowing well the kind of response such a portrayal would elicit, Coetzee engages with controversial racist stereotypes: in these scenes black agency is configured in the act of rape with devastating implications for a nation in which racist whites have regarded miscegenation with abhorrence and the black man as the natural rapist. Lucy's rights as a woman have been displaced by the withdrawal of her rights as representative of the white oppressor. Elleke Boehmer argues that Lucy will neither speak publicly of the rape nor "seek its redress", and rightly puts the question, "through the medium of the tightly patterned narrative[,] whether it is not outrageous to align this acceptance (for which, at least in Lucy's opinion, there is no alternative) with Lurie's acts of unconscious expiation" ("Not Saying Sorry" 348). For Grant Farred, the "ubiquity of violence, especially against women, constitutes the most damning instance of disgrace" ("Mundanacity" 353). Nonetheless, Boehmer's contention that Lucy "insists that what the men did to her was not a historical act, not a symbolic gesture of revenge", despite making the subsequent claim that she "physically, if not verbally, accepts a burden of accountability for the wrongs of the past" ("Not Saying Sorry" 348; 349), does not tally with Lucy's belief that the rapists see themselves as "debt collectors". This last remark suggests this is how Lucy perceives them too. Lucy acknowledges the need for nation-building that could be hindered by the damaging effects of what Lucy Graham identifies as the discourse of "black peril", evidenced for white racists in the prevalence of rape at the current time ("Unspeakable" 434–35).

Critics who have condemned the novel on grounds of race, David Attwell argues, have paid little attention to Manas Mathabane, the black Professor of Religious Studies and chair of the disciplinary committee:

> Mathabane is not mentioned because he falls outside the stereotype the novel is taken to be peddling ... In his dedication to fairness and procedure, Mathabane is, in fact, the novel's true representative of the Enlightenment, and his generally forgiving stance echoes the presence of the clergy associated with the Truth and Reconciliation Commission. ("Race in *Disgrace*" 335)

Attwell points out that all of the committee are black "in the inclusive sense", although "None of these characters act out racial stereotypes ... and the only hint of racial discourse comes from Rassool, who draws the committee's attention to the 'overtones' of the case" ("Race in *Disgrace*" 335). Readers familiar with Coetzee, who has prepared the ground for this novel with *Age of Iron* (1990) and *The Master of Petersburg* (1994) in their critique of political activism, will recognize the complexities of the work that are in play. This bleak rendering of the "new South Africa" rises to the challenge set by progressives like Nadine Gordimer and Lewis Nkosi who, warning of the potentially debasing effects of protest art, advocated more critical reflexivity.

The diptych structure of the novel allows Coetzee to parallel the violation of Lucy with Lurie's own abuse of women, women towards whom Lurie admits he is predatory. In the case of Melanie, Lurie also abuses his position of authority in his role as teacher and mentor. Comparable to Byron's mistreatment of women – "Among the legions of countesses and kitchenmaids Byron pushed himself into there were no doubt those who called it rape" (DIS 160) – Lurie deems the last occasion of his love-making with Melanie to be "not rape, not quite that, but undesired nevertheless, undesired to the core" (DIS 25). Lurie misguidedly warms to and no doubt identifies with Byron, tolerating his countenance because, compared to the kind of violence inflicted upon Lucy, Byron "looks very old-fashioned indeed" (DIS 160).

Lurie realizes it is through loving what he cannot love – women such as Teresa or the equally squat Bev Shaw – that he will reignite his sympathetic faculty and overcome writer's block. In the process he will come to a better self-understanding: "Can he find it in his heart to love this plain, ordinary woman [Teresa]? Can he love her enough to write … music for her? If he cannot, what is left for him?" (DIS 182). After all, he thinks, all the women in his life teach him something. It is not incidental that Teresa transforms into a middle-aged woman in Lurie's mind's eye at the time of his brief affair with the middle-aged Bev Shaw (DIS 181). In the economy of confession the novel promotes, Lurie is confronted therefore with a double-bind: he believes that he must "find himself" through women but inevitably will fail because in doing so, he necessarily continues in a self-oriented and therefore self-deceiving mode of existence.

Recent feminist critics have argued that the male Romantics typically appropriated the (female) other in their quest for autonomy and innovation for, in Claridge's words, the "aggrandizement of the male literary consciousness". Claridge agrees with feminists that the majority of the male Romantics' poems "aimed at recuperating the special potency that accrues to marginalized forces, in this case, woman as that which is not already written" (16–17). Such an evaluation of the male Romantic's literary ego is reflected in Lurie's disingenuous apology to Melanie's father Mr. Isaacs and in his belief that all his relationships with women have "enriched" him: "*Enriched*: that was the word the newspapers picked on to jeer at" following the "trial" (DIS 192).

However, in his attempts to overcome writer's block, Lurie finally turns not to the voice of Teresa but to the comic. Drawing the conclusion that *Byron in Italy*, like he himself, is "going nowhere", he takes up his daughter's toy banjo to compose his opera in the realization that:

> It is not the erotic that is calling to him after all, nor the elegiac, but the comic.
> He is in the opera neither as Teresa nor as Byron nor even as some blending of
> the two: he is held in the music itself, in the flat tinny slap of the banjo strings …
> So this is art, he thinks, and this is how it does its work! (DIS 184–85)

His lofty aestheticism is reduced to the absurd and he finds himself humbled by the ordinary. The "*plink-plunk*" of the banjo he strums (DIS 214) conveys the "language of the other" – authentic truths – observed by de Man in Rousseau's *Confessions*. John Banville is right to suggest in his review of *Disgrace* that "the operatic theme fits oddly into the scheme of the book"; nonetheless, his explanation, that it functions as a "counterpoint to the general minimalist bleakness of the story" (Banville 23), is insubstantial. The opera narrative deliberately draws attention to itself *as disjointed* and, in the model of confession sketched by Coetzee of the confessant searching for self-truths, is a more authentic expression of Lurie's consciousness. Although initially he fails to connect with either Byron or the "female" voice, Lurie's increasing identification with Teresa marks an acceptance of a newer truth and an unspoken but internally articulated ethical transition. The spontaneity he attains on the strings of the banjo characterizes "deeper", authentic truths, signalling that Lurie is learning to speak from the heart.

Disgrace repeatedly makes associations between human and animal behaviour: Lurie's sexual passions are animalistic, predatory; Lucy is treated "like a dog" by the men who rape her (DIS 205), who themselves behave "like dogs in a pack" (DIS 159); Petrus, Lucy's black neighbour, sardonically introduces himself to Lurie as the "dog-man" (DIS 64), only to reject this position as he gains autonomy within the "new South Africa" (DIS 129), in theory, as the white, non-democratic power base is dismantled. (Such a realignment of power can only be a *symbolic* gesture in the novel since in the socio-economic contexts of the novel little has actually changed, evidenced in the ongoing housing and unemployment crises.)[8] The conflict between these two patriarchs reaches its climax when, following Lucy's rape, Lurie helps Petrus to lay pipes on his land. Accruing Freudian connotations, Lurie asks Petrus, "Do you need me here any longer?", to which Petrus responds, "No, now it is easy, now I must just dig the pipe in" (DIS 139). Lurie is reduced to the role of "dog-man" in his work with Bev Shaw and is resituated as other by this newly conferred role. Whilst human behaviour in these examples is degraded and debased by its comparison to animals, this allows Coetzee to distance the narrative from racialized, racist discourse traceable to the Great Chain of Being with its hierarchy of so-called species.

It is finally through dogs – which in *Age of Iron* and *The Master of Petersburg* pertain to Levinas's Absolute Other as the parodic inversion of "God" – that Lurie struggles for atonement. He at first regarded Lucy and Bev's affection for animals as sentimental (DIS 73): animals are of a lower order, he reasons, and though they should be treated humanely this should not be motivated by guilt (DIS 74). Lucy's suggestion that Lurie help Bev at the clinic "sounds suspiciously like community service … like someone trying to make reparation for past misdeeds" (DIS 77). Moreover, Lucy notes her father's initial disdain for Bev Shaw and her husband Bill built, Lucy believes, on the fact that if her father had his way she would devote herself to a higher (rarefied) cultural order: she "ought to be painting still lives or teaching [her]self Russian". Friends like Bill and Bev, on the other hand, "are not going to lead [her] to a higher life". (Nonetheless, Lucy's service to animals, she lets slip, is itself self-interested: "I don't want to come back in another existence as a dog or a pig and have to live as dogs or pigs live

---

8 Unemployment in South Africa rose from 31.2 per cent in 1993 to a high of 41.8 per cent in 2002 (Kingdon and Knight n. pag.). As the *Encyclopedia of the Nations* states, "only about one-tenth" of the dwellings needed to tackle the housing shortage were being built in the late 1990s, "leaving the country with a serious housing shortage" (n. pag.).

ELIZABETH COSTELLO *SUFFERING* [handwritten annotations]

under us" [DIS 74].) In spite of this, Lurie becomes sympathetic to the cause in the wake of Lucy's rape.

The idea that an odious character such as Lurie can find redemption through caring for sick animals where the juxtaposition of animal and human suffering brings the two forms of suffering into relief, in the context of egregious inequality that has been largely racially determined, might well be construed inappropriate. Just as the oppression of women in Coetzee's parody of the TRC corresponds with apartheid's oppressed, it is through alleviating animal suffering that Lurie atones for his abusive attitude towards women. At stake is whether by paralleling very different modes of oppression Coetzee sacrifices specificity and silences the workings of the particular. (Mamdani, writing about the "truths" of the TRC, points out that the TRC read apartheid through the analogy of Latin American dictatorships, thereby diminishing the truth of apartheid. Such an analogy, he argues, erroneously papers over the racialized nature of oppression in South Africa, obscuring "the link between perpetrator and beneficiary" ["Truth" 179]. I realize that to make my point I too am falling back upon an analogy.)

Disgrace was published concurrently in 1999 with *The Lives of Animals* (later republished in *Elizabeth Costello* [2003]): two lectures given by Coetzee at Princeton University in which, standing before his audience, he seemingly adopts the persona of Elizabeth Costello, a moderately successful and eccentric author and academic who has been invited to Appleton College in the States to lecture on the theme of animal rights. Marjorie Garber, in her response to *Lives*, argues that the premise of Costello's position on our treatment of animals resides in what Freud calls the "seduction of an analogy": an ill-conceived yet seemingly [handwritten: actually the reverse] credible appropriation of one term – in *Disgrace* and *Lives* the suffering of animals – to illuminate another: oppressed peoples (LA 80). Such a "seduction" is best illustrated in *Lives* when Costello likens the treatment of animals in factory farms to that of the Jews in the Nazi concentration camps (the animals to humans analogy is reversed in *Disgrace*). Abraham Stern, a Jewish poet, who responds to Costello's polemic in a letter because he cannot stomach breaking bread with her, warns: "The inversion insults the memory of the dead [and] trades on the horror of the camps in a cheap way" (LA 50). The respondent to her talk, Professor Thomas O'Hearne, charges Costello with drawing an analogy between modes of oppression that are of a "different scale" (LA 64). Tested against *Disgrace* we might ask, does Lurie's assuagement of guilt through animals teeter on shaky ethical ground that is based within the text on an ill-conceived equivalence?

To answer this question we can turn to Costello's critique of Enlightenment thinking in which she sets the poets against the philosophers. She pours scorn on the notion that because animals lack the power to reason, their slaughter is justified: in light of this, "reason looks to me suspiciously like the being of human thought", she says (LA 23). She quickly dismisses the charge that she is anthropomorphizing animal behaviour by claiming that animals and humans have the common bond of "embodiedness, the sensation of being" (LA 33). If there is a sense of community between all species, and if we are able to conceptualize death, which is, after all, outside our experience, do we not have the capacity to imagine ourselves as animals (LA 33)? In *Disgrace*, suggestive of the otherness of death, the utter humiliation it engenders, Lurie wonders if dogs, like humans, "feel the disgrace of dying" (DIS 143). Costello refers her audience to her novel *The House on Eccles Street*, which portrays the life of Marion Bloom, wife of Joyce's Leopold in *Ulysses*: if writers can imagine the lives of their characters, she reflects, surely it is possible to imagine animal being? Nevertheless, as "Peter Singer's" daughter suggests (or the animal rights philosopher Singer himself, who appropriates a metageneric device not unlike Coetzee's in his "reflection" on *Lives*), this sentiment is quite obviously flawed (LA 90–91): imagining ourselves into other human beings is very different from imagining ourselves into the being of animals. Costello argues that the poet might be more adequately equipped to comprehend animal existence than the philosopher and urges us "to read the poets who return the living, electric being to language". She concludes that "If the last common ground that I have with [the philosopher she has read in preparation for the talk] is reason, and if reason is what sets me apart from the veal calf, then thank you but no thank you, I'll talk to someone else" (*Lives* 67). It is the sympathetic imagination that ushers in authentic communion with the other.

Lurie passes through a stage of what might be called penitence in Coetzee's model of confession to form a close bond with the dogs under his care and strives to return to the animals – even as corpses – their dignity: "He has learned by now, from [Bev], to concentrate all his attention on the animal they are killing, giving it what he no longer has difficulty in calling by its proper name: love" (DIS 219). The novel closes, but does not offer closure, with Lurie giving up one particular dog with which he has formed an especially close bond for euthanasia: "Bearing him in his arms like a lamb, he re-enters the surgery. 'I thought you would save him for another week,' says Bev Shaw,/'Are you giving him up?'/'Yes, I am giving him up'" (DIS 220). By relinquishing his care of the dog, sacrificing the emotional investment he has made in it, Lurie finds, in one sense, closure for the cycle of self-excoriation and self-revelation in which he has become entangled. He has atoned, albeit minimally, for his transgression, both in working with the dogs and in this act of giving up; the gesture marks a conclusion of sorts to this process.

The denouement reads in stark contrast to Coetzee's singularly unsentimental and highly cerebral prose and corresponds with Lurie's reaffirmation of a Wordsworthian ethic. Lurie's affinity with the Romantics' reworking of the sympathetic imagination underscores the very private nature of truth and reconciliation portrayed in the novel, in turn laying bare the limitations of public notions of "truth" and the compromises they produce, though Coetzee offers no comforting resolution.

Coetzee is hesitant over the redemptive potential of confession and absolution. Whether, ultimately, Lurie is able to say sorry with conviction or sincerity is subject to doubt, though Coetzee certainly gestures in this direction. Firstly, Lurie learns through processes of empathy to give voice to the Teresa character in his opera rather than the salacious Byron with whom he first identifies. Nonetheless, *not sick, just unwanted.*

the motive for this gesture is itself questionable since he can only suppress his violent rage against Pollux through Teresa, "That is why he must listen to Teresa. Teresa may be the last one left who can save him" (209). Secondly, in a gesture of kindness, he gives up the sick dog with which he has formed a particularly intimate bond for euthanasia. Lurie is propelled on to a journey of self-discovery and personal atonement which ultimately is revealed to be morally bankrupt for he visits Melanie's family home and, in an act of what Graham Pechey calls "grotesque obeisance" ("Purgatorial Africa" 381), kisses the feet of her father, all the while secretly lusting after Melanie's even more beautiful sister, the aptly named Desiree. Lurie's failure to atone for the affair signals that this is also a novel about saving oneself.

Coetzee finally draws the animal and opera subtexts together with Lurie's half-ironic notion of introducing a dog into the opera; parodying the Russian nihilists mantra, the ineffectual academic wonders, "surely, in a work that will never be performed, *all things are permitted?*" (emphasis added; DIS 215). However, he symbolically relinquishes his authority as white writer (or is *relinquished of* this authority) when he realizes that as a "figure from the margins of history … [h]e is inventing the music (or the music is inventing him) but he is not inventing the history" (DIS 167; 186). He wonders, "Will this [the Eastern Cape] be where the dark trio [Byron, Teresa and 'the humiliated husband'] are at last brought to life: not in Cape Town but in old Kaffraria?" (DIS 122). History has "come full circle" (DIS 175): Lurie has confronted his past in the realms of the pastoral, but the novel requires us to question the authenticity of his ethical transition despite the implied critique of the TRC. Rather than offering an alternative to public confession, the novel rejects authentic truths both in the public sphere of the University Committee hearings (and by analogy the TRC) and in the private realm of Lurie's self-doubt because neither institutional nor individual truths, the narrative warns us, can be properly tested.

Chapter 9

Coetzee's Acts of Genre in the Later Works: Truth-telling, Fiction and the Public Intellectual

> Would that I could follow your advice, my dear Anya … But alas, it is a collection of opinions I am committed to, not a memoir. A response to the present in which I find myself.
>
> J. M. Coetzee, *Diary of a Bad Year* (67)

> I am immensely uncomfortable with questions … that call upon me to answer for (in two senses) my novels, and my responses are often taken as evasive … my difficulty is precisely with the project of stating positions, taking positions.
>
> J. M. Coetzee, *Doubling the Point* (205)

"What does each revelation I make *cost*?" This is the question that preoccupies J. M. Coetzee as he makes his inaugural professorial lecture "Truth in Autobiography" to the assembly gathered in the halls of the University of Cape Town on the subject of Jean-Jacques Rousseau's *Confessions* (1782) and the genre of autobiography (Coetzee, "Truth" 6). It is the cost of truth-telling that preoccupies much of Coetzee's fiction, crystallized in the later works *The Lives of Animals* (1999), *Elizabeth Costello* (2003) and *Diary of a Bad Year* (2007), which, through their very mode of address, through the radical defamiliarization of the discourses of genre, call into question the ethico-politics of intellectual practice as well as the truths of authorship.

The manner and mode of the lectures in *Lives* and *Elizabeth Costello* and J. C.'s aphoristic opinion pieces in *Diary* allow Coetzee to grapple more openly with the ethico-politics of intellectual practice. Indeed, his apparent direct engagement with contemporary politics (the lectures and opinion pieces range from animal rights, the status of the novel in Africa, intelligent design, the "war on terror" and Harold Pinter's controversial 2005 Nobel Prize acceptance speech on that war) may surprise those more used to a taciturn Coetzee who refuses to nail his political colours to the mast. These lectures and novels invite public debate, albeit confoundingly through the cipher of fiction. Indeed, as I will argue, it is through the *form* of these works, through what I call "acts of genre" (cf. Wright, "Feminist-Vegetarian"; Graham, "Textual Transvestism"), rather than their substance, that the most significant intellectualizing is done. "Acts" captures not only the performative, self-conscious quality of the lectures and the duplicity of genre as it manifests in these works but also the agency an act engenders.

By isolating the "cost" of truth, Coetzee is referring to the *discourse* of autobiography rather than the sincerity of the author: "In terms of the economic life of the discourse, it sometimes costs too much to make certain revelations: they threaten the ability of the discourse to grow, they threaten its freedom", he explains ("Truth" 6). In the economy of autobiography, in other words, what Coetzee calls a certain "blindness" to the truth is required to justify confession because if our eyes are "wide open" then the need for confession quickly dissipates ("Truth" 5). If, as Coetzee argues, "The only sure truth in autobiography is that one's self-interest will be located at one's blind spot" (DP 392), and if we accept Coetzee's maxim "All autobiography is storytelling, all writing is autobiography" (DP 391), deeper self-truths in autobiography and in writing more generally reside in unconscious self-revelations which are thus difficult to locate let alone verify. Even the author of a book cannot fully know its meaning and is therefore denied absolute authority over it. Meaning can reconstruct action or, alternatively, can be reconfigured by a developing consciousness. That Coetzee is concerned with "how to tell the truth in autobiography" therefore does not mean he is concerned with truth per se, but with its telling. In other words, Coetzee is less interested in the truth value of narrative than in the mechanisms by which "truth" – always a category to be questioned in Coetzee – is brought to light. In the later works that foreground intellectual practice, Coetzee focuses not on the truth-value of the public interventions his writer-intellectuals circulate but on the manner and mode by which these interventions are disseminated. We are required to be "blind" to such truths in order that the intellectual, whom we must rely upon to be truthful or at least sincere, can enlighten us.

An increasingly meta-discursive mode in Coetzee's fiction that coincides with his departure from South Africa for Adelaide, Australia in 2002, also for the most part marks a departure in the oeuvre from the postcolonial paradigm at a time, ironically, when South Africa is for the first time properly "postcolonial" following the inception of democracy in 1994. So whilst these later works may seem to have less relevance in a book about postcolonial authorship, they do make important contributions to debates on intellectualism and the author's authority pertinent to the postcolonial field. For instance, in "Lesson 1: Realism" (*Elizabeth Costello*) Costello apologizes to her audience, "I am not, I hope, abusing the privilege of this platform" (she is delivering a lecture on Kafka's "Red Peter" story in defence of animals) (EC 19). In a self-conscious twist in which Coetzee apparently undermines his own procedures, the writer J. C. in *Diary* even disparages Roland Barthes and Michel Foucault's reduction of the authority of the author to nothing more than "a bagful of rhetorical tricks" and reminds us in "On authority in fiction" that "Authority must be earned" (DBY 149). J. C. speculates in "On having thoughts" on his right to air his opinions at all since he has "never been easy with abstractions or good with abstract thought" (DBY 203); yet in these words he repudiates the loftiness of the traditional intellectual that Antonio

Gramsci and subsequently Edward Said have rejected. Coetzee time and again in his fiction and essays signals the conviction that he hasn't earned this right. *Slow Man* (2005), set in Australia and telling the story of Paul Rayment coming to terms with the loss of a leg following a bicycle accident, is a more conventional novel and so for this reason I focus on what I will call the Costello lectures (*Lives* and the lectures collected as "lessons" in *Elizabeth Costello*) and *Diary*. Set in a postcolonial locale, *Slow Man* raises questions about immigration and economic migrancy that fall within the remit of the "postcolonial".

Of course, much of Coetzee's earlier work also disrupts our expectations of genre. *Dusklands* (1974) presents Jacobus Coetzee's divergent accounts, for instance, of the servant Klawer's death, unsettling notions of verisimilitude to which the work's part journal-style narrative gives credence. *In the Heart of the Country* (1977), in diary format, employs a similar device with Magda's multiple versions of her rape and two of the fate of her father. *Foe* (1986) radically revises the colonialist-individualist Robinsonade with the death in the first of three parts of its hero Cruso, whose marginality is compounded by his usurpation by a female narrator Susan Barton. *Age of Iron* (1990) disturbs the genre of the epistle with Mrs. Curren's improbable letter to her daughter (improbable because, as Dominic Head points out, it incorporates dialogue and description [*J. M. Coetzee* 129]). The memoirs *Boyhood* (1997) and *Youth* (2002) are fictionalized accounts of the author J. M. Coetzee's life: the use of the third person narrator, out of place in memoir or autobiography, suggests just this; moreover, the American publisher of *Boyhood* insisted proper names be changed – that is, fictionalized – to protect the identities of the protagonists in John Coetzee's life (Attridge, *J. M. Coetzee* 148–49), and the dust jacket of *Youth* pledges fiction. Rayment's life in *Slow Man* seems uncannily to be repeating itself in the hands of the inimitable novelist Elizabeth Costello who, making a surprise appearance in this novel, is able to recount verbatim the report of Rayment's accident which opens the narrative. Later Rayment will sum up his aberrant and far-fetched encounter engineered by Costello with Marianna, his blind paramour, as an "experiment, that is what it amounts to, an idle, biologico-literary experiment" (SM 114).

It is in the later fictions that Coetzee for the first time engages with the ethico-politics of *public* intellectual practice. Up until this point he has shied away from the publicity such intellectualism entails. Yet the slipperiness that characterizes his writing even here endures. The metageneric play of the Costello lectures and *Diary* self-reflexively strips away layers of intellectual authority to make Coetzee both accountable and not-accountable to the ethico-politics his characters promote. In these later works the figure of Coetzee most obviously haunts fictionalized texts to disrupt the pacts of genre. (Importantly, both Costello and J. C., like Coetzee himself, are both novelists and public intellectuals.) It is the slippage between the two, between author and author-protagonist, that energizes questions about the relationship between public intellectuals and the truths they promote.

The painfully uncharismatic Costello is the persona Coetzee has seemingly elected to perform in a series of real-life lectures at various international venues,

haha yes!

later to be published as "lessons" in *Elizabeth Costello* (the two Princeton lectures first appeared in print in 1999 as *The Lives of Animals*)[1] and we know that similarities exist between Coetzee's principles and Costello's such as their shared vegetarianism.[2] Costello therefore, unsurprisingly, has been referred to variously as Coetzee's "mouthpiece" (Graham, "Textual Transvestism" 219), his "surrogate" (Attwell, "Life and Times" 33) and his "alter ego" (Bell 174). Although Costello is only one character amongst many in the lectures, suggesting that Coetzee cannot simply be ventriloquizing through her, Costello is the connecting thread in the series of republished lectures that otherwise would function as discreet entities. J. C. is the name the main narrator of *Diary* uses to sign himself off in his journal of "strong opinions" – a fictionalized John Coetzee's ruminations on contentious current debates. The similarities between author and narrator don't end there: J. C. is a South African of about the same age as Coetzee who, like Coetzee, has moved to Australia; like Coetzee, he is a novelist whose oeuvre includes *Waiting for the Barbarians* and like Coetzee's, his 1990s book on censorship was quietly received.

So in the Costello lectures and *Diary* the porousness of genre boundaries misleadingly entices us down the path of biographical reading. We are tempted to draw parallels and distinctions between Coetzee and his intellectual-protagonists, work for literary critics not generally regarded with much esteem except in the field of life writing. We should not, however, too easily be seduced into reading either Costello or J. C. as Coetzee, as a number of critics have pointed out, or to interpret the works within their purported genres – broadly speaking, the public intervention. This is the mistake that Ian Hacking makes in his review of *Lives*.[3] The trap of correspondences and similarities may have been laid, yet it is my contention that the puzzlement the texts elicit, especially over Coetzee's performance of Costello on stage that Lucy Graham calls his "textual transvestism" ("Textual Transvestism" 217) and in *Diary* over such obvious signposts to Coetzee's life, encourage us as readers to wrestle with what such performances might mean. It would be all too easy for Coetzee to broadcast his beliefs but such a move would fly in the face of his principled (though overly idealistic and even naïve) disavowal of political rhetoric, that, though "Sympathetic to the human concerns of the left, he is alienated, when the crunch comes, by its language – by all political language, in fact" (DP 394).

---

[1]   Neither the last two lessons, "Eros" and "At the Gate", nor the "Postscript" utilize the motif of the public address and are included as new material in *Elizabeth Costello* (Attridge, *J. M. Coetzee* 194–95).

[2]   For an account of the contexts of the Costello lectures see Attridge, *J. M. Coetzee* (192–96).

[3]   Michael Bell notes this flaw in Hacking's otherwise "penetrating" review (Bell, "What is it like?" 175; Hacking, "Our Fellow Animals").

CRUX OF THESIS?

The later, quasi-fictional works all deliberately violate or disrupt the "pact" of genre, as Coetzee would have it ("Truth" 5), between writer/speaker and reader/audience. Such pacts are, he says,

> negotiated over the years between writers and readers (and always open to renegotiation) for each of the genres and sub-genres, pacts which cover, among other things, what demands may be made of each genre and what may not, what questions may be asked and what may not, what one may see and what one must be blind to. ("Truth" 5)

I am suggesting that *Lives, Elizabeth Costello* and *Diary* ask, what is the cost of truth to the genres of the public lecture and opinion piece? Or, what are the necessary conditions for truth to be spoken?

The question of truth in art is too wide-reaching to address here but can be divided broadly into three categories: firstly, the personal truths of confessional writing; secondly, "transcendental-poetic" truths of the kind associated with liberal humanism and, thirdly, public truths or "socio-cultural" truths that challenge systems of power.[4] What happens when these different kinds of truth are brought to bear upon each other within a single text and how might this affect the purchase of their public interventions? The discourse or pact of the public intervention depends upon our faith in the authority (truthfulness or integrity) of the intellectual who will impart truths to which we are required to be "blind". Once this authority becomes subject to doubt, the intervention itself is threatened. Costello and J. C. violate the pacts of the genres in which they engage, as I go on to explain, in Costello's case, purposively.

If public intellectualism is built, in the words of Said, on "speaking truth to power" (*Representations* 85), we should ask, what then is truth? And, what is Coetzee's investment in truth? Although poststructuralist and postcolonial theories have taught us to be skeptical of truth, for the purposes of this chapter I am concerned with the truths spoken by public intellectuals which are yoked to free speech: based on ethico-political conviction, the capacity to say what we like, to whom we like and when. In turn free speech takes three distinct forms, all of which potentially can be blocked. The first is measured by obligations to society (and, in extreme contexts such as apartheid, regulated by the state through mechanisms like censorship), the second, by self-regulation or self-censorship (the censor within) and the third by unconscious drives, a mode of censorship which supersedes both that of the state and the conscious self. Coetzee's writing even suggests that private thoughts are not, as commonly held in Enlightenment discourse, free from policing. How and when, therefore, can we know that the truth is being spoken? Coetzee's fiction reveals that even truths apparently told freely are subject to doubt. Conversely, it tests the extent to which one's innermost

---

4   In "What is a Classic?" Coetzee elaborates upon two apparently divergent modes of *criticism*, the "transcendental-poetic" and the "socio-cultural" (SS 9).

thoughts and feelings can be brought acceptably into the public domain. How far can one explore and reveal the "depths" of consciousness and conscience (*Youth* 131) and remain within the limits of the ethical?

This is Costello's topic in "Lesson 6: The Problem of Evil". Invited to speak on "the age-old problem of evil" at a conference in Amsterdam (EC 156), she argues "certain things are not good to read *or to write*" (original emphasis; EC 173). She publicly condemns the (real-life) author Paul West's novel *The Very Rich Hours of Count von Stauffenberg* (1980), which, based on factual events, depicts in sickeningly intimate detail the execution of a band of Hitler's would-be assassins: "one cannot come away unscathed, as a writer, from conjuring up such scenes" (EC 172), she believes. Privately, she reflects that such representations are "Obscene because having taken place they ought not to be brought into the light but covered up and hidden forever in the bowels of the earth" (EC 159). Such moralizing, which seems to undo the principles of free speech, is not unlike feminists' response to pornography, feminists who, claims J. C. in "On Paedophilia" (and echoed by Coetzee in "Taking Offense" [GO 26]), have "chose[n] to go to bed with the religious conservatives" (DBY 54).

The position of Anya, the neighbour J. C. employs as his secretary to transcribe his opinion pieces, that acts do not necessarily follow thoughts ("are wicked thoughts really so wicked ... For an old man, after all, what is there left in the world but wicked thoughts?" [DBY 87]) is closer, we might suppose, to Coetzee's own. In "The Taint of the Pornographic" Coetzee sets straight D. H. Lawrence, who exercises taboo in order to exorcize it of its offensive meaning, by arguing that the "moral [Lawrence] is really after is that only a mind already tainted can be touched by taint" (DP 310). Anya is repulsed by J. C.'s writings on paedophilia (which J. C. tacitly defends by evoking an ethic of representation that an adult acting the part of a child is a far cry from child pornography itself [DBY 53]). Nonetheless, she shows compassion for his "private thoughts" (that are about her) and is disturbed by Alan's attempts to poke about in them (DBY 119). Not incidentally placed below J. C.'s reflections "On Compassion", Anya tells him "frankly" that she was "never embarrassed by your thoughts, I even helped them along a little ... And if you want to write and tell me your thoughts, that is OK too, I can be discreet" (DBY 211). Nevertheless, J. C.'s lascivious fantasies about Anya's "derrière[,] so near to perfect as to be angelic" (8), inserted directly below his thoughts "on the origins of the state", on questions of citizenry and subjecthood, certainly threaten to test the moral high-ground he takes in his public interventions, or at least mark a clear division between them.

Costello in "The Problem of Evil" visits the novelist West, who by ill luck is attending the same conference, to warn him of the substance of her talk. Yet "proceed[ing] with the task of watering down her paper" to save West's sensibilities and her face, she realizes that, "Ineluctably she is arguing herself into the position of the old-fashioned censor" (EC 164). Done in her old age with uncritical belief in storytelling (EC 167), of which "She is not sure ... whether she believes any longer in" (EC 39), she tells her audience that as a novelist she "would not let [her]self, not any more" enter scenes of human depravity as those depicted by West (EC 172). She likens storytelling to "a bottle with a genie in it" that once "released into the world" reeks havoc that would be difficult to repair, and concludes that, *"Her position, her revised position, her position in the twilight of life*: better, on the whole, that the genie stay in the bottle" (emphasis added; EC 167). Costello's self-reflexivity and shifting consciousness mark the traits of the critical mindset that are the linchpin of the intellectual, "whose whole being is staked on a critical sense" and requires a willingness to speak out in public (Said, *Representations* 23).

The disjunction between Costello and Coetzee on the problem of representing the obscene and the violent in fiction, however, is strikingly apparent: we only have to think of Eugene Dawn's photographs in *Dusklands*, the scenes of torture in *Waiting for the Barbarians*, the mutilation of Friday in *Foe*, the murder of Bheki, child revolutionary, in *Age of Iron* or the rape of Lucy in *Disgrace*, to see that Coetzee is a novelist more than familiar with representing acts of inhumanity, even, as in the case of *Dusklands* and *Barbarians*, in the most stomach-churningly intimate detail. Violence in *Foe* and *Disgrace* may not be represented explicitly: in the case of Friday's possible genital mutilation, Barton reflects, "What had been hidden from me was revealed. I saw, or, I should say, my eyes were open to what was present to them". Similarly, she reports that when Cruso held Friday's mouth open "to show me he had no tongue" she "averted" her eyes (F 119). Lurie, as focalizer in *Disgrace*, does not witness Lucy's rape but hears it through the walls of a locked toilet door. Yet the suggestive, imaginative capacity of art in each case allows us to conjure what is left unarticulated. So we would be right to question Coetzee's game.

It is my contention that the effect of such a radical disruption of genre – Coetzee's "genre acts" – is to lay bare the author's/speaker's device, turning the critical gaze back self-reflexively upon what Michel Foucault would call the "author-function" ("What is an Author?" 148) and here the function of the intellectual, and rendering the fiction profoundly ethico-political. I enjoin the two terms, ethical and political, where others have tended to polarize Coetzee's writing between the two. "Ethico-political" expresses what Attridge refers to as a "politics worth espousing", one that "is surely a politics that both incorporates the ethical and is incorporated in it, while acknowledging the inescapable tension and continual revaluation that this mutual incorporation implies" ("Trusting the Other" 70–71). Robert Spencer argues that the form of Coetzee's novels "potentially makes them ethically and ultimately (here my emphasis differs subtly but I think crucially from Attridge's) *politically* consequential experiences for their readers" (Spencer, "War on Terror" n. pag.).[5] In Spencer's eyes Attridge relies too heavily on an "under-theorised ethical rhetoric" that is dependent on a commitment that is conceived in "even mystical ... terms" which are "at any rate ... anti-political" ("War on Terror" n. pag.).

? seriously?

Ok, but this is the clarification that has been missing in the book so far.

---

[5]   The unpublished version of Spencer's essay subsequently appeared in *Interventions* (2008) as "J.M. Coetzee and Colonial Violence".

Before I explore the problem of genre I should lay my cards on the table and explain the implied association between a novelist like Coetzee and the public intellectual, who by definition speaks truth to power. To those familiar with the author's work, Coetzee and public intellectualism may seem peculiar bedfellows, though the former occupies the seemingly paradoxical position of shunning publicity whilst he has been known to make a few, very public sallies into public debates. Attwell points out that although there are occasional "lapses" in Coetzee's resistance to being "drawn into the public sphere" ("Life and Times" 26), he is not a public intellectual in the sense that Said means. Firstly, Coetzee is notoriously elusive and "remains, in a particular sense, the least known of South African writers". Secondly, Coetzee is always skeptical of asserting positions; his stories resist "deliver[ing] a usable ethical content" (but for me this resistance signals just the opposite). Echoing Coetzee's sentiment, in "Realism" Costello asks her interlocutor, "am I obliged [as a novelist] to carry a message?" [EC 10]. Thirdly, there is the question of Coetzee's opacity which has frustrated some readers who have missed, Attwell implies, the fiction's nuances and "the enigmas of the public performance". Attwell warns that "mak[ing] a public case on his behalf is … to risk traducing the very qualities of his writing one most respects, including his uncanny combinations of power and instability, intensity and elusiveness" ("Life and Times" 25–26). The utopianism of Said's public intellectual, however, is not lost on Coetzee: "I would deny that the vocation of the intellectual is possible in the absence of a certain idealism and certain ideal standards" ("Critic Citizen" 109); yet, paradoxically, Coetzee's own "public interventions" typically radically disrupt what it means to be one.

On this point Theodor Adorno's discussion of artistic "commitment" proves enlightening. Suggesting that "proper" commitment works at the level of "fundamental attitudes" he distinguishes between "autonomous art" and "committed art" – not unlike the two kinds of criticism "transcendental-poetic" and "socio-cultural" outlined by Coetzee in "What is a Classic?" (SS 9). Whilst Adorno lauds Jean-Paul Sartre's objective in committed literature "to awaken the free choice of the agent [ ] that makes authentic existence possible at all", he concludes that Sartre is unable to conjure the necessary aesthetic resources to make this free choice possible. In Sartre, "What remains is merely the abstract authority of choice enjoined, with no regard for the fact that the very possibility of choosing depends on what can be chosen" (Adorno, "Commitment" 78). On the grounds of what distinguishes the category of the literary, Adorno laments the reductiveness of Sartre's maxim, "The writer deals with meanings" (*What is Literature?*), which Adorno interprets as content-bound. Every word, Adorno contends, is altered by its transposition to literature, and each word and idea assumes new textures in different generic contexts ("Commitment" 76).

For Adorno, art is the dialectic between meaning and form ("Commitment" 79) and his own inclination towards a modernist aesthetic over realism – to the "shock of the unintelligible" ("Commitment" 77) – is evident in his assertion that properly committed art, which resides at the level of "fundamental attitudes" rather than "ameliorative measures, legislative acts or practical institutions", is *difficult*. If we return to Sartre's principle of choice, Adorno reminds us, "what gives commitment its aesthetic advantage over tendentiousness also renders the content to which the artist commits himself inherently ambiguous" ("Commitment" 78). He lambastes Sartre's art as philosophy, what he calls Sartre's "own philosophy", because thoughts are "never [ ] much more than one of the materials for art" (79). Coetzee *REALLY* would most likely sympathize with Adorno's notion of commitment, so it will have been with a measure of surprise that many of his readers encountered in the Costello lectures and *Diary* these out-of-character ventures into the political fray.

Coetzee suggests in "The Novel Today" that (experimental) fiction has the capacity to operate on a different discursive plane from other modes of discourse: this is the source of its power:

Derek takes this up.

> the offensiveness of stories lies not in their transgressing particular rules but in their faculty of making and changing their own rules. There is a game going on between the covers of a book, but it is not always the game you think it is. (NT 3–4)

For Coetzee, then, the very form of the experimental novel – its anti-realist strategies and genre acts – can usefully counterpoint received discourses. We hardly need be reminded that History, against which Coetzee directs "The Novel Today" (1987), is discursive and highly politicized, particularly in the context of apartheid South Africa during which time the talk was delivered. Mediated by the state, History is part of the make-up of the national consciousness and gives credence to the myth of national origins, serving in this case to bolster apartheid ideology. By disrupting the conventions of realism – the pact between novelist and reader – the experimental novel lays bare the workings of narrative and the author-function. What might be the implications of this line of reasoning for the public interventions made by Coetzee's protagonists in the Costello lectures and *Diary*? Put another way, what effect does the process of fictionalizing have upon the validity of Coetzee's sorties into public-political debate?

The later works require us to ask, who speaks: Coetzee the author, who becomes implicated in his narratives as a kind of invisible presence, or the characters he portrays? At the Costello lectures, as Attridge observes, Coetzee chose to respond to questions from the floor in the third person, "I think that what Costello would say is that …" (*J. M. Coetzee* 193), which might well be construed intellectual side-stepping. This would be supported by Attridge's remark that "One negative response to *Elizabeth Costello* has been to complain that Coetzee uses fictional *valid argument* creations to advance arguments … without assuming responsibility for them, and is thus ethically at fault" (*J. M. Coetzee* 197). This is the point that Peter Singer moots in his response to *Lives* (published in the same volume as the lectures). Singer counters like with like by fictionalizing his own position on the lectures to ask whether Coetzee's fictional representations of writers allow him, as a private individual, to withdraw from the public sphere *whilst* making interventions, through characterized personae: "But are they Coetzee's arguments? … Coetzee's device enables him to distance himself from them" (LA 91). Critics who have claimed that Singer misses the point forget that pinning Singer down is complicated by his own self-fictionalizing device.

Like Singer, Garber, in the second of the four "reflections" on *Lives*, also recognizes the distance established between speaker and so-called mouthpiece but makes her conclusion at the point at which the argument made here takes off by asking, "In these two elegant lectures we thought John Coetzee was talking about animals. Could it be, however, that all along he was really asking, 'What is the value of literature?'" (LA 84). However, Garber is somewhat off the mark because, as Dominic Head points out, Coetzee's fiction – and *Lives* is a fiction – functions on "different planes of signification" simultaneously ("Belief in Frogs" 106). Put another way, these later novels are "about" the topics they intellectualize just as they are about intellectualism itself. What is more, Garber's analysis isn't far reaching enough. The later works, *Lives*, *Elizabeth Costello* and *Diary*, question not only the value of literature: Coetzee utilizes literature to expose the weak points of intellectual practice, centring on questions of authority and speaking on others' behalf.

By unsettling ideas of truth and the distance between the voice of author/lecturer and protagonist, Coetzee maintains the paradoxical position of nonposition to which he makes claim in *Doubling the Point* – "my difficulty is precisely with the project of stating positions, taking positions" (DP 205) – and which he clearly favours in his analysis of the Erasmus of *Praise of Folly* (GO 84). It is interesting that an author who so doggedly resists being positioned consistently stages a drama of positionality, inviting us, teasingly, to enter his literary game playing in the struggle for meaning that the act of reading engenders. Attridge contends that those who criticize Coetzee on the grounds of evasiveness are assuming wrongly they are dealing with "arguments presented *as arguments*" where Attridge prefers to think of them as "*arguings*", suggesting process: "They are, that is, events staged within the event of the work" and "invite the reader's participation" (*J. M. Coetzee* 197–98). For Attridge this is an ethical move, born out by the argument I am forwarding here: Coetzee is less concerned with the truths his characters promote than with the modes or "pacts" by which these truths are conveyed, in this way testing the ethico-politics of intellectual practice.

In these works Coetzee incorporates the scene of intellectual debate. Figures like Stern and Norma in *Lives* are given the opportunity to respond to Costello's interventions on animal rights in which she makes the comparison between factory-farmed animals and the Holocaust – Stern as a Holocaust survivor and a poet, Norma as a philosopher and the stereotyped daughter-in-law-as-antagonist. In *Diary* J. C.'s public voice is tempered by the various private ones, including his own; Anya, for instance, who calls herself his "guardian angel" (85), is unafraid to tell him that the implied authority of his "strong opinions" will alienate his reader: "There is a tone … a tone that really turns people off. A know-it-all tone. Everything is cut and dried: *I am the one with all the answers, here is how it is, don't argue, it won't get you anywhere"* (original emphasis; DBY 70). Anya's boyfriend Alan disparages J. C. for his lack of action, a requirement of the organic intellectual of which Gramsci writes. In these words Alan questions J. C.'s intellectual integrity: "I ask myself, If he really believes in these human rights, why isn't he out in the real world fighting for them?" (DBY 197). Through the conduits of Costello and J. C., Coetzee puts ideas on the table, inviting debate rather than imperiously pressing observable truths or offering nullifying directives. This is a more obvious instance of what Laura Wright identifies as Coetzee's dialogism, "in the Bakhtinian sense, [in which he] refuses to claim the narrative position of the monologic insider, the textual presence that has access to the answers, or access to contested notions of the truth" (*Writing* 12).

It is the violation of the pacts of genre of these works that gives the (staged) intellectualism its edge. The initial public-lecture setting of the "lessons" establishes the pact between lecturer and audience (authoritative speaker instructs receptive audience) that is severely tested by the knowledge that Coetzee is presenting fiction. The subject matter of J. C.'s "strong opinions" (*Diary*), which Spencer describes as, "In length, tone and style resemble[ing] nothing so much as the philosophical apercus of Nietzsche or the *Minima Moralia* of Adorno" ("War on Terror" n. pag.) and which Alan calls J. C.'s "morality play" (DBY 97), profess the kind of truthfulness and authority that accrues to ethico-political conviction through their very mode of address – the opinion piece. At stake is whether fiction and intellectualism in this context are a happy marriage and, furthermore, whether Coetzee can successfully or indeed productively align his various personae of author, critic, public intellectual and citizen (or private individual with both rights and obligations to society).

Michael Bell, Graham and Wright all point up the manner in which, through the lectures and lessons, Coetzee performs his so-called alter ego and the effect such a performance generates. Bell contends that Costello is a device that allows Coetzee to express opinions he otherwise would publicly shirk, yet warns that if Costello were a "straightforward mouthpiece" then the readings Coetzee makes *through* Costello of the likes of Lawrence and Ted Hughes would be "disingenuous" (176). Similarly, the disjuncture between Costello and Coetzee is evident, Bell implies, in Costello's tendency "to override the internal niceties of irony in a literary work and go directly for its existential premises" (175). Such a manoeuvre would break with Coetzee's skepticism of positionality. Directing us to a comment by Coetzee in *Doubling the Point* in which he explains that "There is no ethical imperative that I claim access to[;] Elizabeth [Curren in *Age of Iron*] is the one who believes in *should*", Bell concludes that "*Lives* is a closely structured examination of why Coetzee himself cannot readily believe in 'believes in'" (original emphasis; DP 250; Bell 175).

Wright analyzes Coetzee's genre acts from almost an antithetical perspective to Bell by claiming that Coetzee is performing a feminist "rant" "clothed in the auspices of a fiction". She picks up on the question of the pact of genre to which I am referring when she argues that *Lives* "examines the interaction and disjunction *between two modes of discourse*: the seemingly objective rhetoric of a philosophical lecture, and the subjective, lived experience of the polemical diatribe" (emphasis added; "Feminist-Vegetarian" 198). Graham argues that the Costello lectures should be read within the context of female voices in Coetzee's oeuvre which all self-reflexively question "discourses of authority and origin" ("Textual Transvestism" 219). Both Wright and Graham suggest that it is through a form of "excitable speech" (Judith Butler qtd. in Wright, "Feminist-Vegetarian" 196) or, alternatively, "hystericized narrative" (Graham, "Textual Transvestism" 230), which contravene the phallocentric economy of authorship, that Costello's interventions are effectually, that is ethico-politically, made.

What happens when the idea of (secular) belief is mediated, as it is here, through the prism of fiction? Bell notes that in the case of *Lives* the transposition of pieces that were originally staged as lectures to novel form alters the nature of Coetzee's intellectual intervention in important ways: "The[lectures] become part of a horizontal axis of mutual reference between similar fictions rather than vertical penetrations of the interface between fiction and the world of extrafictional responsibilities" ("What is it like?" 174). Through a process of revision, the public impact of the "lessons" apparently is weakened. Though *Diary* is a novel, Coetzee offers tantalizing clues that J. C.'s strong opinions might be Coetzee's own.

Costello in "Lesson 3: The Philosophers and the Animals" tests the pact of the public lecture (and the patience of her audience) with her polemical comparison of the treatment of the Jews during the Holocaust with the treatment of factory-farmed animals. The (fictional) poet Abraham Stern calls her analogy "a trick with words which I will not accept": "If Jews were treated like cattle, it does not follow that cattle are treated like Jews" (EC 94). This supposed trick which deceptively comments on Coetzee's genre trick may not be a trick at all: Costello actually refutes the very concept of a hierarchy of human and non-human animals, basing her animal ethics on natural rights theory rather than utilitarianism.[6] As Singer suggests in his response to *Lives*, a "comparison is not necessarily an equation" (LA 86). On a meta-discursive level, Coetzee through Costello exposes the weak points of analogy in a move with which we are now familiar. Moreover, by referring to her own novel *The House on Eccles Street* and calling upon Kafka's story of the ape "Red Peter" to support her case on our commonality with animals, Costello herself transgresses the pact of the public intervention by invoking fiction to defend a rational argument.

Diary is more than a series of opinion pieces. It presents several distinct yet concurrent "voices", each graphically underscored on the page. The top part is devoted, firstly, in Part One, to the ageing novelist J. C.'s diary of "strong opinions" and in Part Two to more personal diary entries from the "Second Diary" that Anya calls his "Soft Opinions" (DBY 193). The opinion pieces are offset on the lower

---

6   Laura Wright makes such a distinction between modes of animal rights theories ("Feminist-Vegetarian" 209).

part of the page by the personal narrative of J. C. as he first encounters Anya, who is coquettish yet ultimately sincere. Anya's voice shortly interjects as a third and is subsequently joined by that of the disgruntled and jealous Alan, who plots to siphon money from J. C.'s bank account. Finally, the voices of these two gradually displace the personal voice of J. C. which recedes into his second diary. Through syncretized strategies of juxtaposition and defamiliarization – we are obliged to move backwards and forwards through the text if we are to follow the stories simultaneously – private and public first are brought into sharp relief, gradually to reveal the mediation of political thoughts by private ones embodied in J. C.'s transitional consciousness.

Christopher Tayler reads the narrative device in *Diary* as a "comedy of conflicting perspectives, of high rhetoric and low aims" in which "[J]C's political writings … are accompanied by his attack on his credentials as a guru – an attack growing out of the questioning of the novelist's authority" (Tayler n. pag.). Hilary Mantel, critiquing the book's *graphic* effect on the page, corroborates my argument about defamiliarization in her suggestion that the format of *Diary* makes it impossible to "concentrate on the argument" which "shar[es] the space" with another story (Mantel n. pag.). In an analysis not unlike Tayler's, she intones, "above the line [J. C.] continues to assert himself … Below the line he trembles" (Mantel n. pag.). Spencer takes a rather different view: the cacophony of voices in *Diary* means that "the process of dialogue is here built more openly into the very form of the text" ("Colonial Violence" 179), a technique that he defines as "contrapuntal": "made up of interweaving voice parts. This means *not that the thoughts of J. C. are supplanted or discredited in any way* but rather that his too proud and oracular voice is qualified by that of Anya, whose own frequently flippant outlook is modified in turn" (emphasis added; Spencer "Colonial Violence" 180). Whilst the idea that the text incorporates a contrapuntal technique rings true, the very "qualification" of J. C.'s public-political voice suggests a supplanting of sorts, particularly as the "strong opinions" are superseded by the soft ones in the second part. Importantly, Mantel argues, as Anya becomes a stronger presence (she struggles for her place in the narrative, asking, "But what about me[; w]ho listens to my opinions?" [DBY 101]), it becomes painfully apparent that the "strong opinions" of the intellectualizing J. C. are undermined by Anya's greater worldliness (experience being the elixir of creative writing Coetzee's protagonists, including J. C., fruitlessly chase) (Mantel n. pag.). Anya's voice, for instance, cuts across J. C.'s reflections "On paedophilia": "I saw enough of old men and little girls in Viet Nam", she says (DBY 88). J. C.'s reflections on the ageing writer's shift from didacticism to an affirmation of life notably come after Anya's repeated assertions that political diatribes just won't sell.

The multiple voices in *Diary* – what, in a different context, Wright calls Coetzee's dialogism – constitute a mélange of "diaries", each with its respective genre pacts. Firstly, we have J. C.'s contributions to *Strong Opinions*: a volume of opinion pieces from six eminent writers whose brief from the German publisher is "the more contentious the better" and which is likely therefore to compromise the intellectual "truths" of the writing (DBY 21). Secondly, the more personal, unpublished Second Diary, is a kind of journal which, even if more formal than the conventional diary, incorporates the first person pronoun used only sparingly in the "strong opinions" and that, despite J. C.'s claims to the contrary, is a result of his interaction with Anya. J. C.'s "soft opinions" coincide with his decline towards death – a 72-year-old victim to Parkinson's, he apparently dies at the novel's close. The confessional aura of the second set of entries, denoted by pronoun usage and subject matter – in general, a move away from the "hurly-burly" of politics (DBY 171) to private reflection on lived experience – is given more credence by this very fact; as Coetzee argues in "Confession and Double Thoughts", confessants on the brink of death are likely to be more truthful because they have less to lose in telling the truth (DP 284). I would argue that the novel presents us with a third form, a notional private diary situated at the bottom of the page containing the expression of day-to-day thoughts and experiences (notional because it is never referred to as such and, like Mrs. Curren's letter, it includes reported speech). The interaction of these three modes of "speech" constitutes a strategy of demystification. The strong opinions are juxtaposed, firstly, with J. C.'s second diary entries which like Costello's reflections on the lives of animals centre on the experience of being, and, secondly, with the everyday ruminations of the third "diary". On this point Coetzee's essay "Apartheid Thinking" is instructive: under oppressive regimes like apartheid autobiography can usefully be recalibrated within the public sphere to demystify apartheid ideology, the objective of which was to "deform[ ] and harden[ ]" – dehumanize – the heart (GO 164). The "heart-speech" of autobiography would challenge apartheid in the "lair of the heart" (GO 164). In *Diary*, through his more private diary entries, therefore, J. C. is feeling his way to a fuller, more sympathetic understanding of (political) life.

Coetzee's public interventions therefore typically defer to the intensely private. In turn, representations of the private illuminate the interests of the public sphere. (Moreover, "public" is problematized by the private nature of citizenry as well as by the requirements of free speech.) Lecturing on animal rights in *Lives*, Costello is mistrustful of reason – the intellectual faculty – on the grounds that it is the reasoned idea that animals lack reason that is invoked to justify us humans eating animal flesh. Like us, she argues, animals experience the "sensation of being" and therefore deserve our humanity (LA 33). Costello claims that the heart is "the seat of a faculty, *sympathy*, that allows us to share at times the being of another" (LA 34): by sharing experience one makes oneself accountable to one's fellow animals, human and non-human, and to society. It is a feeling towards a sense of community rather than a community of correct feeling. She brings the sympathetic faculty to bear upon the discourses of reason that feed public, intellectual debate. Costello presses the concept of embodiment, setting the process of textual signification in reverse, by comparing the animal imagery in Rilke and Hughes: whilst in Rilke "animals stand for human qualities", Hughes, through "poetic invention" (*Lives* 53), is "feeling his way toward a different kind of being-in-the-world, one which is not entirely foreign to us ... The poem asks us to imagine our way into that way of moving, to inhabit that body" (*Lives* 50–51).

If Costello advocates what Attwell calls a "redemptive, ontological consciousness", "a valorisation of being itself" ("Life and Times" 38), J. C. turns to music: "Music expresses feeling, that is to say, gives shape and habitation to feeling, not in space but in time", he intones (DBY 130). Grouchily bemoaning the "thudding, mechanical music favoured by the young", the old curmudgeon contends that feelings "must have a history too", which leads him to the bleak conclusion that certain "qualities of feeling [ ] have not survived into the twenty-first century" (DBY 130). He pinpoints the ethicality of music, claiming that in "nineteenth-century art-song ... singing meant to convey moral nobility ... [t]he very sound the singer produced ... had a reflective quality" (DBY 131).

These are two examples of what Attwell, drawing upon Said (who like J. C. is talking about music), calls instances of other "*languages*": other modes of "social practice" that can nurture the kind of dissenting mindset that questions the social order and that is the lifeblood of intellectualism. From such modes of experience, we would learn, in Said's words, "to grasp and dissent from our fate as citizens in society, to make and unmake, to construct and deconstruct the forms of life into which we have been formed and from which mortality decrees that we must leave" (qtd. in Attwell, "Life and Times" 38). "Truths" of the kind Costello and J. C. disseminate via the sympathetic imagination might resonate differently from Said's public truth-speaking according to Attwell (who is writing about *Elizabeth Costello*), but they chime with his principle of "several languages" ("Life and Times" 38).

Via his association with Anya which slowly warms to friendship, J. C. makes a move not unlike Costello's in "The Problem of Evil": Anya functions as a kind of sympathetic medium that leads J. C. to moderate his "strong opinions" in the first part to "soft" ones in Part Two, the Second Diary, marked by a shift to the confessional "I". Anya reminds him of her place in the diaries: "I really do hope you will publish your soft opinions one day. If you do, remember to send a copy to the little typist who showed you the way" (DBY 222). Based on Anya's compassion for his "post-physical" needs (DBY 13), it is J. C.'s friendship with Anya that leads him to revise his sense of conviction just as Costello revised hers: "What has begun to change since I moved into the orbit of Anya is not my opinions themselves so much as my opinion of my opinions" (136), he says. Can he stand by the "hard" opinions he has published? Through Anya's eyes, as his sympathetic medium, he can see "how alien and antiquated they may seem" (DBY 137), even though his opinions are "now so strong ... that aside from the odd word here and there there was no chance that refraction through her gaze could alter their angle" (DBY 125). Yet his turn to the Second Diary does indeed signify a change of heart. J. C. defers to the intimacy of death as he remembers a recurring dream of his own death and the presence of a girl (who we assume is Anya) who "was doing her best to soften the impact of death while shielding me from other people" (DBY 157).

Anya too experiences a change of heart, confessing as she signs her penultimate message to J. C., "Anya [an admirer too]" (DBY 227).

The integrity of the intellectual is therefore tested by the question, to what point do I stand my ground? "Lesson 8: At the Gate" in *Elizabeth Costello* stages an all too literary death of Costello – a "purgatory of clichés" – in a parody of Kafka's "Before the Law" embedded in *The Trial* (1925) in which Costello is called upon by the keeper of the gate to prepare a statement of her belief. As in Kafka, her early attempts are rejected (like Costello, K. never passes the test; he is executed "like a dog"). Here is Costello's first offering:

> *I am a writer, a trader in fictions … . I maintain beliefs only provisionally: fixed beliefs would stand in my way. I change my beliefs as I change my habitation or my clothes, according to my needs. On these grounds – professional, vocational – I request exemption from a rule … that every petitioner at the gate should hold to one or more beliefs.* (original emphasis; EC 195)

Not unlike Coetzee's position of nonposition, Costello subscribes to the idea that "Unbelief is a belief" (EC 201). Her words that preface this first attempt, that as a novelist, "It is not my profession to believe … *I do imitations*" (emphasis added; EC 194), hints at Coetzee's device in his acts of genre. Here, Costello stands by the principle of open-endedness in fiction: that the ethico-political purchase of creative writing, channelled by fixed belief, is in danger of being stymied – Adorno's "flat objectivity" ("Commitment" 79). Yet she is forced to reconsider her statement if she wishes to pass through purgatory. Unable to commit herself to a position of "believes in" – "in my work a belief is a resistance, an obstacle" (EC 200), she explains – she reformulates her script. This sentiment, however, jars with her passionate defence of animals and with her belief in the moral bankruptcy of representing evil. Like Coetzee, she seamlessly withdraws behind her private persona as novelist as and when she chooses. She revisits the sympathetic faculty, represented by the language of the heart, which is an alternative "ethical support[ ]" to belief (EC 203). In an environment that is "*Too literary, too literary!*" and which Costello says she must "*get out of* [ ] *before I die!*" (EC 215), she revises her submission to a belief in the experience simply of being. In a passage frequently commented upon by critics, she commits herself to belief in the tiny frogs of the Dulgannon mudflats:

> Excuse my language. I am or have been a professional writer … . In my account, for whose many failings I beg your pardon, the life cycle of the frog may sound allegorical, but to the frogs themselves it is no allegory, it is the thing itself, the only thing … . It is because of the indifference of those little frogs to my belief … that I believe in them. (EC 217)

This, her final statement, is misinterpreted by the judges as allegory: "These Australian frogs of yours embody the spirit of life, which is what you as a storyteller believe in". Acquiescing to this misunderstanding, as she also acquiesces to the Polish woman's advice to "Show [the judges] passion and they will let you through" (EC 213), compromises Costello's (un)belief. She remains silent: "she reins herself in. She is not here to win an argument, she is here to win a pass, a passage" (EC 219). In other words, in her incarnation here as novelist rather than public intellectual, she compromises her belief whilst albeit silently holding to her first statement, that of unbelief. These are her writerly principles, which are in fact what Head calls Coetzee's "enduring faith in fiction" for its capacity to function as another universe of discourse. The judges' wilful misreading of Costello's statement, as Head points out,

> brings with it another paradox: the writer cannot escape the imposition
> of metaphorical levels on his or her expression, and this may produce the
> nightmarish sense of being misunderstood (as in Costello's parodically
> Kafkaesque experience "at the gate"). In this sense, the frustration of Costello is
> a way for Coetzee to explore and express the limits of fiction and of the writer's
> authority. ("Belief" 115)

J. C. makes an affirmation of life in the Second Diary, ironically, as he is eased towards death by Anya. He reflects on the softening of opinions in the ageing writer, who experiences a "growing detachment from the world". Whilst the "syndrome" is often attributed to "a waning of creative power", "from the inside the same development may bear a quite different interpretation: as a liberation, a clearing of the mind to take on more important tasks". He notices a shift in Tolstoy from didacticism to the question of "how to live" (DBY 193). It is this question which colours the Second Diary to which J. C. is guided by Anya, who promises to see him on his passage to death: "I can't go with you but what I will do is hold your hand as far as the gate" (DBY 226).

Coetzee's morbid fascination with the effect of imminent death upon the writer, which at heart expresses an anxiety about authority in fiction, is a trope that resurfaces throughout the oeuvre. In the face of death any inhibitions Mrs. Curren may have harboured in expressing her convictions are easily dispelled. Paul Rayment in *Slow Man*, apparently surviving his accident, imagines preparing a statement of belief "When he arrives at the gate": "When I was living I did not understand, father, but now I understand, now that it is too late; and believe me, father, I repent, I repent me, *je me repens*, and bitterly too" (original emphasis; SM 34). To whom Rayment confesses is left in doubt, given that Coetzee chooses not to capitalize "father". Could this be the authorial father (replacing the Divine), who in the guise of Elizabeth Costello turns out to be a mother after all? Costello tells Rayment that "you came to me, as I told you: the man with the bad leg" (SM 88–89): fitting material for a book.

I began this chapter with Coetzee's question, what does each revelation I make cost? By this Coetzee means, what cost to the discourse of genre does truth-telling entail? In these later, quasi-fictional works Coetzee may appear to be making public interventions in the familiar format of the public lecture and the opinion piece. Indeed, the similarity in belief and personal traits between Coetzee and his characters in the works discussed here might seem to bear this out. But scratch below the surface and quite a different story emerges. The forum of the public lecture in *Lives* and *Elizabeth Costello* and of the opinion piece in *Diary* provides an opening for the more private, sympathetic voice to emerge, one less certain of intellectual truths. Costello's son John in "Realism" asks, "Isn't that what is most important about fiction: that it takes us out of ourselves, into other lives?" (EC 23). If Coetzee transgresses the pact of the public intervention through the medium of fiction, so too do Costello and J. C. by invoking the sympathetic faculty, and in Costello's case fiction too.

Wright argues that, "by enacting Elizabeth Costello in *The Lives of Animals*, Coetzee gets a rant and a sentimental voice presented *through rational argument*" (emphasis added; "Feminist-Vegetarian" 212). However, the argument can be reversed: public intellectualism can be measured by the sentimental voice and by fiction. Coetzee is always heedful of the paradox of authorship, that getting one's voice heard is always at the cost of imposing authority, humorously implied in Costello's parody of the myth of Genesis when she comforts Rayment in *Slow Man*: "I will teach you how to speak from the heart[; o]ne two-hour lesson a day, six days a week; on the seventh day we can rest" (SM 231). Coetzee utilizes fictive forums to test the limits of the intellectual's authority, which as I have shown is itself a worthy intellectual endeavour. This does not mean that Costello or J. C.'s polemics are for nought: Coetzee's fiction is too complex to be reduced to single planes of signification or straightforward allegory. Through its paradoxes of postcolonial authorship Coetzee's oeuvre, in Adorno's words, sets about "awaken[ing] the free choice of the agent", and ultimately this is the fiction's ethico-political currency.

Works Cited

Primary Sources

Coetzee, J. M. *Age of Iron*. 1990. London: Penguin, 1991.
———. *Boyhood: A Memoir*. 1997. London: Vintage, 1998.
———. "Critic and Citizen: A Response." *Pretexts* 9.1 (2000): 109–11.
———. *Diary of a Bad Year*. London: Harvill Secker, 2007.
———. *Disgrace*. London: Secker & Warburg, 1999.
———. *Doubling the Point: Essays and Interviews*. Ed. David Attwell. Cambridge Massachusetts; London: Harvard UP, 1992.
———. *Dusklands*. London: Vintage, 1998. First published 1974.
———. *Elizabeth Costello*. London: Secker & Warburg, 2003.
———. "Elizabeth Costello and the Problem of Evil." *Salmagundi* 137–38 (2003): 48–64.
———. *Foe*. 1986. Middlesex: Penguin, 1987.
———. *Giving Offense: Essays on Censorship*. Chicago: Chicago UP, 1996.
———. *The Humanities in Africa. Die Geisteswissenschaften in Afrika*. Intro. Heinrich Meier. Munich: Carl Friedrich von Siemens Stiftung, 2001.
———. *In the Heart of the Country*. 1977. London: Vintage, 1999.
———. *Life & Times of Michael K*. 1983. Middlesex: Penguin, 1985.
———. *The Lives of Animals*. With Wendy Doniger, Marjorie Garber, Peter Singer and Barbara Smuts. Ed. and intro. Amy Gutmann. Princeton: Princeton UP, 1999.
———. *The Master of Petersburg*. 1994. London: Minerva, 1995.
———. "The Novel Today." *Upstream* 6.1 (1988): 2–5.
———. *Slow Man: A Novel*. New York: Viking, 2005.
———. *Stranger Shores: Essays 1986–1999*. London: Secker & Warburg, 2001.
———. "Truth in Autobiography." Unpublished Inaugural Lecture. University of Cape Town, 1984.
———. *Waiting for the Barbarians*. 1980. London: Minerva, 1997.
———. "What is Realism?" *Salmagundi*. Spring/Summer (1997): 60–81.
———. *White Writing: On the Culture of Letters in South Africa*. London & New Haven: Yale University, 1988.

Secondary Sources

Achebe, Chinua. *Hopes and Impediments: Selected Essays: 1965–1987*. Oxford: Heinemann, 1988.

———. *Things Fall Apart*. 1958. African Writers Series. London: Heinemann, 1986.

Adorno, Theodor. "Commitment." *New Left Review* 87–88 (1974): 75-89.

———. "Notes on Kafka." *Franz Kafka*. Ed. and intro. Harold Bloom. Modern Critical Views. New York; Philadelphia: Chelsea House Publishers, 1986. 95–105.

Ahmad, Aijaz. "Jameson's Rhetoric of Otherness and the 'National Allegory.'" *Social Text* 17 (1987): 3–25.

Alexander, Neville. *An Ordinary Country: Issues in the Transition from Apartheid to Democracy in South Africa*. 2002. New York and Oxford: Berghahn Books, 2003.

———. "A Plea for a New World: Review of *Foe*, by J. M. Coetzee." *Die Suid-Afrikaan* 10 (1987): 38.

Attridge, Derek. "Age of Bronze, State of Grace: Music and Dogs in Coetzee's *Disgrace*." *Novel* 34.1 (2000): 98–121.

———. "Expecting the Unexpected in Coetzee's *Master of Petersburg* and Derrida's Recent Writings." *Applying: To Derrida*. Ed. John Brannigan et al. Basingstoke and London: Macmillan, 1996. 21–41.

———. "J. M. Coetzee's *Disgrace*: Introduction." *J. M. Coetzee's* Disgrace. Ed. Derek Attridge and Peter D. McDonald. Spec. issue of *Interventions* 4.3 (2002): 315–20.

———. *J. M. Coetzee and the Ethics of Reading: Literature in the Event*. Chicago: Chicago UP, 2004.

———. "Trusting the Other: Ethics and Politics in J. M. Coetzee's *Age of Iron*." *The Writings of J. M. Coetzee*. Ed. Michael Valdez Moses. Spec. issue of *South Atlantic Quarterly* 93.1 (1994): 59–82.

Attwell, David. "'Dialogue' and 'Fulfilment' in J. M. Coetzee's *Age of Iron*." *Writing South Africa: Literature, Apartheid, and Democracy, 1970–1995*. Ed. Derek Attridge and Rosemary Jolly. Cambridge: Cambridge UP, 1998. 149–65.

———. *J. M. Coetzee: South Africa and the Politics of Writing*. Berkeley, Los Angeles; London: University of California Press, 1993.

———. "The Life and Times of Elizabeth Costello: J. M. Coetzee and the Public Sphere." *J. M. Coetzee and the Idea of the Public Intellectual*. Ed. Jane Poyner. Athens, Ohio: Ohio UP, 2006. 25–41.

———. "Race in *Disgrace*." *J. M. Coetzee's* Disgrace. Ed. Derek Attridge and Peter D. McDonald. Spec. issue of *Interventions* 4.3 (2002): 331–41.

———. *Rewriting Modernity: Studies in Black South African Literary History*. Scottsville: U KwaZulu-Natal P, 2005.

Bakhtin, Mikhail. *Problems of Dostoevsky's Poetics*. Ed. and trans. Caryl Emerson. Intro. Wayne C. Booth. Theory and History of Literature 8. Manchester: Manchester UP, 1984.

Banville, John. "Endgame: *Disgrace* by J. M. Coetzee." *New York Review* 20 January 2000: 23–25.

Barnard, Rita. "Dream Topographies: J. M. Coetzee and the South African Pastoral." *The Writings of J. M. Coetzee*. Ed. Michael Valdez Moses. Spec. issue of *South Atlantic Quarterly* 93.1 (1994): 33–58.

———. "'Imagining the Unimaginable': J. M. Coetzee, History and Autobiography," Rev. of *Doubling the Point: Essays and Interviews* by J. M. Coetzee and ed. by David Attwell. *Postmodern Culture* 4.1 (1993). Online posting. http://muse.jhu. edu/journals/postmodern_culture/v004/4.1r_barnard.html.

Barthes, Roland. "The Death of the Author." *Modern Literary Theory: A Reader*, 2nd edn. Ed. Philip Rice and Patricia Waugh. London: Edward Arnold, 1992. 114–18.

———. *Mythologies*. 1957. Selected and trans. Annette Lavers. London: Vintage, 2000.

Beckett, Samuel. *Molloy, Malone Dies, The Unnamable*. 1959. London: John Calder, 1976.

Begam, Richard. "Silence and Mut(e)ilation: White Writing in J. M. Coetzee's *Foe*." *The Writings of J. M. Coetzee*. Ed. Michael Valdez Moses. Spec. issue of *South Atlantic Quarterly* 93.1 (1994): 111–27.

Beinart, William. *Twentieth-Century South Africa*. Oxford: Oxford UP, 1994.

Bell, Michael. "What Is It Like to Be a Nonracist? Costello and Coetzee on the Lives of Animals and Men". *J. M. Coetzee and the Idea of the Public Intellectual*. Ed. Jane Poyner. Athens, Ohio: Ohio UP, 2006. 172–92.

Bhabha, Homi. "The Other Question—The Stereotype and Colonial Discourse." *Screen* 24 (1983): 18–36.

———. "Postcolonial Authority and Postmodern Guilt." *Cultural Studies*. Ed. Lawrence Grossberg, Cary Nelson and Paula Treichler. London and New York: Routledge, 1992. 56–65.

Biko, Steve. *I Write What I Like: A Selection of His Writings*. 1978. Ed. Aelred Stubbs C. R.. Oxford: Heinemann, 1987.

Blanchot, Maurice. *The Work of Fire*. 1949. Trans. Charlotte Mandell. Stanford: Stanford UP, 1995.

Boehmer, Elleke. *Colonial and Postcolonial Literature*. Oxford: Oxford UP, 1995.

———. "Not Saying Sorry, Not Speaking Pain: Gender Implications in *Disgrace*." *J. M. Coetzee's Disgrace*. Ed. Derek Attridge and Peter D. McDonald. Spec. issue of *Interventions* 4.3 (2002): 342–51.

———. "Transfiguring: Colonial Body into Postcolonial Narrative." *Novel* 26.1 (1993): 268–77.

Bourke, Richard. *Romantic Discourse and Political Modernity: Wordsworth, the Intellectual and Cultural Critique*. Hemel Hempstead: Harvester Wheatsheaf, 1993.

Breytenbach, Breyten. *Buffalo Bill*. Johannesburg: Taurus, 1984.

———. *End Papers*. London: Faber, 1986.

———. *Mouroir: Mirrornotes of a Novel*. 1983. New York: Farrar/Straus/Giroux, 1984.

————. *The True Confessions of an Albino Terrorist*. London: Faber and Faber, 1984.

Brink, André and J. M. Coetzee. Eds. *A Land Apart: A South African Reader*. Boston and London: Faber and Faber, 1987.

Brown, Wendy. "Wounded Attachments." *Political Theory* 21.3 (1993): 390–410.

Burgess, Anthony. "The Beast Within: *Waiting for the Barbarians*." *New York* 26 April 1982. 88.

Butler, Judith. *Bodies That Matter: On the Discursive Limits of "Sex"*. New York and London: Routledge, 1993.

————. *Gender Trouble: Feminism and the Subversion of Identity*. Thinking Gender. London and New York: Routledge, 1990.

Cartwright, Justin. "Stranger than Fiction." *The Guardian* 19 April 2001. Online posting. http://www.guardian.co.uk/g2/story/0,3604,474849,00.html.

Cavafy, C. P. "Waiting for the Barbarians." 1904. *Scanning the Century: The Penguin Book of the Twentieth Century in Poetry*. Ed. Peter Forbes. London: Penguin, 2000. 5–6.

Chatterjee, Partha. *The Nation and Its Fragments: Colonial and Postcolonial Histories*. Princeton: Princeton UP, 1993.

Claridge, Laura. *Romantic Potency: The Paradox of Desire*. New York: Cornell UP, 1992.

Clingman, Stephen. "Beyond the Limit: The Social Relations of Madness in Southern African Fiction." *The Bounds of Race: Perspectives on Hegemony and Resistance*. Ed. Dominick LaCapra. Ithaca and London: Cornell UP, 1991. 231–54.

————. "Letter to Mr. Félix Faure, President of the Republic." *Émile Zola, The Dreyfus Affair*. Ed. Alain Pagés. New Haven: Yale UP, 1996. 43–53.

Conrad, Joseph. *Heart of Darkness*. 1902. New York: New American Library, 1950.

Dangor, Achmat. *Bitter Fruit*. Cape Town: Kwela, 2001.

Defoe, Daniel. *Robinson Crusoe*. 1719. New York: Bantam Books, 1981.

————. *Roxana: the Fortunate Mistress*. 1724. London: Simpkin, Marshall, Hamilton, Kent & Co., n.d.

Derrida, Jacques. *Acts of Literature*. Ed. Derek Attridge. London; New York: Routledge, 1992.

————. "On Forgiveness." *On Cosmopolitanism and Forgiveness*. Thinking in Action. London and New York: Routledge, 2001.

————. *Writing and Difference*. Trans. and intro. Alan Bass. London: Routledge, 1978.

Dirlik, Arif. "'Like a Song Gone Silent': The Political Ecology of Barbarism and Civilization in *Waiting for the Barbarians* and *The Legend of the Thousand Bulls*." *Diaspora* 3 (1991): 321–52.

Dostoyevsky, Fyodor. *The Idiot*. 1868. Oxford World's Classics. Oxford: Oxford UP, 1992.

————. *The Possessed*. 1872. Trans. Constance Garnett. Foreword Avrahm Yarmolinsky. New York: Modern Library, n.d.

Dovey, Teresa. *The Novels of J. M. Coetzee: Lacanian Allegories*. Craighall: Ad. Donker, 1988.

———. "*Waiting for the Barbarians*: Allegory of Allegories." *Critical Perspectives on J. M. Coetzee*. Ed. Graham Huggan and Stephen Watson. Basingstoke; London: Macmillan, 1996. 138–51.

Easton, Kai. "Coetzee's *Disgrace*: Byron in Italy and the Eastern Cape c. 1820." *Journal of the Commonwealth Literature* 42.3 (2007): 113–30.

Eckstein, Barbara. "Iconicity, Immersion and Otherness: The Hegelian 'Dive' of J. M. Coetzee and Adrienne Rich." *Mosaic* 29.1 (1996). Online posting. 13 September 2007. http://0-lion.chadwyck.co.uk.pugwash.lib.warwick.ac.uk/searchFulltext.do?id=R01529661&divLevel=0&area=abell&forward=critref_ft.

Emants, Marcellus. *A Posthumous Confession*. Trans. and intro. J. M. Coetzee. London: Quartet, 1986.

Erasmus, Desiderius. *Praise of Folly*. 1509. Trans. Betty Radice. Intro. A. H. T. Levi. London: Penguin, 1971.

Fanon, Frantz. *Black Skin, White Masks*. 1952. Trans. Charles Lam Markmann. London: Pluto Press, 1986.

———. *The Wretched of the Earth*. 1961. Trans. Constance Farrington. Penguin: London, 1990.

Farred, Grant. "The Mundanacity of Violence: Living in a State of *Disgrace*." *J. M. Coetzee's* Disgrace. Ed. Derek Attridge and Peter D. McDonald. Spec. issue of *Interventions* 4.3 (2002): 352–62.

Felman, Shoshana. "Women and Madness: The Critical Phallacy." *The Feminist Reader: Essays in Gender and the Politics of Literary Criticism*. Ed. Catherine Belsey and Jane Moore. 2nd edn Basingstoke; London: Macmillan, 1997. 117–32.

———. *Writing and Madness: (Literature/Philosophy/Psychoanalysis)*. Trans. Martha Noel Evans and Shoshana Felman. Ithaca: Cornell UP, 1985.

Ferguson, James. *The Anti-Politics Machine: 'Development,' Depoliticisation and Bureaucratic State Power in Lesotho*. Cape Town: David Philip, 1990.

Foucault, Michel. *Discipline and Punish: The Birth of the Prison*. 1975. Trans. Alan Sheridan. London: Penguin, 1991.

———. *Madness and Civilization: A History of Insanity in the Age of Reason*. 1965. Trans. Richard Howard. London: Routledge, 1989.

———. "What is an Author?" *Textual Strategies: Perspectives in Post-Structuralist Criticism*. Ed. Josué V. Harari. Ithaca, New York: Cornell UP, 1979. 141–60.

Freud, Sigmund. "A Child is Being Beaten: A Contribution to the Study of the Origin of Sexual Perversion." 1919. *The Standard Edition of Complete Psychological Works of Sigmund Freud*. Vol. 17. Ed. and trans. James Strachey. London: Hogarth and the Institute of Psychoanalysis, 1955. 175–204.

———. "Lecture XXXIII: Femininity." 1933. *The Standard Edition of Complete Psychological Works of Sigmund Freud*. Vol. 22. Ed. and trans. James Strachey. London: Hogarth and the Institute of Psychoanalysis, 1964. 112–35.

Gallagher, Susan Van Zanten. *A Story of South Africa: J. M. Coetzee's Fiction in Context*. Cambridge, Massachusetts: Harvard UP, 1991.

———. "Torture and the Novel: J. M. Coetzee's *Waiting for the Barbarians*." *Contemporary Literature* 29.2 (1988): 277–85.

Gilbert, Sandra and Susan Gubar. *The Madwoman in the Attic: The Woman Writer and the Nineteenth-Century Literary Imagination*. Yale UP, New Haven, 1979.

Gilroy, Paul. *Against Race: Imaging Political Culture Beyond the Color Line*. Cambridge: Harvard UP, 2000.

Glenn, Ian. "Game Hunting in *In the Heart of the Country*." *Critical Perspectives on J. M. Coetzee*. Ed. Graham Huggan and Stephen Watson. Preface Nadine Gordimer. Basingstoke: Macmillan, 1996: 120–37.

Gordimer, Nadine. *Burger's Daughter*. 1979. Harmondsworth: Penguin, 1980.

———. *The Conservationist*. 1974. London: Penguin, 1978.

———. *The Essential Gesture: Writing, Politics and Places*. Ed. Stephen Clingman. London: Jonathan Cape, 1988.

———. *The House Gun*. 1998. London: Bloomsbury, 1999.

———. "The Idea of Gardening: *Life and Times of Michael K* by J. M. Coetzee." *New York Review of Books* 31.1 (1984): 3–6.

———. *July's People*. 1981. London: Penguin, 1982.

Graham, James. "Abject Land: Rethinking the Connections between Women, Land and Nation in Doris Lessing's *The Grass is Singing* and Chenjerai Hove's *Bones*." Unpublished paper, 2007.

———. "An Abject Land? Remembering Women Differently in Doris Lessing's *The Grass is Singing* and Chenjerai Hove's *Bones*'." *English Studies in Africa*. 50.1 (2007): 57–74.

Graham, Lucy. "Reading the Unspeakable: Rape in *Disgrace*." *Journal of Southern African Studies* 29.2 (2003): 433–444.

———. "Textual Transvestism: The Female Voices of J. M. Coetzee." *J. M. Coetzee and the Idea of the Public Intellectual*. Ed. Jane Poyner. Athens, Ohio: Ohio UP, 2006. 217–35.

Gramsci, Antonio. *Selections from the Prison Notebooks of Antonio Gramsci*. Ed. Quintin Hoare and Geoffrey Nowell Smith. London: Lawrence & Wishart, 1971.

Gray, Stephen. *Southern African Literature: An Introduction*. Cape Town: David Philip; London: Rex Collings, 1979.

Grossvogel, David I. "*The Trial*: Structure as Mystery." *Franz Kafka*. Ed. and intro. Harold Bloom. Modern Critical Views. New York; Philadelphia: Chelsea House Publishers, 1986. 183–98.

La Guma, Alex. *In the Fog of the Season's End*. Harare: Baobab Books, 1992.

Hacking, Ian. "Our Fellow Animals." Rev. of *The Lives of Animals* by J. M. Coetzee, and *Ethics into Action: Henry Spira and the Animal Rights Movement* by Peter Singer. *The New York Review* 29 June 2000: 20–26.

Head, Dominic. "A Belief in Frogs: J. M. Coetzee's Enduring Faith in Fiction." *J. M. Coetzee and the Idea of the Public Intellectual*. Ed. Jane Poyner. Athens, Ohio: Ohio UP, 2006. 100–17.

———. *J. M. Coetzee*. Cambridge: Cambridge UP, 1997.

Higgins, Linda and Brenda Silver. *Rape and Representation*. New York: Columbia UP, 1991.

Holiday, Anthony. "Forgiving and Forgetting: the Truth and Reconciliation Commission." *Negotiating the Past: The Making of Memory in South Africa*. Ed. Sarah Nuttall and Carli Coetzee. Oxford: Oxford UP, 1998. 43–56.

Holland, Michael. "'*Plink-Plunk*': Unforgetting the Present in Coetzee's *Disgrace*." *J. M. Coetzee's* Disgrace. Ed. Derek Attridge and Peter D. McDonald. Spec. issue of *Interventions* 4.3 (2002): 395–404.

Hulme, Peter. *Colonial Encounters: Europe and the Caribbean 1492–1797*. London: Methuen, 1986.

Irigaray, Luce. *The Irigaray Reader*. Ed. and intro. Margaret Whitford. Oxford: Blackwell, 1991.

———. *This Sex Which Is Not One*. 1975. Trans. Catherine Porter. Ithaca: Cornell UP, 1985.

Jameson, Fredric. "Metacommentary." *PMLA,* 86.1 (1971): 9–17.

———. *Postmodernism: Or, the Cultural Logic of Late Capitalism*. North Carolina: Duke UP, 1992.

———. "Third-World Literature in the Era of Multinational Capitalism". *Social Text* 15 (1986): 65–88.

JanMohamed, Abdul R. "The Economy of Manichean Allegory: The Function of Racial Difference in Colonialist Literature." Ed. Henry Louis Gates Jr. *"Race," Writing, and Difference*. Spec. issue of *Critical Inquiry* 12.1. (1985): 59-87.

Jolly, Rosemary Jane. *Colonization, Violence, and Narration in White South African Writing: André Brink, Breyten Breytenbach, and J. M. Coetzee*. Athens, Ohio: Ohio UP; Johannesburg: Witwatersrand UP, 1996.

Kafka, Franz. "Before the Law." 1919. Trans. Edwin Muir and Willa Muir. *Franz Kafka: The Complete Stories*. Ed. Nahum N. Glatzer. Centennial edn. 1946. New York: Schocken Books, 1983.

———. *The Castle*. Trans. Willa and Edwin Muir. London: Minerva, 1992.

———. "A Hunger Artist." *Franz Kafka: The Complete Stories*. Ed. Nahum N. Glatzer. Foreword John Updike. 1946. New York: Schocken Books, 1983.

———. "The Hunger Strike." *Parables and Paradoxes: In German and English*. 1935. New York: Schocken Books, 1961.

———. "In the Penal Colony." Trans. Edwin Muir and Willa Muir. *Franz Kafka: The Complete Stories*. Ed. Nahum N. Glatzer. Centennial edn 1946. New York: Schocken Books, 1983.

———. "My Destination." *Parables and Paradoxes: In German and English*. 1935. New York: Schocken Books, 1961.

———. *Parables and Paradoxes: In German and English*. 1946. New York: Schocken Books, 1961.

———. *The Trial*. Trans. Willa and Edwin Muir. 1925. Harmondsworth: Penguin Books, 1953.

Kandiyoti, Deniz. "Identity and Its Discontents: Women and the Nation." *Colonial Discourse and Post-Colonial Theory: A Reader*. Ed. Patrick Williams and Laura Chrisman. Hemel Hempstead: Prentice Hall/Harvester Wheatsheaf, 1993. 376–91.

Kant, Immanuel. "The Categorical Imperative." 1785. *Ethics*. Ed. Peter Singer. Oxford Readers. Oxford: Oxford UP, 1994. 274–79.

———. *The Moral Law: Groundwork of the Metaphysic of Morals*. Trans. and analyzed H. J. Paton. 1948. London: Routledge, 1991.

———. "The Noble Descent of Duty." 1788. *Ethics*. Ed. Peter Singer. Oxford Readers. Oxford: Oxford UP, 1994. 39–41.

———. "On a Supposed Right to Lie from Altruistic Motives." 1785. *Ethics*. Ed. Peter Singer. Oxford Readers. Oxford: Oxford UP, 1994. 280–81.

Kingdon, Geeta and John Knight. "Unemployment in South Africa: A Microeconomic Approach." Centre for the Study of African Economies. Online posting. 13 January 2007. http://www.csae.ox.ac.uk/resprogs/usam/default.html.

Knox-Shaw, Peter. "*Dusklands*: A Metaphysics of Violence." *Contrast: Southern African Literary Journal* 14.1 (1982): 26–38.

Kossew, Sue. *Pen and Power: A Post-Colonial Reading of J. M. Coetzee and André Brink*. Amsterdam and Atlanta: Rodopi, 1996.

Krog, Antjie. *Country of My Skull*. London: Jonathan Cape, 1999. London: Vintage, 1999.

Lawrence, D. H. *Lady Chatterley's Lover*. 1928. New York: Modern Library, 1957.

 A Propos of Lady Chatterley's Lover. London: Mandrake Press, 1930. 9–10.

Lazarus, Neil. "Modernism and Modernity: T. W. Adorno and Contemporary White South African Literature." *Modernity and Modernism/Postmodernity and Postmodernism*. Spec. issue of *Cultural Critique* 5 (1986–87): 131–55.

Leatherbarrow, W. J. "*The Devils* in the Context of Dostoevsky's Life and Works." *Dostoevsky's* The Devils*: A Critical Companion*. Ed. W. J. Leatherbarrow. Illinois: Northwestern UP, 1999. 3–59.

Levinas, Emmanuel. *Totality and Infinity: An Essay on Exteriority*. Trans. Alphonso Lingis. Hague; Boston; London: Martinus Nijhoff, 1979.

Li, Victor. "Globalization's Robinsonade: Cast Away and Neo-Liberal Subject Formation." Conference paper. Rerouting the Postcolonial. Northampton University: n.p., 2007.

Lowry, Elizabeth. "Like a Dog." Rev. of *Disgrace* by J. M. Coetzee. *London Review of Books* 21.20 (1999): 12–14.

Lukács, Georg. *The Meaning of Contemporary Realism*. Trans. John and Necke Mander. London: Merlin, 1962.

Mamdani, Mahmood. "The Truth According to the TRC." *The Politics of Memory: Truth, Healing and Social Justice.* Ed. Ifi Amadiume and Abdullah An-Naim. New York: Zed Books. 176–83.

Mannoni, O. *Prospero and Caliban: The Psychology of Colonization.* New York: Praeger, 1964.

Mantel, Hilary. "The Shadow Line: *Diary of a Bad Year* by J. M. Coetzee." *New York Review of Books* 55.1. 17 Jan. 2008. Online posting. http://www.nybooks.com/articles/20936.

Marais, Michael. "J. M. Coetzee's *Disgrace* and the Task of the Imagination." *Journal of Modern Literature* 29.2 (2006): 75–93.

———. "Places of Pigs: The Tension Between Implication and Transcendence in J. M. Coetzee's *Age of Iron* and *The Master of Petersburg*." *Journal of Commonwealth Literature* 31.1 (1996): 83–95.

Marx, John. "Postcolonial Literature and the Western Literary Canon." *The Cambridge Companion to Postcolonial Literary Studies.* Ed. Neil Lazarus. Cambridge: Cambridge UP, 2004. 83–96.

Mbeki, Thabo. "When is Good New Bad News?" *ANC Today: Online Voice of the African National Congress* 4.39 (2004). Online posting. 29 March 2007. http://www.anc.org.za/ancdocs/anctoday/2004/at39.htm.

McDonald, Peter D. "*Disgrace* Effects." *J. M. Coetzee's* Disgrace. Ed. Derek Attridge and Peter D. McDonald. Spec. issue of *Interventions* 4.3 (2002): 321–30.

———. "'Not Undesirable': How J. M. Coetzee Escaped the Censor." *TLS* 19 May 2000: 14–15.

———. "The Writer, the Critic, and the Censor." *J. M. Coetzee and the Idea of the Public Intellectual.* Ed. Jane Poyner. Athens, Ohio: Ohio UP, 2006. 42–62.

Memmi, Albert. *The Colonizer and the Colonized.* 1965. Trans. Howard Greenfeld. London: Souvenir Press, 1974.

Merivale, Patricia. "Audible Palimpsests: Coetzee's Kafka." *Critical Perspectives on J. M. Coetzee.* Ed. Graham Huggan and Stephen Watson. London; New York: Macmillan, 1996. 152–167.

Millin, Sarah Gertrude. *God's Step-Children.* 1924. 2nd edn. London: Constable, 1951.

Morphet, Tony. "Two Interviews with J. M. Coetzee, 1983 and 1987." *TriQuarterly* 69 (1987): 454–64.

Moses, Michael Valdez, "Solitary Walkers: Rousseau and Coetzee's *Life & Times of Michael K.*" *The Writings of J. M. Coetzee.* Ed. Michael Valdez Moses. Spec. issue of *South Atlantic Quarterly* 93.1 (1994): 131–56.

Mulisch. Harry. *The Discovery of Heaven.* Trans. Paul Vincent. New York: Viking, 1996.

Ndebele, Njabulo S. *The Cry of Winnie Mandela: A Novel.* Claremont: David Philip, 2003.

———. "Memory, Metaphor, and the Triumph of Narrative." *Negotiating the Past: The Making of Memory in South Africa*. Ed. Sarah Nuttall and Carli Coetzee. Oxford: Oxford UP, 1998.

———. *South African Literature and Culture: Rediscovery of the Ordinary*. Manchester; New York: Manchester UP, 1994.

Nietzsche, Friedrich. *The Use and Abuse of History*. Trans. Adrian Collins. 2nd edn. Indianapolis: The Library of Liberal Arts, 1984.

Nixon, Rob. "Aftermaths." *Transition* 72 (1997): 64–77.

Nkosi, Lewis. *Home and Exile*. 1965. London; New York: Longman, 1983.

———. "Fiction by Black South Africans: Richard Rive, Bloke Modisane, Ezekiel Mphahlele, Alex La Guma." *Introduction to African Literature: An Anthology of Critical Writing*. Ed. Ulli Beier. London: Longman, 1979. 221–27.

Offord, D. C. "*The Devils* in the Context of Contemporary Russian Thought and Politics." *Dostoevsky's* The Devils: *A Critical Companion*. Ed. W. J. Leatherbarrow. Illinois: Northwestern UP, 1999. 63–99.

Orwell, George. "Politics and the English Language." *Orwell and Politics*. Ed. Peter Davison. London: Penguin, 2001.

Parry, Benita. "J. M. Coetzee. *White Writing*." Review. *Research in African Literatures* 22.4 (1991): 196–99.

———. "The Moment and Afterlife of *Heart of Darkness*." *Conrad in the Twenty-First Century*. Ed. Carola Kaplan, Andrea White, and Peter Mallios. London: Routledge, 2004. Unpublished version.

———. *Postcolonial Studies: A Materialist Critique*. London and New York: Routledge, 2004.

———. "Resistance Theory: Theorising Resistance." *Colonial Discourse/ Postcolonial Theory*. Ed. Francis Barker et al. Manchester; New York: Manchester UP, 1994. 172–96.

———. "*Robinson Crusoe*." Lecture. University of Warwick. N.d. N. pag.

———. "Speech and Silence in the Fictions of J. M. Coetzee." *Writing South Africa: Literature, Apartheid, and Democracy, 1970–1995*. Ed. Derek Attridge and Rosemary Jolly. Cambridge: Cambridge UP, 1998. 149–65.

Peace, Richard. *Dostoevsky: An Examination of the Major Novels*. Cambridge: Cambridge UP, 1971.

Pechey, Graham. "Coetzee's Purgatorial Africa: The Case of *Disgrace*." *J. M. Coetzee's* Disgrace. Ed. Derek Attridge and Peter D. McDonald. Spec. issue of *Interventions* 4.3 (2002): 374–83.

———. "The Post-apartheid Sublime: Rediscovering the Extraordinary." *Writing South Africa: Literature, Apartheid, and Democracy, 1970–1995*. Ed. Derek Attridge and Rosemary Jolly. Cambridge: Cambridge UP, 1998. 57–74.

Petersen, Kirsten Holst. "An Elaborate Dead End? A Feminist Reading of Coetzee's *Foe*." *A Shaping of Connections: Commonwealth Literature Studies—Then and Now*. Ed. Hena Maes-Jelinek, Kirsten Holst Petersen and Anna Rutherford. Sydney: Dangaroo Press, 1989: 243–52.

Plomer, William. *Turbott Wolfe*. Intro. Laurens van der Post. London: Hogarth Press, 1965.

Poyner, Jane. "Truth and Reconciliation in J. M. Coetzee's *Disgrace*." *Scrutiny2* 5.2 (2000): 66–77.

The Presidency, Republic of South Africa. "The Order of Mapungubwe in Gold: Awarded to John Maxwell Coetzee." Online posting. 24 April 2008. http:// www.thepresidency.gov.za/orders_list.asp?show=69.

Rajan, Tilottama. *Dark Interpreter: The Discourse of Romanticism*. Ithaca: Cornell UP, 1980.

Rhys, Jean. *Wide Sargasso Sea*. 1966. Ed. Angela Smith. Penguin Modern Classics. London: Penguin, 2000.

Roberts, Sheila. "'Post-colonialism, or the House of Friday'—J. M. Coetzee's *Foe*." *World Literature Written in English* 31.1 (1991): 87–92.

Rody, Caroline. "The Mad Colonial Daughter's Revolt: J. M. Coetzee's *In the Heart of the Country*." *The Writings of J. M. Coetzee*. Ed. Michael Valdez Moses. Spec. issue of *South Atlantic Quarterly* 93.1 (1994): 157–80.

Rosner, Victoria. "Home Fires: Doris Lessing, Colonial Architecture, and the Reproduction of Mothering." *Tulsa Studies in Women's Literature* 18.1 (1999): 59–89.

Patricia Rozema. Dir. *Mansfield Park*. Mirimax. 1999.

Rudicina, Alexandra F. "Crime and Myth: The Archetypal Pattern of Rebirth in Three Novels of Dostoevsky." *PMLA* 87.5 (1972): 1065–74.

Sachs, Albie. "Preparing Ourselves for Freedom." *Spring is Rebellious*. Ed. Ingrid de Kok and Karen Press. Cape Town: Buchu Books, 1990. 19–29.

SAHRC. *Inquiry into Racism in the Media: Interim Report*. Online posting. http:// www.gov.za/reports/2000/racism/pdf.

Said, Edward W. *Culture and Imperialism*. 1993. London: Vintage, 1994.

———. *Orientalism*. 1978. Harmondsworth: Peregrine, 1985.

———. "Permission to Narrate." *Journal of Palestine Studies* 13.3 (1984): 27–48.

———. *Representations of the Intellectual: The 1993 Reith Lectures*. London: Vintage, 1994.

———. "The Text, the World, the Critic." *Textual Strategies: Perspectives in Post-Structuralist Criticism*. Ed. Josué V. Harari. Ithaca, New York: Cornell UP, 1979. 161–88.

Samuelson, Meg. "The Rainbow Womb: Rape and Race in South African Fiction of the Transition." *Kunapipi* 14.1 (2002): 88–100.

Sartre, Jean-Paul. *Being and Nothingness: An Essay on Phenomenological Ontology*. Trans. Hazel Barnes. 1957. London: Routledge, 1989.

Scarry, Elaine. *The Body in Pain: The Making and the Unmaking of the World*. Oxford: Oxford UP, 1985.

Schreiner, Olive. *The Story of an African Farm*. 1883. Harmondsworth: Penguin, 1979.

Serote, Mongane Wally. *To Every Birth Its Blood*. Johannesburg: Ravan, 1981.

Singer, Peter. "Unspeakable Acts: *The Body in Pain: The Making and the Unmaking of the World,* by Elaine Scarry." Review. *New York Review* 27 February 1986: 27–30.

Sinnott-Armstrong, Walter. "You Ought to be Ashamed of Yourself (When You Violate an Imperfect Moral Obligation)." Normativity. *Philosophical Issues* 15 (2005): 193–208.

Slemon, Stephen. "Post-Colonial Allegory and the Transformation of History." *Journal of Commonwealth Literature* 23 (1988): 157–68.

Smith, Pauline. *The Beadle*. London: Cape, 1926.

———. *The Little Karoo*. 1925. London: Cape, 1952.

"South Africa: Housing." Encyclopedia of the Nations. Online posting. 25 January 2009. http://www.nationsencyclopedia.com/Africa/South-Africa-HOUSING. html.

South African Government Information. "Spotlight on Matriculants' List of Set Books." 19 April 2001. Online posting. 14 July 2007. http://www.info.gov. za/speeches/2001/010420945a1006.htm.

Spencer, Robert. "J. M. Coetzee and Colonial Violence." *Interventions* 10.2 (2008): 173–87.

———. "J. M. Coetzee and the 'War on Terror'." Unpublished paper, 2007.

Spivak, Gayatri Chakravorty. "Can the Subaltern Speak?" *Marxism and the Interpretation of Culture*. Ed. Cary Nelson and Lawrence Grossberg. Urbana and Chicago: U of Illinois P, 1988: 271–313.

———. *A Critique of Postcolonial Reason*. Cambridge, MA: Harvard UP, 1999.

———. "Theory in the Margin: Coetzee's *Foe* Reading Defoe's *Crusoe/ Roxana*." *Consequences of Theory: Selected Papers from the English Institute, 1987–88* 14. Ed. Jonathan Arac and Barbara Johnson. Baltimore and London: Johns Hopkins UP, 1991. 154 80.

———. "Three Women's Texts and a Critique of Imperialism." *"Race", Writing and Difference*. Ed. Henry Louis Gates Jr. Chicago: Chicago UP, 1985. 262–80.

Tayler, Christopher. "Just Like Life: *Diary of a Bad Year* by J. M. Coetzee." *The Guardian* 1 Sept. 2007. Online posting. http://books.guardian.co.uk/reviews/ generalfiction/0,2159966,00.html.

Tiffin, Helen. "Post-Colonialism, Post-Modernism and the Rehabilitation of Post-Colonial History." *The Journal of Commonwealth Literature* 23.1 (1988): 167–81.

Truth and Reconciliation Commission. "Transforming Society Through Reconciliation: Myth or Reality?" Public Discussion. Cape Town. 12 March 1998. Online posting. www.truth.org.za/papers/recon2.html.

———. *Truth and Reconciliation Commission of South Africa Report*. 6 vols. London: Macmillan, 1999.

Turgenev, Ivan. *Fathers and Sons*. 1862. Trans. Rosemary Edmonds. Romanes Lecture "Fathers and Children" by Isaiah Berlin. London: Penguin, 1975.

Watson, Stephen. "Colonialism and the Novels of J. M. Coetzee." *Critical Perspectives on J. M. Coetzee*. Ed. Graham Huggan and Stephen Watson. Basingstoke and London: Macmillan, 1996. 13–36.

———. "Speaking: J. M. Coetzee." *Speak: Critical Arts Journal* 1.3 (1978): 21–24.

———. "The Writer and the Devil: J. M. Coetzee's *The Master of Petersburg.*" *New Contrast* 22.3 (1994): 47–61.

Watt, Ian. *The Rise of the Novel: Studies in Defoe, Richardson and Fielding.* 1957. London: Hogarth Press, 1987.

Wenzel, Jennifer. "The Pastoral Promise and the Political Imperative: The Plaasroman Tradition in an Era of Land Reform." *MFS* 46.1 (2000): 90–113.

West, Paul. *The Very Rich Hours of Count von Stauffenberg.* New York: Harper & Row, 1980.

Whitford, Margaret. "Introduction." *The Irigaray Reader.* Ed. and intro. Margaret Whitford. Oxford: Blackwell, 1991.

Wollstonecraft, Mary. *Maria, or, the Wrongs of Woman.* 1798. Intro. Anne K. Mellor. New York; London: W. W. Norton, 1994.

Wood, Marcus. *Blind Memory: Visual Representations of Slavery in England and America 1780–1865.* Manchester: Manchester UP, 2000.

Wright, Laura. "A Feminist-Vegetarian Defense of Elizabeth Costello: A Rant from an Ethical Academic on J. M. Coetzee's *The Lives of Animals.*" *J. M. Coetzee and the Idea of the Public Intellectual.* Ed. Jane Poyner. Athens, Ohio: Ohio UP, 2006.

———. *Writing "Out of All the Camps": J. M. Coetzee's Narratives of Displacement.* New York; London: Routledge, 2006.

Yarmolinsky, Avrahm. "Foreword to *The Possessed* by Fyodor Dostoevsky." Trans. Constance Garnett. New York: Modern Library, 1936. v–ix.

Yeğenoğlu, Meyda. *Colonial Fantasies: Towards a Feminist Reading of Orientalism.* Cambridge: Cambridge UP, 1998.

Zinik, Zinovy. "The Spirit of Stavrogin." *TLS* 19. 4 March 1994.

Zola, Émile. "J'Accuse! Lettre au Président de la République." *L'Aurore.* 13 January 1898. Online posting. http://www.francealacarte.org.uk/education/enseigner/resources/alevel.

———. "J'Accuse! Lettre au Président de la République." Trans. and notes Shelley Temchin and Jean-Max Guieu. 2001. Online posting. http://www.georgetown.edu/faculty/guieuj/Iaccuse.htm.

Index

The Wretched of the Earth 25, 104,
130, 147
see also neo-colonialism
Farred, Grant 160
Felman, Shoshana 34, 38 1n., 42, 46,
51–52
feminism 36–38, 48–49, 95, 161, 172,
177–78
see also Irigaray, Luce; Gilbert, Sandra
Ferguson, James 158
Flaubert, Gustave 30, 136
Foe 1 1n., 6, 8, 12, 37, 91–109, 133, 169,
173
forced removals, policy of 11
see also apartheid legislation
Foucault, Michel 5, 16, 173
Discipline and Punish 63
Madness and Civilization 10, 33, 53,
54, 59–60, 62, 63–64, 67
Freud, Sigmund 5, 19, 28, 34, 36, 37–38,
68, 163
see also Oedipus myth

Gallagher, Susan Van Zanten 8, 23 3n., 35,
44, 58
Garnett, Constance 131
genre 2–3, 5–6, 16–17, 45–46, 76, 96–97,
107, 167–68, 169, 170–71, 175,
177–78
see also autobiography; parable;
pastoral; *plaasroman*; *Robinson
Crusoe*
Gilbert, Sandra
and Gubar, Susan 49
Gilman, Charlotte Perkins 49
Girard, René 10
Giving Offense 10, 11, 28, 59–60, 136–37,
140
see also censorship
Glenn, Ian 36, 42
Gordimer, Nadine 5, 67
Burger's Daughter 9, 115
The Conservationist 6
The Essential Gesture 4, 53, 71, 85,
111, 129, 139
The House Gun 149
"The Idea of Gardening" 70–71, 114
July's People 9

Graham, James 157–58
Graham, Lucy 40, 41, 160, 170, 177–78
Gramsci, Antonio 53, 71, 134–35, 168–69
see also intellectualism
Gray, Stephen 157
Grossvogel, David I. 74–76, 77, 78
Gubar, Susan
see Gilbert, Sandra
guilt, (colonial) 25–26
see also shame

Hacking, Ian 170
Head, Bessie 34
Head, Dominic 10, 15, 26, 31, 39, 44, 58,
73, 89, 107, 111, 114–15, 141,
145–46, 176, 183
Hegelian dialectic 21, 64, 68
history, discourse of 8, 16–17, 18, 58
Holiday, Anthony 151
Hughes, Ted 177, 180–81
Hulme, Peter 12, 92, 96–97, 103

"Idleness in South Africa" 22–23, 83
see also White Writing
imperialism 19, 26, 45, 49, 58, 94
In the Heart of the Country 1 1n., 2, 4, 6,
11, 33–52, 103–04, 122, 169
intellectualism 174
see also Gramsci, Antonio; Orwell,
George; Said, Edward W.
interregnum 53, 113, 134–35
see also Gramsci, Antonio
intertextuality 92–93, 96–97, 101, 131
"Into the Dark Chamber" 7, 64
Irigaray, Luce 5, 38, 51
see also feminism

Jakobson, Roman 42, 46
Jolly, Rosemary Jane 17, 21
Jameson, Fredric 82, 130–31
on postmodernism 27–28
on "national allegory" 71–72, 89
JanMohamed, Abdul R. 58, 67

Kafka, Franz 5, 7, 70 1n., 73, 78
"Before the Law" 76, 182–83
"The Burrow" 76
The Castle 75